THE

ANDY McNAB

DOSSIER

CONFIDENTIAL

www.andymcnab.co.uk

ANDY McNAB

⮫ In 1984 he was 'badged' as a member of 22 SAS Regiment.

⮫ Over the course of the next nine years he was at the centre of covert operations on five continents.

⮫ During the first Gulf War he commanded Bravo Two Zero, a patrol that, in the words of his commanding officer, 'will remain in regimental history for ever'.

⮫ Awarded both the Distinguished Conduct Medal (DCM) and Military Medal (MM) during his military career.

⮫ McNab was the British Army's most highly decorated serving soldier when he finally left the SAS in February 1993.

⮫ He is now the author of eleven bestselling thrillers.

BRAVO TWO ZERO

In January 1991, eight members of the SAS regiment, under the command of Sergeant Andy McNab, embarked upon a top secret mission in Iraq to infiltrate them deep behind enemy lines. Their call sign: 'Bravo Two Zero'.

IMMEDIATE ACTION

The no–holds–barred account of an extraordinary life, from the day McNab as a baby was found in a carrier bag on the steps of Guy's Hospital to the day he went to fight in the Gulf War. As a delinquent youth he kicked against society. As a young soldier he waged war against the IRA in the streets and fields of South Armagh.

SEVEN TROOP

Andy McNab's gripping account of the time he served in the company of a remarkable band of brothers. The things they saw and did during that time would take them all to breaking point – and some beyond – in the years that followed. He who dares doesn't always win . . .

Nick Stone, ex–SAS trooper, now gun–for–hire working on deniable ops for the British government, is the perfect man for the dirtiest of jobs, doing whatever it takes by whatever means necessary…

REMOTE CONTROL
⊞ Dateline: Washington DC, USA

Stone is drawn into the bloody killing of an ex–SAS
officer and his family and soon finds himself on
the run with the one survivor who can identify the
killer – a nine-year-old girl.

> 'Proceeds with a testosterone surge'
> *Daily Telegraph*

CRISIS FOUR
⊞ Dateline: North Carolina, USA

In the backwoods of the American South, Stone
has to keep alive the beautiful young woman who
holds the key to unlock a chilling conspiracy that
will threaten world peace.

> 'When it comes to thrills, he's Forsyth class'
> *Mail on Sunday*

FIREWALL
⊞ Dateline: Finland

The kidnapping of a Russian Mafia warlord takes
Stone into the heart of the global espionage world
and into conflict with some of the most dangerous
killers around.

> 'Other thriller writers do their research, but
> McNab has actually been there'
> *Sunday Times*

LAST LIGHT
✚ Dateline: Panama

Stone finds himself at the centre of a lethal conspiracy involving ruthless Colombian mercenaries, the US government and Chinese big business. It's an uncomfortable place to be . . .

> 'A heart thumping read'
> *Mail on Sunday*

LIBERATION DAY
✚ Dateline: Cannes, France

Behind its glamorous exterior, the city's seething underworld is the battleground for a very dirty drugs war and Stone must reach deep within himself to fight it on their terms.

> 'McNab's great asset is that the heart of his fiction is non–fiction'
> *Sunday Times*

DARK WINTER
✚ Dateline: Malaysia

A straightforward action on behalf of the War on Terror turns into a race to escape his past for Stone if he is to save himself and those closest to him.

> 'Addictive . . . Packed with wild action and revealing tradecraft'
> *Daily Telegraph*

DEEP BLACK
⊞ Dateline: Bosnia

All too late Stone realizes that he is being used as bait to lure into the open a man whom the darker forces of the West will stop at nothing to destroy.

'One of the UK's top thriller writers'
Daily Express

AGGRESSOR
⊞ Dateline: Georgia, former Soviet Union

A longstanding debt of friendship to an SAS comrade takes Stone on a journey where he will have to risk everything to repay what he owes, even his life . . .

'A terrific novelist'
Mail on Sunday

RECOIL
⊞ Dateline: The Congo, Africa

What starts out as a personal quest for a missing woman quickly becomes a headlong rush from his own past for Stone.

'Stunning . . . A first class action thriller'
The Sun

CROSSFIRE
Dateline: Kabul

Nick Stone enters the modern day wild west that is Afghanistan in search of a kidnapped reporter.

> 'Authentic to the core ... McNab at his electrifying best'
> *Daily Express*

ANDY McNAB
BRUTE FORCE

CORGI BOOKS

TRANSWORLD PUBLISHERS
61–63 Uxbridge Road, London W5 5SA
A Random House Group Company
www.rbooks.co.uk

BRUTE FORCE
A CORGI BOOK: 9780552153799

First published in Great Britain
in 2008 by Bantam Press
an imprint of Transworld Publishers
Corgi edition published 2009

Addresses for Random House Group Ltd companies outside the UK
can be found at: www.randomhouse.co.uk
The Random House Group Ltd Reg. No. 954009

The Random House Group Limited supports The Forest Stewardship Council (FSC), the
leading international forest certification organisation. All our titles that are printed on
Greenpeace approved FSC certified paper carry the FSC logo. Our paper procurement
policy can be found at www.rbooks.co.uk/environment

Typeset in 11/14pt Palatino by
Falcon Oast Graphic Art Ltd.
Printed in the UK by CPI Cox & Wyman, Reading, RG1 8EX.

2 4 6 8 10 9 7 5 3 1

PART ONE

1

Tripoli docks
October 1987

I sat well back in my seat and listened as Colonel Gaddafi's latest day-long rant burst from the radio like an Arab Fidel Castro on speed. I pictured a big mike blocking his craggy features as he denounced Reagan, Thatcher and all things Western, so all you could see was a mad mop of black curly hair and angry flecks of spit flying in every direction.

I was in the passenger seat of an old box like Russian jeep. Africa was littered with the things, bare metal showing through the green paint where thousands of boots and hands had worn it away.

I was sweating big-time, and it had nothing to do with the weather. This might be North Africa, but it was October. It was cold. The leaking was to do with the wet-suit I had on over my clothes. Apart from my sweatshirt, tracksuit bottoms and trainers, I was totally sterile: no money, no weapon. I wasn't going to need any, not even a watch. Time wasn't going to matter on this job. I had to react to events as they happened, not when the little hand hit five. I would give my cover documents to Lynn at the very last minute.

Sitting back in the seat and completely still – that's the secret of not being seen. The jeep looked just like any one of the ten-year-old American pimp-mobiles we were parked alongside: empty. I had my binos up, eyes on target. My main area of focus was the pair of big holes at the arse end of the ship from which six-inch-thick ropes snaked towards the quayside.

The life of the docks continued around us. The quay was jammed with boats unloading TVs and white goods to feed Libya's consumer boom. This was an oil country and then some. Arabs from all over, brown and black, made up the labour force. The overseers were all ex-pats. The air was filled with German, French, British and American accents. So much for the sanctions against what the White House called the mad dog of the Middle East. All the old imperialists had their noses in the trough. Everyone was helping themselves to the huge salaries offered by this former Italian colony.

The driver was listening intently, hands resting on the enormous black steel steering wheel. 'What's he on about?' I didn't even bother looking over at him.

He powered down the small transistor. 'The whole world is going down the gurgler, as per usual.' The voice was softly spoken, the accent cut-glass.

Although the British embassy had long since closed – along with everybody else's – as part of their sanctions against the Colonel for his habit of sponsoring global terrorism, everybody, Brits included, had left a couple of spooks behind. Colonel Lynn was one of them. Gaddafi remained one of the biggest threats to world peace, and his black-leather-jacketed heavies tended to come to the UK and murder anyone speaking out against the regime, so we needed people with their ear to the ground.

Lynn wasn't a field operator. He was our man in Havana – only in Tripoli. In his late thirties, of average build, he looked and spoke like a history teacher – but his fresh-from-the-shower smell screamed officer, and his aura marked him out as a high flier. He spoke the language and knew the players. He'd probably been born here; for all I knew, his dad had been ambassador or something. Colonel Lynn – I never had found out what his first name was – ate, drank and breathed the place. He was what the Firm called an Arabist.

He was all right, I supposed – just not the sort of guy I'd phone up and ask out for a brew and a sticky bun. A bit too keen for me; a bit too full of devotion to the cause. He probably kept a picture of the Queen under his pillow. And he was also just a bit too keen to tell me how to do my job. He didn't like people like me. There was just a hint now and again of disgust at what people like me got up to. Even though he was part of it, he was from the hands-clean side of the fence and everyone on my side was not much more than a necessary evil.

'Don't forget to confirm the cargo before anything else.'

'OK. What if it isn't there?'

'It is.'

'So why check it?'

15

'Because I need you to tell me when you get back that you physically saw it.'

The target ship was parked up between two Libyan navy patrol boats in the military section the other side of the harbour. I deliberately didn't say 'moored' because it got a rise out of Lynn. He knew about boaty stuff. I didn't know many of the technical terms and I didn't need to learn them. That was the navy's job. As far as I was concerned it was parked up, and that was fine.

Lynn had a small sailing boat of his own in a marina about fifteen Ks away. I'd spent the last four days living in it while he briefed me. The sitting and eating area downstairs was full of pictures of him and his wife in the creeks of north Norfolk. Nelson country, he called it.

I'd fucked up; by showing a spark of polite interest in a shot of the two of them standing outside their local, the Hero, I had opened the door to a serious history lesson, beginning with how the great man had been born a few miles up the road from their home.

The Egyptian-registered *Bahiti* could carry up to 150 tonnes of cargo. When the chairman's wife smashed a bottle of Cairo's fizziest against its side, all the bodywork was probably a gleaming white. Twenty or so years of saltwater and neglect had streaked it with rust. A crane was mounted at the bow for loading and unloading. The rest of the topside was flat, apart from the bridge tower at the back end. It looked like a miniature oil-tanker.

Lynn had his binos up too as forklifts hummed around us, laden with yet more crates and what looked like a consignment of dustbin lids. A group of dockers leant against walls smoking, waiting for the next job to come along or some German to bollock them for being Arabs.

'You see the man on the gangplank now?'

I nodded.

'Black leather jacket? Papers in his hand?'

'Yeah, I've got him.'

'That's Mansour.'

I knew plenty about Mansour from Lynn's briefing. He was in his forties and worked for Libyan intelligence. He was medium height and stocky, with brushed-back hair and a very neat moustache.

'He calls me Leptis.'

'Leptis?'

'Just a name he gave me.'

'You two mates?'

'Hardly.' He dropped his binos for a moment and turned to me. 'Need-to-know, Nick – and you don't need to.'

He was right. I didn't need to know – I didn't even want to. All this spookery was way beyond my pay scale.

'You sure that's him? He looks fatter than in the pictures.'

'Absolutely certain. He's over-indulged the falafels, that's all. A sign of privilege. He's overpaid.'

Mansour pointed and shouted, and generally seemed to take over the show as he walked up the gangplank. Two bodies emerged from the hold, headed for Mansour and started talking.

'Stand by – that's Two Cells.'

Lynn confirmed. 'Yes, that's Lesser.'

2

Benjamin Lesser – it didn't sound quite hard-core or Republican enough to belong to PIRA's top bomb-maker. I'd only just got over the Nelson history lesson when Lynn embarked on a lengthy explanation of the origins of the name. It boiled down to the fact that Benjamin was a Celtic name as well as an Eastern European one. It meant favourite son. Benjamin was also a Catholic saint, which qualified it for a place in *The PIRA Book of Baby Names*. In the year 424 he was tortured by the king of Persia for preaching. Reeds were thrust under his nails and into all the tenderest parts of his body. After this torture had been repeated several times, a barbed stake was shoved up his arse as a show-stopper. PIRA still did much the same thing to its victims fifteen hundred years later, so the history lesson wasn't a total waste of time.

I'd nicknamed Ben Two Cells. It suited me to think of him as stupid. It cheered me up.

'I suppose need-to-know means you can't tell me who the woman is?'

'I don't know her, actually.' Lynn took a couple of seconds to check out the hauntingly beautiful, dark-skinned face. 'Probably one of Mansour's people checking the cargo.'

Two Cells' dark brown wavy hair was a bit longer than it had been in the briefing pictures, down to his shoulders and centre-parted, but it was definitely him. He towered over the Libyan, and probably everybody else aboard. He was at least six four, and built to build. I expected a bomb-maker's hands to be like a pianist's, but Benny Boy's were the size of shovels.

'Remember, you've got to make it look like an accident. And the ship must be preserved at all costs for the Spanish to capture.'

'Yep, I've got it.'

He'd told me enough times over the last few days. This had to be the best-briefed job I'd ever been on. But all the briefing in the world wasn't going to help me drop Two Cells without it looking like exactly what it was. I might be able to channel him into the killing ground, but if anything went wrong I'd have to contend with a good eighteen stone of seriously unsaintly Two Cells throwing one of those super-sized fists at me. If it made contact, I'd be over the side.

Mansour and the woman made their way back to the quay and disappeared into the maze of warehouses as Two Cells went onto the ship and started chatting with the skipper.

Liam Brian Duff was a lot more than a sailor boy. He'd been caught up in the events of Bloody Sunday, and joined the IRA the very next day. He was just sixteen. The following year, he was caught trying to bomb a government building.

Sentenced to six years, he shared cells in the Maze prison with some major league Republican icons. By the time he was released, Duff was quite the rising star. He came back onto British radar when he was arrested by the French police five or six years ago. He'd been travelling with a false passport on his return from a Hezbollah training camp in Lebanon – evidence of his role in fostering the international ties the IRA and Sinn Fein were building with the Middle East, and most particularly with Gaddafi's Libya.

I kept my binos trained on the ship as Duff checked the crane was lowering the boxes into the hold correctly. Then Lynn gunned the engine and I put them in the foot well as he drove us out of the port and along the coast road.

'Take a different route. We don't want to get stuck at another checkpoint.'

Lynn nodded.

We'd had a close shave on the way to the docks. Gaddafi's boys had set up a checkpoint where there hadn't been one on our dry run a few hours earlier. Our papers were good and our cover story had held – we were Dutch oil-workers in transit, a couple of guys making an honest dollar in Colonel G's workers' paradise. After scrutinizing the papers and turning them round a few times, the sentry had waved us on our way, but I wasn't in a hurry to risk an action replay. We had far bigger things to worry about.

3

He parked on a rocky headland about a K from the port. The rocks glistened in the light from the docks, and so did the plastic bottles and general crap spread across the beach. It looked more like a landfill site than a holiday destination. Perhaps that was why Club 18-30 had given it a miss this year.

'Everything in place? Any questions?'

'Yep – and no.' I clambered out of the jeep, leaving my cover docs on the seat. I grabbed the re-breather and fins from the back, and checked the karabiner was still hooked into the netting of the rope sack. All the gear I was going to use to get on board was inside.

Without ceremony, Lynn was gone. He didn't want to be in the vicinity if I got lifted.

I started to sort myself out on top of the landfill. I got the re-breather on my back. It was a commercial system, the sort underwater photographers use when they don't want to frighten the fish. A normal scuba tank is noisy and streams bubbles; re-breather apparatus prevents both by reusing the air you exhale.

One of the small tanks on my back was pure oxygen; the other was normal air. The plastic tub between them was filled with soda lime. As I breathed out, the exhaled air was piped into the tub. The soda lime retained the carbon dioxide but let oxygen through, along with a little top-up from the oxygen bottle. It was ingenious, but that didn't mean I liked using it. If I'd wanted to fuck about underwater I'd have joined the navy.

I attached my navigation aid, a 12cm luminous ball compass mounted on a hard plastic sheet. It hooked onto the re-breather harness and dangled down my chest, a bit like a map case.

Fins in one hand, the sack in the other, I waded into the sea. It was freezing. The mask covered my face. I tightened the straps, dipped my head underwater and took a few breaths to make sure there was a tight seal.

I put the fins on, and kicked off slowly and steadily. I'd insisted on calling them flippers in front of Lynn. At least it made me smile.

I'd hooked my left arm through the net and I kept my hands down by my stomach while I finned. Its weight kept the rest of my body submerged.

As I rounded the headland, I could see the lights of the docks in the distance. I lifted the plastic plate, checked the compass bearing was direct onto the boat I was after, and started to fin myself down about five metres below the surface. I took slow, normal breaths, which echoed in the silence. The soda lime gave the breathing mixture a citrus, acidic taste.

I knew not to rush. If I did, the board would push

22

upwards and I wouldn't be able to keep on-bearing. I pumped the fins methodically and kept my eyes glued to the luminous markings of the ball compass.

It wasn't long before the dock lights glared overhead, and the silence was broken by a cacophony of turning screws and clanging hulls, and the demented buzz of a powerboat skimming across the harbour. I kept the ball compass up in front of me and stuck to my bearing.

Even though I kept the pace slow and constant, I was starting to feel the strain now. Vast, barnacle-encrusted hulls hung in the water on either side of me. I just kept on-bearing; that was all I could do, short of popping up and checking.

Two sleek, chiselled shapes rode the swell ahead of me, left and right of a larger, blunter craft.

4

I dived under the keel of the *Bahiti*. Pockmarked with
barnacles and swirling seaweed – in sharp contrast to the
patrol boats at either end – it was like the roof of a sea
cave. The steamer's idling engines throbbed above me
and metal clattered against metal.

Two huge brass propellers glinted in the murky water
ahead; they would start turning soon, to take us out of
port – but not just yet, I hoped.

The quay was now behind me. The *Bahiti*'s bulbous
stern swept out above the waterline and I kept out of
sight beneath the overhang. I unclipped the compass and
let it drop.

I finned up slowly, brushing my hand against the hull
from time to time to steady myself. The vibration from
the engines pulsed up my arm. My head broke the
surface; I was still sheltered by the overhang.

There was clamour and movement above me.
The world was unmuffled. I took off the mask and
let it hang by its tube as I undid the catches on the

re-breather and sent it the same way as the compass.

Finning to keep my head above water, I felt around in the net and pulled out the modified mine magnet. Well, not so much modified as minus its mine. It was about twenty centimetres by twenty, with a thin rubber cushion cemented to one side to prevent a resounding clang inside the ship as the thing grabbed onto the hull, followed by a shower of grenades from the deck.

I clipped the karabiner to the steel handle I'd welded onto the other side of the magnet, where the mine had been, then hung onto the net sack and waited for the crew of the *Bahiti* to get their shit together.

For the best part of an hour the clanking and shouting and general fucking about carried on seven or eight metres above me, then the final one of the crates the Libyans had spent the last few hours loading slid into place a few inches the other side of the hull.

There were only six crewmen – this rust-bucket was about cargo, not Caribbean cruises – but you wouldn't have known it from the amount of hollering and swearing as the gangplank was heaved aboard. By now my fingers were wrinkled and skeletal and had lost every shred of feeling.

The engines rumbled into action and the hull vibrated like a jackhammer. The back rope was released from a bollard on the quay and splashed into the water about a metre from my head before being hauled aboard.

The water behind me started to churn. I didn't know if this thing was going to get towed out by a tug, or leave under its own steam. It didn't matter either way, so long as nobody came and started messing about anywhere near me.

The boat moved slowly away from the quay, but my legs still came up to the surface; I'd had to keep my fins on in case I got pinged and had to swim for it. Now we were under way, I could kick them off. I didn't plan to hang around much longer. I had to get on board before Liam and his mates got up a decent head of steam.

It wasn't long before the lights of the harbour were behind us. The headland emerged from the shadows on my left.

The propellers were kicking up a storm. My hands and arms were numb from the cold, and the strain of holding onto the net.

I fished out a one-metre pole that could extend to ten. Next came a rolled-up ten-metre caving ladder with 12.5mm tubular alloy rungs suspended on galvanized 4mm steel wire, and a spring-mounted, four-pronged hook at the top. The whole thing weighed no more than about three kilos.

All I had to do now was rig the ladder onto the pole, extend it one metre section by one metre section, twisting it to lock each time. Soon it was fully stretched and vertical, scraping against the side of the ship.

Spray splashed my face. With my arm still hooked into the netting I started to manoeuvre the ladder hook until it grappled onto something solid on the deck. The closest thing I could see was the housing for the mooring rope.

The water buffeted against me as we gathered speed and I had to fight to keep my pole arm steady. At least I didn't have to worry about noise. My efforts were entirely focused on getting that hook to engage. There was no point worrying about the magnet; if it gave way, it gave way. Why worry about what you can't change?

I just hoped that anyone on the bridge was looking straight ahead and not pissing around on the wings. Fuck it, I'd soon find out. The captain and his mate should be up there behind the steering wheel. The other four would be fucking around with the engines and whatever other stuff you needed to keep the ship afloat and pointing in the right direction. I didn't know much about life on the ocean wave, but I couldn't think why any of them would be hanging around at the stern, staring idly at the wake. That was the sort of thing I would have done.

I had so much seawater in my mouth I was starting to gag. My eyes stung. I felt like I was in one of those tidal exercise pools and someone had turned the dial to max. I bounced up across the surface one second and got dragged down by the sheer weight of water the next. I had to get some better leverage. With my left hand hooked into the net, I pushed against the hull with my feet and tried to brace myself.

The harbour lights faded into the distance. Isolated settlements glowed weakly along the coast.

On the sixth or seventh attempt, the hook finally snagged. On what, I didn't know, but it was holding. I gave it a sharp tug, then another. It held.

I released the karabiner from the magnet, let the net fall and gripped the ladder with both hands. My legs were swept from under me as I flailed in the *Bahiti*'s wake, hoping like fuck that I wasn't going to be sliced into a million little pieces by the churning propeller screws.

5

You don't climb caving ladders the same way as you do traditional, rigid ones. You go up them side-on, using your heels, not the balls of your feet. That way you don't get tangled and fuck up.

I moved one hand up a rung and the corresponding foot. Then another. And another. Then I was out of the water. The ladder flapped around in the wake as I bounced around at a forty-five degree angle.

I kept on going, hand over hand, foot over foot. The only lights I could see now were on the ship itself. If the ladder came unstuck or I fell, it was going to be a long swim back.

A couple of rungs from the top I could see that the ladder's hook, or at least one prong of it, was caught on the rope hole – and that it was too small for me to climb through.

I scrabbled to get one hand onto the bottom rail, then two, heaving myself up and onto the deck with the world's biggest chin-up. I kicked the ladder and pole away. They dropped into the boiling white foam eight metres below.

I moved straight into the shadows at the rear of the bridge tower, peeled off the wetsuit and binned it over the side as well. My head and hands were still ice cold, but my body was drenched with sweat.

The priority now was to get below. There were hatches all over the place. They were all tied down, but that didn't matter; I knew exactly where I was going and how to get there. As you looked towards the bow, there was a door to the right of the bridge tower. I edged my way to the corner and lay flat on the deck. I eased my head round at ground level.

The door was open, just as Lynn had said it would be. Weak yellow light spilled from inside. I drew level and checked down the narrow corridor. Layers of badly painted cream gloss adorned the walls, and stairs led off to the right and left. The lino-covered floor was impregnated with grit to prevent slipping.

I could hear voices on the bridge above me, muttering in Arabic-accented English, then Duff – it had to be him, because he was giving orders – replying. The engines thundered below. I couldn't see any sign of movement. I crossed the threshold and headed straight downstairs.

The engine noise got louder with each step I took. The louder the better, as far as I was concerned. An open door to my left reminded me of watching *Voyage To The Bottom Of The Sea* as a kid: the *Seaview*'s had been exactly the same.

I heard voices from the engine room but I didn't check them out – the door I wanted was opposite and just short of it.

The cargo hold was lit, but it felt like a dungeon. Crates and alloy boxes were stacked in two sections to within a few feet of the ceiling, leaving an alleyway between them just wide enough for a man to squeeze through, and another around the sides. The whole lot was lashed down with nylon nets and ropes.

The place stank of oily wood and grease. The floor seemed to be covered with wheat – its normal payload, perhaps – but these crates and boxes weren't going to be full of Shreddies, that was for sure. I stepped over the dark brown detonator cord that ran left and right of me then around the side of the cargo.

I had to climb on top of the stack before I found a spot where the net was slack and there was a space just big enough to move around in.

I unclipped the green metal retainers on the top wooden crate, and hauled up the netting so I could get the lid open. I didn't really need to check. I had spent years humping boxes exactly like these all over the world when I was in the infantry. The contents were as the stencilling described: it was a general-purpose machinegun in its transit chest. The butt and barrel had been removed and placed in receptacles cut into the interior framework. Even the GPMG's cleaning wallet, a green nylon bag, was exactly where it should have been. The whole lot was factory fresh.

The 150 tonnes of weapons were bound for the Provisional IRA. I wasn't going to unload each box to make sure Lynn was right, but he'd told me there were a thousand AKs; a million rounds of ammunition; loads of GPMGs; 450 hand grenades; rocket-propelled grenade launchers and grenades; SAM ground-to-air launchers and missiles, each one capable of downing a British army helicopter; anti-tank launchers, and thousands of electric dets and fuses. There were even a couple of crates of flamethrowers, apparently, and to top it all off, two tonnes of Semtex explosive, lovingly fashioned in the old Czechoslovakia.

Mansour was organizing the shipment. It was en route to the west coast of Ireland, and from there to the streets of Derry, Belfast and the UK mainland. It seemed bizarre to me that the task wasn't to sink the thing. That, it seemed, was Two Cells' job if the shipment was compromised.

He wouldn't fuck about. According to Lynn, he was the best of the best when it came to making IEDs, and prepared to die for the cause. He'd even offered himself up as a suicide bomber – to wrap himself around Maggie and then press the detonator button – but the boyos thought he was too good to waste.

The dim glow of a torch appeared at the far end of the aisle, heading my way. I flattened myself against the stack.

The beam slewed across the gap between the crates and brightened with every footstep. Its owner moved closer to where I was hidden. As he came into the light from the corridor, he switched off the torch. He passed below me.

I moved my head fractionally and saw Two Cells walking towards the entrance I'd just come through. His hair hung lank and greasy down the back of his neck.

He closed the door behind him.

I jumped down and headed over to see what he'd been up to.

Not that I couldn't already guess.

31

6

He'd glued the timer power unit directly to the bare steel to the right of the bow. I could still smell the Evostik.

The TPU consisted of a blue wooden box about twenty centimetres square and four deep. The top was screwed down and the detonator leads emerged from a small hole in its side. The det itself, an aluminium cylinder the size of half a cigarette packed with HE, was gaffer-taped to a length of brown det cord. Essentially washing line with a high-explosive filling, it snaked away down the aisle.

The boy knew exactly what he was doing. He'd left a good fifteen to twenty centimetres of cord hanging before he'd attached the det, in case any moisture or shit had contaminated the end of the line. He wanted to make sure that when he was detonating, he was only detonating good HE.

I followed the ring main of det cord along the floor, down the narrow aisle between the weapons and ammunition boxes and the hull. I saw the first device straightaway.

The tin dustbin lid was flush against the hull, held in position by two wooden stakes wedged back against the cargo. The det cord disappeared into a hole drilled centre-rear, from which a bead of yellow PE extruded; I knew Two Cells would have knotted it inside the lid before feeding it back through to continue the ring main.

Twelve charges had been set around the hull. Lynn was right: this boat wasn't going to be taken alive. In fact, Lynn had been right about everything so far.

Two Cells had used a dustbin lid because its shape would do the most damage. Instead of the *brisance* – the shattering effect of the explosion – dissipating in all directions, it would be sufficiently focused to cut a dustbin-lid-sized hole through the hull.

The det cord running along to the next charge would detonate in a split second and so would all the others.

I went back to the GPMG box and took out the cleaning wallet, a small tool roll with slots.

There was no need to follow the ring main any further than the first charge. The business end was back at the TPU.

The wallet contained a combination tool, a sort of purpose-built Leatherman used to split the weapon so you could clean out the carbon deposit that glues itself to weapons after firing.

I used the flat-head screwdriver bit to remove the four brass screws holding down the lid. Two Cells had been taking no chances. He didn't want anyone or anything getting inside to mess with the device by mistake. He was the only one going to kick this thing off.

My job was to disarm the devices while making it look

like a malfunction. I also had to kill Two Cells, and make it look like an accident. As Lynn must have said to me a hundred times, the charges must not go off. The shipment must be preserved at all costs. That suited me fine. I didn't want to spend the next few days bobbing up and down in the Med.

The TPU was made out of a mechanical Parkway timer, the kind you used to be able to buy on a key ring as a parking reminder. They were made illegal when it was discovered that more of the things ended up inside TPUs than in motorists' pockets.

The Parkway was a small disc powered by a spring mechanism. You put your money in the parking meter, turned the disc to twenty minutes, say, and away it would tick. When the twenty minutes were up, the disc would hit zero and the device would start ringing. Bomb-makers didn't care about that – they just needed a small and reliable mechanical timer. Keep it simple, stupid: you didn't have to worry about anything going wrong – you just set it for any delay up to an hour and walked away.

The TPU only had four main components: the twelve-volt battery that would provide the power to initiate the det connected to the ring main; two short lengths of steel about twice the size of a sewing needle, and, of course, the Parkway timer, all Evo-stuck down to prevent anything moving that shouldn't. A thin blue wire linked the negative terminal to one of the leads from the det.

The positive lead was only partially glued down; it coiled its way to a small steel rod glued vertically on top of the Parkway's zero marker. Another wire joined the second det lead to the second rod, embedded horizon-tally into the wood so the two would complete the circuit when the time ran out. For the time being, a rubber pad was wedged between the two to stop the current completing its journey.

All Two Cells had to do was turn the Parkway to what-ever time delay he wanted, pull out the rubber pad, and let the TPU do the rest.

7

I felt myself break into a smile. These things always worked better when they were kept simple, but you had to be really smart to put them together this competently. I'd been wrong to call him Two Cells. This boy really knew what he was doing.

My smile widened. I double-checked the joints between the terminal wires and the det leads and knew exactly where he'd learnt his craft. Unless he was an Afghan, it was right here in one of the terror training camps in Libya or Algeria. Nobody else used this variation of the Chinese pigtail to join their wires.

The Chinese labourers working for the Western Union in the Wild West used it to repair downed telegraph lines. They took the two cut ends, crossed them left over right to make the first part of a reef knot, and then twisted the two ends together. They didn't finish the reef knot because it just wasn't practical. The wires hung between poles, making it close to impossible to tie the second part of the reef – and the half reef and pigtail twist both guaranteed conductivity and held the connection, even with a couple of vultures sitting on the wires, waiting for Jesse James to come by and leave them lunch.

When we went to teach the Mujahideen, we found that they flapped a whole lot more than the average Chinaman. They'd do the half-knot but forget the twist, or do the twist but forget the half-knot. So we taught them the complete reef knot, left over right, right over left, then a pigtail twist with what was left of the wire – exactly as Big Ben had done here. It wasn't long before the TPUs we taught the Muj, and the tricks we'd learnt from PIRA, were being taught in the crazy colonel's terror schools.

All I could do now was hang around and wait. I climbed back into the gap between the GPMGs and the deck. I lay there curled up, trying to listen for other noises above the steady thud of engines, my nostrils filled with the aroma of gun oil. It reminded me of every armoury I'd ever been in.

As I lay there with the rope net digging into my back, I started to worry about the amount of information I'd been given. The more I knew about a job, the more I could see that I was just a little, dispensable cog in a very large and ugly machine.

To my way of thinking, the less I knew the better. It meant I really was their last chance, they really needed me – and that therefore they weren't completely fucking me over.

Why did I have to make Big Ben's death look like an accident? And why bother saving the shipment? We were a big Firm; we had enough kit to go round; we didn't need this lot. Why not let the whole cargo go down and make sure it didn't fall into the wrong hands?

Too little air, too many questions and too much gun oil were giving me a headache. Fuck it, I just wanted to get the job done.

A shout – pure Belfast – came from the stairway. 'Ben! Come – *now*. We've got a big focking problem! A plane – flying low!'

I wriggled out of my hiding place and ran like Superman to the door. I jammed my ear against the cold steel.

'Where from?'

'The north; so low I could see the pilot.'

'Military?'

'Air force.'

'Must be from Gibraltar. The Brits, they've got us.' He was more pissed off than scared.

Another voice joined in, this time an Arab. 'No, no, no – it's the Spanish. I can hear them on the radio. Spanish customs. They're heading straight for us.'

'They may get us.' It was Big Ben again. 'But they're not laying a finger on this lot. Get ready to jump ship.'

There was a blast of noise from the engine room, then a lot of hollering.

As I clambered back up onto the GPMGs, the engines slowed to a hum.

Lights went on in the hold and I heard movement below me.

8

I watched Lesser hunch over the TPU, remove a penknife from his jeans and unscrew the lid. He turned the Parkway anticlockwise, lifted out the rubber pad and dropped it and the knife onto the deck. Then he made his way back the way he had come. He was walking, not running. Good drills: he didn't want to break a leg and be stuck down here when the device kicked off. He wanted to make sure he could get upstairs before the Parkway did its bit.

The moment he'd disappeared, I legged it towards the TPU. He'd set the Parkway to fifteen minutes. I grabbed the rubber, jammed it into place and turned the dial back down to zero.

I picked up the knife and cut the ring main about three metres from the detonator. Whatever happened now, only three metres of det cord would ignite. It had the power to rip through human flesh, but it wasn't going to do much damage to the ship.

I edged round beside the first dustbin lid and waited.

Big Ben would be back. He was too professional and committed to just shrug his shoulders when it didn't detonate.

I kept reminding myself that his death had to look like an accident. I imagined the frantic activity up on deck as they tried to get the boats away before it detonated.

The fifteen minutes passed.

He'd give it maybe another two, three at the most. I felt a sneaking admiration for him. Me, I had no commitment to anything. Maybe that was because no one had any commitment to me.

I heard the beat of a helicopter's rotors above the ship, and then Ben's large and menacing frame filled the doorway. There could be no finesse in this. It had to be short and sharp. He mustn't get near the TPU.

Head down, teeth clenched, I jumped out and rammed him against the stack of crates.

My head was buried in his gut, my neck taking the strain. He bellowed like a wounded animal and his two clenched fists pile-drove down each side of my spine. I took the pain as best I could; my kidneys felt like they were exploding.

I struggled to force up my head, trying to get my hands round the back of his so I could make contact with the fucking thing. It would be OK to damage his face. It had to be. His face was going to get the worst of it anyway.

I could smell his stale sweat and the nicotine on his breath. His greasy hair fell over me like a clump of seaweed. Then he simply brushed me away as if I was an annoying kid.

His entire focus was on the TPU.

I grabbed his arm as he moved away from me and used his momentum to swing him around. He turned, and I let go. He banged his head against a stanchion and went down on his knees. I grabbed hold of the three metres of det cord still connected to the TPU, flicked it like a skipping rope over his back, whipped out the rubber pad and dived for cover.

The det cord kicked off and the concussion wave hit me, short and sharp, as my face was sprayed with warm blood. The detonation rattled around the cargo hold.

I jumped back up, in case he was doing the same.

He lay on the deck. The det cord had crossed his chest and the left side of his head. The explosion had cut a deep groove in his flesh and muscle, as if someone had run a chainsaw all the way down his body. He was still alive, still kicking out to fight the pain, but not shouting. He still had a job to do. He dragged himself towards the TPU, smearing blood over the carpet of wheat grains.

I wiped his blood from my eyes. I knelt next to him. He tried to push forwards, but it was no good. I put my right hand over his mouth and nose and my left behind what was left of his neck and pushed them together. He fought it. His hands came up but he knew it wasn't going to help him. His eyes burned with hatred and defiance.

After thirty seconds he started to struggle furiously, with all the frenzied strength that a man draws on when he knows he's dying. But no matter what he did now, he wouldn't be getting up.

His hands scrabbled at my face. I bobbed and weaved to avoid them, but maintained the pressure on his nose and mouth.

Gradually at first, his frenzy subsided. Soon there was

no more than a spasmodic twitching in his legs. His hands stopped grasping. Moments later, he was unconscious.

I gave it another thirty seconds. His chest stopped moving. Another thirty and I released him. He slumped face down in the wheat grains, grease and dirt.

9

Fuck knows what was happening on deck. I could hear helicopters in the hover.

I didn't know what I was looking for, but I went through his pockets anyway. They were empty. Maybe his wallet was with the rest of his gear in a cabin or up on the bridge. I rolled him over. The edge of a bloodstained piece of card peeped from the top of his shirt pocket. I pulled it out and turned it over.

Her face had been charred by the det cord, but she was as hauntingly beautiful in the photograph as she had been alongside Mansour on the gangplank. Thirties, maybe. Palestinian. Her piercing sea-green eyes gazed straight into the camera: passionate, obsessive, almost manic. Those eyes had burned into Lesser's with fierce love. They seemed to stare into mine with nothing but blame and reproach.

I legged it back to the door, across the corridor, and into the engine room. The engines were idling. I killed the lights. The stench of diesel fumes and grease was overpowering.

I tucked myself behind a couple of tool lockers.

I could extract myself when the ship had been towed into port. If I got lifted before that, at least I would be out of sight of the crew. I took deep breaths, sucking in the diesel fumes as I tried to re-oxygenate myself. What was left of Big Ben looked exactly like it should have done. He'd been cut almost in half by the det cord. To whoever found him, he must have gone in, cut the det cord to stop the ring main going off while he sorted out whatever the problem was, and the TPU had kicked off.

Shouts in Spanish echoed around the ship. Their search had begun. I sucked in more air and tightened myself up, as if that was going to make me smaller behind the lockers.

The doors opened and a torch beam flicked around the engine room. The main lights came on. Two seconds later, the muzzle of a 5.56mm assault rifle was pressing into my cheek.

I let them shout and holler. It was pointless trying to explain, even if they did speak English. I put my hands behind my head. It's always best to do that.

They pushed me down onto the floor, and gave me a proper going over. My hands were plasticuffed behind my back. A couple of unseen hands hauled me to my feet and dragged me towards the stairs. Lads were already at work on the device. I wasn't the only one who'd been well briefed. I just hoped I was part of their int.

I came out of the door into brilliant sunshine. I squinted like a mole. There wasn't a cloud in the blue Mediterranean sky.

The ship bobbed up and down in the swell. There were a couple of coastguard cutters tied up alongside. I looked down onto the deck of the first one and saw five pairs of eyes burning up at me. It didn't take a brain surgeon to work out what had happened. Duff's eyes burned the fiercest.

The Spanish boss looked over at me too. There was lots of nodding and more shouting. He had a series of pictures on a clipboard. He bellowed something at his troops and I was pushed to my knees. Then, like a fucking idiot, he gave me a nod and carried on. That was me well and truly fucked, even if there were a couple of lads in the crew who couldn't work out what I was.

I was helped down into the second cutter. As soon as I was aboard, the handcuffs were taken off and I was given a bowl of hot chocolate.

'You fucking shite! We'll get you one day!' Duff yelled his farewell as we pulled away.

He might have been right, for all I knew. But they'd have to join the queue.

PART TWO

10

Dun Laoghaire, Republic of Ireland
December 2007

If I drank any more tea I was going to die of tannin poisoning, but how could I turn her away? Ruby was getting too much of a kick out of going up to the counter and ordering like a grown-up. Besides, it was fun watching the eight-year-old coping with the motion of the ferry as she waitressed the cups back to us.

She waved excitedly at Tallulah and me from the queue and then grinned and pulled a face at a girl behind her who seemed to be doing a Steven Spielberg of her trip with a handheld camcorder. They both laughed and fell into the kind of animated conversation that girls of any age seem to be able to have with complete strangers.

'How old is that girl behind Ruby? Or is she a woman? When do you start calling a girl a woman? Twenty? Thirty?'

Tallulah looked up from her magazine and followed

my gaze. 'Depends, I guess. Some are women at twenty. Some are still girls at thirty.'

I looked out of the window. Only a few minutes ago all I could see was slate-grey sea and clear blue sky; now a frost-covered Ireland was filling it up fast. Last time I did this crossing by boat, I was a young squaddie aboard a Royal Corps of Transport ferry from Liverpool docks. The boats were flat-bottomed for beach landings, which turned the Irish Sea into a rollercoaster – and the ride usually lasted all night. Catamarans with jet engines were definitely the way to go. Stena Line's finest had whisked us here in ninety minutes flat. In fact, the crossing had taken us less time than it had to get from Tallulah and Ruby's house to the M4. The traffic leaving London had been so bad I wondered if I'd missed an announcement about an outbreak of the Ebola virus in Piccadilly.

Ruby delivered the latest two cups with a theatrical flourish as the tannoy announced we would soon be docking at Dun Laoghaire. Would all car passengers kindly return to their vehicles?

Or, in our case, Avis's vehicle: a supercharged Mercedes C Class estate, with all the bells and whistles. They were so proud of it when I collected it from the Mayfair office, I didn't like to trouble them with the news that I was taking it out of the UK.

'So what were you plotting and scheming with your new best friend up there?'

'She's nice. I said about the surprise. I said me and Tally don't even know where we're going for our holiday!'

'What did she say to that?'

'She said have a happy Christmas.'

'And that's exactly what we will do.'

'Where?'

I pretended to start spilling the beans but caught myself just in time. 'Nearly got me!'

'That's lovely! The whole family. Come on, Ruby, say cheese!' Up close I could see that Ruby's new friend looked more Eastern European than Irish, but the accent was pure Belfast.

Ruby turned and started waving at the lens.

I stood up and smiled apologetically. 'Just off to the toilet.' Old habits died hard; I just never felt comfortable in front of a camera.

'What's your mammy and daddy's names then?'

Tallulah wasn't impressed. 'Sorry, I feel uncomfortable about you filming my daughter. Please stop.'

By the time I'd got back Tallulah had gathered up the dozen or so magazines she'd bought at various motorway service stations yesterday and Miss Spielberg had gone.

Tallulah was on edge. 'I just don't like it. You never know where the footage could end up. There are some weird people out there.'

I wasn't about to disagree. Ruby's dad Pete had caught me on film not so long ago in Iraq, and when he was killed I'd ended up on a nationwide TV tribute to the guy. I was only on screen for a nanosecond, and I doubted I'd have featured in Gary Glitter's personal collection, but I didn't like it one bit.

11

I'd forgotten what it was like to travel with an eight-year-old. Ruby had a bladder the size of a walnut and we'd had to stop at almost every service station on the way to the ferry yesterday. Every time we did, Tallulah had found another couple of magazines she needed. I kind of understood, but couldn't help feeling that *Heat* and *Grazia* weren't going to fill the void left by Pete's death; it was the size of the Grand Canyon. I felt it too, and I'd only known him for about five minutes.

This had been a bit of a last-minute affair, so we hadn't been able to fly; every seat had been booked on every plane out of the UK since about September, and so had every hotel room from Land's End to the tip of Jockland. I'd only phoned Tallulah a few days ago to see how she and Ruby were doing, and discovered that actually neither of them was doing very well at all. Tallulah couldn't bear the thought of their first festive season alone without Pete, so I'd offered to take them away. Luckily for us, the cottage was still available, and since

Brits were wary of the Irish Sea in winter there was space on the ferry.

Tallulah stood up. She was tall, and her long wavy blonde hair made her seem even taller. She looked and dressed like a Notting Hill trust-fund hippie, but nothing could have been further from the truth. She and Pete had worked hard for everything.

The car deck was freezing and stank of diesel fumes. Coats and bags were stuffed into impossibly small spaces and doors and tailgates slammed before the wacky races to get out of the docks and onto the motorway began.

We squeezed between a couple of trucks to get to our gleaming Merc. It had cost a fortune to hire – even though I hadn't bothered with the insurance waivers – but I couldn't just cram these two into a budget hatchback after all that they'd been through in the last few months.

The car was packed to the gunwales with towels and duvets and brightly coloured suitcases. Somewhere underneath it all was my stuff: toothbrush – one; pants, socks, T-shirts – three: one on, one clean, one in the wash. Including their present, it fitted into a small holdall.

I pointed at the pile of bedding. 'You think I'd take you guys to a place with bare mattresses?'

Tallulah shifted in her seat. 'Just in case.' She shrugged. 'I'm a worrier.'

I gave her a smile and touched her lightly on the shoulder. She was doing her best, but I could see the tension in her face, and feel it in her shoulder muscles. She was finding her feet again, expanding her comfort zone inch by inch. It was painful to watch. She had a house to look after all on her own now, and, more importantly, her dead partner's child. I knew how she felt. I'd found myself in a similar position a few years ago, and fucked up big-time.

'Ruby!'

I looked across the deck. A few cars away, the girl with the camcorder was making her way towards us. Squeezed into the front passenger seat of the BMW behind her was a big, muscular guy with dark skin and a black leather jacket who glowered at me like a jealous boyfriend.

The girl beamed at Tallulah. 'I'm so sorry I bothered you. I spend so much time with a camera in my hand, I seem to end up filming everyone and everything.' She held out her hand. 'Mairead O'Connell.'

'Tallulah. Are you with a TV station?'

Mairead laughed. 'Nothing so glamorous. I'm Richard Isham's press secretary. Half my job is recording who he meets and what they talk about.'

12

We rolled off the ramp and into a bright sharp day. Exhaust fumes misted the air.

'Who's Richard Isham?' Tallulah said. 'Should I know?'

'Not really. Another one of these Irish politicos who's desperate to show that he's a fully paid-up member of the Good Lads' Club.'

Ruby tapped me on the back. 'What's that say? I can't read those words.'

She was pointing at the big sign saying *Welcome to Dun Laoghaire.*

'It's how the Irish write Dun Leary. Rhymes with dreary, dearie.' I was rather pleased with that one.

Tallulah smiled. 'That your theory, O'Leary?'

'What's this game?' Ruby demanded.

'It's just finished. I can't think of any more rhymes. But do you like games?'

'Yeessss!'

'Good. You'll like Christmas Day then.'

'Why?'

'That would be telling.'

The 200-mile drive to Donegal should take four or five hours, which meant closer to six, once we'd factored in regular stops for Ruby to empty the walnut and Tallulah to stock up on copies of *Irish Homes and Gardens*. At least we'd hit the village before the shops closed, and that was the main thing. Otherwise we'd have to do our shopping on the way, and there was barely room in the back for a pint of milk, let alone food and drink for the week.

Tallulah had stayed in the back with Ruby, which meant I still had a pile of duvets for company. I'd hoped she'd sit up front with me for this leg. When people sit in the back, it's not long before they get fed up leaning forward and trying to involve the driver; he ends up fading into the background. But fuck it, this wasn't my party. These two were grieving and needed each other.

We followed signs to Dublin. I could have used the Merc's Gucci sat nav, but I thought it might register back at Avis HQ. I didn't want alarm bells ringing in Berkeley Square and them sending in the stormtroopers to get their car back. Anyway, I couldn't be arsed to read the manual, and I knew my way round Dublin well enough. I just had to aim for the M1 and eventually peel off northwest.

'Nick, can we have the radio on?'

I winked at Ruby in the rear-view. 'Good idea. What kind? Talking? Music? We don't need the radio for that. I can sing.'

Her face fell. I'd overstepped the mark again somehow. Maybe her dad had used to sing to her in the car. I was walking on eggshells, and I was shit at it.

I hit the buttons and the Merc filled with perfect sound from about twenty separate speakers.

> *God Rest Ye Merry, Gentlemen,*
> *Let nothing you dismay*

I checked the rear-view. Ruby's mouth was moving with the words.

> *Remember Christ, our Saviour,*
> *Was born on Christmas day*

I checked Tallulah. She gave me a fleeting smile.

> *To save us all from Satan's power*
> *When we were gone astray*

I grinned. 'Quite a big ask for one bloke . . .'
Tallulah shot me a tense, not-in-front-of-the-children look. 'Maybe he just needed more friends to help him.'

> *O tidings of comfort and joy,*
> *comfort and joy,*
> *O tidings of comfort and joy.*

I didn't know her well enough to respond. Best to look at the road and shut up. By the time we'd hit the city out-skirts half an hour later, Ruby was asleep.

13

We turned off the N14 at Letterkenny and onto the N56 for the next fifty miles to Dungloe. The cottage was just a couple of miles beyond that.

As Tallulah nodded off too, my thoughts drifted to Little Miss Camcorder on the ferry. If she was working for Richard Isham, I was glad Tallulah had stopped her getting any more footage.

Richard Isham had joined the IRA at the age of twenty, a couple of years after the Troubles broke out. By the time of Bloody Sunday he was already high up in the Derry command.

When he was convicted of terrorist crimes by the Republic of Ireland's Special Criminal Court in 1974, he declared he was a member of PIRA and proud of it. They sentenced him to nine months' imprisonment.

After his release, he became increasingly prominent in the political arena. Our paths had crossed when he was in contact with the Firm during the hunger strikes in the early eighties, and later in the early nineties, by which time he was a fully fledged member of the IRA Army Council.

We never had the proof, but were pretty sure that Isham was responsible for a string of murders of members of the security forces, Protestant paramilitaries and alleged PIRA traitors.

Worst of all, in my book, he was a high-ranking member of PIRA's Northern Command in 1987, and had advance knowledge of the Enniskillen bomb. He and his mates could have stopped the carnage if they'd wanted to.

There was a lot of blood on Isham's hands, and if the lovely Mairead really was his press secretary, she was doing a good job at keeping it under wraps. After the Good Friday Agreement, any media investigation into his background had been actively discouraged, if not suppressed, and his membership of the Good Lads' Club was being protected on all fronts.

Which made me wonder briefly where the heavy in the front of the BMW fitted in. I had a feeling PR wasn't his game.

14

Ruby had fallen asleep again after our last 'comfort stop', as Tallulah called them, and Tallulah had finally come up front to get a better view.

'Knocks spots off Herne Hill.' She turned and looked at me, doing her best to relax.

I wanted to tell her that she didn't have to try so hard, that I knew coming with a relative stranger on this trip was a big deal, but I didn't know how.

'This is so good of you, Nick.'

'What? Agreeing not to sing?'

'You know very well. I want you to know . . . well, I couldn't have faced . . . Ruby's really excited.'

'So am I. I can't wait to play with the present I got you. I'm glad she's asleep.'

'Why?' She looked concerned.

I nodded towards another road sign. An Clochán Liath. 'She might have asked what that meant.'

Tallulah smiled. She hadn't just bought *Top Of The Morning* or whatever Irish *Hello!* was called – she'd also got herself a guidebook. 'I don't know how to pronounce it, but it's how they write Dungloe – it refers to the grey-coloured stepping stones which the townspeople once used to cross the river.' She read on: ' "The hills and cliffs of North West Donegal are still relatively unfrequented and little restraint is put on walkers. There are walks to suit all ages and interests. In the immediate vicinity you will find stunning unspoiled beaches, forest walks, quiet country roads and a wealth of historical sites to explore." '

'And a wide selection of pubs. I've done a bit of research too . . .'

'No you haven't. That applies to every village in Ireland.' She gave a little laugh. It was a rare thing, and sounded good.

'Everything OK?'

She looked down at her lap. 'Mind if I ask you some-thing, Nick? There must be plenty of other ways you could have been spending Christmas. What would you normally do? Family?'

I shook my head. 'Telly and the microwave. You're doing me a favour.'

She hesitated. 'Thing is, Nick, I need to make sure we're clear about something—'

'I think we'd better stop right here.'

I pulled up outside a small mini-mart. It was only just past four but already getting dark. The shop window lights reflected off the pavement. The woman who looked after the cottage was going to stick a pint of milk and a few other basics in the fridge when she came in to air the place and make sure the immersion heater was on, but we had to buy everything else. I switched off the engine. 'She's still asleep. You stay. What's her favourite cereal and stuff?'

'Shouldn't I – I mean, if I'm cooking . . . ?'

'This is your holiday. I'll do it. It's OK, there's a microwave. Prepare to be amazed. Man and machine in perfect harmony. Organic or ordinary?'

'What?'

'Baked beans.'

15

The hundred-year-old, two-storey stone farmhouse stood on a secluded twelve-acre site approached by a quiet tree-lined lane, two miles further on from a long, sweeping bay where huge Atlantic breakers pounded the shoreline. Tallulah seemed to find it all so beautiful I thought she was going to burst into tears.

'It's bigger than I was expecting . . . You said cottage.'

'Four bedrooms.'

She looked relieved, and I suddenly knew what she had been worrying about.

I turned away and took in the view. There was nothing but fields and hills as far as the eye could see. Not another building in sight, not even a barn. The house was surrounded by trees and blackberry bushes. The ground itself looked peaty with long grass and heather between rocky outcrops.

Ruby climbed out of the car. As if on cue, a couple of rabbits scampered into view to complete the fairy tale.

A big white porch led to the front door. I retrieved the

key from under a flower pot, turned the lock in the heavy oak door and ushered Ruby and Tallulah inside.

I followed them into a large kitchen with exposed ceiling beams. I put the kettle on the hot Aga. There was an old oak table and chairs, and a dresser that looked as ancient as the house, but also all the mod cons: fridge/freezer, dishwasher, washing machine, tumble dryer. And I was pleased to see there really was a microwave.

The snug living room had an open fireplace with a stack of turf next to the hearth and a dark mahogany parquet floor covered with bright rugs. Comfy-looking armchairs and a huge sofa completed the picture.

There was a separate dining room with oil lamps and antique mahogany furniture. Glazed double doors opened onto the back garden.

'You two go bag the best rooms and I'll unload the car.'

I was going to leave them to it but Tallulah followed. 'Ruby can explore.'

We went back into the kitchen and I switched on more lights. It was only then that I spotted the flowers on the table, and a bottle of wine and a card. Tallulah opened it.

'It's from Dom!' She was thrilled. 'This is Dom's place? I should have guessed as soon as you said Donegal!'

'Friends in high places.' I was rather pleased with myself.

'All the time we knew them, Pete always said we'd visit and we never . . .'

Her head dropped. A tear rolled down her cheek. I never knew what to say or do at times like this. Arranging the trip was the best I could manage.

'Thank you. It's lovely. I want to make sure you know

this. Things are hard for us right now and I really appreciate everything you're doing . . .' She paused. She fidgeted.

'Sounds like there's a bit of a but on its way?'

'But . . .' She smiled. '. . . it's just that, please, you mustn't worry about treading carefully. Everybody we know is still being so kind and understanding. I didn't realize how much I needed to get away from the . . . the . . . the whole widow thing. Do you know what I mean?'

I sort of nodded.

'Thank you. I don't want you thinking you have to second-guess us the whole time and wrap us up in cotton wool. This should be your holiday too.'

I spent longer than I needed to outside, and when I came back with my arms full of gear she was gone. I dumped it all on the floor. It took several more trips until the car was empty, and by then the kitchen looked like a bomb had hit it.

Tallulah reappeared. She'd composed herself. I helped her ferry their stuff – which meant everything apart from my small holdall – to the two rooms Ruby had bagged. Both were upstairs.

Tallulah had a big double with an old panelled ceiling. Ruby had the single next to it. They also had the only bathroom.

'And what have you picked for me, Ruby? The barn?'

She pointed downstairs. 'It's nice. There's a basin.'

16

I tipped out my holdall on the double bed and studied the badly wrapped parcel. I wondered if I'd bought the right thing.

It was strange to think of myself having a family Christmas – if you could call it that. First, because it wasn't my family. Second, because my own family's Christmases had been a nightmare. My stepdad would get pissed the night before and come home and beat up my mum. The presents were normally clothes for school, and the dinner was always crap because my mum would be in shit state. The only good bit was not having to go to school.

I threw my few clothes into a chest of drawers and listened to the sound of laughter drifting downstairs. They had lost a partner and a father, but they still had each other. I had no one, male or female; no friends, let alone a partner. I hadn't been lying. They were doing me a favour. At least this trip meant I got to talk to someone normal for a few days.

'Nick?'

Tallulah stood in the doorway.

'One other thing . . .' She didn't quite know where to look. 'It's just that I don't want you to think this can go beyond friendship . . . for now, anyway. Everything is still very raw . . .'

'That's not why I'm here.' I edged past her into the corridor. 'Fancy a brew?'

Her eyes suddenly sparkled and I felt her breath on my cheek. 'At the same time, Nick, don't run away from it.'

'Milk and sugar?'

As I disappeared to the kitchen, I heard her laugh out loud for the very first time.

17

I woke up early. It was still dark outside but I could tell the weather was going to be against us. Rain splattered the window. This was more like the Ireland I knew. I liked it. I'd had some good Christmases here in the army.

I got up and went and filled the kettle. While I was waiting for it to boil, I grabbed a lighter and a couple of old newspapers and headed for the living room. It would be nice for the girls to come down to a roaring fire. I was rolling and twisting a few pages as kindling when a photograph made me do a double-take. It was definitely him: the word *Bahiti* in the headline said so.

Liam Duff was kissing and telling. In fact, to quote his actual words: 'Since the Republican leadership has sold out, I might as well too.'

The article beneath his picture was a taster for what was to come – broad-brush stuff to make sure the readers ordered next week's copy. 'For many years I was loyal to the Republican cause, but I also supplied information to the British when I felt the leadership had strayed from its principles.'

He went on to say that the *Bahiti* operation had been betrayed by someone in the organization – not him – and that the legendary IRA bomber Ben Lesser had been murdered by the British. Strong stuff.

I put a match to the pyramid of paper sticks and sat back on my haunches. I checked, but the other papers I'd brought in pre-dated this one, and so did the ones in the kitchen. Last week's edition, when Duff would have spilled the beans, was nowhere to be found.

I laid a slab of turf on the blazing kindling and it began to glow. I added a couple more and put the guard across. I wasn't too worried. The paper was old, and there couldn't be anything to link me to it or Dom would have said something – if Special Branch hadn't got there first. For all that, Duff was an idiot. If he thought guys like Richard Isham would take this lying down, he had another think coming. He was going to be spending the rest of his days on the run.

I felt myself break into a smile. Not a bad idea: I could do with a bit of exercise myself.

18

It was weeks since I'd been near a gym or done any road work and I missed the endorphins. I poured water over a teabag and went and threw on my running gear. By the time I came back the brew was ready and it was just coming to first light. I drank it looking out of the window. The rain had done Avis a favour. The newly washed Merc gleamed like it was straight from the showroom.

I jogged down the drive in my usual steady rhythm. My ears and hands burned with cold, and my nose started to run as I breathed in freezing rain. I'd always liked running in winter. Maybe it was because I got wet and muddy, so the run felt a bit more gruelling, and I had accomplished more. How many thousands of miles had I run in my time as an infantryman and SAS trooper, then since? Eight years a soldier . . . Ten years in the Regiment . . . About twelve since I'd left. Thirty years, man and boy. I got to the bottom of the drive. Fifty weeks times thirty was one thousand five hundred. Left or right? Even Stevens. I turned left.

One thousand five hundred, times five for the number of runs per week . . . and an average of ten miles a run. Fuck me, seventy-five thousand miles. How many times round the earth was that? There might be a spot for me in the *Guinness Book of Records*.

Once over my first wind, my breathing became deep and regular and I was warm. I liked this. Running was when I got a lot of my best thinking done.

The sky was getting lighter, and the scenery around me was rugged. I passed a thatched cottage. They must have been early risers. Smoke curled from the chimney and I smelled burning turf. Probably not a second-homer like Dom; maybe a farmer or fisherman.

I pounded on methodically. At least Tallulah was talking about her grief. Not like some people who shoved it all deep down inside, slammed the lid and threw away the key. But hey, I liked it that way. Less to say and less to think about.

I hadn't known Pete well, but I missed him. It wasn't just because he'd saved my life during a fire-fight in Basra. It was because in a very short space of time I'd come to love him like a brother.

Pete and Dom – Poland's answer to Jeremy Bowen – had been embedded with British troops in Southern Iraq. It was my job to make sure each story they covered wasn't their last. Dom wasn't one of those bunker journos that gave their action-packed report from the safety of a Green Zone balcony. And that was my big problem. I spent every waking hour either pulling him down or away from something or someone that was trying to kill him.

Dom was one of those people who believed he could

walk through a battle zone without a scratch. Pete had nicknamed him Platinum Bollocks; he said he was the sort of guy who seemed to walk into nothing but good.

He lived in Dublin with his wife and stepson. They also had a holiday cottage in Donegal, and when I phoned, he didn't hesitate to let us have it. He felt he owed me as much as I owed Pete, and he probably wasn't wrong.

I pounded into a neat, sleepy village – a handful of houses scattered around a crossroads. There was one shop that doubled as the post office and pub. The air was thick with the smell of the sea.

Tallulah and Ruby had never been far from Pete's thoughts.

'You got family, Nick?'

'I did have, once.'

I could still remember the sudden rush of pins and needles in my legs.

'A little girl that looked a lot like your Ruby, as a matter of fact. Her parents were killed; I was her guardian. I never really got the birthday thing right . . . in the end I had to ask someone more reliable to take over.'

Somebody once told me I lived that part of my life with the lid on, and I guessed they were right. It was the way it had to be.

I saw a sign for a nature walk. Pete had said Ruby and Tallulah were into all that stuff.

I remembered asking him if there'd be things he'd miss when he left the front line and started taking pictures of flowers and squirrels instead. I could still hear his reply. 'Sure. The camaraderie. The brotherhood. Even when you're up to your neck in shit, you're surrounded by mates.'

He'd been in Kabul when Ruby's mum had fucked off to Spain with the bloke who built their extension. It was Dom and all the other guys who kept him afloat.

I rounded a bend and the sea spread out in front of me. A huge, horseshoe-shaped bay with breakers the height of houses. The harbour looked like it had seen better days. Now the stocks had declined and the EU quotas had come in, it looked like tourism had taken the place of fishing. Every shabby little building seemed to be a scuba-diving or windsurfing school.

The road skirted the bay. I ran towards a cluster of disused huts and shacks on the headland.

It had taken me a long time to put all the pieces together, but I eventually discovered Pete had been killed by an operator in the Firm who'd been using it as a cover for a heroin-running operation. I knew him as the Yes Man. For years he'd been my boss. I killed him. I also killed his two Northern Ireland-born enforcers, Sundance and Trainers.

Tallulah knew none of this, and she'd never learn it from me. She had enough on her plate. Her husband of just a few months was dead, and he'd been an orphan. With no other family to hand Ruby over to, his daughter was now her responsibility.

I turned and headed back towards them.

19

I'd met Tallulah a couple of days after Pete was killed. Dom went missing, and I flew back to London with my forearm brassed up by a 7.62 short.

I'd been parked on a hard plastic chair in the A&E department at Guy's Hospital for the best part of four hours the next morning when two Polish builders alongside me got very excited about something on the TV. I looked up to see the crystal clear, black and white nightsight images of me tumbling into the Basra sewage and Pete being my hero.

It was being played over and over, not only because it was great bang-bang footage, but also as a tribute to Pete – and Platinum Bollocks, of course, for filming it. Luckily, the Poles didn't make a connection between the face on the screen and the one sitting next to them.

When she opened the door of their house in Herne Hill, Tallulah was wearing a baggy red jumper and her feet were bare. The shock of long, blonde, wavy, hippie hair I'd seen in Pete's photographs and movie clips was tied back to the nape of her neck.

I remembered her reaction as I unzipped the side pouch of my Bergen and handed her the bag containing Pete's belongings.

'Thank you so much for doing this, Nick. You don't know what it means to me.'

She'd begun lifting out his things one by one. She almost caressed each item.

Then she came to his almost-new wedding ring and her shoulders convulsed.

I turned up from the lane and my trainers slapped along the drive. The rain had stopped. The sun was up; the Merc glistened.

Might something happen now between Tallulah and me? Maybe it would, maybe it wouldn't. I was scared by the possibility, but if it happened I'd go with it. But for now, it was early days. I liked the idea, but at the same time, it frightened me.

I leant against a tree to do my stretches. The cottage looked even more beautiful in this light, and I asked myself if I'd done the right thing turning down Platinum Bollocks' offer of a set of permanent keys.

Dom had read English Literature at Krakow University, done his national service and sailed into a job on the news desk of a Polish national newspaper. The rest was platinum-plated history. By the time I met him in Basra, he was the star of TVZ-24, a Polish channel with offices in Dublin.

He was tall and annoyingly good-looking, even when a thick layer of desert dust had given him a horror-film face. His *Top Gun*-style dark brown hair, blindingly white teeth and firm jaw line were featured most weeks next to his wife's equally good looks in Poland's answer to *Hello!*.

Dom had had another agenda while he was in Basra, I discovered. He was running a private investigation into the heroin trail from Afghanistan. It was a trail that eventually led him to the Yes Man. Pete was murdered as a warning, but Dom was like a dog with a bone. He ended up being bundled onto a rendition flight to Kabul, where I'd tracked him down and rescued him.

So yes, he owed me big-time, but no one knew that more than Dom himself. When I asked if I could borrow their cottage over Christmas, he said that he should really be handing me the deeds. I laughed. Of all the countries in all the world, Ireland would never be the wisest place for me to settle – Good Friday Agreement or no Good Friday Agreement.

It was just after nine. I pictured Tallulah messing around with the coffee grinder and the bacon sizzling in the pan. If it wasn't, I'd get it on the go. I wasn't as useless in the kitchen as I let on. I knew my way around a frying pan as well as a microwave.

I leant forward in a stretch. The rain hadn't cleaned the car quite as well as I'd thought. There was a muddy smudge along the door sill. Finger marks. There was also a depression in the mud beneath it, like the hollow a woodland animal makes when it sleeps.

I turned and walked away. I went in through the front door, and immediately threw the bolts behind me. Then I ran to the back of the house and did the same, and ran round and made sure every window was secure and kept the curtains closed. And then I went upstairs.

How the fuck was I going to explain to the girls their holiday was over before it had even started?

20

I put my ear to Tallulah's door. I could hear them talking. Either they'd shared a bed or Ruby had crept in during the night or when she woke up.

I called out. 'Room service – any teas or coffees for you ladies?'

'Teas please!' There was a smile in Tallulah's voice. 'And if some toast and honey finds its way onto the saucer as you're passing that would be lovely!'

Ruby giggled. 'Can I help? I'm a waitress!'

'No, no, no – you ladies stay exactly where you are. It's holiday time. Breakfast in bed.'

I ran downstairs to the kitchen and grabbed a knife. Fuck knows who or what was out there, but if they burst through the door right now all I had to defend us with was Mr Sabatier's finest.

I put the kettle on and threw some bread in the toaster.

I didn't know if there was a device under the car, but I had to assume there was. I hadn't seen a command wire so I didn't know if it was remote-controlled, but again, I couldn't take any chances. The smart money was on a pair of eyes up the hill, watching and waiting – either for all of us to come and get in the car, or, more likely, just me. Why would these two be the target?

The toast popped up and I took butter and milk from the fridge. The priority had to be keeping Tallulah and Ruby safe, preferably without them even knowing what was happening. They'd had enough trauma and distress to last them a lifetime.

I put the toast, butter and honey on a tray, and poured boiling water over a couple of teabags. There were shouts from upstairs. Ruby was enjoying the whole room-service thing.

'Waiter! Where *is* my breakfast?'

How would I get them out of here?

I was going to stay. I wanted to know what was under Mr Avis's pride and joy.

I piled the teapot, mugs and a little jug of milk on the tray, and then I picked up the phone and dialled a Dublin number.

'Dom. Nick. Listen, mate, can you come and collect the girls this evening? About five?'

Platinum Bollocks was concerned. 'You argued? They not liking it?'

I just said I needed him to get his arse up here to collect the girls, but only after five.

'Just give me two rings on the phone as you approach, and drive round the back of the house. Stay in the car, engine running, and they'll come out and jump in. Don't ask, mate, just do. I'll explain it all later, OK?'

I put down the receiver and picked up the tray. I

carried it upstairs and tapped on the door. 'Everybody decent?'

'Enter.'

They were sitting up in bed, all smiles. I put the tray down in front of them with a flourish.

'OK.' I grinned. 'Not only breakfast in bed, but a huge surprise.'

Ruby looked excited. 'What kind of surprise?'

'You sure you're ready for this?'

'I'm sure, I'm sure!'

'OK, we're in Ireland, right?'

'Right.'

'And you know they do things differently in different countries?'

'Yes.'

'Well, guess what happens differently here? In Ireland, today is Christmas Day!'

They both looked at me like I'd gone mad.

'Yeah, it's a fact. Finish your breakfast, take as long as you like. When you come down, it's present time.'

Tallulah stared at me with an arched eyebrow.

I tried to signal back that I'd explain later, and turned for the door before she had time to react.

They didn't appear downstairs for another half hour. Good. Only another six or seven hours of daylight to go.

'Is it really Christmas early here, Nick? Tally says you're joking.'

'Well, she's right; but the thing is, I can't wait any longer. I'm too excited. I want you to open your present.'

Tallulah shot me another disapproving glance.

I shrugged. 'OK, I'd better break it to you guys gently. It's a terrible forecast, so I thought we should have something to keep us busy. It's going to tip with rain any minute, and pour all day.'

Tallulah went to the window and raised her hand to the curtain.

'No, Tallulah, let's leave them closed. Keep it cosy. Anyway, we'll need to be in the dark in a minute.'

She looked at me strangely, but complied.

'Here we go.' I handed Ruby a badly wrapped box about the size of three stacked DVD cases.

She tore it open and she was so ecstatic I thought the ceiling was going to fall in.

21

Two hours later, Ruby had beaten me to a pulp too many times to count on the Wii tennis court, and every time Tallulah asked me a question about what was going on I somehow fobbed her off. She'd given up in the end and disappeared into the kitchen.

'Lunch is ready.' Her voice floated in from next door.

I looked at Ruby. 'You ready, champ?'

She nodded reluctantly and put down her Wii remote. We followed the smell of food.

'It's not raining, Nick. It doesn't even *look like* it's going to rain.' It sounded as if Tallulah had had enough. 'Let's get out this afternoon. What about a walk on the beach?'

'Nah, I fancy staying round here. Let's watch some telly.'

I flicked it on. The politicians of Northern Ireland were having a Christmas love fest for the cameras. Richard Isham gave Ian Paisley the full voltage, everlastingly sincere two-handed shake. He was looking fatter and healthier than when I'd bodyguarded him during his informal talks with Downing Street, when he'd decided politics provided a quicker route to power than Semtex had done.

It was never a surprise to me when these guys switched horses. Former terrorists were turning into statesmen everywhere on the planet, and had done since the dawn of time. Menachem Begin slaughtered British soldiers on the streets of Jerusalem and ended up on the red carpet when he arrived at 10 Downing Street as Israel's premier. Nelson Mandela and the ANC were outlaws who went on to run South Africa. Even Hamas is now the voters' friend in the West Bank. At this rate, it won't be long before Osama Bin Laden becomes a Goodwill Ambassador for the UN.

The peace process had produced the same result here, but that didn't mean everything in the garden was rosy. Even before 9/11, when the Americans had their first really big taste of the terrorism turkey, PIRA hadn't just raised funds in Boston and New York from tenth-generation Irishmen who thought of them as freedom fighters who played the fiddle in pubs in their spare time. They'd also made a fortune domestically from gambling, extortion, prostitution, bank robbery – and most of all, drugs. The police and army were too busy getting shot at and bombed, so there had been no one around to stop it. PIRA kneecapped dealers periodically as a public relations exercise, but only as a punishment for going freelance.

Richard might be having a kiss and a cuddle with Ian at Stormont right now, but deep down in the belly of the island, old habits died hard. There was just too much money at stake and they didn't want anyone else muscling in. Drugs were their big thing; they'd been running the trade for the last thirty-odd years.

Tallulah was now completely confused. 'You've been in front of that screen all morning. Is something the matter, Nick? You seem to be listening out for something. Are you expecting someone?'

'Father Christmas?' Ruby grinned.

I was going to have to switch to Plan B, whatever the fuck that was. 'OK, you're right. Tell you what, I'll go and take a shower when we've finished this fantastic food, and then we'll make some plans.'

22

I found the immersion heater in an airing cupboard next to the bathroom and switched it off at the mains. Then I took a very long shower.

Assuming it was me they were after, who had a motive? The list was as long as my arm. I stopped thinking about the motive – what about the opportunity? Who the fuck knew I was here? More than that, who would be able to spring into action so quickly?

Dom? No. The housekeeper? Ditto. The shopkeeper, or somebody in one of the villages who'd recognized me? Almost impossible, unless they'd been on the streets of Derry and Belfast in the eighties and recognized my face twenty-odd years on.

And absolutely nobody else knew I was here. Why should they? I had no one to tell where I was going. It wasn't like I had family or an employer who needed to keep in touch. And we hadn't been followed. I would have known.

I yelled loudly as the water ran cold and went back downstairs with a towel around me.

'Looks like the boiler's on the blink. I'll phone Dom, see if there's a quick fix.'

I picked up the phone in the kitchen and talked without dialling. 'Can I speak with Dom, please? It's Nick, a friend. It's a personal call. He'll know who I am.' I hummed a bit as I waited. 'Hi, mate – listen, the boiler's playing up. Yeah, it's run cold. Oh shit, really? That's not good. You think so? OK, that's great. See you at about five then?'

I went back. Tallulah gave me the arched eyebrow treatment again. I beckoned her into the kitchen.

'What's happening, Nick? You're behaving very—'

'I'm not sure, but I think there's somebody outside. Don't worry, they're after me, not you. But Dom is on his way to collect you as a precaution.'

23

The house phone rang twice moments before a set of headlights swept up the drive. He drove straight to the back of the house and left the engine running

The girls were ready. I shepherded them out to the car and saw them safely into the back before approaching Dom's window.

'Do you know who I mean when I say Liam Duff?'

'He's a household name.'

'Since when?'

'Since he was murdered last week.'

24

I hadn't seen a command wire earlier on. I didn't even know if there was a device. But if there was a command wire, there would still be somebody out there, watching and waiting for me to get into the car. Maybe the same guy who'd given Liam Duff the good news with a Black and Decker drill before finishing him off with a single shot to the head. Dom had checked out some pictures of the murder scene. He'd seen some serious shit in his time, but they had really turned his stomach.

I crawled out of the back door of the house, hugging the walls as I made my way to the front. I had a small torch I'd found in the fuse cupboard in my left hand and the kitchen knife in the other.

At the corner of the house I got down on my stomach and used my elbows and the tips of my boots to inch myself towards the car. Frozen water and mud seeped through my jeans and fleece, triggering some major league goose-bumps. Faster movement could give me away, and this way I had time to look and listen as the ice-cold wind rustled the grass and peeled a layer or two of skin off my face.

When I got to the car, I rolled onto my back and wriggled until my head was under the chassis. I made sure my fingers covered the lens of the torch before I switched it on. If I *was* being watched, it would be from the high ground the other side of the road, but I didn't want to make it any easier to spot me than I had to.

The beam brushed across it at once – a lunchbox-sized Tupperware container fixed under the driver's seat. Two big magnets had been stuck to the base with Isopon so it was quick to slap into position.

I still couldn't see a command wire. There was no antenna for a remote detonation.

I'd already shut myself off from the outside world. My entire focus was on this box.

There was a tiny hole with blackened edges in the lid of the container; it looked like it had been melted with a hot needle. A length of thin, eight-pound fishing line glimmered in my pencil-thin torch beam as it stretched from the hole towards the front of the vehicle. It was as taut as a bowstring; I didn't have to see where it went to know it was tied to a fish-hook that would have been snagged to the front offside wheel.

That meant I could rule out any remote detonation. There wasn't anybody on the hill. This device was going to explode the moment the car moved, and that pissed me off. There were innocent people involved here. The bomber might at least have had the decency to make sure he had eyes-on and killed only the intended target.

And the target had to be me: otherwise why place it under the driver's seat?

I wasn't going to touch it yet. I wasn't going to do anything for now but shine the torch around the semi-opaque Tupperware. It was fairly thin plastic, but the tiny beam wasn't strong enough to allow me to see inside.

The frozen ground numbed my back and hands. I found two more strands of fishing line, about three or four inches long, coming out of the other side. The priority had been to find out if it was armed, and how – and now I knew.

Every device has a safety catch. You place it, arm it, and then pull the safety pin. The three or four inches of fishing line would have started as just one or two, taped on the outside of the box to avoid them snagging. The fact that they'd been pulled meant the device was now rigged and ready to detonate. And any bomb-maker worth his salt would also have rigged an anti-handling device. Until I knew what kind this one carried, I couldn't cut the fishing line attached to the wheel and pull the box away.

I wriggled out from under the car and walked back to the house. Rummaging in the kitchen drawers, I kitted myself out with a dinner knife and a couple of cigarette lighters. Then I walked back to the car and went back to work.

25

My first job was to deal with the fishing line leading to the front wheel. No way was I just going to cut it with the knife. There was no telling how much tension it would take to trigger the thing, and cutting would create tension. Instead, I flicked the lighter and played the flame close to the device so there'd be no line left dangling to snag or pull.

The prime initiation mechanism was now dead, but that wasn't the same as saying the whole IED was. I still had to assume there was an anti-handling device.

I flicked the lighter again and held the tip of the dinner knife in the flame until it glowed. It took so long my thumb got scalded.

I put the knife straight to the two-strand end of the box and managed to cut through the plastic for a few seconds before the steel went cold. Then I had to roast my thumb all over again. I finally cut a two-inch square hole, and shone the torch inside.

There were no surprises. My fingertips touched a thin

plastic sheet about halfway down. It would be sitting on top of a slab of PE. A clothes peg had been glued in place at each end. The torch beam also caught the outline of a test tube. A ball bearing glinted inside. I'd found the anti-handling device.

I probed further. I could feel a drawing pin in the jaws of each of the clothes pegs. They were touching, and therefore completing an electrical circuit. I felt for the plastic disc that would have sat between them until whoever had placed the bomb yanked it away with the two strands of fishing line.

I pressed open the peg and eased the disc back into place. The drawing-pin terminals were separated again. The circuit was broken. That just left the anti-handling booby trap.

The bomber had wedged a little bit of cardboard under one end of the Tupperware box to create enough of a gradient for the ball bearing to roll to the bottom of the tube. As soon as it rolled back up, either because the car was mobile, or because the device had been disturbed, the ball bearing would touch the two nails protruding from the rubber bung in the open end. The nails were connected to wires. A second circuit would have been completed when the ball bearing bridged the gap.

I pulled one wire free, took a deep breath and pulled the box gingerly from the chassis. It wasn't easy; the magnets were strong, and I didn't want to jerk the device.

Keeping it nice and level in case there was yet another anti-handling mechanism I hadn't spotted, I lowered it to the ground next to me. I wriggled out into the open air then reached back and retrieved it.

I carried it into the house. It weighed a good couple of

kilos, more than enough PE to blow all three of us to smithereens. Half a kilo would have killed the driver, especially if the charge had been shaped to direct most of the *brisance* up my arse and through the top of my head. Whoever had placed it didn't give a shit about collateral damage.

I placed the bomb on the kitchen table then went into the front room and switched on the TV. I didn't have to wait long. As I hopped from channel to channel, my old mate Richard Isham appeared on the screen.

'You were at his funeral today,' the reporter said. 'Any thoughts on Liam Duff you'd like to share?'

Isham did his best to conjure up a look of infinite grief. 'I've known him since we were both in the cages of Long Kesh. He was a popular and likable person.'

Yeah, right. Until about two weeks ago.

Isham said he'd been drafting a speech when the call came through to tell him of Duff's murder. 'The news came as a tremendous shock and surprise – especially the horrific way in which he had died.'

How had he reacted to the revelation that Duff had been a British double agent?

Isham gave a shrug of his shoulders. 'Philosophically.'

Any thoughts on who'd murdered him?

The camera pulled back for a wider shot of the funeral cortège, and I caught a fleeting glimpse of Little Miss Camcorder. She was filming the interview.

Isham was swift to align himself with the London and Dublin governments. 'Neither of them believe Republicans killed him. The IRA said it did not kill Duff and I believe them. You have to remember, Special Branch and the British intelligence agencies are forever

93

trying to undermine and work against the peace process. Investigations in the past have found evidence of British agencies being involved in dirty tricks and criminal acts, including murder. The jury is out on this one.'

I'd seen enough.

I went back to the kitchen and switched on all the lights. Only now did I risk peeling off the lid. It was a simple but extremely well-made device. Every component had been glued onto the sheet of plastic resting on top of the big yellow block of plastic explosive. All the wires connecting the clothes-peg and test-tube circuits to the battery in the corner were glued down. This wasn't amateur hour.

I disconnected the wires from the battery terminals one at a time, and then removed the battery altogether. I touched the ends of the wires to earth them, and then twisted them together. It could take less than two ohms of current to set one of these off, and you generate that just by rubbing your hands together. Now no amount of electrical leakage in the house or even a freak thunderstorm could detonate this thing.

I prised the plastic circuit board away from the yellow slab and cut the two wires leading from it. None of this red wire, blue wire business – I just cut whatever I could.

Once the det was out, I twisted its wires together and put it to one side. All that was left was the block of Semtex. They hadn't skimped. There was enough there to blow up an armoured Land Rover. Without a detonator, the PE was harmless. You can even burn it, which was exactly what I intended to do.

A lot of care and attention had gone into the construction of the circuit. All four drawing pins had been roughened with emery cloth to ensure a good contact. Even the nails inside the test tube had been rubbed down, and the ball bearing had been polished free of any contamination. And most significant of all, every one of the connections between wires was finished off with Chinese pigtails.

If nothing else, I knew where this fucker had been to bomb school.

26

I dug a hole about a foot deep with a big cooking spoon not too far away from the back door, threw in the det and replaced the earth. I'd connected a metre or so of two-strand wire I'd ripped from a table lamp to its terminals. I couldn't just leave the device lying around. The easiest way to dispose of it was with a controlled explosion, and then to burn the PE separately.

I touched the wires to the battery terminals, but the plan went the way of all the others I'd made this Christmas. There was no dull thud in the mud as the circuit was completed. Yet the wiring was correct, and the det hadn't been tampered with. It was very rare for a det to malfunction, so that could only leave the battery. I touched the terminals to my tongue, with no effect. No mild fizz. Batteries keep their charge better in cold conditions, so it could only mean the fucking idiots had used a dud and not tested it.

I took the bulb out of the torch, connected the wires to

it and switched it on. There was a dull, reassuring thud and a tremor in the mud.

I scooped a few handfuls to one side and threw in the slab of PE. I held a lighter to a corner. It ignited, and burned rapidly with a hiss and a bright white flame. All it was doing was combusting as it would have done if the det had initiated it, but much more slowly. It still generated enough heat to melt metal, and made short shrift of the Tupperware and the circuit board. I pushed the mud back over the residue and went back inside.

The girls had taken their suitcases with them. The only stuff left was the Wii machine, my holdall and the mountain of bedding. I packed, locked up, went out, opened the boot and threw it in.

I drove down to the road and turned left. Dom had checked out Duff's address. I checked the maps. It was sixty-four Ks to the north. An hour maybe, an hour and a half at the most.

Who would have murdered him? Dom had got out of his car and taken me out of earshot. The papers were full of conjecture. One of them had even conducted an opinion poll. Most of their readers thought it was PIRA, but some suspected the Brits. Who knew what beans the old sailor boy had been about to spill? The only question I wanted an answer to was: whatever individual, faction or organization was responsible, had they also planted the device under my car?

The link looked cast-iron, which was why I was going to Duff's to see what I could see. The police had probably bagged everything up and taken it away, but I might see something that they had missed.

As I drove, the same question ricocheted around in my

head. Who knew both how to find me, and how to construct and plant a device? Unless it was some totally random hater of tourists or Merc drivers, he probably knew how to find me again. That was a good thing, as far as I was concerned. Next time I'd be waiting.

I pulled into town and parked outside the Spar. Before getting out of the car I checked for anyone watching or waiting. I memorized the last three digits of any passing plate for later.

I got out, zipped up my muddy fleece, and headed into the shop. The old guy behind the counter didn't look startled or surprised to see me alive. It was a fair assumption he wasn't the tout. He asked me how my Christmas was going, which was probably a superfluous question given that I was clutching a pack of manky, two-day-old sandwiches, some ready-salted, and a can of Coke. *No, mate, this ain't quite the way I'd imagined the festive season turning out.*

Back out on the dimly lit street I didn't stop to check who was looking and waiting, just got back into the car and drove. If they were there, I'd soon know about it.

Maybe it was Dom they were after? Maybe they'd confused us. There were a good few people who might feel they had a score to settle with him. Dom had lifted a lot of lids over the years that everyone from PIRA to the Firm would have preferred to remain sealed. It was Dom who'd reported the story about the busting of the drug-smuggling ring the Yes Man ran over here. But he was only the messenger. He didn't claim any credit for it. I was the one who'd made enemies of the drug chain that would have to start all over again . . .

After fifty minutes I turned off the main road and onto

98

a narrow lane. The track that led to Duff's house was a mile and a half further north.

Maybe my enemy was inside the Firm. Maybe the bomb-maker hadn't been shown how to use pigtails in one of the Middle Eastern camps before coming home to put it into practice; maybe he was one of the original trainers now working for the Firm?

The Firm had the motive. Sundance and Trainers were small fry, low life like me. No one would be pissed off about them becoming history. But the Yes Man?

I came to the track leading to Duff's cottage, and carried straight on. Parked right across the gate was a white Ford with the word Garda emblazoned in black across the fluorescent yellow flash along its side. The two officers inside watched me intently. I was probably the first sign of life they'd seen all shift.

I'd have to carry on north. I couldn't turn round and come back past them again. They'd probably already logged my number.

I pushed the Merc another three or four miles before I finally hit the junction I wanted. I turned right and had gone no more than half a mile when my mobile rang. It was Dom.

'Nick, I've just received a really weird message from the station . . . A man called, fifties maybe. English. He said—'

'Don't say it. Have you got to where I thought you were going?'

'Yes.'

'I'm on my way.'

27

The first time I'd gone to Dom's house, the cab driver told me that on the Dublin Monopoly board, the streets in his area were the purple squares. As soon as we'd got there, I could see why. These were big, fuck-off, four-storey houses set back from the road. They had huge rectangular windows, so the grand could look out on the less fortunate. Raised stone staircases led one floor up to very solid and highly glossed front doors.

It was just coming to first light as I drove down the road. I wasn't going to try and hide the car or be covert. What was the point?

Lights were still on in several of the houses and curtains were open to display the gilded furniture and big chandeliers to best effect.

I was still trying to work out what to say to Tallulah and Ruby. I'd keep up the dud boiler story until it went to rat shit.

I drove past 6 Series BMWs and shiny 4x4s. The last time I'd walked past so many brand-new cars I'd been in a Middle East showroom. This place was knee-deep in euros.

The hall light of No. 88 shone through a glass panel over a wide, shiny wooden door. I couldn't see any light or movement through the front windows or upstairs. I guessed they'd all be in the kitchen area at the back.

I parked right outside the house. I wanted to be able to keep an eyeball on Mr Avis's forty grand's worth.

A car went past. Its last three digits weren't any of the combinations I'd memorized. I got out and went and knocked on the heavy iron lion's head on the front door.

The voice that answered a few seconds later was female and Irish. 'That you, Nick?'

'Yup. Failed Boiler Maintenance Man of the Year.'

It wasn't just the housing jackpot Platinum Bollocks had hit. Siobhan looked stunning even in jeans, trainers and a black sweatshirt.

She stepped aside. 'Come on in.'

I crossed the threshold and started wiping my shoes on a big square of matting until I noticed Tallulah's and Ruby's shoes lined up next to a pair of men's trainers. The highly polished black and white chequered tiles looked clean enough to do surgery on. This was a no-shoes zone.

'Dom explained about the boiler. I'm so sorry. It's never happened before.'

'He should try paying the bill. It works for me.'

She was already walking down the chandeliered hall. 'Tea or coffee?'

'Coffee – strong. I might be back on the road.'

'Stay here, there's—'

'Hot water?' I laughed a bit too long.

Subject dropped. Mission accomplished.

We passed the open door to a reception room and finally arrived in the kitchen.

It was a large knock-through that took up the whole of the rear of the building. I was in a world of stainless steel and glass, limed oak and spotlights. Four gas rings seemed to float in a polished granite island in the middle of the room.

Dom and Tallulah were on stools. Ruby was tucking into a bowl of cereal at the table in the corner.

I gave an exaggerated gesture of surrender. 'Well, I tried. No chance of a plumber this side of New Year. But I've got a mate coming over from London. I'll meet him off the ferry and take him up there. Soon as it's fixed, I'll give you a call.'

Dom looked at me as if I'd barked at the moon.

Ruby looked up from her cornflakes. 'I like it here.'

'You mean the TV's bigger?'

She grinned, caught out. 'Can we stay, Tally?'

Siobhan jumped in. 'Yes, why don't you stay a bit longer? We three girls could have a good catch-up.'

Dom got off his stool. 'OK, Nick – let's you and me go do some boiler talk.'

I followed him through double doors that had been punched through the dividing wall. He offered me a blue velvet two-seater one side of the low coffee table and sat down opposite. I had a good view of the car. Good; that meant they had a good view of me.

The fireplace to my left was tiled. The black grate was far too shiny ever to have been used. The mantelpiece was covered with all the usual pictures of two people's lives together, but no framed prints of Dom being heroic with a microphone. There was, however, a gold award that looked like the Flying Lady on a Rolls Royce. *Veiled Threats*, the documentary that had made Pete and Dom famous, had scooped the Emmys a couple of years back.

'OK, Nick, let's cut to the chase. This isn't about the boiler, is it?'

'Something's come up. I've got to go back to London and I didn't know how to tell them.'

'Work?'

'Sort of. I don't know how long I'll be. Just a couple of days, with any luck. Do you mind letting them stay, keeping an eye on them?'

'They're not in any danger, are they?'

'Why do you ask?'

'You keep glancing out of the window. Not expecting Leptis to make an appearance, are you?'

I looked up sharply.

'The message to the station I phoned you about – he said to tell you he knew what was happening at the house, and he knows what it's all about. He has the answers. He said to go and see him soon as you can. He said you'd understand.'

'And he said his name was Leptis? No mistake about that?'

He shook his head. 'You sure this shouldn't be a police matter?'

28

I said goodbye to Tallulah in the front room, in full view of the street. I waved my arms about, demonstrating some of the shots I'd use to beat Ruby at Wii tennis next time I saw her. She thought I was mad. Seconds later I stormed out of the house, slammed the car door and drove off much too fast.

I headed for the ferry terminal and bought a one-way ticket. To anyone watching, this was one man's Christmas that hadn't gone well.

I checked my rear-view all the way to the dock. I took note of the cars behind, and even stopped for a brew on the five-mile route between Ballsbridge and Dun Laoghaire. I checked who drove in with me, and if they followed me back onto the road. I checked anyone who got out of their cars or even just looked at me.

I saw nothing suspicious, and that scared me as much as it would have done if I had. Apart from the dud battery, these guys were good. They would come at me again; the only questions were where and when. For all I knew, they might brass it out on the boat and come and check the device was still where they'd placed it, and try and sort out whatever had stopped it from detonating.

29

I drove the Merc up the ramp, to where one of the crew directed me behind a van and next to a small truck. I rearranged stuff busily in the glove compartment and watched the wing mirror to see who came in behind me.

Maybe this ferry was their next killing ground. A risky place for a murder, but my body wouldn't be found until the ferry docked in Holyhead and my car failed to move. By the time one of the crew came to see why and found me slumped over the steering wheel with two extra holes in my head, a biker, the driver of a car near the off ramp or even a foot passenger could be well on their way.

An SUV pulled up carrying a family of four. Mum told the kids to hurry up or they wouldn't get good seats upstairs. Dad told them there was no rush, they had reservations. Mum told them to hurry up anyway.

I climbed out of the Merc and stretched. I scanned the car deck like I was looking for a friend. I couldn't see any obvious threat; no vanload of heavies in bomber jackets, no biker keeping his helmet on.

People squeezed between vehicles as they made their way towards the stairs either side. I got back in the Merc, as if I was waiting for the rush to die down. I tidied a couple of duvets on the passenger seat next to me, and a couple of bottles of wine I'd rescued from the kitchen table as I left the cottage.

The last car was on board and the ramp had gone up. The final trickle of passengers had made their way to the stairs. The crew would soon be doing a check to make sure no one had stayed behind.

I gathered the duvets and bottles and got out. I put the bottles on the deck then went and lifted the tailgate. I made as if to throw the duvets in, but bent down and pushed them under the chassis instead. I closed the tailgate again and blipped the key fob. I went back round to the driver's door, and looked around. No crew watching. I bent to pick up the bottles and rolled under the truck alongside me.

I hadn't bought my ticket with cash or practised any sort of tradecraft. I continued to act as if I didn't know the device had been planted. I kept everything overt, to try and bring whoever was responsible back to the car.

Who the fuck was it? Only three people in the world knew what 'Leptis' meant: Colonel Lynn, the Libyan spook who'd coined it and me. Unless . . . *shit* . . . Lynn may have mentioned it in a report, which meant it was sitting in a file. Anyone at the Firm with the appropriate level of clearance would have had access to it.

Whoever they were, I really wanted them to find me

now. I wanted to be picked up. I wanted some fucker to come and have another go.

I reached under the Merc and grabbed the duvets. I wriggled to get one of them under me, and pulled the other over the top. The steel plates of the deck were freezing cold, and the air temperature wasn't much better. I kept the wine bottles within reach. They were the only weapons I had.

30

When the ship cast off and began to move with the swell, I felt for a moment like I was back in the cargo hold of the *Bahiti*. I just hoped this wasn't fate coming full circle and propelling me towards a hot date with a length of det cord.

1987 had been a good year for Lynn and me, but a terrible one for PIRA. In February, Sinn Fein had fielded twenty-seven candidates in the Irish general election but they'd only managed to scrape about a thousand votes each. It showed how out of touch PIRA were. Few people in the south gave a toss about reunification with Northern Ireland; they were far more concerned with other issues like unemployment and the crippling level of taxation. Ordinary people really did believe that London and Dublin could work together to bring about a long-term solution to the troubles.

PIRA and Sinn Fein were in danger of being marginalized, and must have decided they needed a morale booster. Their knee-jerk reaction was the murder, on

Saturday 25 April, of Lord Justice Maurice Gibson, one of the province's most senior judges. I saw the celebrations first-hand in PIRA's illegal drinking dens that weekend. I even had a few pints myself as I hung around. The players loved what had happened. Not only had they got rid of one of their worst enemies, but recriminations were flying left, right and centre between London and Dublin. The Anglo-Irish accord, which had done so much to undermine PIRA's power base, was now in question itself.

Barely had the hangovers receded when, two weeks later, PIRA suffered its biggest loss in a single action since 1921. On 8 May, at Loughgall in County Armagh, the Regiment ambushed and killed eight of PIRA's East Tyrone Brigade while they were attempting to bomb a police station. I was there, and I knew that we'd been acting on a tip-off from an undisclosed but highly placed source.

PIRA was reeling. From a force of 1,000 hardcore players in 1980, its strength had already been cut to fewer than 250, of which only fifty or so were members of active service units. Our successes had cut this down to forty, which meant that the operation at Loughgall wiped out one-fifth of PIRA's hardliners at a stroke. If this carried on, the remaining members of PIRA would soon be able to share the same taxi. A couple more tip-offs and they might be history.

Loughgall was followed by a disastrous showing by Sinn Fein in the British general election. The Catholic vote was switching to the moderate SDLP. Then, in October, during Sinn Fein's annual conference in Dublin, Spanish forces seized a small freighter called the *Bahiti* in the Med, and Colonel Gaddafi's early Christmas present to PIRA.

The humiliation was complete. No wonder PIRA wanted revenge, and some sort of publicity coup to show people like Gaddafi and those Irish-Americans who contributed to Noraid that they hadn't completely lost their grip.

On 11 November, Remembrance Day, PIRA planted a 30lb bomb with a timer device at the town memorial in Enniskillen in County Fermanagh. I arrived on the scene soon afterwards and saw the carnage with my own eyes. Eleven civilians lay dead in the mountain of rubble and twisted steel, and more than sixty were seriously injured.

Outrage at the atrocity was instant and worldwide. In Dublin, thousands lined up to sign a book of condolence. In Moscow, not a place well known for its community care, the Tass news agency denounced what it called 'barbaric murders'. Even Gaddafi disowned them. But worst of all for PIRA, even the Irish-Americans appeared to have had enough.

They'd fucked up big-time. They'd thought the bombing would be hailed as a victory in their struggle against an occupying power, but all it had done was show them up for what they really were. It might be one thing to kill 'legitimate' targets like judges, policemen and members of the security forces – but murdering innocent civilians while they were honouring their dead at a Remembrance Day service?

PIRA's very existence was at stake, leaving the field wide open for the UDA and other Protestant paramilitaries to have the drugs rackets to themselves. There were no sectarian divides when it came to money – just normal competition and greed. PIRA and the UDA used to get together on a regular basis to carve up the drug, prostitution and extortion rackets, even to discuss demarcation lines for different taxi firms and sites for gaming machines. They had the infrastructure, the knowledge and the weapons to be major players in the world of crime. With cooperation from other terror organizations throughout the world, the possibilities were endless.

And that was why people like Richard Isham had taken a brisk pace forward and announced they were turning from the gun to the ballot box.

31

The boat was docking and I still had no definitive answers. No one had come for me or even checked the car. I'd been hoping they would; I'd been hoping I could jump someone and beat a few answers out of them.

As things stood, the only thing I knew more or less for certain was that it could be any one of three groups of people who were after me: PIRA, the Firm or the Mujahideen. They were the only people, as far as I knew, who used Chinese pigtails in their IEDs. The Muj could be ticked off the list straightaway. Even in mountainous Donegal, a carload of Bin Laden lookalikes would be just a little bit conspicuous.

The Firm have phenomenal electronic firepower at their beck and call. Using the Echelon system, GCHQ could capture radio and satellite communications, mobile phone calls, emails and other data streams nearly anywhere in the world. Was that how they'd tracked me to the house, by pinging my mobile phone? If so, it was lucky I spoke to Dom on the landline or they'd know where I was right now.

Would they have taken innocent lives just to get to me? Yes. They'd killed Pete to try and get to Dom. They wouldn't care; it would just look like an attempt by RIRA – the Real IRA, resurgent elements of PIRA hardliners who refused to buy into the peace process – to kill an ex-member of the SAS and put themselves on the map.

I had no contacts, let alone friends, on the inside at Vauxhall Cross. No official points of contact, no mates I could turn to. Even my old contacts in the RUC (now PSNI) or Irish Special Branch couldn't help me if the Firm was involved. The Firm trumped every other card in the pack.

This message from Leptis ... Maybe it wasn't Lynn trying to help or 'having the answers'. Maybe he'd simply been roped in to channel me to his home, the next killing ground?

I would have to assume the worst – that Lynn was being coerced – and act accordingly. But first, I would have to find him.

It was ten years since I'd last seen him. An ex-spook like him would hardly be in the phone directory or have a Facebook page, and I didn't have him on speed dial.

PART THREE

32

I drove off the ferry and into Holyhead. I parked up near
the first internet café I could find and paid for an hour.

If they were following me they'd soon find out where
I was heading. I checked the windows and there was still
nothing obvious to tell me anyone out there walking the
streets, sitting in a parked car or just mincing about
window-shopping had a trigger on me. Maybe they
didn't have to now: they'd just lift me at Lynn's place,
once I'd found out where it was.

My first port of call was obvious: I tried a site that
searched the telephone directory. I didn't know Lynn's
first name, but had to insert at least an initial. It was
going to be a laborious process. I started with A Lynn and
Norfolk as the location, and got over a hundred results
straightaway – just for the site's free directory enquiries
listings. There were many more listings on the electoral
roll and birth, marriage and death records, but you had
to pay to view them. This wasn't going to work. I could
plough through a couple of thousand free listings,

and still not have a result. He could be ex-directory.

The only clue I had to a more specific location came from our twenty-year-old conversation at the Tripoli docks, and what he had told me in his office ten years ago, when he was forced into early retirement after a deniable job he'd sent me to do in America had gone very wrong, and his head had rolled.

After the Tripoli job, Colonel Lynn came back to the UK and acted as liaison between the MoD and SIS. He'd sent me to Washington to deal with a renegade operator, and I had. But others, mostly Americans, got caught in the crossfire, and since this all happened inside the White House, I wasn't exactly flavour of the month. Since then he'd treated me as if he was a bank manager and I was asking for a bigger overdraft, trying hard to be nice but never quite managing to conceal his disdain. I didn't mind. I'd been used to that kind of shit since I was a kid. As long as he didn't expect me to look up to him with reverence.

I still remembered asking to be put on the fulltime pay-roll, permanent cadre as a K, a deniable operator. His words stung in my memory.

'After your total lack of judgement, do you really think that you would ever be considered for permanent cadre?' His face flushed. It was the first time I'd ever seen him angry. 'Think yourself lucky you are still on retainer. Do you really think that you would be considered for work after you –' his voice got louder and his right index finger stabbed the air more vigorously with every point – 'one, disobey my direct order to kill that damned woman. Two, actually believe her preposterous story and assist her assassination attempt in the White House. God, man, your judgement was no better than a love-struck school-boy's. Do you really think a woman like that would be interested in *you*?'

He couldn't contain himself. It was as if I'd touched a raw nerve.

'And to put the tin lid on it, you used a member of the American Secret Service to get you in there . . . who then gets shot! Do you know the havoc you have caused, not only in the US but here? Careers have been ruined because of you. The answer is no. Not now, not ever.'

That was when I realized this wasn't just about me, and it wasn't early retirement at the end of his tour next year. He'd been given the push. He had been running the Ks, the deniable operators, at the time, and someone had had to pay. People like Lynn could be replaced; people like me were more difficult to blow out, if only for financial reasons. The government had invested several million in my training as a Special Air Service soldier. They wanted to get their money's worth out of me even after I got out. It must have killed him to know that I was the one who'd fucked up, but he was the one to carry the can – probably as part of the deal to appease the Americans.

I didn't feel sorry for him for long. The Intelligence Branch, the top tier in the Firm's food chain, looks after its own. Even if one of the IB has been given the sack for such gross misconduct as fiddling with kids and getting blackmailed for it, he or she goes into a feeder system where they get work somewhere in the City or in a sports organization. That ticks two boxes: it keeps tabs on them, but also it keeps them sweet, and, more im-portantly, quiet. Me? Once I was no longer useful, I wouldn't be so lucky. Maybe this really was my time.

At that last meeting he told me what his future held. He didn't need to become a share dealer or the chair of the Sack Race UK Committee. He had the family mushroom farm. He'd talked, too, about sailing and Norfolk, and opening your window and smelling the sea. His farm couldn't be more than a mile inland.

I Googled 'Norfolk+mushrooms', got 33,000 results, changed the search to 'Norfolk+sailing' and up popped about thirty sailing clubs. I tried phoning one from my mobile. Fuck it, if they had my number they would be following anyway. They might as well know where I was going. If this didn't draw them out nothing would. I only got voicemail. Of course – these would just be little set-ups; there wouldn't be anyone around to answer.

One club said it was in the homeland of Admiral Nelson, and I remembered he'd mentioned a pub called the Hero. I Googled it. It was in a place called Burnham Overy Staithe, about halfway along the top edge of Norfolk.

I started to punch in the pub's number then thought better of it. Lynn would be expecting me – why else would he have sent the message? But what if I was wrong and the Firm wasn't after me? Charging around the village asking questions could be a mistake – this was backwoods country, where blood was thicker than water and neighbours were actually neighbourly.

No matter; if the pub landlord couldn't tell me where he lived, Google Earth might be able to.

I went back and zoomed in on the area. The whole north coast was a patchwork of farmland. And what did a mushroom farm look like when it was at home? I didn't have a clue, but Mr Google did. He told me: 'A mushroom farm would consist of a number of environmentally controlled growing sheds and because the conditions are fully controlled, high temperatures are not a problem. A pack-house and cold store are also required along with offices and staff facilities. An area of concrete and a pasteurization room would be required for the production of compost.'

I went back to Google Earth and the overview of Burnham Overy Staithe. I moved the cursor left and right, up and down from the centre of the village, and finally found what I was looking for: a line of three large, low-level outbuildings, with a large farmhouse, some smaller sheds and a couple of cars. The farm sat in a triangle of land, bordered on all three sides by B roads. I noted the lat and long, and the road names.

I got back in the car and headed northeast towards Manchester. From there, I'd drive cross-country, southeast to King's Lynn. I'd then hit the North Sea, and turn right.

33

One question bugged me all the way to Manchester. If the Leptis message was from Lynn, how could he be sure I'd find him? Maybe he had faith in my tradecraft skills. It had only taken me half an hour in the internet café and I was on my way. So would he be expecting me? Maybe he was lulling me into a false sense of security, making me think I was making the running, when all the time he was channelling me into the killing ground.

What if the detonator battery had been dead because it was meant to be? I wasn't sure where that thought got me, but it didn't matter. Lynn would soon be telling all I needed to know.

It took me five hours of driving at, or under, the speed limit so I didn't get pulled over, but eventually I was in amongst the flat, endlessly boring fields of Cambridgeshire. Rain fell in a constant shower. The road was elevated in places and there were dykes either side, waterways draining the fenland, and miles and miles of jet black earth growing spuds or carrots or whatever.

A mile or two from King's Lynn, I stopped at a garage and bought sandwiches and a bottle of Coke, and fold-out road maps of the coast. I also filled up with fuel. You always start an op with a full tank.

As I walked back across the forecourt I could already feel the breeze off the North Sea. King's Lynn was at the bottom corner of the Wash. The Great Ouse ran through it, which was presumably how the ships made it into the docks.

Back behind the wheel, I crossed a ring road lined with burger franchises and furniture, electrical and DIY super-stores. I pulled into the car park. I needed kit to protect myself, and to get into that house of his and lift him.

As I moved down the aisles I found myself doing something I always did, no matter where I was in the world. Even in Tesco, I'd check out the cooking in-gredients and cans of domestic cleaner, and work out which would go with which to make chaos. Mix this and that, then boil it up and I'd have an incendiary device. Or boil all that down and scrape off the scum from around the edge of the pot, then add some of the stuff from the bake-a-cake counter and boil it up some more until I just had sediment, and I'd have low explosive. Twenty minutes in any supermarket would be enough to buy all the ingredients for a bomb powerful enough to blow a car in half, and you'd still have change from a tenner. It's even easier in a DIY store.

But I didn't need any of that today. I came out of various stores the proud owner of a glass-cutter and parcel tape, a day sack and a twenty-one-piece screw-driver and tool set. At £4.99 it was an absolute rip-off. They'd last about five minutes, but that was all I'd need.

The most important item of all was a Stanley knife, a box-cutter. These things strike fear into people, even though it takes quite a frenzied attack to do any lasting damage. The major organs are out of reach of the inch-long blade, and there are only a few places on a body where an artery is that close to the skin.

Next stop was Norfolk Country Pursuits. It looked more like an army surplus store than the hunting, shooting, fishing establishment I'd been expecting. The window displays were piled high with everything from targets and rubber ducks to tents and camouflage gear.

The counter was a long glass showcase. The old guy behind it studied my face for signs I was about to pull a sawn-off shotgun from under my jacket and demand the contents of the till.

'Morning. Got a bit of a squirrel problem I need some help with.'

He looked blank. 'Squirrel problem?'

'Yeah, the problem is, my wife loves them and I don't. I just want something to scare the little buggers away with. One of these, maybe?' I tapped the glass over an air pistol that looked like a Colt 45.

His face lit up. I was a respectable married man, and more likely to have a wallet in my coat than a sawn-off.

'Weihrauch HW45. Best spring-powered on the market.'

'Sounds perfect. Eighty pounds? Will you throw in some pellets?'

His smile widened. I hadn't even haggled much.

'And do you sell Maglites? I need the smallest one.'

Something else had caught my eye. Lynn might have

124

sent me a message to come to him, but I wanted it to be on my terms.

Norfolk Country Pursuits also did a fine line in night-vision aids: weapon sights, monoculars, binoculars.

'My wife's mad about foxes and badgers. She'd love one of these for watching the buggers dig up my garden. Which one's the best, without breaking the bank?'

'Don't like the scopes and monoculars myself, if I'm honest with you. Too much strain on the closed eye, and you end up with no night vision in the other. Big fan of the binos version though. Nothing could be easier. They give you depth perception too. When you view a scene through binoculars, each eye is viewing things from a slightly different angle.

'These ones look good. She'll like the yellow trim.'

The old guy looked like he was going to hyperventilate with joy. I'd just parted company with the best part of another eight hundred quid for the National Geographic Explorers.

'There's a lovely range of ladies' waxed jackets in my sale, if you—'

I pulled out my wallet and handed him my card. 'I think that's enough spoiling for one day.'

He sighed as he handed me the bag. 'Now – new legislation, sir. I'm obliged to remind you that it is an offence for any person, regardless of age, to be in possession of an air weapon in a public place without a reasonable excuse. A reasonable excuse might be carrying a gun to and from a target shooting club or to and from land on which you have permission to shoot. It would also include taking a gun to and from a gunsmith for repair or service or taking a new gun home from the dealer. So please, do keep the pistol in its packaging until you get home.'

I turned to go and he sighed. 'There's a lot of crazy people out there who would use them to actually hurt people.'

34

I hit the main artery out of town towards the bypass. I remembered the place from a job I'd done up here about five years ago. Except that wasteland and shit terraced houses had been replaced by big DIY and frozen-food stores and car outlets.

I followed the road towards the coast. The idea was to hit the sea and head east. According to the map it was about thirty miles to the mushroom farm. I wouldn't really need it: once I hit the coast road I wasn't going to miss it. I drove slowly. I didn't want to get there too early and have to hang around.

The grass either side of the road suddenly became very neatly manicured. Even the molehills had been flattened. Signs started to let me in on the secret. Sandringham was just up the road. I was sure I'd know when I got there: the air would smell of polish and fresh paint.

I carried on to Hunstanton, where the road met the sea. It was very much like any other UK coastal town, up on high ground, a bit of a cliff and a hill going down to the beach. Victorian buildings proudly lined the esplanade, but the glory days were gone. Now they all looked a bit tired.

There was the obligatory Tesco on the outskirts, and the green area on the high ground was covered with hundreds of white and cream boxes with satellite dishes on the roof so holidaymakers could come all this way and do exactly the same thing as they did at home.

I checked the rear-view regularly, mentally registering every vehicle behind me.

Bright lights flashed hopefully outside a couple of amusement arcades. I cruised about, following the one-way system around the town, looking for a steamy-windowed café that had what I needed.

I found one down by the Sea Life Sanctuary. The attraction was closed, but the car park was open. As I locked up the Merc and headed across the road, the sea looked as dull and cloudy as the sky.

The cappuccino I ordered came in a cup the size of a soup bowl. I grabbed a packet of ready-salted and a cheese and pickle sandwich, and logged on. As I lifted the bread and tipped in the crisps, my eyes never left the Merc, nor the two or three cars that had come into the car park after me.

I hit Google Earth and carried out a recce of the target. The days of having to do walk- or fly-pasts to get some imagery with a Hasselblad camera were long gone.

I kept checking the Merc.

The only other diners were two or three young lads in Guns N' Roses hoodies, hunched over burger and Cokes. All our tables had plastic tomato-shaped red and brown sauce squeezers, the kind that had been around in every

Greasy Joe's since I was a kid. By the look of these particular ones, they *had* been. Dried sauce clung to the spouts. My two halves of cheese and pickle got a burst of something vinegary as the target came up on the screen.

I wanted to make it as difficult as possible for anyone that might be waiting for me. I gave my eyes a good rub to wake them up and stared at the screen.

The farm stood on a triangle of land bordered by three B roads. The site probably covered three acres. The farmhouse itself was set back from the road at the base of the triangle and there were two large outbuildings – probably the packing houses and cold stores – along either side, accessible from both roads. A further three buildings, which I took to be the growing sheds, stood in the middle of the plot. I zoomed in. It looked like mushroom rustling wasn't big business around these parts. I couldn't see any fences or floodlights.

I zoomed out to check the surrounding area and couldn't see any other buildings for at least a kilometre. Most were on the coast and around the road coming into the target area. That meant there'd be no ambient light, which suited me perfectly.

I squashed my sandwiches down a bit and got stuck in as I checked the Merc again. Crisp fragments showered the plate and my lap.

The plan was simple. I would park up short of the target on the road from the coast, and work my way towards it from within his grounds, to avoid being channelled along any of the roads. I'd gain entry to the house, grip Lynn and get him to tell me what the fuck was going on, whether he liked it or not.

If the Firm were waiting for me, too bad. I'd cross that

bridge when I came to it. I'd still try to get to Lynn, get him out of there and find out what I needed to know.

I thought about Ruby and Tallulah getting into the car with me as we set off for the beach, and the front wheel pulling the piece of plastic away from between the jaws of the clothes peg. These were real people; they weren't pond life like me, up to their neck in this sort of shit. If Lynn didn't have a pretty fucking good explanation for all this, I'd kill him.

I had my final munch of sandwich and sat back and made the coffee last while I studied the target until every detail of the area had soaked into my head.

It was starting to get darker and even more miserable out there now the rain was returning. The lights of the amusement arcade flashed even brighter. I rubbed my eyes. I hadn't slept for thirty-six hours.

I examined the area around the target in more detail. If it went tits up, where would I run? What was my best escape route? It was no good heading to the right of the house, hitting a field and paralleling the road – only to find there was a raging river in between me and my car.

35

Though the rain had stopped the sky was still overcast, making the night even darker. The grass at the apex of the triangle where the road forked each side of the target was soaked.

Two large wrought-iron gates hung from stone pillars, with nothing either side of them. They were closed, and the driveway had grown over long ago. This must have been the entrance to the house when it really was just a house. Maybe Nelson and Lady Hamilton had a couple of nights out here.

Day sack over my shoulder, binocular night-viewing aid hanging round my neck, I had left the car at the entrance to a field about two hundred from the target. The pistol was tucked down the front of my jeans and the box-cutter was in the pocket of my fleece. I was glad to be moving as I bypassed the gates and hit the hard standing. It was freezing.

A lot of what-ifs raced through my mind as I approached. I'd be finding out some answers soon enough.

The family photo I'd seen on Lynn's desk in 1998 showed his wife, two kids and a Labrador. The kids had looked about nine and eleven. That would make them university age now. They would surely have come home for the Christmas vacation. What if they were still here? What about his wife? What if the wife was alone but Lynn came back while I was there? What if one or both of the children were at home? What if the whole family were out? What about the Labrador? That particular one would be dead, but Lynn would have bought another. His sort loved the smell of wet dogs in the kitchen.

I hunched down, my back against the wall of one of the breezeblock growing sheds. Judging by the complete absence of compost smell and no sign of activity from the refrigeration units, business wasn't exactly booming on the mushroom front. There were no lights at all, anywhere.

I watched and listened as the trees rustled in the wind, then switched on the night-viewing aid. The electronics kicked in with a gentle hum and the National Geographics treated me to a fantastically sharp black and white negative picture. The old guy at Norfolk Country Pursuits hadn't let me down.

I settled into the hedge and scanned the front of the Lynns' family seat. It was gracious, rectangular and Georgian, with six huge windows top and bottom and a grand doorway dead centre.

I wondered what their forebears would have made of the family having to convert three acres of front lawn and

132

driveway into a fungus farm. Apoplectic was the word that came to mind.

There was smoke from the chimney but no other immediate signs of life. None of the interior lights were on either, or heavy curtains had been drawn.

I started to shiver. Time to get moving again. I worked my way around the side of the house, aiming for the rear.

Cats or foxes had scattered frozen-food packaging and the odd banana skin from the solitary refuse bin. The cartons told me they'd contained meals for one.

Light spilled from a downstairs window to the right of the back door, and through a gap in the curtains from another to the left. I stood back from the house, in the shadows, and heard a toilet flush on the first floor. There was no sound of a TV or radio. No dog barking.

A muddy Volvo 4x4 was parked on the cracked tarmac.

I stayed where I was, just looking and listening, sweeping the area with the binos now and again in case anything or anyone out there was doing the same.

I moved a step or two in the direction of the un-curtained window, close enough to see that it belonged to the kitchen. I let the binos hang from my neck. I was still in shadow, but there was too much light for them now.

I sat on the tarmac, my back against the Volvo, and waited.

Whoever had just taken a leak upstairs would have to turn the lights off at some stage, or come and make a brew in the morning.

Twenty freezing minutes later, Lynn appeared at the window, kettle in hand. He was wearing a dark blue dressing gown over striped pyjamas. He really was a toff. The little that was left of his greying hair was wet and slicked back.

His lips weren't moving, and he gave his full attention to the tap. Moments later, he was gone.

I flicked up the collar of my jacket to give me some protection from the biting wind as I waited for him to return to the kitchen to finish making what I hoped was just the one brew.

He did, fleetingly, mug in hand, then the crack of light from the curtained window strengthened.

I packed my binos away in the day sack and crossed the open ground towards it. He was sitting on a packing case, nursing his brew by a big wood-burning stove with glass doors. The room was bare. Not a stick of furniture or a single painting on the wall. Battered tea chests littered the floor.

I checked my watch as he raised the mug to his lips. Was he waiting for his wife to come home? Not by the look of things. The empty room and the food cartons were telling me a different story.

I kept watching him through the gap between the curtains, making sure my mouth was far enough away from the glass not to leave any condensation. Maybe his retirement had been a front. Maybe he hadn't left the Firm at all, and was just relocating. Maybe the reason he'd summoned me was to come and help him with his packing.

I wanted to get moving, take action, do something positive. I went back to the kitchen window. The sink was empty, and there weren't any pictures on the fridge, or happy snaps on the walls. This room, too, had been stripped.

The light went off in the living room and a hand came through the doorway and hit the kitchen light switch. A dressing-gowned shadow, thrown by the glow of the wood-burning stove, moved towards the stairs.

I waited for a light to come on above me. Nothing. I edged slowly round to the front of the house. Again, no light at all to help me locate him.

I'd kept the carrier bags from my shopping trip. I'd wrapped my passport, phone and credit cards in them, and stuffed them inside my jacket. I'd made the decision to take them with me instead of going into the house sterile; Lynn knew who I was, and if I got caught now, I'd be dead.

I headed back to the rear, took the mini-Maglite from my pocket and, holding two fingers over the lens to minimize the light, shone it through the living-room window. It was a simple latch job on a sash. The frame was old softwood, and its paint was peeling. A spider's web covered a Chubb window lock screwed down tight.

I moved across to the back door and shone the Maglite into the keyhole. It was an ordinary domestic four-lever. But it's no good attacking a lock if the thing is firmly bolted.

I pushed gently on the panel beside the lock, then pulled the handle towards me, to see if there was any give. There was about half an inch. I ran my hands down to the bottom of the door and pushed hard and slow. It gave an inch, then moved back into position. I did the same at the top. It also gave way, and I eased it gently back into position. No bolts; only the one lever lock to deal with.

You could spend hours picking a lock only to find out

that the fucking thing was already open, so I always took my time and checked the obvious. Holding my breath, I twisted the handle. No such luck; the door was locked.

The next move was to check all the most likely hiding places for a spare key. Some people leave theirs dangling on a string the other side of the letter box or on the inside of a cat flap, others under a dustbin or just behind a little pile of stones by the door. I checked the old rusting paint tins by the door, along the top of the door frame and in all the obvious places. Nothing.

I got down onto my knees and looked through the keyhole. I shone the torch through and had another look. There was a glint of metal.

What a dickhead.

He'd left the key in the lock.

36

With the Maglite in my mouth, I opened the screwdriver set and worked one of them into the keyhole. The key obscured most of my vision, but I could see that the teeth were up in the wards of the lock. When it had a firm purchase I started to turn the key clockwise, at the same time pulling the door towards me to release the pressure of the frame on the latch and the deadbolt.

The key turned until it hit the lock; it would need a lot more pressure now to open it and that might make a noise. I took a deep breath. If Lynn suddenly appeared with a shotgun, I'd have to switch to Plan B – which would probably involve running like fuck.

I gave the key the final twist and the screwdriver snapped in my hand. The cheap metal head was jammed against the key and there was no way to get another one in.

I went back to the living-room window and took the roll of parcel tape from my day sack. Pulling it off the roll very slowly to eliminate noise, I covered the whole pane with the stuff, then made a handle, something for me to hold while I scored around the edge with the cutter. I punched the pane gently with my fist and it cracked and popped. I pulled back on the tape handle and the glass came away in my hands.

I lowered the day sack behind the curtain and slid through the gap, immediately feeling the heat from the burner.

I'd have to clear the house room by room. I had to make sure no one else was here. I'd remain covert for as long as possible, and only go noisy if he did. It wasn't much of a plan, but it would have to do.

I kept the Maglite close to the floor so I could see my way through the living room. The burner still glowed, but didn't throw out enough light to prevent me from standing on a cat or tripping over a log pile.

I reached the door that led into the front hall. My ears started to sting now that the warmth was returning to them. I went down on my knees, eased it a little further ajar, listened for a moment and then looked through.

The first room I had to clear was the kitchen; it was the nearest.

I held the pistol out in front of me. I hoped that it would buy me at least two seconds of hesitation from whoever I might have to point it at.

That was where the box-cutter came in. If the shit really hit the fan, it would drop my assailant but not totally fuck him up – and give me enough time to decide if I would have to get a frenzy on and slice him to shreds before he did something similar to me.

There was nothing in the hallway. I moved forward and pushed the kitchen door fully open. Nothing.

I went back into the hallway.

Still nothing.

I thought about the single mug and the ready-meal cartons. Fuck it, I'd just go straight upstairs and find him.

Focusing my eyes and the weapon on the top landing, I placed my left foot very carefully on the bottom step, then my right.

I stopped and listened.

I lifted my left foot again and put it down on the second step, easing my weight down gently on the carpet, hoping the board wouldn't creak beneath it.

I moved slowly but purposefully, eyes wide, weapon up. The glow from the wood-burner threw my shadow against the wall.

Adrenalin took over. If Lynn was waiting for me, he'd be armed. A shotgun, at least. I was drenched with sweat. My heart was pumping so hard I could feel it hammering against my chest.

It started to get darker and colder as the glow of the embers faded. All I could hear was the sound of my own breath.

Moving like this is physically demanding. Every movement has to be so slow and deliberate that every single muscle is tensed; your body needs more oxygen, and your lungs, in turn, need to work harder. And on top of all that, somebody could be waiting to kill you at any moment.

I reached the landing. There was a smell of polish and mothballs. There was a door to my left. The corridor to my right ran the length of the house. Knees bent, shoulders hunched over, box-cutter now in my left hand and pistol in my right, I started to move along the

Afghan runner at its centre. I checked the crack under each of the doors I passed for any signs of life.

The first was to my left, facing the rear of the house.

Nothing.

I turned the handle and went in.

Nothing.

No one.

I moved down to the next door on the right, facing the front of the house.

I could hear snoring.

I carried on along the corridor and listened outside the next room. Nothing. And there was no noise from any of the other five.

I put the box-cutter back in my fleece, fished out the torch and twisted the lens.

At this point I'd normally have pressed my right thumb down on the weapon's safety catch, checking that it was off and ready to go, before entering the target room. Then I'd have pushed the mag in the pistol grip to make sure that it was engaged.

No need for any of that with this fucking thing. I just hoped my bluff was going to work.

I lifted the latch, and none too gently. Once you've decided you're going in, you might as well get it over with. I pushed the door a few inches, brought up the torch and used my body to open the door fully.

I moved immediately to the right, to avoid silhouetting my body in the doorway. The curtains were still open.

I closed the door most of the way with my shoulder, and the torch beam hit a pile of clothes draped over a wooden chair, then a watch and a glass of water on a bedside table. There was a body in the bed. It stirred, maybe as a reaction to the change in the air pressure as the door opened, or the fact that light was now shining in its face.

His head turned and his eyes opened wide. He wouldn't be able to see me, just the torchlight. I tilted it to make sure he caught sight of the pistol.

I moved quickly and knelt astride him, pinned him to the bed with the duvet taut across his chest.

I cut the light and dropped the torch onto the bed. I didn't want him to see my face yet. I wanted to keep him confused.

He started to react. 'What . . . ? Who the . . . ?'

He gave a grunt as I pressed the pistol against his clenched teeth. He tried to resist. I grabbed the back of his balding head with my left hand and forced the weapon down harder. Metal scraped against enamel until he eventually opened up.

I pushed the muzzle as far into his mouth as it would go.

37

He struggled for a while, not trying to escape, just trying to work out what the fuck was going on, and to breathe. He was flapping, and snorting like a horse. I moved with his chest as it arched up and down. Finally he lay still. No one will really fuck around once they realize they have a pistol in their mouth and it's not coming out.

I leant towards his left ear. His cheek smelled of coal tar soap. 'You have two choices. Die if you don't help me, live if you do. Nod if you understand.'

The pistol moved up and down.

It's always better to take your time at moments like this. If you've got somebody who's flapping and you say, 'OK, what's all this shit about Leptis?', he can't talk because he's got this weapon stuck in his mouth, so he gets all confused about what you expect of him. It's better to do it as a process of elimination. Then, once he got in the swing of things, I could grip him and get him spewing out everything he knew.

'If there's anyone else in the house, nod slowly.'

There was no movement of the pistol.

'Dogs?'

No movement.

'Anyone turning up before first light?'

No movement.

He gagged and his Adam's apple worked overtime. With his jaw wide open he'd lost his ability to swallow.

'It's Nick Stone. You remember.'

The pistol moved up and down, with purpose.

'That Libyan in Tripoli called you Leptis. Yes?'

He nodded.

'The only people who have that information are the Libyan, you and me, right?'

He nodded again.

'You put it in a report?'

His cheeks inflated and his lips bubbled. Saliva oozed from his mouth and down his chin. I could hear all the breathing and slurping, but there was just a touch too much hesitation. He was doing some serious thinking about what to say next.

'Don't second-guess. You don't know what I want to hear. Just tell the truth. If not, you're no good to me. Understand?'

The pistol moved up and down. I could feel his chest rising and falling more and more quickly; he was fighting for oxygen and there were too many obstructions.

He nodded.

Light sliced through the darkness outside. In the middle distance, towards the coast, two sets of headlamps moved along the road I'd parked beside.

'You still work for the Firm?'

Side to side.

Both vehicles had stopped about two hundred up the road, and both sets of lights cut.

'How many are coming?'

I pulled the weapon from his mouth and slammed it down on top of his head. Partly to control him, partly out of anger, I screamed with him. '*I wasn't the only fucker in that car . . .*'

I pulled out the Explorers, turned them on and slung them back round my neck. I jumped off him and grabbed one of his socks and shoved it into his mouth, pulling down on his jaw to force him to take it all. Noise comes from the throat and below, not the mouth; for an effective gag, you have to ram the obstruction down as far as it can go, so that when your prisoner tries to scream, the sound can't amplify in the mouth. I also wanted him to be more worried about choking than raising the alarm.

I tied his shirtsleeve as tightly as I could around his mouth and at the back of his neck so I could use it as a lead, but kept his nose uncovered because he had to be able to breathe. Moans and groans sounded from the back of his throat as I dragged him onto the floor. I kept my Timberland over the sleeve to keep him down as I checked the darkness outside with the binos.

Now they'd checked out the Merc, the two cars moved towards the fork in the road, lights off and slow. I lost them for a few seconds behind the farm buildings.

They split, one down each side of the triangle.

The driver of the one to the right stuck his head out of the window for a clearer view. His passenger had something with him that gave off a gentle glow. As they passed the house, I pulled Lynn from the bedroom and towards the stairs. I dropped the pistol and grabbed the torch. I wouldn't be able to bluff these guys. I twisted open the lens.

The front door was the best option, then out into the open and use the outbuildings for cover. Then over fields to wherever, now the car was compromised.

It didn't matter where I was heading for now; the only thing that did was getting out of the shit and keeping Lynn with me. I hadn't found anything out yet.

I dragged him down the stairs. Blood glistened on his head and face. He stumbled as he tried to grab the shirt to ease the pressure on his mouth at the same time as following the torch beam.

We reached level ground.

I focused the light on the front door and pushed him against the wall, kicking him down onto the carpet to control him as I took the box-cutter out of my fleece, turned the torch off and released the Yale.

No time to be tactical. I wanted to be outside, in the dark and in cover.

I wrenched him off the floor and dragged him diagonally across the wet grass.

38

My Timberlands hit the hard standing and we got in amongst the growing sheds. My plan was simply to head for the gates and then out into the open to make them think I was going back to the Merc. They didn't have night-viewing aids, or they would have used them.

Lynn tripped and sprawled along the concrete. I turned and yanked the shirt, giving him a taste of Timberland toecap for good measure. The fucker was stalling.

At that moment, a body crashed into me from behind with the force of a moving car, tearing Lynn from my grip. I spun, landing on my back.

I tried to turn to face whoever had banged into me but the body was already on top of me, crushing the air from my lungs. I arched my back, kicking, bucking, struggling to get my hands up to his mouth, but he was ahead of me. Hands the size of shovels gripped my arms and then moved down until he had me in a bear hug.

The top of his head pushed hard against my chin. I

twisted like a mad man. Sixteen, seventeen stone of him pressed down on me, keeping my arms against my sides.

I tried to kick and buck out of position, then to head butt him. He did exactly the same, growling at me through clenched teeth.

He let go of my arms and decided to throttle me instead. Massive fingers closed around my throat and his saliva sprayed my face as he strained to push my Adam's apple out through the back of my neck. My head felt like it was going to explode.

I managed to grab a handful of hair at the back of his head and jabbed the box-cutter repeatedly into his face.

He screamed.

I slashed and slashed. Three, four, five times. Blood dribbled onto my face and then spurted. I must have hit the artery.

The boy jerked around. His blood poured into my mouth. I could taste the iron and feel the warmth. I kept jabbing, waiting for him to let go.

He finally screamed like a pig and his hands flew to his ravaged face. I pushed him off and rolled away, looking around wildly for Lynn. He was on the ground too and there was another body on top of him, raining punches.

I stabbed the box-cutter into the leather-jacketed back but couldn't go deep enough so I ran it into the back of his head and down into his neck. He shouted with pain but managed to roll away and jump to his feet. I lashed out again and felt his stubble against my hand as I tore the blade across his cheek.

Taking the pain, he drove his shoulder into my ribcage

and the back of my head slammed against the breeze-blocks of the growing shed.

Stars exploded behind my eyes. The box-cutter fell from my hand and I followed it onto the ground and he came down on top of me. Blood from his face splashed onto mine.

I knew I had to keep on twisting. I kept my arms above my head. I tried to kick, buck, head butt, anything to get out of the move. He knew exactly what he was doing. Like a skilled wrestler, his body moulded onto mine. The stubble on his cheek ground against mine. His breath stank of tobacco and greasy food.

His hands shot up and clutched at my throat. His saliva sprayed my face as he rammed his thumbs into my Adam's apple. He was on a mission to crush the life out of me.

I struggled to get my hands around his throat too, but he just tensed his neck muscles and breathed between his teeth.

My head swelled to bursting point.

I was going to black out.

He had me, elbows out wide as he tightened his grip. I couldn't move my arms. I writhed and kicked and flailed and knew it wasn't working. There was nothing else I could do.

I felt him suddenly go rigid. He moaned and his head jerked back. Air gushed out of him like a punctured balloon and I rolled clear.

The shaft of the garden fork that was sticking out of his back thudded against the concrete as he fell. He thrashed about on the ground like a game fish under a harpoon.

Lynn stood above us, ripping the shirt from his mouth,

gagging for air. I could see his silhouette against the lights that now shone from the house. I could hear shouting and it definitely wasn't English.

I staggered to my feet and grabbed him. I dragged him by his pyjamas out onto the road and into the field. I pushed him down onto the frost-hardened mud, maintaining my grip on him as I fought to fill my lungs with oxygen.

My Adam's apple felt like it was still in a vice.

'Nick—'

'Shut the fuck up – not now!'

We needed transport, and theirs was the nearest.

More shouts came from the house. Screams of anguish filled the air from the growing sheds.

'Come on, keep up.'

I powered up the binos and moved towards the road at the base of the triangle. Their cars had approached from either side of the house. They were probably parked up behind it.

We moved as fast as we could over the frozen mud. Lynn was finding it hard in his bare feet. I had to keep pulling him forward, then stopping to scan through the binos for the shape of a car on the road or beyond the trees and bushes that lined the fields.

We were about twenty from the base of the triangle. The house was immediately to my right. Still no sign of a vehicle.

A figure appeared from the rear of the house. Lights sprang on a few seconds later, reversed a short way along the base road, swung back up the drive, then turned back towards us.

'Keep the fuck down!'

I had another squint through the binos. Two guys were carrying the body and a third was helping the other casualty to the road.

I ripped off my day sack and fumbled inside the flap as the car drew level with the first cooling shed.

It stopped when I was still about seven or eight metres from the road.

I sprinted for it, not bothering to check if Lynn was behind. I got to the driver's door. The window was down. He'd been shouting to the others with the engine still running.

I pulled open the door and swung the screwdriver down hard into the top of his shoulder.

He roared like a wounded bull and made a wild grab for it. He looked up at me. I could see his face in the lights of the dash. It would have looked perfectly at home on the front seat of Little Miss Camcorder's BMW.

I grabbed a handful of hair, yanked him out onto the road and kicked him down.

'Come on, get in there!' I yelled at Lynn. 'You drive.'

The lads were streaming towards us from the cooling sheds. I threw the day sack over the roof at them, not that it was going to slow them down much, then pulled the bino strap off my neck and threw them too. As the closest one dodged to avoid them I dived into the back seat. 'Go! Go! Go!'

Lynn put his foot to the floor and mounted the verge. We bounced back down onto the tarmac and nearly stalled.

'Calm down! Put it in first – let's go! Let's go!'

As we fishtailed up the road, Mr Norfolk Country Pursuits' binos bounced off the rear window.

We drove up to the fork and then on towards the coast. The Merc was going to have to find its way back to Mayfair on its own.

39

Our next objective wasn't complicated: to get the fuck out of the immediate area before they cordoned it off, or night was turned into day by searchlight-toting helicopters.

I wiped the blood from my face as the car weaved with the road.

I sat up as it began to narrow. Lynn made few concessions. I caught sight of his expression in the glow of the dashboard: eyes narrowed, jaw clenched, concentrating with every fibre of his being on the tunnel of light thrown by the headlamp beams and framed by the high hedges either side of the road.

The rev counter gradually fell from the red. Without as much as a sideways glance, he smiled for the first time. Fuck me, I was sharing a getaway car with Stirling Moss in stripy pyjamas.

'Where's the nearest ATM?'

'Holt. About fifteen minutes away.'

Life had to change now. I could no longer leave a trail

behind me. With every new direction I took, I needed to shed my skin. First job was to draw the max from my two accounts, then bin the cards. No more money trail. Then we had to get some clothes and get the fuck out of the land of Country Pursuits.

The lane became a blur as Lynn forgot to relax his right foot again. I checked behind and saw no lights.

'Bit slower . . .'

I didn't want to end up in a ditch now we'd got this far.

Despite the gash I'd left on his pate and the streaks of mud on his dressing gown, he was completely unruffled, and so typically English it was as if we were slightly late for dinner.

'Who are they, Nick? Anyone we know?'

I shrugged. 'The Firm's still top of my list, though that doesn't totally explain the leatherwear. I was in Ireland yesterday. A device was shoved under my car. By them, I reckon; that's why they had no weapons. We've all come straight off the ferry.'

Another corner was coming up fast. He dipped the lights to check if anything was coming the other way, then switched back to full beam.

My feet kicked against some shit in the foot well. I looked down and saw a sliver of light. I reached down and recovered a laptop with a mobile phone connected to it by a cable. Sellotaped to the lid was a sheet of A4, a printout of a video grab. It was a close-up of my face from Pete's Basra footage. Would the Firm need to rely on that? They'd have far better mug shots of me on file – but maybe none that were quite so up-to-date.

I opened the top and tapped the keys to take it out of screensaver. A Google Earth map came up. The cursor hovered on the road where I'd parked the Merc, at more or less exactly the location of the lay-by.

'Has to be the Firm ... The device wasn't the only thing they put in my car.'

'Tracker?'

I nodded. They'd probably slipped it behind the Merc's bumper or under the chassis, held in place by a strong magnet, maybe even connected to the car battery. Fuck it, who cared? Lynn, maybe – it meant both of us were targets. They were trying to kill him as well.

I pulled the mobile away from the laptop and threw it out of the window as Lynn missed the apex of another bend, confirming that the only thing he really knew how to drive was a desk. My own mobile swiftly followed.

I asked him about the Leptis message, but all I got was a blank stare. 'Why would Vauxhall Cross need to use you to lead them here? I draw a pension; they know where I live. So why not just hit you and me separately? Why the message?'

We screamed through another village. I couldn't stop myself doing some phantom braking as he narrowly missed a couple of parked cars.

A sign for Holt flashed by. The dashboard clock said nearly 2 a.m. Lynn went straight across a raised round-about on the edge of town.

'OK, slow down. We're out of the shit, at least for the time being. Drive normally now. I need an ATM, not a fucking ambulance.'

40

We reached Holt and parked up outside Lloyds on the main street.

'Wait here, engine on.'

It was a nice, well-to-do town: lots of candle shops, cafés and estate agencies. That meant people around here probably liked to be nice too.

I got £400 out on both my cards and was back in the car asap, now in the front passenger seat. I snapped my cards in half.

'Where's the charity shops?'

We went down the high street and into a small square. Lynn drove slowly while I ran backwards and forwards between the car and the shop doorways and threw the nice people's bags of cast-offs into the back of the car like it was a rubbish cart. I didn't care if any CCTV saw us. We'd be shedding another layer of skin soon.

'OK, out of town now, towards Norwich – and slowly. How far is that?'

'About twenty miles.'

As we headed back into the darkness I hit the interior lights and ripped open the bin-liners.

'What about your family? You'd better phone them and get them out of the way.'

He shook his head and a muscle twitched briefly in his jaw. 'No need.'

'OK. So now we get dressed and cleaned up. Then we dump the car and train it to London.'

'I don't know what we can—'

'Need to know, Colonel, remember?' I grinned. 'And you don't need to know anything until you need to know it. Don't want you giving away the game plan.'

I gave him the once-over. The blood on his head had dried a little and the swelling had begun. It wouldn't have been that noticeable if he'd had any hair to cover it. 'Right now we need a nice quiet stretch of river so we can clean ourselves up, then we're going to need to find you a hat.'

He seemed to relax again and pointed at the rear-view. 'You're no oil painting yourself, Stone. If I need a hat, you need the full *shemagh* . . .'

His foot went back on the pedal.

'And slow down,' I yelled. 'We don't want to get stopped.'

We had to dump the car once we got into the city – somewhere it wouldn't stick out and get pinged too quickly. Main streets and multi-storey car parks were out, because of the CCTV, but we couldn't leave it anywhere too isolated either – it would stick out like a sore thumb.

'When's the first train?'

Lynn finally lifted his foot off the gas.

'Not sure; it used to be some time before six – to get into London for the start of the working day.'

The clock on the dash read 02.38.

41

Norwich
0334 hrs

I kept about two hundred behind Lynn as we walked into the city centre. It was bitterly cold. His breath hung in clouds behind him. The streets were well lit, so it was head down all the way, hands in pockets. My ears and nose were numb, and my hair was still wet from the river. It would have nudged me into hypothermia if I hadn't kept moving.

I must have looked pissed. The shoes the Red Cross shop had provided were plastic, and skidded on the icy pavement. Their jeans were two sizes too small; the zip only did up halfway. At least the jumpers fitted. I had two of them on over a T-shirt, and a shabby black rain-coat.

There'd only been one hat, a fake-leather Russian thing with ear muffs, which I'd given to Lynn.

Now that we'd shed another skin – the car – we

needed to get out of here asap. We'd parked it near some council houses, opposite the entrance to the city airport. I'd left the keys in the ignition. With luck, it would be nicked. It was only about a mile to the station, but each step felt like Scott pushing for the Pole.

The roads narrowed as we got closer to the city centre. Lynn had suggested we RV by the skips behind the Big W, the warehouse to a general store a couple of hundred from the station. He said I wouldn't be able to miss it.

He wasn't wrong. The massive metal and concrete block had the world's biggest yellow W shining out over a stadium-sized car park it shared with Morrisons.

The recycling area was piled high with folded cardboard boxes and overflowing skips. Lynn wasn't the only one to suggest it as an RV. Crushed beer cans and empty vodka bottles were strewn across the greasy concrete. The smell of vomit and cigarettes probably meant it was a hang-out for kids rather than dossers.

We each stood on a folded box to insulate ourselves from the ground. If anything, my plastic shoes were conducting the cold. I swayed from foot to foot for a moment, then grabbed him by the lapels and shoved him against the wall. He didn't see it coming.

'What the fuck's happening?'

He looked genuinely shocked.

I realized I liked shoving him about. 'It's the Firm, isn't it? Who else has the resources to track me over the water, plant a device, and follow me all the way to your stately fucking home when it doesn't detonate?'

My breath billowed across the narrow gap between us.

'Then I get a message that Leptis has the answers.'

He was getting really scared. I didn't blame him. He'd seen my handiwork with the box-cutter.

'Now, only you, me and your old mate Mansour know about Leptis – and a bloody great filing cabinet in Vauxhall Cross.'

'Maybe they want both of us . . .'

'There are fucking easier ways, don't you think?'

'Maybe they wanted you to find the device . . .' He started to calm down again. He'd sensed he wasn't in danger; that I was just pissed off.

'It was a pretty serious chunk of Semtex.'

'But the battery was flat.'

'What about Liam Duff?'

I released my grip a little and he shrugged. 'You said you were in Ireland. I was wondering if that was down to you.'

'You're a fucking nightmare.'

'You made pretty short work of those men at the farm.'

He needed another shove. 'I don't fucking believe it! You were quite happy to order shit like that from the comfort of your air-conditioned office, but seeing it up close is a whole different ball game, isn't it? Get real, Lynn. What the fuck do you think I did to Ben Lesser on the *Bahiti* – cuddle him to death?'

'I just think that you could have shown some restraint, reasonable force . . .'

'The only way to stop being on the receiving end of that shit is by being on top; being as violent and quick as you can. Get them before they get you. What do you call that trick with the fork? A spot of gardening?'

It was falling on deaf ears. There was the same look of disdain on his face as he had always given me.

'Fuck it. Just listen. Get a ticket to Liverpool Street.'

Lynn was busy tying the flaps under his chin.

'Use a machine. Here.' I gave him £100.

'I'll be on the train, but we split up. Don't speak to anybody. Get yourself a paper, something to do. When we get there, go left out of the main entrance, then right onto Bishopsgate. Right again takes you onto Wormwood Street. There's a Caffè Nero. Go in, buy a cup of coffee, sit down and wait.'

'Then what?'

'I've already told you. You'll know when you need to know.'

42

0524 hrs

My feet were blocks of ice. I was desperate for a brew.

'OK, remember. Talk to no one. Just buy your ticket, and keep your head down.'

I gave him five minutes and then followed.

The station was an old Victorian building with a new car park and taxi rank. There were already quite a few cars parking up, pumping out clouds of cold CO_2. They couldn't have come far. The taxis' engines were hot and so their exhausts were clear.

I kept my head down but kept a lookout as best I could as Lynn disappeared into the building.

I concentrated on vehicles that weren't belching. Maybe the car we'd lifted had a tracking device too. Maybe they had driven like madmen from the coast, following its signal. Then put two and two together and realized that unless we were going to hide here, there were only three ways out: plane, bus or train.

I checked the board. The next train out was 05.40. I bought myself a paper and fell in behind a couple of guys with briefcases, long overcoats and scarves up to their ears, who were moaning about some injustice or other at the office as they shoved their cards into the ticket machine. I was tempted to suggest they try my life for a day.

I headed for the café with my second-class single safely in my pocket and saw Lynn sitting in the corner, warming his hands on a steaming paper cup.

'Coffee – large, please, to take away. And a couple of those.'

The girl, whose name tag said she was called Giertruda and wished me a safe journey, shoved the two Danishes in a bag as the machine behind her gargled away.

I was soon back in the cold concourse, pissed off that Lynn was still in the warm. But so what? So far, so good.

I watched him come and join the throng of commuters heading for the waiting train. He got into the next carriage up from mine.

I still couldn't be absolutely sure about Lynn. He might have saved my arse with the gardening fork, but he might now want to save his own by giving me up to the Firm. But for now, I just had to keep both of us from being lifted. Especially me.

I settled into my seat and the first notice I read warned me that assaults on staff were taken seriously and would result in prosecution. Onboard cameras would be collecting evidence all the way.

No doubt about it, the UK had become a surveillance society. We have 1 per cent of the world's population, but

20 per cent of its CCTV cameras. The Holloway Road in north London has 102 in two miles. One 650-yard stretch has twenty-nine of the fuckers – one every twenty-odd yards.

All good news for people like the Firm, who needed to know things, but a nightmare when it's being used against you. And that was why it was imperative we got out of the UK, soon as.

PART FOUR

PART FOUR

43

Liverpool Street station
0740 hrs

The cafés and restaurants around the station were heaving with commuters up to their eyes in woolly coats and clutching their coffees. They, too, kept their heads down as they rushed to work over wet pavements under a grey and depressing sky.

I was behind Lynn once more as he headed for the RV. This time I was putting surveillance on him, watching his every move. Maybe he would talk to someone, or slip into a phone box. Maybe he'd think better of throwing in his lot with me, and decide to jump in a cab and head for Vauxhall Cross.

I had no idea if he had the bottle for this sort of thing. Or if he thought he knew which side his bread was buttered – and he thought, wrongly, it wasn't my side.

I bumbled on in the cold, not looking directly through the window of Caffè Nero, but checking things out all the same. If a trigger was on the coffee shop and a weirdo walked past staring hard at the place, it would be a good bet that he was the target. The weather was in my favour. I couldn't see anyone hanging about, but that didn't necessarily mean they weren't.

I walked past another coffee and sandwich shop that was busily helping itself to some City money. People were filling their faces and sharing office gossip. The attraction of the place for me was that Caffè Nero was in line of sight.

I bought a pastry and the biggest available cup of coffee, and sat at a table that gave me a good trigger on the RV.

I watched as people walked past from both directions, on both sides of the street. Everyone wore a coat and trailed a cloud of breath. Were they doing walk-pasts to see if we were in there? This wasn't paranoia, it was attention to detail.

No one went in and came straight out again; no one walked around muttering into their collar. All of which meant they weren't there, or were very good indeed.

If there was one thing I hated more than clearing an area before a meet, it was the meet itself. It was at simple events like this that people got killed, in the way that, these days, a traffic cop stopping a car for jumping a red light might land up getting shot by the driver.

I sat, watched and waited. It wouldn't look abnormal to the staff or anyone else for me to be spending this amount of time in here. They could have been forgiven for thinking I was a dosser paying for temporary shelter with a large coffee. Not that anybody would have cared. The thing about cities is that the slickers and the dossers have no choice but to rub shoulders. It wasn't as if I was the only strange-looking person in town.

I checked around me again, just to be sure that I wasn't sitting next to a trigger. Stranger things have happened.

I watched for another five minutes past the RV time, finished off the coffee and Danish, and walked outside. As I pulled the door of Caffè Nero towards me I saw the back of Lynn's Russian hat in the queue. The flaps were still tied under his chin. He looked even weirder than I did. I walked past him and did my surprised, 'Hi! What are you doing here?'

He turned, smiled that happy, I-haven't-seen-you-for-a-while look, and we shook hands. 'Great to see you, it's been . . . ages.' He beamed.

'Coffee?' I took a look around. All the seats were taken. 'Tell you what, you got time for a Micky D?'

We left the coffee shop and I headed left. He fell into step beside me and shot me a quizzical look. 'What the devil is a Micky D?'

'McDonald's.'

'Is that where we're really going?'

'No. Not yet anyway. Keep your head down.'

I walked backwards to watch the oncoming traffic and flagged down a cab.

'Golden Lane Estate, mate.'

It was only a ten-minute walk, but that was ten minutes more exposure to Big Brother.

'Who are we meeting, Nick?'

'No one. I've got something there for when I'm in the shit. I think this is the moment, don't you?'

44

The Golden Lane Estate was originally built for essential workers – firemen, nurses, that kind of stuff. But in the eighties housing boom it all went private and now belonged to architects and traders. They're nice little two-bedroom flats rubbing shoulders with the City.

The only subject I had really liked at school was history, and I'd lapped up the sales leaflet I found when I went to check it out. In the eighteenth century it was a warren of slums and red-light areas. By the end of the nineteenth the slums had been replaced by warehouses and train yards. The Great Cripplegate fire of 1897 began in an ostrich-feather warehouse and swept away most of the remaining residential buildings.

By the start of the twentieth century only 6,000 people lived here. Then, on a single night in December 1940, the Luftwaffe destroyed virtually every building in the area. The bombsite lay abandoned until an architectural competition in 1951, and the Golden Lane Estate was born in all its glory: one eleven-storey block, twelve terrace blocks, and a leisure centre with a twenty-metre swimming pool and two all-weather tennis courts.

We couldn't go straight to the cache. I was going to have to clear the area, in case it had been discovered and it was linked to me as a known location. If that was the case, they would have a trigger on it to see if I turned up.

We were more or less level with the entrance to the estate. If I'd been triggered as I left the station or the coffee shop, they would now be behind me, thinking that I was heading for my security blanket. Unless the area was covered by enough CCTV cameras to cover me electronically.

Two attractive women approached from the opposite direction, sandwich-bar paper bags in their hands. I would have no more than three seconds in which to check. They passed, laughing and talking loudly. Now was the time. I turned to give them an admiring glance, in the way men think they do unobtrusively. The two women gave me a 'You should be so lucky' look and got back to their laughing.

There were three candidates beyond them. A middle-aged couple dressed for the office turned the corner behind me. They looked too preoccupied, staring into each other's eyes for as long as possible before getting back to the grindstone. Then again, good operators would always make it look that way. The other possible was coming from straight ahead, and on the estate side of the street. He looked like a builder; he was wearing blue jeans and a thick, dark blue shirt with the tail hanging out, the way I would if I wanted to cover my weapon and radio.

I turned back in the direction I'd been heading. If they were operators, the couple behind me would now look as

171

though they were exchanging sweet nothings, but actually be reporting what I was getting up to, on a radio net, telling the Desk and the other operators where I was, what I was wearing, and the same for my friend. And if they were good, they would also say that I could be aware, because of the look back.

I carried on to the end of the estate and turned left. The couple were still with me. I stopped outside the last of the shops to read the cards in the window selling everything from second-hand vacuum cleaners to personal massage, before turning left again. Three corners in a circular route isn't natural. A good operator wouldn't turn the third corner, but if the lovers came past, I would bin the RV anyway. Better safe than sorry.

A target going static short-term is always awkward for a surveillance team. Everybody's got to get in position, so that next time the target goes mobile they've covered every possible option. That way, the target moves to the team, instead of the team crowding the target. But was there a trigger here? I'd find out soon enough.

Nothing happened during the five minutes it took me to read every card. Lynn stood nervously beside me.

'Don't worry. They're not going to hit us here in the middle of the city. If they know we're here, they'll wait.'

Moving off again, I eventually turned back onto Goswell Road and into the estate.

I went towards the chute where the big wheelie bins stood, where they threw the rubbish down onto the ground floor, and picked up a little plastic key fob hidden behind a pair of large metal doors.

A glass- and steel-framed security door led into the

stairwell. I rested the fob against the pad alongside it and it clicked open.

I didn't go into an apartment. I could never have afforded one here. My fob came from the Pizza Express about five minutes away. It was sheer luck: I'd found a set of keys in the toilet about five years ago. The dickhead had stuck his address on it. The keys didn't interest me – they'd have had them changed anyway. What did was the fact I could now enter and exit a secure area.

I led Lynn down into the basement, where the residents had little lock ups for bikes and all that kind of shit.

I ducked under a tent that had been hung between the cages to dry and went and stood in the far corner, in front of a sign listing fire hazards.

I checked the flat screw heads. All of them should have had their recess at forty-five degrees. It was a simple telltale and one that any professional would have noticed. But that was exactly what I wanted them to see, to give them a false sense of security when they opened up the cache.

The screws were still in position. I twisted them open with a 5p piece. The next tell-tale was on top of the loose brick behind the board. I pulled it out gently, checking the top right-hand corner to reveal a disc-shaped piece of mortar that rested on top. I watched it fall into the small holding area as I removed the brick from the wall. No mortar disc? I would have walked away.

A clingfilm-wrapped bundle sat snugly in the holding area. It contained a passport, driver's licence and credit card in the name of Marc Richardson, and 6,000 US dollars in small denomination bills.

I checked that everything was exactly the way I'd left it: the end of the plastic cover cutting through the second S of the word passport.

I undid the package, removed its contents, replaced them with Nick Stone's passport, driving licence and credit cards, and wrapped it up again and slid it back in the hole.

'I'm shedding a skin.'

I slipped my new identity inside my Red Cross raincoat. 'I always knew there'd be a time when someone like you wouldn't want me around any more. This is my safety blanket.'

He didn't say a word – just took off his hat and ran his fingers absently across the scabs on his pate. I was beginning to sense a vulnerability in him that I hadn't expected. Fear I could have understood – but what I now saw in his eyes was sadness, and I couldn't think why. He was retired, he had a pension, a family, a big country seat. He should have been dancing a jig from dawn till dusk. *Resignation*, that's what it was – almost like he'd lost the will to live.

He put his hat back on and did up the flaps. 'No weapon?'

'No need. Next stop City Airport or the Eurostar.'

I headed out of the basement. 'I've got my new life. Now we'd better fix you one, so we can get out of here.'

45

I did have a weapon tucked away, but it was in another safety blanket, for use if I had to stay in the UK.

Everybody finds their own way to build an alternative ID, and, more especially, hide it. The second one was in northwest London, behind a bakery. It used to be in a safe-deposit box, but the police now had the power to open them up at will.

I wasn't worried about real people finding the caches. They'd probably just take the cash and sell the weapon and passport. It was the Firm that concerned me.

They would always be on the hunt for safety blankets. They knew any deniable operator worth his salt would have one. If mine was compromised, they'd have my new ID, my credit card details; they could let me run from the UK, allowing me to think I had evaporated, then just wait and see where I pitched up with my new passport and card, and do whatever they felt like doing.

I thought about Marc Richardson, who I'd bumped into in Zurich a couple of years earlier and set out to clone. He was a bit younger than me, but we looked vaguely similar.

I'd found him working in a bar in Mühlegasse, a notorious gay cruising ground. It's the best kind of place for what I had in mind, whatever country you're in. Marc had been living and working in Zurich for a couple of years. He had a steady job, and shared an apartment with his Swiss partner in the city. Most important of all, he had no intention of going back to England. I learnt all this as I got to know him over a couple of weeks; I'd pop into his bar when I knew it was his shift, and we'd chat. I met other gay men there, but they didn't have what Marc had. He was the one for me.

When I got back to the UK, I signed up to an online genealogical site and set about scouring the registers between 1960 and 1965 for his date of birth and his father's and mother's names. He hadn't liked to talk to me about his past, and I could never get anything more out of him than where he was born; trying to dig any deeper would have aroused suspicion. Besides, his partner was getting all territorial. It only took an hour to find him.

Marc Richardson the Second was soon the proud owner of a brand-new ten-year passport, complete with biometric chip. The Identity and Passport Service didn't provide it, of course. Brendan Coogan did.

Coogan was either a stickler for detail or just liked a laugh, because he even handed me the booklet that came with real passports. I nearly fell onto Coogan's kitchen floor laughing when I read it. I'm glad I didn't. His house made NHS wards seem almost sterile.

It told me that the IPS took Marc's security and privacy

very seriously. The new British biometric passport met international standards, and they were confident that it was one of the most secure available. It featured many new security features which would show if the passport had been tampered with, and the facial biometrics on the chip would help link the passport holder to the document.

What was more, the data on the chip, Marc's photo and personal information would be protected against theft through the use of 'advanced digital encryption techniques'. The chip would complement the security features currently inherent in the passport, including the 'machine readable zone' on the personal data page.

The chip contained Marc's signature (from a joke bet I'd got him to sign that England would win the next World Cup) to show the encoded data was genuine; the place of issue; a secure access protocol; and the benefit of Public Key Infrastructure (PKI) digital encryption technology, which provides protection against changes in encoded data. I'd never felt so secure.

I opened up an accommodation address in Marc's name, then went to the council offices and registered him on the electoral roll. I also applied for a duplicate of his driver's licence, which arrived from the DVLA just a few days later.

Over the next few months I signed up with several book and record clubs; I even bought a collection of porcelain thimbles out of a Sunday supplement, paying with a postal order. In return, I got a fistful of bills and receipts, all issued to the accommodation address.

Next I wrote to two or three of the high street banks and asked them a string of questions that made it sound as if I was a serious investor. I received suitably grovelling letters in reply, on the bank's letterhead. Then all I did was walk into a building society, played stupid, and said I would like to open a bank account, please. As long as you have your address on the appropriate documentation, they don't seem to look much further.

I put a few quid in my new account and let it tick over. After a few weeks I got some standing orders up and running with the book clubs, and at last I was ready to apply for a credit card. As long as you're on the electoral register, have a bank account and no bad credit history, the card is yours. And once you have one card, all the other banks and finance houses will fall over themselves to make sure you take theirs as well.

I thought about going one step further and getting myself a national insurance number, but there was really no point. I had money to use and a card that would get me out of the UK. Cash payments can be flagged up by airlines as out of the norm. With a card, I could go online, book, print off my boarding card, and be away in a matter of hours. The UK blanket was created in the same way.

I replaced the key fob, then gave Lynn another hundred pounds. 'We need a change of clothes. But first, we've got to go to Woolworths.'

I half expected him to ask me who that was.

46

'Catford Bridge station, mate. Near the old dog track.'

The minicab driver nodded as if he knew exactly where that was, and then got busy with his sat nav as we climbed into the back of the Espace. He was then far too busy talking football into a Bluetooth headset to pay us any further attention, let alone take time to admire our new baseball caps and anoraks

Twenty minutes later, Lynn and I exchanged a glance as we crossed Vauxhall Bridge. Vauxhall Cross, the head-quarters of MI6, was ahead of us on the South Bank. It looked like a beige and black pyramid with its top cut off, and large towers either side. There was even a terrace bar overlooking the river. It only needed a few swirls of neon and you'd swear you were in Las Vegas. I wondered if he had half a mind to stop the cab, run to the gate and throw himself on the mercy of his old employers.

I could see the cogs whirring in his head as he looked out of the window.

'Don't even think about it. If you did, you'd come

out in a bin-liner. This is the only way, believe me.'

He turned and gave me a slightly sheepish expression.

South of the river, London got grimier and more down-on-its-luck by the mile. By the time we'd reached our destination, I was starting to feel as depressed as Lynn looked.

I had a look around while he paid the driver. We walked uphill from the railway station, and the wreck of the old dog track soon came into view.

We carried on past rows of not-so-good-looking thirties bay-windowed terraces. Some of the occupants had gone for the seventies pebbledash or Roman stone cladding upgrade. Others had opted for the fixed one-sheet double-glazing that no one can escape through when the house gets torched. They were all in need of an urgent visit from a window cleaner and net-curtain washer.

Coogan's street looked in even shittier state than the rest. The two-metre-wide stretch of mud at the front had been given over largely to brambles and dandelions. A couple of council recycling wheelie bins stood against a low wall, but most of his shit seemed to have been thrown from an upstairs window and missed. Most of the cars parked along the kerb looked like they should be up on bricks.

Brendan and Leena had been in the passport business since the seventies, after they'd had to do a runner from the Free State for forging welfare coupons. For the last six or seven years Nigerians buying multiple passports for their multiple mortgages on their multiple buy-to-lets were keeping them generously afloat, but people like me had been their mainstay in the eighties and nineties. I'd first met Brendan during the Struggles, Troubles or the War (what you called it depended on who you were). We used to be sent down to Lewisham to be fitted up with the appropriate documents. I'd used him many times since then at my own expense. He was the best.

I told Lynn to stay out of sight while I rang the doorbell. Brendan himself answered. His face didn't break into a big smile and he didn't throw his arms around me. He just rolled his eyes, tutted and ushered me in. Just how I liked it with the old fucker.

'I have a friend.'

'Would that be a friend with money?'

'Yes.'

'A welcome awaits.'

I waved Lynn over and we stepped across the PVC threshold and into Minging Central. The stench of rotting vegetables and old newspapers reminded me of a run-down corner-shop.

He led us into the sitting room. The red velour curtains were closed. A green three-piece was arranged around a small TV. A raincoat hung over the back of the nearest armchair. A small dark wood table with two chairs stood against one wall. The fireplace was decorated with green thirties tiles, and an equally ancient gas fire had been fitted into the grate. It was doing its asthmatic best to fug up proceedings.

'Glad to see you still don't go for the minimalist look . . .'

He wasn't biting; he never did.

'It would be the usual you're after, would it?'

'My friend here has lost his passport and we need to travel tomorrow.'

He looked at me with a twinkle in his eye. 'And for some reason you choose not to avail your fine up-standing selves of Her Majesty's Passport Office's new premium same-day service?'

'Sometimes the old ways are the best. My friend wants to get away from his wife, her divorce lawyer and the Child Support Agency. He'd prefer not to be traced . . .'

Brendan looked at Lynn and raised an eyebrow.

I grinned. 'Second time round, lucky bastard. Young, beautiful, but, as it turned out, a bit too fond of the Bolivian Marching Powder.'

Coogan laughed. 'The young ones can be just as big a nightmare as the old ones. That's why I stayed with the missus – even though I'm never short of offers.' He cackled to himself.

'Where is the lovely Mrs Coogan? Still making that ginger cake?'

'She does, she does, and no, we haven't any left. She's down at bingo, thank God. She'd be fussing all over you by now and giving you all my biscuits.'

'Could you at least bring yourself to part with two cups of tea?'

He cackled some more as he disappeared into a kitchen that, if the smell coming out of it was anything to go by, was the source of the Ebola outbreak I thought might have brought London to a standstill a few days ago.

The look on Lynn's face told me this was a totally different world for him. A few hours ago he was in his lovely farmhouse, inhaling the sea air and staring out over acres of glorious countryside. Now he was in this minging thirties terrace with this minging old man. He'd probably never seen anything like this in his life, except perhaps when he was delivering coal and food parcels to the family servants at Christmas.

Brendan reappeared with three steaming mugs and half a packet of HobNobs and led us upstairs with a deep sigh. 'Things are a lot more complicated these days, you have to understand. The days of just pressing the printer button are long gone. Welcome to the brave new world of biometrics.'

'That sounds like a posh way of saying your prices have gone up – again.'

He looked pained. 'That it would be, that it would be. Seventeen hundred pounds, in fact. Half now, half tomorrow morning, when you collect.'

'No VAT?'

'Oh, I don't like to bother those nice people at the Excise. They've got quite enough to worry about '

'What about a discount for old times' sake? My friend has been mauled by lawyers. I told him it was twelve hundred.'

'Fifteen?'

'Done. It'll be in dollars again. Shall we say at 1.90?' I didn't want to spend the whole day rug-trading, but I had to go through the motions. I didn't want to disappoint him.

He turned just short of the landing and looked down at me. At last I got a full smile from him. It always took a while. 'I don't think that would be terribly helpful, do you? There would be complicated calculations and even some change involved. Let's say two dollars a pound. I'll lose some in commission when I exchange, don't forget. A businessman has to watch his margins.'

47

I looked around his workshop. He might have embraced the new technology, but not with open arms. He wasn't working in a stainless-steel hyper-tech bubble, that was for sure. It looked like all his equipment had been salvaged from skips and second-hand shops. Still, if it did the job . . .

'We've brought the usual selection of passport photos, but he hasn't had time to get a new name for himself—'

'Not a problem any more, old son. Do you have yours handy?'

I handed it over.

Brendan waved at Lynn. 'And does your friend have a shot of himself looking like—' he glanced down at a scrappy bit of A4 – 'like Mr Adrian William Letts?'

He took the selection of Woolies' photo-booth pictures from Lynn and gave them the once-over. 'And so he does, thank you. Now, Exhibit A.' He beamed at my passport as if he had just taken hold of yet another new grandchild. 'Supposedly the very pinnacle of travel documentation, brought out after 9/11 to satisfy the US State Department's demands. But in its unseemly haste to dance to their tune, the Passport Agency failed to introduce adequate security measures.'

He might have been the world's oldest man, and the most minging, but he was both an artist and craftsman. Even his language and his facial expressions changed once he got into full flow. 'They say there's a secure microchip in here. But weak encryption, plus lack of basic radio shielding, has produced a chip that can be read by electronic eavesdroppers.'

He grinned. 'Some of my ill-intentioned ilk struggled, but it took me just two weeks to figure out how to clone it. The authorities didn't exactly make it hard for me. They posted the standards for e-passports on several websites – including the International Civil Aviation Organization, the United Nations body that developed the standard.'

He opened the passport. 'Inside, as you see, is a laminated page containing the holder's picture, passport number, name, nationality, sex, signature, date and place of birth, and the document's issue and expiry date. Nothing special so far.

'But at the bottom of the page are two lines of printed numbers and letters, which can be read by a computer when the passport is swiped at the MRZ – the Machine Readable Zone – at the immigration desk.'

He flipped it over. 'The RFID, the Radio Frequency Identification microchip, is right here, surrounded by a coil of copper-coloured wire.'

He shook his head in disbelief. 'Governments claim the new biometric chips can only be read over a distance of two centimetres, but I'm reliably informed those in British passports can be read from over a metre away. I don't know anyone who's done that yet, but we've contacted chips at thirty centimetres. That's twelve inches in old money.

'Me and Leena have a day out at Heathrow now and again with the reader in her handbag. You can buy one off the internet for two hundred quid. It takes around four seconds to suck out the information and Bob's your uncle. So there's no more need to chat up strange men in bars . . .'

Brendan giggled away to himself as he handed back my passport and cracked open another packet of his beloved HobNobs.

Lynn suddenly looked more animated than he had done all day. 'What's in the chip that's so worthwhile getting at?'

'Ah, there are three important files. One contains an electronic copy of the printed information on the passport's photo page. The second holds the electronic image of the holder. The third is a security device which checks that the previous two files haven't been accessed and altered.

'The government says the biometric chips are protected by what they call an advanced digital encryption technique. In other words, without the MRZ key code it is impossible to steal the passport holder's details if you do not have their travel document.

'They're talking bollocks, of course.' He laughed so hard that flecks of HobNob flew out of his mouth to join the rest of the shit on the carpet. 'The first big flaw is that someone like me can try to access the chip as many times as he likes until he cracks the MRZ code, unlike, say, putting a pin number into an ATM machine, where the security system refuses access after three wrong attempts.

'The second flaw is that there are easily identifiable recurring patterns in the MRZ key codes. Bizarrely, the ICAO suggested that the key needed to access the data on the chips should be comprised of the passport number, the holder's date of birth and the expiry date, in that order. That's about as secure as living in a bank vault but leaving the key under the mat.

'I got myself a helper, a young computer whiz-kid, and he developed a brute-force program that repeatedly tries different combinations of data to discover a password. The old programs could take months, but not any more. Those Indian fellers are smart, aren't they? Once Leena has sucked out six or seven passports from the tube I can crack the MRZ in a couple of days, four at the most.'

He chuckled away to himself. 'Brute force, now that's the way to crack a nut, eh, Nick?'

'Every time, Brendan.'

He got back into work mode. 'But remember, information cannot be added to a cloned chip, so anyone using it to make a counterfeit passport will have to use a picture that bears a reasonable resemblance to the previous owner. Sure, there are facial recognition systems in the chip – precise measurements of key points on your face and head – but they are not yet in operation. In any case, the technology throws up between 20 and 25 per cent false negatives or false positives. It won't be reliable for years to come.'

He beamed at Lynn. 'Adrian's got the same hairstyle as your good self.'

He got back to his waffle. 'So it's down to the Mark 1 human eyeball at airports and such like. People have great difficulty matching faces to pictures, even trained immigration officials. That's why photographs have never been introduced on credit cards. As long as your friend here bears a fair resemblance to the person on the chip – or grows a beard – he'll get through a border post. Or your money back.' He laughed again, but we didn't get hit by HobNob shrapnel this time. 'The beauty of it is that nobody knows that their passport is being cloned. Nobody's reported their passport stolen. After all, they still have it.'

He stood up and held out a hand. 'So that'll be half now and the rest tomorrow morning . . .'

I peeled off the dollars. 'Jesus, Brendan. Money for old rope.'

He allowed himself another giggle. 'I know, son, I know. I only wish I was thirty years younger; I'd have such fun with all this new technology. I've just got into cloning those Oyster cards everyone seems to be using – piece of piss! You fellers want a couple?'

'No, we're OK, mate. Off tomorrow, remember?'

He pocketed the down payment and started rummaging about in his desk drawer. 'It gets better. You know the ID card scheme your Gordon Brown is so keen on? It'll use the same technology. So I'll have access to around fifty pieces of information about you: your name, age, all your addresses, your national insurance number and biometric details; everything a feller could possibly need.'

He pulled out a signature tablet, the type used in US stores to check signatures electronically.

'Now, Mr Letts. If you would just sign your name . . .'

48

Where to spend the night? I wouldn't put Brendan on the spot by asking if he had a spare room. Besides, I wanted us to have a reasonable chance of surviving the night. Nor could we use a hotel, or even a B&B. If we'd been spotted in the area, the Firm would have the police checking every spare bed within a one-mile radius. We had a lot of walking to do through residential streets, away from the cameras' gaze, until it was time to find somewhere to hide.

The Black Cat shopping centre down the road – well, I called it that anyway – was perfect. I'd hung about there for about nine hours once while the Irishman sorted out a few documents for me. It wouldn't be the most comfortable night Lynn had ever spent away from home, but at least it meant we'd drop off the face of the earth until Brendan had done his stuff.

We could evade surveillance only for so long. If it was the Firm after us, they'd have covered all the motorways and transport hubs. Those cameras would be in overdrive.

We walked for two hours or so and landed up in Honour Oak Park. We sat on a bench like two perverts and froze. At least the rain was holding off, and by about 4.30 it was getting dark. Soon I could see the stars and clouds of my own breath. It was going to be another sub-zero night.

'Time to go.'

We made our way back to Catford. The evening commute was in full swing, which was good for us. I got Lynn his first ever doner kebab and chips and he definitely didn't like it.

'Better get them down you; it's the only shop without a camera.'

I'd bought two each.

'They're horrible when they're cold. The grease . . .'

We sat on a bench the other side of the shopping centre, opposite a big black plastic cat draped over the welcome sign.

Lynn picked at his kebabs, then pushed them to one side, so I got them down my neck while he turned his attention to the chips and stewed tea.

Ten minutes later we headed outside. The car park was lit, but the recycling skips that supermarkets provide to make us all feel like we're saving the planet were in deep shadow. One of them was for clothes. I leant in and pulled them out by the armload.

'Insulation. You need more between you and the ground than you do on top.'

It was so dark here I could hardly see his face, even though real life continued not more than 100 metres away. Traffic ground its way along the street and people ran for buses.

The wind had picked up and we arranged the clothes as best we could to provide some sort of mattress. I kept my arms tight against my sides and pulled up my collar to conserve as much warmth as I could. If I had to move my head I'd turn my whole body. I didn't want the slightest breath of wind down my neck.

Lynn started shivering. He hadn't spent half his life being cold, wet and hungry like I had.

I gave him a nudge. 'Duff – was he really a source?'

'Yes.' Lynn sat up. 'We turned him in the early eighties. He was arrested by the French coming back from a Hezbollah training camp with a false passport. Duff was an idealist, but he was also a realist. He was staring down the barrel of a very long prison sentence. We could spring him. All he had to do was accept a golden hand-shake and give us the occasional little bit of information. Nothing major. Nothing life-threatening. Just gossip, really.'

Once he had taken that first step, there would have been no way back. The handlers would have started off slow, but the die was cast. He would have taken money from the British government. They'd have made it impossible for him to get out without a PIRA bullet in his head.

'Early eighties? So he was working for you at the time of the Tripoli job? I thought I'd never had so much int on a job – now I know why.'

'He'd got a bit stroppy by then, so we upped the ante. We said we'd kill his younger brother. Well, someone like you would.'

After that, Lynn said, Liam Duff became quite an asset. He had the ear of hard-bitten players who wouldn't have trusted their own grannies but seemed to take a shine to him.

'Why break cover after all this time? Missed you after your retirement, did he?'

Lynn wasn't going to bite. 'When I left the service, he was still in prison for his part in the *Bahiti* but was released early as part of the Good Friday Agreement. From what I've heard, the peace process unhinged him. He never forgave Isham and the others for what he saw as selling out. A bit ironic, considering what he'd been up to all those years and the fact it got him early release.'

'Who killed him?'

'That's the sixty-four-thousand-dollar question.' He half shivered, half shrugged. 'Until you turned up, I'd have said the answer was obvious. Now I'm not so sure. PIRA insist it wasn't them, and we're supposed to believe them these days. There are plenty who think British security forces are still trying to undermine the peace accord . . .'

49

I lay in my pile of discarded clothes; they smelled like
stale margarine. What a dickhead Duff was. Why expose
yourself if you don't have to? Money and vanity are
more dangerous than a box-cutter. Maybe he'd thought
he had immunity in the aftermath of the Good Friday
Agreement. Even a couple of years ago, he would have
been found in a plastic bag on the Armagh border, leaking badly.

'You know anything more about how he was killed?'

'He got some close attention from an electric drill, and
then he was shot.'

PIRA got the Black and Deckers out for at least fifty
people it claimed were informers during the Troubles.
Duff's disclosure came after they'd formally declared
that they were abandoning violence. But maybe in his
case they'd been prepared to make an exception.

Northern Ireland might be on the brink of a new era of
peace, but someone had clearly decided that Duff wasn't
going to live to see it. If he'd left Ireland he might still be

alive: plenty of informers and double agents had been spirited away to start new lives abroad. By staying in Ireland, Duff had signed his own death warrant. He'd been living in a remote area of western Ireland, in a run-down cottage with no electricity or running water. But even in Donegal there is nowhere that anyone can completely hide themselves away, as I had very quickly found out.

I nodded. 'Plenty of people have that MO.'

'I really did think it might have been you. That maybe you still worked for the Firm – or perhaps had a few scores to settle of your own . . .'

He had a point. 'This PIRA traitor Duff was on about – the one who gave up the *Bahiti* – you know who it was? He had to be pretty high up the food chain to know about the job.'

He didn't even blink. 'That information, Nick, is something that would get you killed.'

'You really think it could have been the Firm?'

'Duff had already revealed there was a Brit on board who killed Lesser. He would undoubtedly have exposed even more details about us. Then, of course, there is the question of a device under your car. It's not too hard to put two and two together . . .'

'You think it's the Firm tying off a few loose ends?'

'More each time I think about it.'

'But why go to such elaborate lengths to drop us two? There has to be more to this than a bit of spring cleaning.'

I rolled over and looked up at the sky. Whatever – it didn't matter right now. What did was getting out of the UK to re-form, regroup and sort our shit out.

Lynn was starting to read my mind. 'Where next, Nick?'

'Not sure yet.'

He sat up and adjusted the pile of clothes to insulate his back against the bricks. 'I have a place in Italy.'

I thought for a second. 'It'll be a known location. They'll check it.'

'You aren't the only one who has a safety blanket, you know. I was about to move there myself – until you interrupted my packing.'

'It's secure? No one knows about it? You can't be found?'

'No one. Not even my children.'

50

We lay huddled for two, maybe three hours. I wasn't sure and I couldn't be arsed to expose any skin to the cold to check my watch.

The sound of adolescent voices came from over to our left, full of fucks and shits, getting louder as they approached.

There was only room for one of us right behind the bins. I motioned for Lynn to make himself scarce. He shuffled backwards, dragging his bundle with him.

The shouts and laughter came closer, until one of them stopped no more than a few feet away. 'Hold on . . .'

I looked up at him.

'Oi, mate, get a fucking job.' I was treated to a fourteen-year-old's sneer from beneath a grey hoodie. I'd have had mine up too, if I'd had one.

Four of his mates gathered round to share the entertainment. More hoodies, baggy jeans, trainers. It was obviously a big night out.

'You a mether, or what?'

They crowded round the gap between the bins.

I wasn't going to get up just yet. There wasn't any need.

'No, mate. I'm just here, that's all.'

I thought of myself at their age, doing exactly the same as they were, always in a gang. The only difference was the clothes. These lads were much better dressed.

They were just bored, with no job prospects apart from serving up fries or stacking shelves. No wonder they were roaming about, trying out phone boxes for cash, not going out to do anything specific – if it was there they'd do it. Climb through the window of a house if it was open; try a few car doors. Anything to show the rest of the pack they were one of them. If you've got nothing, you've got nothing to lose.

Even their faces were the same as those around me when I was a kid. Black, white, Indian, mixed. On a housing estate, colour doesn't matter. Everyone's in the same shit. Everyone's parents are unemployed. Everyone's on benefits. Everyone's in the dustbin. Even dogs think the flats are interchangeable.

Another one shouted, 'Oi, mate . . .'

It was a white lad this time. I could just make out a chin full of zits under his hoodie. 'You got any fags? Give us a fag.'

A couple of them were getting a bit restless. It was time to stand up. Pack mentality: they were starting to think about other things than just taking the piss. I could feel it. I'd done it myself.

'No, mate. I don't smoke. Can't afford 'em.'

These lads were getting more confident.

'Yeah, but you're on the dole, aintcha? You're getting money, aintcha?'

'A little.'

I knew what was coming. The zit-faced one whipped out a blade. 'Fucking give us it then.'

There was no point debating this. I stepped forward and grabbed his hand and bent his palm back towards his forearm. My momentum gave me more power in my grip, and he went down, more with surprise than pain.

The knife clattered to the ground. The others did a kind of war dance, ready to have a go but not sure what to do now one of them was down. But one of them would, eventually.

Zit-face lay there in shock. I folded the knife and put it in my pocket. 'OK, lads, now just fuck off.'

'Cunt!' The first black lad made his move. He aimed a kick at me, but wasn't fast enough. I grabbed his leg and pulled him towards me, at the same time kicking down hard on the calf muscle of his standing leg. He fell onto his back.

The others shouted, 'You cunt!' but no one else was in a hurry to make the mistake he had.

I held onto his leg. I had to do something short, sharp and drastic to stop this from escalating. I stamped down on the side of his knee. I wasn't going to break it; just give him the worst pain he'd ever experienced. He howled like a wounded animal.

'Now fuck off.'

I let go of his leg and put my hand in my pocket. I threw about £50 at Zit-face but kept my eyes on the rest of them, just in case.

'You've got to watch what you're doing, lads. Don't

take things at face value. Someone else might have got hold of that knife and jammed it in one of your necks. One or two of you would have been down and dead – just over a few fucking quid. You've got to start switching yourselves on . . .'

I gave the two lads on the floor a tap, letting them know it was OK to get up.

'Take the money, go and get pissed, do whatever, just fuck off and let me get my head down.'

They did. They took the money and ran – all except the black lad, who hobbled. He'd be all right. I watched them disappear back the way they'd come, pausing occasionally to turn and shout at me in an effort to regain some dignity. 'You cunt! You fucking mad man wanker!'

They faded into the darkness and eventually their shouts were drowned by traffic.

Lynn emerged from behind the bins. 'Next time I stay on show. Safety in numbers . . .'

'With your accent? Red rag to a bull. But there won't be a next time. We're moving round the corner. They might go and get pissed with my cash and come back with a gun. Come on.'

As he gathered up his stuff, I did my bit for the environment. I recycled the knife into the empty-can skip.

We went and dug ourselves in behind the not-so-trendy skips, the ones filled with actual rubbish and shite from Tesco. Lynn had had at least one new life experience today, an encounter with hoodie culture. He might be about to have his second, coming face to face with a real rat.

It was time to think about the next phase. 'So anyway,

what are they wearing round Genoa this time of the year?'

He gave it some thought. 'It'll be fairly mild, but still cold. Smart coats mostly, but you'll get away with a ski jacket. A lot of people head for the Alps at the weekend.'

'OK, we'll buy some gear in the morning. But we won't wear it yet – we'll take the bags to the airport. We'll travel separately, take a shower, then come out in our new gear. Throw away your old clothes in dribs and drabs around the terminal. Don't try to force big bundles into a bin – remember the CCTV.'

51

Gatwick airport
0800 hrs

I headed straight to the check-in area in the South
Terminal with the two plastic carrier bags that contained
my next layer of skin. If we'd been flying anywhere
longer haul than Europe I would have bought myself
some hand luggage so I blended in, but for short hops it
didn't matter. So many people fly to places like Brussels
and Milan for the day that travelling without even a
newspaper doesn't raise an eyebrow. The flight seemed
to be on time.

I asked at the information desk about soap and a towel
and went up the escalator to Gatwick Village. I spotted
Lynn in an overcoat with a velvet collar and a dark
brown fedora, sitting at a table in a coffee shop, staring
forlornly into a large frothy cup. Giving him a wide
berth, I carried on to the showers tucked away behind
Starbucks.

After we'd picked up Lynn's passport and Leena had filled us up with her ginger cake, made especially for me once she found out I was coming, we'd split up for the shopping frenzy.

The very last item on my list was airline tickets for me and Mr Adrian William Letts. Since I had a card, it was easily done online. The 24-hour internet café even printed out the boarding passes there and then.

We'd arranged to meet where the minicab had dropped us off by Catford station at 5 a.m., before travelling separately again to the airport.

I finished my shower, and emerged in my new not-so-man-about-Santa-Margherita-Ligure gear: jeans, Nikes, blue polo shirt and matching ski jacket from a 24/7 supermarket with a clothes section. No red or yellow Euro coloured jeans for me.

I got rid of my old stuff in several bins, and headed for departures.

The flight was busy and there was a scrum around the gate. I never understood what the rush was about. The plane wouldn't leave until the last passenger was on board, and there were seats for everyone. And in my experience, last on got the seat next to the beautiful girl everyone else had avoided in case it looked like they were trying it on.

I just hoped the only vacant seat wasn't next to Lynn. He hadn't just gone native, he'd turned into Don Corleone.

PART FIVE

52

1250 hrs

Cristoforo Colombo International Airport is quite small,
despite the grand name and the fact Genoa is a big
industrial city of close to a million inhabitants. Built on a
reclaimed peninsula about fifteen Ks outside the city, it's
only got the one terminal. But it's always busy if you're
Irish or a Brit. The 1995 Schengen Agreement allows EU
countries to remove their internal borders and let citizens
travel freely from country to country. For security
reasons, the UK and Ireland were the only two countries
to remain outside the agreement. It pissed Lynn off
big-time.

'The upshot is, you have to join the bloody United
Nations queue for just two booths to have our passports
checked. By the time you've got to the front and they've
had a quick flick-through, all the taxis have gone and
there's a long wait between buses.'

'Just as well we won't be using them then, eh?'

I was feeling confident. I knew my passport chip was going to say exactly what was written on the page.

To my right I could hear Lynn being very cool and casual, giving it plenty of '*Buongiorno*' and '*Grazie*'.

If his passport didn't pass the test and the carabinieri jumped him, I'd carry on alone. From here, fuck it, I could drive to Russia, or get a train and be there within sixteen hours. Or I could even drive to Serbia or Kosovo. No heavy surveillance there: just ask Radovan Karadzic. It'd only take a few hours. It'd actually be quicker than driving from London to Dundee.

We both sailed through. Brendan had earned his fifteen hundred. Well, sixteen if you counted the hundred I gave him on top for his next three months' worth of HobNobs and a bunch of something nice for Leena.

Rather than getting any of the transport I could see outside, the buses that took you down to the train station, Genoa Principale, or a cab from the rank, I headed for the Hertz office. I thought I'd give Avis a miss. I wasn't worried they'd tie me in to the missing Merc because I was using my cover docs – but their cars didn't seem to be doing me any favours.

Lynn had said the forty-K drive to Santa Margherita Ligure took about fifty minutes. We could have taken a taxi, but Lynn had a theory that every cab driver in Italy worked either for the Mafia or the government. Besides, we might need to make a quick getaway from his safe house if it turned out not to be so safe after all, and I wanted instant wheels.

I left Lynn outside and went to the Hertz desk alone.

The less time we were seen together the better. The girl processed my card, licence and passport with a big smile, and minutes later I had the key fob to a blue Fiat Punto in my hand and was heading for the car park. It was possible they had cameras at entrance and exit as an anti-theft measure, so I'd told Lynn I'd pick him up just outside.

He was waiting where I'd told him to. I'd taken the piss out of his Don Corleone overcoat, but now he looked like every other smartly dressed Italian in sight.

Lynn directed me onto the tollbooths for the A12. The Italians did two things well, I'd always thought: dictators and motorways. The one thing they didn't seem to go in for, I said, was CCTV cameras.

Lynn laughed. 'You worry about surveillance in the UK, but the Italians are among the most spied-upon people in the world. Seventy-six telephone intercepts per hundred thousand people each year.

'It's hilarious. The Italian constitution guarantees privacy of information, and they even set up a national data-protection authority in 2003, but wiretapping and electronic eavesdropping are a national sport – not only by the secret services, but also by the judiciary. Prosecutors routinely order wiretaps, citing the fight against the Mafia as their justification. The cost to the Italian taxpayer is enormous.'

'I always thought "Italian taxpayer" was a contradiction in terms. Who carries out the wiretaps?'

'The newly privatized Italian Telecom – which the press has been having a go at for years for working hand in glove with the secret services.'

The two-lane autostrada cut straight through the

mountains on its way to the sea. Everyone was driving at 160km an hour and about a metre apart. A mother with a cigarette in her mouth still managed to bollock her kids and her husband as she pulled into the fast lane to overtake us. A motorbike somehow cut her up, and she went berserk. Italians really do talk with their hands.

Lynn didn't bat an eyelid. He was now in full university lecturer mode. 'A former director of security at Telecom, who had close links with the secret services, was sent to prison not so long ago, together with a former anti-terrorism chief, as a result of a wiretapping scandal.

'Private conversations of politicians and public figures are taped wholesale. Prosecutors and judges routinely leak details to journalists.'

We went into a tunnel that seemed to go on forever. Not long after we emerged, Lynn pointed ahead at a small service station cut into the mountainside on the right. 'Groceries are cheaper here than down in the town.'

Typical officer.

A lad with a bumbag was filling petrol tanks and taking payment. He was chatting away with the driver in front of us but it looked like they were about to come to blows. There was a small car park to one side for the Autogrill.

We weren't back on the road for long before the Rapallo turn-off, which was actually past Santa Margherita Ligure. Paying our two and a bit euros at the toll, we drove into a neat little coastal town, and then stayed by the sea for the next five or six Ks. As we drove over the last hill and Santa Margherita spread out below us it was like a scene from a French Riviera movie of the fifties or sixties. I was half expecting David Niven to come over the crest in an open-top Austin Healey.

53

'Mussolini used to come here for his holidays.' Lynn waved his hand at the palm trees and grand old hotels and villas. 'A lot of northern Europeans retire here.'

I wasn't surprised a fascist dictator came here with his bucket and spade. The whole place looked so well behaved even the flowers stood to attention. But fuck that. 'If everything goes to rat shit in the next ten minutes, what are the escape routes?'

Lynn looked and sounded a bit more lively. Maybe he thought that because we were out of the UK, we were out of danger. 'Back to the airport at Genoa, or the one at Pisa's about a hundred and fifty kilometres.' He was getting the hang of this. 'Portofino's just down the road. If we have to dump the car, the train station is near the centre of the town. It's on the main line to Genoa, Pisa and Rome. Buses run from outside the station. From the harbour, passenger ferries connect the town with other resorts up and down the coast, even off-season.'

I looked at him. 'You buy or rent?'

He waved his hand again. 'There's no need to worry about traceability. I wouldn't be here with you now if there was any chance of that.'

'Lots of cash about?'

'Property here is now the dearest in Italy, outside of central Rome. It's the only place where the market's gone up every single year since the Second World War. No more building has been allowed and the only thing they can do is dig into the mountains and build car parks in the countryside. But everybody wants to be here. The Russians and oil sheiks are sending prices through the roof.'

I had to remind myself that this was the man who'd shopped at a service station out of town instead of the local Co-op because his cornflakes were half a euro cheaper.

My impression that Santa Margherita Ligure was like a film set was holding out. The place seemed to be entirely populated with stars or extras. Even on a winter day, the sun was strong and everybody had their Gucci sunglasses on. A glamorous woman glided past on a moped. As she turned to flick ash from her cigarette, I caught the Chanel logo on the back of her leopard-skin helmet.

Every shop we passed seemed to be selling either shoes or pashminas. There wasn't an amusement arcade, Mr Whippy machine or hoodie in sight. Maybe I should have gone to university like Lynn and become our man in Tripoli, rather than fucking about at the bottom of the pond.

We passed a taxi rank on the seafront. All the cabs were white Q7 Audis and big, over-the-top Italian estate cars or Mercedes. I wondered what had happened to mine – or rather, Avis's. Had they done all the forensics and returned it to them yet, or had it been reported as stolen and my credit card maxed out in non-return charges?

'That low hill above the waterfront is an interesting place. The castle was built in 1550 as defence against the Saracens.'

He wasn't the only one pointing. We passed a big statue of Christopher Columbus with his arm stretched out to sea. One bit of pub quiz trivia I'd remembered from school: he'd set sail from Genoa.

The harbour was small and obviously catered for smart yachts, but it still had a fishing fleet. Several boats were unloading opposite a market. A breakwater stretched about three or four hundred metres into the sea, towards a cluster of massive floating gin palaces. I got the system: the bigger the boat, the further out it parked.

We found a space along the seafront. It was lined with more beautiful old buildings. The arches underneath were inset with cafés, ice cream parlours, bars and restaurants. At the front, elegant Italians in sunglasses and overcoats sat drinking coffee. Behind them, in what looked like caves, were dining areas lined with dark wood panelling and bottles of wine.

Lynn nodded up at one of the apartment blocks. 'That's me. Great view of the harbour one way, the Basilica the other. Well worth a visit, Nick, to view the gilded chandeliers. Come on, we can see them while I pick up the keys.'

A tour of the Basilica? Just what fucking planet was this guy on?

'The British Embassy is in Rome, yeah?'

'There's a consulate in Genoa, but yes, that's where the embassy is.'

'How far by road?'

'Three hundred miles, just about spot on.'

'How long would it take to drive it?'

'Five and a half hours, maybe a bit longer this time of year. Why, do you want to go to Rome?'

I shook my head. 'It's how long it would take them to drive here I'm worried about.'

The Basilica, it turned out, was stunning. Fifty-metre high ceilings, massive chandeliers, and more saints' relics and old women on their knees than you could shake a stick at.

Lynn hadn't brought me here for the view. He headed straight for the furthest confession box, felt under the seat and pulled out two keys taped together.

'I make sure there isn't anything in the UK to connect me with here.'

54

The apartment had two bedrooms and was very simple and very white after what I could smell was a new lick of paint. The building was nineteenth century, with high ceilings and shutters on the windows. The furniture was modern and new. I doubted Lynn had chosen it. In the living room, a pair of high glass doors opened onto a small Juliet balcony overlooking the Viale Andrea Doria, the road that ran along the harbour front and carried on the four K or so to Portofino. Beyond it was the harbour and the Mediterranean.

I picked up a pair of binoculars. Lynn probably spent hours boat spotting.

'We still assuming it's the Firm?'

'What's to tell us it isn't? Who else had the resources to find me in Donegal so fast? Who else could have made and planted a device so fast? Who else knew about Leptis? OK, anybody could have bought a tracker and followed me to yours, but the other stuff still points in the direction of Vauxhall Cross.'

'But why would they bracket us together? We're hardly a job lot.'

'It must be linked to Duff somehow. They're cleaning house. It must all come back to the Tripoli job.' I looked up at him sharply. 'Were there drugs on the *Bahiti*?'

'You mean anything the Yes Man could have been involved in?'

I must have looked surprised.

'I might have left the building, Nick, but I still have friends who haven't. I knew what he was up to all those years, but nobody would listen. He had the ear of the right people. When early retirement came up, I was glad to cut and run, wash my hands of the whole thing.' He looked up. 'You know about Hannibal?'

'Elephant Boy? Crossed the Alps?'

'Precisely. Well, we're in Hannibal country here. I've been thinking about his catchphrase: "We will either find a way, or make one."'

'Which one's your money on?'

'Make.' He smiled. 'Mark my words, Hannibal knew what he was talking about. He was only in his twenties when he was given command of Carthage's forces. That's Tunisia, these days. Within two years, by 219 BC, he had subjugated all of Spain, which violated Carthage's treaties with Rome. The Romans demanded Carthage surrender Hannibal to them, and the city refused. The Romans declared war, and so began the Second Punic War. But then came his masterstroke: instead of waiting for the Romans to arrive, Hannibal carried the war to their doorstep.

'That September he set out to cross the Alps with fifty thousand men and forty elephants. He did it in just fifteen days, despite heavy losses of men and animals to bad weather and hostile mountain tribesmen. His army went on to defeat the Romans in the battles of Ticinus and Trebia and occupy northern Italy.'

'And which bit of that applies to our situation exactly?'

'The thought that maybe we should carry the fight to them. Maybe we should contact the friends I still have on the inside, find out why this is happening and what we can do to end it.'

I scanned the harbour and road below for guys sitting well back in their car seats, or a fishing boat bobbing about with a guy looking back at me through binoculars. I finally put them down and turned to him. 'There's another way of looking at Hannibal, you know.'

Lynn did a double-take, as if he was surprised I might have an opinion on anything other than what to look for in a kebab or a box-cutter. He might have guessed rightly that I didn't even get close to a GCSE in ancient history, but what he didn't know was that when I was in my twenties, I'd done a paper for my case study on battle-field strategy at the school of infantry in Brecon. The other guys did Rommel, Montgomery and Che Guevara, but Hannibal Barca was the boy for me. He ranked right up there alongside Alexander the Great, Napoleon Bonaparte and the Duke of Wellington in my book, as one of the greatest generals of all time.

'He might be famous for taking his army and elephants across the Alps, but he gets more cred from me for leading a successful campaign for fifteen years, far from home, and only by surviving off the land and his tactical wits.

'He was a soldier's soldier. He shared the same

hardship and dangers as his men. Even his enemies said he never asked others to do what he couldn't or wouldn't do himself. No army's ever held its own so long, against such odds.'

'You're saying we do nothing?'

'I'm saying let's wait and see. Hannibal showed war can be won by avoiding battle instead of seeking it. He got results by attacking the enemy's communications and by flanking manoeuvres. So we don't have to carry the battle to them. Not yet, at least. We're in a safe house, let's draw breath and do some thinking.'

'That's all well and good, but we could have a window here that's not going to be open long. There must be deals to be made – there always are. I can catch one of my friends at home—'

'Not while I'm still about. You can call if you want, but I won't be staying. You'll be on your own when they stuff you in a bin-liner.' I shook my head. 'There's something else Hannibal once said: "When you make friends with the elephant keeper, expect the elephant."'

I looked along the walls for phone points. Nothing. Lynn knew his stuff. This really was a safe house. 'I'm going out to recce a few things. Give me the keys. If I'm not back in one hour thirty you're on your own. They'll have me.'

55

The first thing you do when you arrive somewhere is work out how to get away again in a hurry. If we had to do a runner and got split up, I wanted to know where to run to. I wanted to be able to nominate RVs.

I was mugged by sunshine the moment I stepped out of the main door. I pulled on my sun-gigs; they were hanging on a string I'd bought in the London ski shop.

I kept the harbour on my right for about 200 metres, then turned and came back inland on parallel, narrow streets between elegant old buildings. Was nothing ugly in this town?

I mapped it all in my head as I climbed the low hill dominating the waterfront. Behind the castle Lynn had pointed out was a maze of overgrown passageways prowled by semi-wild cats. Further up the slope was a church with a spookily illuminated Madonna in a rocky grotto, and a public park made up of a series of terraced gardens. All good RVs: Lynn would know them.

I found a Co-op mini-market on Corso Giacomo

Matteotti and went in and bought one of yesterday's English broadsheets for the price of a paperback, and a couple of baguettes to take back to the apartment. I couldn't find anything resembling cheese and Branston so I settled for a couple filled with, well, Italian stuff.

I followed the road down into Piazza Caprera, which contained the Basilica. The area was pedestrianized. There was a big Christmas tree in one corner, and strings of unlit white bulbs were draped between shops and the church, waiting for last light.

Everybody was wrapped up, though it didn't feel very cold to me. I went into a café and ordered a cappuccino. The place mat had a history of the town in three languages. Maybe that was where Lynn had hoovered up all his knowledge.

'Santa Margherita has a long history,' it told me proudly, 'dating back to the Roman town of Pescino, which was razed first by the Lombards in 641 and then the Saracens in the 1100s. In 1229 it became part of the Republic of Genoa, was raided by Venice in 1432, and by the Turks in 1549. It fell to Napoleon, who renamed it Porto Napoleone, then to Sardinia and in 1861 it joined the new Kingdom of Italy.'

Fine, but the only marauders I needed news of were whoever jumped us in Norfolk.

I got to grips with the front page of the newspaper. Pakistani former prime minister Benazir Bhutto had been assassinated in a suicide attack. She was leaving an election rally in Rawalpindi when a gunman shot her in the neck and then detonated himself. At least twenty other people died in the attack and several more were injured.

I couldn't be arsed to read on. I put the paper on the

221

table and stretched my legs and arms as I looked out over the piazza. Two immaculately dressed Italian women walked past arm in arm, yabbering away to each other. It seemed impossible to speak Italian without sounding as if you were either having an argument or trying to talk someone into bed. There had to be worse places on earth to sit and pass the time of day. For a moment I almost forgot I was being chased by men in leather jackets who wanted to kill me.

A plan started to form in my head. After my coffee, I'd walk back to Lynn's apartment and we'd have a long discussion about his career since our last contact in 1998. Somewhere in there lay the answer to what bound us together and why someone wanted us both dead.

My cappuccino arrived and I took a sip and went back to the paper.

I scanned the inside pages. Jack and Katie were the most popular first names given to children whose births were registered in Northern Ireland in 2007. *Time* magazine's Person of the Year was Vladimir Putin. In Britain, the Foreign Secretary was about to visit Libya to tie off some loose ends in the Lockerbie agreement. I could imagine the chaos on the ground as British and local security tried to keep him safe from fundamentalists. Glad it was their problem; I had enough of my own.

I folded it up, paid the bill and started back towards the apartment.

56

Lynn was sitting at the table. His laptop was open as wide as the smile across his face.

'Good news, Nick. It's not the Firm.'

'You've spoken to them?'

'It's the internet, Nick! Don't worry, I surf off my neighbour's wi-fi – silly boy doesn't even have a password. We're safe, it's OK!'

I shoved my face into his. 'You pissed? Do they know where we are?'

'They just know it's Italy. Nick, it's OK – they can't trace Skype. It's VOIP traffic, there are no fixed lines. The packets are routed around the network on any one of a number of different routes. We're safe here.'

'They *know* it's Italy, or you told them?'

'I told them. Listen, the question's been bugging me ever since those cars turned up at the farm: why would the Firm use you to lead them to me when they knew all along where I lived? I know you think this will end in bin-liners, but you'll have to trust me – the same as I trust my old friends.'

'Friends? Are you paying their mortgages?'

'No.'

'So why trust them?'

'That's not how it works in my world, Nick – one of them is godfather to my son.'

I turned to the window. The sun glittered on the sea.

'OK, it's done. Damage-limitation time. What did they say?'

'Just that it isn't them. They said we should come in from the cold, get their help.'

It would be great if this shit didn't belong to them. They might even be able to help, if only because Lynn was involved. It would have nothing to do with the low life following in his wake.

Lynn joined me at the window. 'I told them we could meet at the Autogrill. It's a public area, Nick.'

'When?'

'They suggested six thirty tonight.'

I looked at my watch. It was already four o'clock. 'So they're not coming from Rome?'

'They were at the consulate in Genoa.'

'Is that the first call you've made to them?'

'Yes. I didn't just say we'd come to them. I arranged an RV . . . and they do not know about the flat.'

'Did you say what car we'd be in?'

'No.'

'What direction we'd be coming from?'

'No.'

57

The apartment keys were back under the confessional seat, and the Fiat was stuck in a line of traffic. It was still hot and humid outside, but the sun was getting lower. We were heading for the Rapallo toll to get back on the A12, where we'd turn north towards Genoa, spin round at the exit just beyond it, and then to the Autogrill.

The queue we were in wasn't anything to do with the toll plaza yet. We were still way back in the town. It was the sheer volume of traffic clogging the maze of narrow streets that had been built for horses and carts. There were traffic lights at every junction, and only about fifty metres between them. That didn't faze the mopeds and motorbikes that buzzed around us like flies. They all managed to keep moving; we managed about twenty metres at a time before the lights changed.

I'd been checking the mirrors, doing all my normal anti-surveillance stuff: not looking, but at the same time looking. The unconscious absorbs everything like a sponge. If you come home and the doormat has been disturbed, you'll know it – even though you've never paid it any special attention. You don't know why you know it, you just do. Or when you get to your desk at work in the morning and your pen isn't at the exact angle you left it, little alarm bells ring in your unconscious. Everything is registered.

And what had registered with me was a particular motorbike. I couldn't even make out the exact make and model just yet, but the bells had rung and I'd listened.

It was behind us, maybe four or five cars back, and it had been behind us for the last three or four sets of lights. Why wasn't it cutting through like the rest of them? It wasn't as if it was a big old bike like a Honda Goldwing with panniers and fairings, so bulky it couldn't manoeuvre. It wasn't an old guy's bike either, the sort of big menopausal BMW that retired dentists buy without really knowing how to ride, and don't risk in traffic in case it gets scratched. This was just a slim road bike. The rider had a shaded visor over his plain black helmet, a black bike jacket and jeans. He looked local, but wasn't acting it. There was something wrong.

Lynn was in a world of his own. He kept looking at his watch and willing the traffic to part like the Red Sea. That was just fine. I wasn't going to tell him what was behind us. I didn't want him sparked up and turning in his seat to see for himself. The rider would be straight onto his radio to tell the rest of the team that we were aware, and that wouldn't be good. Whatever they had planned, they might bring it forward. They certainly weren't going to lift off and come back another day. If they knew that we knew, they were going to take action.

We were following the river that ran through from the

high ground beyond the motorway down to the sea. We limped towards the next set of lights.

We inched forward another thirty metres, our best bound so far. The bike stayed behind us as the rest of the two-wheeled traffic weaved its way as far as it could get.

'How many more turns before we hit the tolls?'

Lynn sighed as he checked his watch.

'Don't worry about it – we've got lots of time before the RV. We take a right up here, and then round the corner there's another set, and then we turn left. Then it's straight up to the toll plaza, about a kilometre.'

I nodded and played it casual, checked the wing mirror. I could see the top of the helmet behind the line of cars.

We rolled another twenty metres and the bike pulled out a fraction to make sure he still had eyes on target. It was a blue Yamaha VFR. The rider's helmet was down, as if he was checking the machine. There was fuck-all wrong with that machine. It moved when it had to.

I indicated right and the dash clicked away while we waited. It looked like I'd get through on the next green.

If the Yamaha was part of a surveillance team – or a hit team – there would be cars ahead of us by now, trying to pre-empt so the surveillance wasn't so obvious, trying to get ahead of the junctions so they could take us once the bike had told them what direction we'd committed to.

Other cars might be behind us, caught in the traffic, trying to close in, but it didn't matter too much. The stark fact was, there wouldn't just be a lone bike following us. They'd be all over the place. If I was heading the team, I'd send a car or bike straight to the tollbooths.

The lights turned to green. We went right and onto

another junction about seventy metres further on. The lights were at red. A green sign pointed left to the autostrada. I hit the indicator while a dozen or so bikes and mopeds pushed past. The VFR went with them. I checked my wing mirror. He'd had no choice: I'd been the last car through.

Lynn checked his watch again and tutted.

58

The lights changed and I followed the traffic left. As I drove, I swivelled my eyes to check a filling station and shop car parks. Less than fifteen metres from the junction, there he was. The VFR was static between two parked cars. The rider was going through the motions of sorting himself out, but I knew from where he'd positioned the bike that he would have eyes on the junction.

And I knew what he'd be saying into his radio: that I was now heading towards the tollbooths and not turning right and going back into town. In other words, I wasn't doing anti-surveillance.

I pointed ahead. 'We're definitely on the straight now for the toll road, are we?'

'Yep, not far – thank God.' He checked his watch again.

The bike hadn't come with us. There were others ahead, for sure.

The road widened after one K into the toll plaza, as Lynn had said it would. Cafés and shops lined the route to the six or seven booths. So did parked cars and trucks. One in particular caught my attention. It was a dark blue Golf. If you'd jumped out to grab a coffee or a paper, you would have nosy-parked. This one had reversed in, ready to go.

As I drew level, I could see it was two-up. Both sat well back; no conversation, no movement. The side windows were tinted but the windscreen had a direct view of the tollgates. Both guys had black hair, days of growth, black leather jackets. I'd know that look anywhere.

I checked the rear-view as I got to the booth. The Golf cut out into the traffic at the same time as the VFR appeared in the distance.

I took my ticket and the barrier went up. We had two choices: left towards Genoa and the RV, right to head south, further down the coast.

I took the right.

'No, Nick, we want left, towards—'

I put my hand on his to stop him pointing. 'Shut the fuck up.'

The Golf was coming with me.

The Yamaha reappeared as we spiralled up to the autostrada. Good, just the bike and the Golf to contend with so far. With luck, everyone else would have been staking out the RV. Now that we were committed, they would be gunning it down to the next junction.

'We're going the wrong way. We're going to be late.'

'Listen in. Do not look back. Just look at me or ahead.'

He shuffled around in his seat, trying to decide what to do.

'We're being followed, got that? I thought you said Skype was safe . . .'

'It is, Nick. I don't know what's going on.'

'Well I fucking do.'

A sign said the next exit was a K away. I moved over to the right-hand lane, making it easier for them.

'This can't be them. I trust them—'

'Trust them or not, they've stitched us up.'

The Golf had followed us into the right-hand lane.

'We're going to try and lose them, dump the car and then do a runner.'

The slip road curled steeply to the right. The surface was canted; our wheels juddered on the rumble strips that lined the concrete drainage ditch.

Lynn turned to see what I kept checking in the mirror.

'For fuck's sake! Don't let them know!'

It wouldn't have mattered. The Golf came up close, with the Yamaha following. They were coming for us now we were out of view of the autostrada anyway. It was the best time and the only place to do it.

The Golf was going to ram us into the ditch. The rider would then pull up and drop us with a weapon.

'Fucking hold on!'

I rammed the wheel to the left and moved out into the centre of the road then hit the brakes so hard Lynn's head banged on the dash.

The Golf had been coming up alongside. Now it nearly overshot us. The bonnet was ahead.

I hit the wheel hard and sharp, banging into it and turning immediately back to the centre. There was a screech of metal and its rear windscreen shattered. The driver's arms flailed at the steering wheel as the Golf lurched then disappeared into the ditch. It flipped twice, landing on the driver's side.

The Yamaha braked so hard his back wheel smoked as it slid out from underneath him. I racked the wheel hard and clipped him. The bike banged against the concrete wall that towered up to the autostrada. The rider fell off and tumbled end over end along the tarmac. His machine spun in mid-air.

I put my foot down to clear the area, tyres squealing. Little Fiat Puntos weren't made for this sort of thing. I pumped the brakes to slow down before I hit the exit booth, and came to a screeching halt just in time. I handed over my eighty cents to a woman who didn't even glance up. This was Italy, after all. She'd seen worse.

I was pouring with sweat as we hit the road. 'Tell me where to go. Somewhere to dump this fucking thing and get on a bus so we can get out of here. Tell me.'

59

We sat on the bus for Chiavari, still heading south along the coast, away from Santa Margherita. Our seats were halfway along the single-decker and out of view of any vehicles that followed. We'd dumped the Punto in a residential street and Lynn had navigated us to a bus stop. We'd bought our tickets at the roadside machine and jumped on.

His head hung down. He was feeling shit for compromising us, and so he should. But I had to keep him revved up. We still had a lot to do.

'Fuck it. Don't worry, it's done. We all fuck up. Besides, they were going to hit us anyway.' I leant over. 'I guess we now know it's the Firm.'

His head jerked up. 'Do we, Nick? It couldn't have been Skype. It's secure. All the Firm knew was our RV. They wouldn't have had operators scouring the whole length of the autostrada just to follow us in. Why bother, if they knew where we were going?'

He had a point.

'And if they'd got a fix on us from the call, why wait until we were on the road? Why not hit us at the flat? Why take the chance of the surveillance being compromised, why take the chance of us not going to the RV?'

He was right. We still did have a place to hide.

The bus stopped for a couple of waffling women and some kids with day sacks. The air conditioning kept everything nice and cool and calm. It was helping me, for sure.

We got to the edge of Chiavari and the bus stopped. I stood up and Lynn followed. We might as well stay on the outskirts of this place and move back to the flat once it was dark.

We went into a café to keep out of sight of the road. I nursed an espresso as I visualized the opening of my cache down on the Golden Lane Estate. I picked up the menu and gave it to Lynn. 'Might as well order some food, eh?'

I played with my coffee. In my mind's eye, the screws were still in place. The mortar was still in place. Even the clingfilm; everything was as it should have been. I swallowed the shot and shuddered – only partly because the coffee was so strong. Mainly it was the thought that whoever knew about my cache would have my passport details, and everything else would have followed. They would have trawled through any credit card movements. My passport would have been pinged by the biometrics as soon as it was put under the reader at Genoa, and that would have confirmed that the tickets I'd bought on the credit card weren't a decoy. The hire car would have turned up on their screens, and all they had to do was check the camera information coming out of the toll-booths.

It all pointed back to the Firm, no matter what Lynn believed.

They would have some intelligence-sharing agreement in place with the Italians. They'd be able to link into their cameras and access plate-recognition machinery at the tollbooths without even leaving their desks. The Italians wouldn't have had to know what was going on. The request would have been entirely routine, and submitted with a big pile of others.

Once they knew where we'd come off the autostrada, they would have had to start checking the old-fashioned way, and they wouldn't have involved the Italians in that, for sure. Meanwhile, they would have been looking for us electronically, waiting for credit cards to be pinged.

Lynn was busy waffling away to the waiter when I realized that there was someone I'd overlooked – someone else who knew about my passport.

The waiter left.

'Can you get me a phone card?'

'We calling Vauxhall Cross?'

'Fuck Vauxhall Cross.'

A few seconds later a couple of paninis appeared, along with glasses of chopped-up carrot and celery.

I asked for a cappuccino.

60

The phone rang six times.

I cut straight in when I heard her voice. 'Just phoning to say thanks for the ginger cake; it was lovely – as always.'

But she didn't screech with delight as she usually did at the sound of my voice, or launch into intimate details of her latest bingo adventure.

She was in shit state.

'Something terrible . . . I . . . It's . . .' She gulped in air.

'What's happened, Leena? Is it Brendan?'

There was a long silence.

The phone clattered to the floor.

Traffic raced up and down the coast road and I pressed my ear hard against the receiver.

'Leena?'

I heard a rustle as the phone was retrieved. I could hear her breathing.

'Leena?'

'They mugged him . . . right outside Costcutter . . .

they killed him ... He was only going to get his HobNobs.'

I wanted to commiserate with her, but there was no time. I needed information out of her before she dissolved. 'Who did it?'

'The police don't know yet. It's so awful. So many strange things today.'

'Strange things?'

There was another long silence.

'Talk to me, Leena. This is important.'

'Well ... just this morning, he had some people from the old country turn up ... and then this ... I told him I'd go later, but he wouldn't hear of it. Said I had enough to do ... and now ...'

I heard her distressed breathing retreat as she replaced the receiver.

I redialled and got the engaged tone. She'd taken it off the hook.

The street lights had come on without me noticing. I walked fast to the café.

Lynn had waited for me to return before starting on his panini.

I took a bite and leant towards him. 'We're fucked.'

His eyes widened. 'What, more than we were ten minutes ago?'

'I'll explain later. We've got to take the passports as compromised. We've got to get to an ATM. I'll draw out as much as I can then I'll bin the card. Then it's straight to the flat.'

Within an hour we were back in the middle of a bus, this time heading north. My ripped-up card was buried in a couple of Chiavari bins.

Lynn's eyelids drooped and he kept rubbing his face. His stubble rustled under his fingers.

'It's going to get worse than this, believe me. We've tried it your way. There's only one place we can go now.'

'Where's that?'

'Libya.'

PART SIX

61

The warm breeze carried the smell of the sea and the sound of raised voices. Then I heard the rev of engines, the blast of a horn, more shouting and the squeal of tyres.

I opened my eyes. Lynn was sitting in his chair by the window that opened onto the Juliet balcony. He was staring out across the harbour. I wondered how long he'd been there.

I swung my legs off the bed, hauled myself into the kitchen and started going through the cupboards, but all I could find was some decaf. I heaped two big spoonfuls into a cup, waited for the kettle to boil and poured myself a small measure of water. I tried to kid myself that the dark black stuff was the real McCoy, but it wasn't working, so I dragged a chair from the dining table and plonked myself next to Lynn. He had his binos stuck to his face and was tracking a large yacht as it made its way out to sea.

'Spotted him yet?'

He lowered the binos. 'Who?'

'Mansour.'

It didn't raise a smile.

'I hope you're right about this.'

'And our alternative is what, exactly? Apart from you and me, Mansour is the only man on the planet who knows the significance of the name Leptis – a nickname he coined for *you*. He's also one of very few who knew Ben Lesser was on board the *Bahiti*. Lesser's dead. Duff's dead. You're supposed to be dead, and I'm assuming I am too. In the whole equation, the only man left standing is Mansour. Either he's pulling the strings here, or he must know who is.'

Lynn pulled a face. 'Bomb-making wasn't part of his repertoire.'

'I told you last night, that's nit-picking. Training and supplying PIRA, the relationship with Lesser, the *Bahiti* shipment . . . they were all handled by Mansour. I don't give a shit whether it's the Firm or the Tellytubbies who are trying to kill me. Mansour will know what all this is about, and if not, maybe he'll know a man who does. We're going to find these fuckers and get them before they get us.'

We'd debated it long enough. He knew I was right.

He shrugged and handed me the binoculars. 'Magnificent, isn't she, don't you think?'

I lifted them to my face. The yacht was now under sail. 'How do you drive one of those things anyway? Does it operate like a car?'

Lynn scowled. 'Not "it", "she". If you insist on calling her "it" you will bring us bad luck.'

Like ours could get any worse.

62

Lynn had gone off on one last night about the sort of
vessel we'd need for the trip. Even he had to confess
we'd need something with more bollocks than a sailing
yacht to get to Tripoli if we wanted to get there before the
end of the year.

I was scanning the harbour for the kind of thing I
thought might be up to the job – not that I had a clue
what we were really looking for. But you didn't have to
be an expert to appreciate some of the seriously Gucci kit
that was out there. In amongst the fishing boats, the
speed boats and the yachts were an array of gin palaces
that told me certain people were riding out the recession
just fine, thank you very much.

Some of them were huge, with double funnel stacks,
tenders as big as Lynn's apartment and more radars than
Heathrow airport. One of them even had a helicopter on
the back.

Lynn picked himself up from his seat and wandered
into the apartment. I heard him clattering around in the

kitchen. 'We're going to need a boat that's fast and has range. How far is it to Tripoli, anyway?'

'No idea.' I carried on scanning the harbour. It was another world out there. How did these people make so much fucking money?

Then, in amongst the kitchen noises, I heard the sound of Bill Gates' welcoming Windows ditty.

Lynn was hunched over the laptop, still surfing off his neighbour's signal. A few moments later his printer whirred and the first of the Google Earth maps of Tripoli landed on the table. I'd been impressed with his work this morning. With nothing to go on except seriously out-of-date information, he'd pulled up the Libyan Yellow Pages online and started burning through his Skype credit, giving it hubba-hubba to all and sundry.

Fuck knows who he was calling, but he managed to get some kind of confirmation that Mansour was still alive and living in Tripoli. I had to trust him on the Skype front. Whatever the risks, they were less than him showing his face on the way to a public phone – which the Italians would probably have been monitoring anyway.

I went back to studying the harbour. Lynn had pointed out the little dinghy he pottered about in. I tracked on down the line of boats on the far side of the marina. The bigger the boat, the closer it was to the open sea. By the time I'd panned down to the end of the sea-wall, adjusting the focus as I went, I half expected to see Roman Abramovich waving at me.

The really big numbers were crawling with crew. Hulls were being scrubbed down, decks swept and paint applied to metalwork.

My binos swept past them and headed out towards the open water.

More boats bobbed up and down just beyond the marina, a mixed bag, all of which still cost more than your average house – on second thoughts, make that ten average houses. I tried to work out whether there was any significance to them being out there, and decided that their owners were too tight to pay harbour fees.

I kept panning, then stopped. Something sleek and dangerous slipped into the field of view – not as big as anything I'd seen on Abramovich Row, but probably no less damaging to the bank account.

It had a matt black hull and a shiny grey upper deck. Antennae sprouted from the roof. A radar revolved on a beam just above and behind the main cabin. The thing looked like an ocean-going Ferrari. And to top it all, there was a really good-looking woman sunning herself on the front deck. I adjusted the focus again. She looked Chinese or Japanese; it was hard to tell at this distance. Oriental, anyway. Her eyes were closed and her face angled towards the weak, wintry sun.

A guy suddenly appeared on deck. I followed him as he edged round the cabin, crept up on her and dropped something down her sweater. Even though the boat was 500 metres away, I heard her squeal.

She jumped up, pretending to be cross, and threw it back at him. Ice-cube attack. The guy ducked and it splashed into the sea. Too bad he didn't follow it. Now that would have been funny. He was neither young nor beautiful. But then with a boat like his he didn't have to be. I narrowed my eyes and peered at him. Well fed, comfortable, tanned and pushing fifty. Lucky fucker.

'What did you say?' Lynn was back, standing beside me, holding two cups of coffee.

I hadn't realized I'd spoken aloud.

I took one and sniffed it. It didn't smell any better than the last cup. 'What's that black and grey Batship out there?'

He peered out to sea.

I pointed.

'That thing?' He made it sound like we were looking at the boating equivalent of a Ford Fiesta. 'It's a Predator 95-100.' His lip curled. 'A Sunseeker.'

All of a sudden it was an it, not a she. 'How fast does it go?' I kept my eyes on the deck. The girl was running after Fatman, arms and legs flailing like windmills. I watched as the two of them disappeared below deck. A moment or two later somebody drew the curtains on a porthole just above the waterline.

'Fast. Probably in excess of thirty knots – forty mph to you, Nick. Why do you ask?'

63

'The confidence and power of this craft is simply awe-inspiring. Performance levels can be adjusted depending on your preference of engine and drive systems. Accommodation is as generous as it is comfortable, whilst an immense upper deck saloon is fitted with a stylish bar and galley. On deck, ample sunbathing space and a retractable bimini top over a huge cockpit area make for effortless entertainment.'

Lynn had pulled the blurb for a Sunseeker Predator 95-100 off the web and read from it as he paced the room. We'd already established he was wrong about one thing. The Predator had a top speed of fifty knots. In excess of sixty-five mph. We could almost be in Tripoli tonight, if we wanted.

Lynn read on. Its vital statistics were awesome: length overall – 28.77 metres; fuel – diesel; propulsion – direct gear drive through triple Arneson surface drives, or submerged twin-props in semi-tunnels. I wasn't sure what it all meant, but I was impressed.

Next came the important bit. It had a fuel capacity of 8500 litres or 1870 gallons. If we hammered it at roughly thirty knots – forty mph – Lynn calculated that we'd be able to go around 350–400 miles on a full tank. As Libya was 700 miles away, we were looking at one refuelling stop, possibly two; and a total journey time of around twenty hours.

Lynn stopped reading from the laptop and came and sat back down in his chair. 'Why don't we take something a little bigger – something with more range? That way we won't have to refuel.'

I shook my head. I was still eyes-on the boat. Fatman and his oriental eye-candy remained below. They'd been down there for an hour.

'The bigger the boat, the more people on board. Fewer people makes it easier to lift. By the way, can you drive one of these things?'

'Of course.' He sounded indignant. I guessed piloting a Predator was like falling off a log if you happened to be a member of some posh yacht club on the north Norfolk coast. He frowned again.

When he spoke, he kept his eyes on the sea. 'How are we going to refuel if the police – actually, more likely the Coast Guard – know that the boat's been stolen? That thing—' he waved an arm in the direction of the Predator – 'is two to three million pounds' worth of vessel, brimming with every bit of kit imaginable – radar, GPS, the whole lot. A Sunseeker is a floating computer. It's probably got a tracker device on it, too They'll be onto us in hours – maybe minutes. Then what?'

I thought he'd finished, but he was only just warming up.

'Just how do you intend to get to Tripoli? I know the Colonel's back in the fold, but they don't just throw their doors open to foreigners, you know. I know the Libyans. This is a society that's been shut off for decades. Even if we evade the Italian authorities, we'll have the Libyan navy to contend with. After the Americans bombed Tripoli in '86, Gaddafi spent serious money beefing up their defences.'

'I said lifted, not stolen. Anyone on board comes with us. We've just got to make sure everything appears completely normal, because they – the owners, whoever they are – are coming with us. Nobody's going to report the boat stolen if it isn't stolen, and that way we can get *them* to refuel. As for the Libyan navy, fuck 'em. The Colonel has got plenty on his plate already – a people-trafficking problem, for starters. My guess is the Libyan navy will be looking out, not in.'

I wasn't an expert, but I remembered seeing something on the news a few years back – seventy migrants dying on one ship when they'd tried to reach Europe illegally from Libya. They'd died of hunger and thirst after the boat broke down and drifted for ten days before being spotted by an Italian steamer. The poor bastards had come from all over Africa – Somalia, Sudan, Nigeria, Ivory Coast, you name it – and Libyan middlemen had promised them safe passage to a new life in Europe.

Of course, there had been a catch – in this case, a shit boat that had broken down almost as soon as it had left Libyan waters. The Europeans had finally demanded action and Gaddafi, by now intent on greasing his way back into the international fold, promised to tighten things up. We'd be doing what the authorities least

249

expected – going against the human tide. Besides, we were in a big sleek boat that meant cash coming into the country.

Lynn drew breath to speak, but I cut him short. 'Listen, it's not a drama. I don't know yet what we're going to do with Candy Girl and Fatman. Unless, of course, you want to kill them . . .'

'Christ, no.'

'Then let me worry about them. If the nav systems give our position away, let's turn 'em all off. We'll buy a bog-standard GPS down the marina and do our own navigation – or get to work with a compass, if necessary. Can you do that?'

'Of course.'

'OK, now we're talking. I'll take first stag. We'll do one hour on, one hour off. We maintain eyes-on that Predator the whole day, to make sure it's just those two. If there's anybody else on board, I need to know. If they leave during the day, tough – it's back to square one.'

I glanced at him to see if he'd got the message. A thin sheen of sweat glistened on his bare head.

He got to his feet. A look of resignation passed across his face. 'What are we going to do with the Predator when we get to Libya?'

I raised the binos. The curtains were still drawn. I could feel Lynn's gaze on the back of my neck. 'I may not know how to drive one of those things, but trust me, I know how to sink them.'

64

It looked as if the sun had brought all the beautiful
people of Europe out to play, bang in front of Lynn's
apartment. It was not yet dark, but the restaurants and
bars around the marina were already starting to fill up.
We had passed the day stagging, on and off – never a
drama for me, but Lynn's boredom threshold was clearly
a lot lower than mine. When he wasn't watching the
boat, he slept, until I told him to go out and check what
time the marina's fuel station closed and, while he was
about it, to buy what we needed for a twenty-hour boat
trip – food, drink and a cheap GPS.

Lynn still puzzled me. He'd told me he'd spent years
setting up the apartment, exactly for this kind of
contingency – but I was sure he wasn't telling me the
whole story. I knew he was getting a bit of a rush as we
stayed one step ahead of the bad guys, but he still wore
his defeated look the rest of the time. There was a
wedding photograph on the dressing table in front of the
balcony window, and yet he hadn't even mentioned

Mrs Lynn in passing since we'd left the mushroom farm.

I was beginning to understand why Fatman had dropped anchor where he had. He and Candy Girl had stayed below deck the entire day. The good news was that nothing else had stirred on the Predator. According to the blurb, the 'Master Stateroom' boasted a double berth, a nineteen-inch flatscreen TV, CD/DVD/Radio surround-sound speaker system, air conditioning and a hand-held fire extinguisher. It looked as though the last two were going to come in very useful.

At five o'clock, Lynn came and sat down next to me. I handed him the binos and he passed me the laptop. 'It's not going to be a piece of cake, is it?'

He'd downloaded an article entitled 'Middle-Power Approaches to Maritime Security – Italy'. It told us that the Italians had a coast guard, a customs service, a maritime extension of the carabinieri and a navy, all charged with policing their national waters. The Guardia Costiera alone had 10,000 personnel and almost 400 ships stationed at 118 bases – most of which looked as big, sleek and impressive as the ocean-going Ferraris I'd clocked on millionaires' row in the marina, except with pop-guns on-deck. The coast guard, the customs service and the navy also operated a variety of fixed- and rotary-wing aircraft equipped with radar and electro-optical sensors that could cut through the night.

Had we bitten off more than we could chew?

I didn't have time to think about it. Something was happening aboard the Predator.

Lynn handed me the binoculars.

They were standing on the back deck. She was wearing a dress that didn't leave much to the imagination. He was doing his best to keep up, with white jeans and a powder-yellow sweater draped over his shoulders. His stomach strained against a white polo shirt.

He pressed a button and a thing like a car boot swung open – the Predator's 'hydraulic opening stern garage'. Inside was a smart-looking tender with a powerful outboard. With another press of a button, a winch lifted the tender a few feet into the air. Fatman gave it a quick once-over then swung it out and lowered it into the water. He was so smooth he didn't even get his shoes wet.

I'd seen enough. I handed Lynn the binos and told him to keep watching. I headed for the stairs.

65

The seafront was brimming with people doing what Italians do best: strolling, chatting, flirting and posing. The air was heavy with the smell of perfume and reverberated with the clip-clop of heels on the cobbles. A moped shot past and backfired, causing a ripple of outrage amongst the promenaders.

Viewed from the back, almost every couple were dead-ringers for my targets. I dodged a taxi and weaved my way past shop windows filled with merchandise and designer labels. The town stretched away from the har-bour up into the hills. Above me, lights twinkled.

Across the marina, the tender had already come along-side. Fatman was onto the quay quicker than I'd have given him credit for – something I'd need to remember later.

After tying up the dinghy, he did the gentlemanly thing and helped Candy Girl ashore. I got my first really good look at them in the lights along the seafront. She was Eurasian rather than Chinese, and absolutely stunning. He was over-fed and greased up, and twenty to thirty years her senior. They didn't get a second look as they made their way towards the centre of town.

I tucked in around twenty metres behind them. The bells rang twice as they passed the church; it was six thirty. The girl was doing her best to slip her arm around Fatman's waist, but she wasn't finding it easy. They crossed the main square and headed down an alley. As I rounded the corner, I saw them duck into a doorway. I followed them inside, down some stairs and into a basement with bare rock walls. With its low lighting, little round tables and wine bottles stacked to the roof, it was the chicest cave I'd ever been in – including some pretty well-appointed Al-Qaeda hangouts in Afghanistan.

Fatman caught the waiter's eye and they were led to a table not far from the bar, still holding hands. I grabbed a stool, picked up a menu and pretended to check out the wine-list. The other tables were all heaving with glitterati picking away at bread, olives and cheese, sipping at their wine and not paying me the least attention. Candy Girl started to speak with a high, nasal American twang. She was still holding Fatman's hand, but looked around the room, checking out the other diners, maybe hoping to spot an even richer target, while he stuck his nose into the menu. Her gaze swept my way and for a brief moment our eyes met.

The spell was broken when, like a dickhead, Fatman clicked his fingers for some waiter-attention. When he opened his mouth, he confirmed what I'd already suspected: he was a Brit.

66

'Pack up, we're moving.'

Lynn sprang to his feet as if a firework had gone off under his arse. The thought crossed my mind that he'd been sleeping while on stag, but that wasn't Lynn's style. He wasn't a skiver; he did his bit. Which made me think it was more likely he'd slipped into one of his daydreams – so deeply he never even heard me come back into the flat. Fuck knew where he went when he drifted off, but my guess was that it involved Hannibal, the Romans and, somewhere in amongst it all, his wife.

'What do you mean, pack up?'

'What does it sound like? Fatman is stuffing his face. He's hoovering it up. We don't have long. When he leaves the bar, I want us to be ready. So pack, go to confession and stand by.'

I told him what I knew: that the girl sounded American, possibly Canadian, and Fatman was a Brit. Then I asked if there had been any movement on the boat

– some sign that there might be somebody else on board. Lynn grunted. Negative.

He was standing with his back to the window, eying me suspiciously as I fished under the bed for my day sack. 'What are you going to do?'

'I'm going to swim aboard.' I twisted my head to talk to him. 'Kitchen knives?'

He pointed to a drawer on the far side of the stove.

My fingers brushed the edge of the day sack, I grabbed hold of it and pulled. It slid out from under the bed.

'Pack everything – and I mean *everything* – you're going to need: clothes, cash, passport – even though it's compromised. Bung it all in a plastic bag. Tie it up. Make it waterproof. And you can do the same for mine.' I chucked my day sack at him.

I picked myself up, ran into the kitchen and opened the drawer. I soon found what I was looking for: a couple of cooking knives – the two biggest ones – and shoved them down the back of my jeans.

'Do people carry weapons on those things – to ward off pirates, that kind of shit?'

'Depends.'

'On what?' I really didn't have time for Twenty Questions.

'He didn't look like the kind of chap who'd carry a gun.'

I wasn't so sure. In my experience, blokes like Fatman loved guns. Guns were almost as good as Viagra – they made them feel big and important. 'Tell me one more time, because this is the last time I'm going to hear it: can you drive that boat?'

Lynn finally hauled himself into action. He walked

past me, heading for his bedroom. 'Yes, I can drive a Sunseeker. And yes, Nick, if it isn't full of fuel, I can take care of that too. How will I know when you've got control of the situation?'

'I'll signal you by torch, possibly flash some headlights – or whatever it is that boats have. Don't worry, when you see it, you'll know.' All he had to do then was lock up the apartment, make his way down to the shoreline and steer his little dinghy out to the Predator.

He disappeared into his room and I took my seat by the window. Ten minutes later, he reappeared and sat down again. We lapsed into silence.

After forty-five minutes, I clocked our unlikely couple as they made their way back along the dock towards the tender. Fatman was all over the girl like a wet dress.

Time to go. No ceremony. I simply told Lynn I'd see him on the Sunseeker.

Down by the harbour people were still strolling, talking, staring. I walked across the road, hopped over the wall and hit the shingle. I glanced back. Nobody seemed to have paid me any attention.

Moving between the boats, I approached the water's edge. The sea was calm. The hubbub from the cafés and bars drowned out the sound of the waves lapping against the shingle. I fixed the position of the Sunseeker, checked the knives were secure in my pocket and stepped into the ice-cold water.

67

The Predator had a platform at the back that was almost
level with the water's surface. I pulled myself aboard
and listened. All the lights on the upper deck were off.
The interior, visible behind two thick glass double doors,
was bathed in a soft glow filtering up from a stairwell to
the left of the driver's station. I heard the hum of an
electric motor from somewhere below – some pump or
other doing its thing. I caught what sounded like a cross
between a groan and grunt from the middle of the boat,
followed by a high-pitched moan. It sounded like I'd
walked onto the set of a bad porn film.

I picked myself up and walked slowly towards the
doors. It had taken me fifteen minutes to reach the
Predator – in a steady breaststroke, to avoid being heard
or seen from the shore, or by anyone who happened to be
on the decks of the gin palaces I had to swim past.

Lynn told me that almost all the boat owners he'd ever
known kept their keys somewhere on the outside of the
vessel. He kept his in one of three small lockers on

the rear deck of his yacht. Many didn't bother with locks at all; some even left their keys in the ignition.

With a nice puddle gathering around my feet, I grabbed the doors and pulled.

They slid apart and I was greeted by the smell of leather and polished wood. The boat equivalent of that new car smell.

I stepped into the warmth and stood stock still, taking in my surroundings.

To my left were two large leather armchairs and a drinks cabinet; to my right, an L-shaped leather bench seat and a table.

I moved forward. The thick carpet cushioned my footsteps and absorbed the water that still dripped off me. I reached the top of the stairs and pulled out the bigger of the two knives.

I stepped down and passed through a galley. The sound of grunting and moaning grew louder. It was coming from directly ahead of me – the Master Stateroom. There wasn't any point stopping to listen; I was deafened as it was. I opened the door.

A moment before Candy Girl rolled off the bed, I saw everything – far more than I wanted to, in fact. Fatman was lying on his back, groping away, but she, of course, had been doing all the work. Nobody had bothered to turn out the lights, so in the full glare of the spots, there really wasn't anywhere to hide. A tattooed phoenix reared up from between her cheeks to the small of her back as she rolled into a ball between the bed and the cupboard, gaping like a fish.

Fatman tried to grab some duvet. 'What? What the fuck d'you want?'

But in all the excitement the duvet had long since left the bed and he ended up staring at me, naked as the day he was born.

'Shut the fuck up, dickhead!' I pointed the knife. Aggression with just a hint of insanity. They needed to think they were about to die, so anything else was a bonus.

The girl slunk deeper into the corner.

Fatman – pumped up on Vitamin V, sex, or just flapping so much he didn't really know what he was doing – tried to stand up. It wasn't a pretty sight. I lunged forward and punched him in the face. He fell back and hit his head on the wood panelling behind the bed. Blood trickled from his nose. It had to be over the top: I wanted to dominate the room from the word go.

Tears cascaded down her face – as they do when you think your nose is going to be fucked up. 'Please, just let me go . . .'

'Get on the bed.'

She crawled onto it and sat shivering next to Fatman.

Blood dribbled from between his fingers as he held them against his face. He put one hand up and stared at the results. Then he started to sob.

'Please, whatever it is you want, just take it, take it . . .'

The voice was estuary English – Kent, maybe, or Essex. I wondered how he'd made his money. Cars, perhaps. Swimming pools? I'd soon find out.

I put the tip of the knife to his throat and asked who had given him permission to speak, but he was in shock; I wasn't even sure he heard me.

'Listen, mate, if it's money you want, you can have it – all the money I've got, OK? OK, mate . . . ?'

I applied some pressure with the knife; not enough to break the skin, but enough to get his attention. For a moment or two he stopped jabbering, long enough for me to ask if he had any weapons.

His eyes widened. 'No, mate, no weapons here. Honest. I swear. No, oh please, dear God, no . . . Look just take it all – anything you want . . .'

'Shut it.'

He fell silent again.

'The boat – how full are the tanks?'

'The boat? It's the boat you want . . . ?' Relief flooded into his eyes. 'Take her, mate. Take her. Just let me go, OK? Please. She's half full. There's almost a thousand gallons of diesel in the tanks. Enough to get you well away from here. Only leave me, OK? Let me go. I got a wife, kids. Lovely girls. Fifteen and thirteen. Please. Let me see 'em grow up, eh? I'm begging you. Let me go and I won't tell anyone. The keys are under the dash. Just take the fucking thing . . .'

I prodded him again. Like a lab-monkey with an electrode up its arse, Fatman was beginning to associate pain with obedience.

'What's your name?'

'Gary.'

'Gary who?'

'Spratley. Gary Spratley.'

'Where are you from, Gary Spratley?'

'Barking.'

Barking, London. Noted for its world-class marinas and jet-set living. 'Who's this?' I nodded towards Candy Girl.

When she looked at me her eyes were as hard as the

lacquer on her exquisitely manicured nails. 'My name's Electra.'

I might have guessed.

'What do you do, Gary?'

'I'm a yacht-broker.'

'Not your boat, then?'

'Mine? Fuck no. I'm handing it over to a client. A Russian. He was meant to be here to take delivery last week, but the bastard hasn't showed. I was looking after it till he turned up . . .'

Electra's kiln-hardened glaze just got harder. 'What? This isn't your boat? I'm wasting my time with a fucking salesman?'

I left them to it and opened the door of the en suite and took a peek inside. The porthole was about ten inches long and five inches wide. The only way off the boat was the way I'd got on.

Both their mobiles were on a shelf behind the bed. I grabbed them and shoved them in my pocket, then gestured with the knife.

Electra stood and let her hands fall from her perfectly enhanced breasts, eying me defiantly. I bundled her into the bathroom and told her if she made a sound, I'd be back to give her some fresh tattoos

Gary, meantime, was coming with me.

'Please.' I thought he was going to start crying again. 'Wh-What are you going to do?'

He bent down to pick up his black Speedo-style underpants.

'You got an account or credit card for fuel?'

Gary's Adam's apple bobbed like a yo-yo. He looked like he was about to be sick again. 'Sure. Company card.'

He produced his wallet and I nodded. A platinum Amex. That would do nicely.

'Get dressed and clean your face up. Then you're going to fill up the boat.'

'Yeah, sure. Just don't hurt me, OK? Please.' He started hopping around on one leg, trying to get the Speedos on.

Spratley was an idiot who'd give me no trouble at all. The girl, though, I wasn't so sure about.

68

Hurtling across the ocean at speeds in excess of fifty miles per hour was an unnerving experience when your entire view forward came courtesy of Jack Shit. The sea was like treacle beneath the gunmetal sky. We'd been pounding through it for almost seven hours. At least there was no wind to speak of, and the mild conditions were forecast to stay with us at least as far as our refuelling stop: the port of Cagliari in southern Sardinia.

Every available headlight and spotlight on the Predator was switched on and angled forward, but at the speeds we were travelling, we'd only have a split second's reaction time if anything appeared out of the gloom.

Lynn sat at the wheel, in the big leather seat in the helm station, staring past the wipers into the blackness. Other shipping didn't worry him – he seemed confident the radar would take care of whatever was out there – but the other crap – the odd tree carried into the Med, or the occasional container washed off the deck of a cargo ship – transformed him into Colonel Doom and Gloom.

Now we were travelling at speed and well away from the mainland, there seemed little point in keeping the two below trussed up. I'd locked Gary and Electra in separate guest cabins. It wasn't quite what they'd been used to, but now her sugar-daddy dream had gone to rat shit it looked like Electra would tear him apart.

I sat next to Lynn at the driver's station, staring into the blackness, aware that, for him, this was all moving at a pace he was desperately uncomfortable with – and that it wasn't going to get any easier.

Lynn finally broke the silence, asking me how I intended to 'put ashore' when we reached Libya.

I told him I needed a stretch of coastline as close as possible to Tripoli. This wasn't as tough as it sounded. The rule when coming ashore was to head for the lights and then veer a little to the left or the right. If we ended up on some endless, sandy beach miles from nowhere, great, no one was going to spot us – but we'd look like a right couple of dickheads in the morning, scratching our arses and wondering what to do next.

Better to come ashore as close to civilization as possible, get into the city and blend in as best we could in a country where foreigners were still eyed with suspicion.

Either way, I reckoned that was going to be the easy bit. 'You still confident about finding a man who'd presided over Libya's foreign intelligence operations, in a country that's still effectively a police state?'

Lynn continued to stare straight ahead, only glancing down from time to time to check our course on the GPS.

'I know him extremely well.'

'You'd better tell me what to expect.'

Mansour was a few years older than Lynn. 'Like me, he

was a classicist – he graduated from Tripoli university then joined the army, passing out from the Tripoli military academy. He spent the next four years as an ordnance officer, working extensively with the Soviet weapons advisers who were crawling all over Libya by then, busy arming Gaddafi to the teeth.

'Mansour is from the Al-Waddan tribe, whose power base is some Godforsaken hole out in the desert, several hundred kilometres south of Tripoli. Tribe matters in Libya, and the Al-Waddan family wasn't part of the elite that helped hoist Gaddafi to power, as far as I know. But somehow Mansour managed to transcend all that.'

Lynn started fucking about with a couple of dials; I thought he was actually starting to enjoy himself.

'Mansour is highly intelligent and cultured – the fact that he has a classics degree should tell you everything you need to know. He has a natural flair for languages – speaks fluent English and is damn-near fluent in Russian and German too. This, and the fact that he didn't eat his peas with a knife, ensured that it wouldn't be long before he was recruited by military intelligence. But above all, the powers-that-be recognized that Mansour could blend in.'

'When did you first come across him?'

'I was posted to Libya in the mid-eighties, just before things went tits-up between London and Tripoli. The Colonel was well into his campaign to support what he called "liberation movements", the Provisionals amongst them. GCHQ provided us with some intelligence drawn from comms traffic between Tripoli and the Republic, but essentially we were in the dark.

'I was dispatched to Tripoli, ostensibly to carry out a review of our embassy's security, but with a brief to keep

267

my eyes and ears open. We had some assets in-country. It was my job to collate everything they knew – put the whole int package together and advise on possible . . . outcomes. We knew that Libyan military intelligence was trying to muscle in on Gaddafi's foreign operations and that the army and the Jamahiriya Security Agency were locked in a power struggle for control of the operation.'

Some of this I remembered from the *Bahiti* job. The JSA was Libya's main intelligence agency; their version of the CIA. It was divided into 'internal' and 'external' security directorates – the former responsible for maintaining Gaddafi's iron grip on Libya's fickle tribal society, which owed him very little and had, on a number of occasions, risen up against him; the latter for Libya's operations on foreign soil, including its support of terrorist organizations like the Provisional IRA.

69

Lynn punched a few buttons on his hand-held GPS, then continued. 'What made Mansour interesting was his background. The JSA were pretty bloody amateurish on many levels – it was only really in the early eighties that they began to constitute a serious external threat to the West.

'Mansour was as independent-minded as they came in the Colonel's Libya, and well trained, having done stints with both the Stasi and the GRU during the seventies and eighties. From what we could make out, he was the architect of the Libyan army's attempt to muscle in on the Colonel's foreign operations – and was well equipped to do so thanks to his Soviet connections.'

I presumed that the JSA weren't overjoyed to have him on their patch. 'So, how did he get in on the act with PIRA?'

'Basically, he turned himself into a one-stop shop. He got things done. You can imagine, Nick, how the Libyan bureaucracy must have come close, on occasion, to driving even the Provisionals mad. But Mansour was *Istikhbarat al-Askaria* – military intelligence. He was Libyan army, and an ordnance officer to boot, and the Provos loved him. It meant they could cut out the middlemen and walk right into the store. Semtex? Not a problem. RPGs? By the truckload. SAM-7 shoulder-launched surface-to-air? Piece of cake.

'Furthermore, because of his links with the GRU, the Soviet army's military intelligence arm, he could arrange for all the training to take place in Libya. And then, one day, even he surpassed himself: he offered PIRA the complete package – weapons, training *and* the shipment.'

'And that's when you turned up?'

Lynn shook his head. 'Sadly, WPC Yvonne Fletcher was gunned down outside the Libyan People's Bureau in the middle of London and, in the ensuing fall-out, our embassy was shut down and our operation with it. After that, the picture started to go fuzzy again. We knew that the rivalry between the JSA and the *Istikhbarat* had intensified, but from the weapons that were pitching up on both sides of the Irish border, it was pretty bloody obvious to us that a shipment or two had got through.

'So in '87 we decided to put a stop to it. Well, get you to put a stop to it.' Lynn glanced at me. 'There were two big planned shipments to the Provisionals that year. The *Eksund* – a JSA-funded operation – was the first, and intercepted by the French. The next one was the *Bahiti*, handled by the *Istikhbarat*, Mansour's group.'

My mind drifted back to the night Lynn spoke about this nickname of his. He checked his watch. I checked mine. It was coming up to three o'clock.

I disappeared into the galley and made us a couple of

strong, black coffees. Gary had had the boat stocked up for his client, and from Harrods Food Hall by the look of it. There was tinned caviar and Russian champagne on board, but, more importantly right now, ground Colombian coffee – the perfect antidote to the way I was feeling.

When the bitter black liquid started to get to work, I asked Lynn what I'd been dying to ask him from the beginning: why Leptis? What was it about that name?

70

Lynn was in full flow now. Maybe it reminded him of the old days.

'I'd read his file, seen photographs of him, knew his vices, and then, blow me, I went and ran straight into him. At some diplomatic do or other. It must have been a month before the Yvonne Fletcher shooting. What an impressive fellow he was, too. Think Omar Sharif . . .'

'Did he know who you were?'

Lynn shook his head. 'Unless, of course, we seriously underestimated the Libyan intelligence machine.'

'So what did you talk about?'

'He simply asked me who I was, what I was doing in Libya and how I liked his country. I told him I'd just visited Leptis Magna – the most majestic place I'd ever been to on God's earth. The only place I've got hopelessly lost – lost in the beauty of my surroundings. I knew, of course, that we shared a common enthusiasm – Classics; him at Tripoli, me at Cambridge – but I meant every word. Not unnaturally, that's what we spoke about for the rest of the evening: the Romans in Libya. But something about my enthusiasm for Leptis Magna tickled him. He christened me "Leptis". Never called me anything else.'

'That was it?'

'There was a bit more to it than that. He told me he was a great admirer of Septimus Severus. Severus was born in Leptis and went on to become emperor.'

The list of O-levels I'd never got close to was headed by Latin and Greek, but a little voice in my head told me that, ancient history or not, I should listen to every word of this – not just because Lynn was a real anorak when it came to this sort of stuff, and I could see how his passion for it bound him to Mansour, but because I knew there was a whole lot more to it than met the eye.

'So Leptis Magna is a ruin, basically – and you told him that it was the hottest thing you'd visited since you'd been in Libya?'

'My dear fellow, you have to understand that Leptis isn't any old ruin – it is the finest surviving example of a city of the ancient world, and by far the best preserved. When we were at Cambridge, my wife and I dreamed of visiting Leptis together, knowing full well that it was damn-near impossible to get near it.'

'Because by then Gaddafi had taken control?' Lynn's wife was at Cambridge with him. I made a mental note.

'Precisely. Gaddafi took over in '69 after executing a perfectly planned coup. He came to power on a particularly interesting ticket: a mix of Arab pan-nationalism and egalitarianism that saw almost all traces of Western influence in Libya washed away within the next few years. He chucked out the British and Americans, closed

273

down their military bases, threw out the Jews and the Italians, nationalized all the banks and threatened to do the same with the foreign oil companies.

'Then, in the mid-seventies, he disappeared into the desert, emerging months later with a manifesto for the Arab revolution, enshrined in something he called "The Third Universal Theory" – the Colonel's view on how to solve the ills of global society.

'The West looked on Gaddafi as a joke, with his loop shades and light blue suits, but it didn't appreciate – I guess none of us did – that the Third Universal Theory wasn't just for the Libyan masses; it was supposed to be a blueprint for everybody. Which was why, when the world didn't embrace his ideas, the Colonel decided to implement them by force.'

'And Mansour was the enforcer?'

'One of them, yes. This, to me, was what made his remark about Septimus Severus so intriguing. You see, Nick, Septimus was proclaimed emperor by his own troops after the assassination of the emperors Commodus and Pentinax in AD 193. Septimus was a soldier, but a soldier with a vision – he saw Leptis Magna as a potential rival to the power of Rome. He saw Africa as the empire's real centre of gravity.'

'Like Gaddafi and Libya?'

'Precisely. Gaddafi was the Great Leader; the man who would unite Africa against the corrupt capitalism of the West. And, despite the blue suits, for a while he really did give us a run for our money.'

'Sounds like you admire him.'

'Gaddafi?' Over the relentless pounding of the waves on the bottom of the boat I caught Lynn's laugh. 'I think

Gaddafi *is* a joke. But when I returned to London I wrote a brief, which I wanted the suits to take very seriously indeed. I pointed out that the Colonel was underpinned by some extremely smart people – people like Mansour. Plotters. Cultured, intelligent Arabs. Not the nomadic ragheads of Whitehall myth and prejudice. You see, Nick, Septimus Severus really was a visionary, and his city, which he renovated following his victory against the Parthians in AD 203, became a lasting testament to his achievements. That's why I'd always wanted to visit Leptis Magna; and that's what I told Mansour.'

'And the brief?'

'I told them that we needed to pay heed to the lessons of history. Mansour's remark about Severus betrayed his ambitions. It told me he was intent on seeing through the Colonel's vision – and that we needed to pay a great deal of attention to that.'

'Pound to a penny the suits shelved it.'

Lynn turned to me and smiled. 'Of course. What did some upstart Classics scholar, a major with ten years' army experience, know? But within a year, Gaddafi's revolutionaries had taken over the Libyan People's Bureau in London, poor Yvonne Fletcher was dead, the Berlin night club had been blown up, the Americans had bombed Tripoli, and, and, and . . .'

He wasn't wrong. The rest was history.

71

I pretty much had the whole picture now. Lynn's brief
encounter with Mansour saw them bonding over ancient
history at a diplomatic party in Tripoli in 1984. Not long
afterwards, Britain's relations with Libya broke down
over the death of Yvonne Fletcher and the embassy was
pulled out. Meanwhile, Mansour accelerated his plans to
arm Britain's Public Enemy Number One, PIRA – only
we got wind of it and decided to shut down the arms
pipeline once and for all. That's when somebody must
have dusted off Lynn's brief and decided to send him
back in – undercover this time.

'What happened to Mansour after the *Bahiti*?'

'Gaddafi had more than $300 million personally
invested in those two shipments. The *Eksund*'s seizure
by the French was bad enough; but when
the Spanish took the *Bahiti* . . .' Lynn checked the
handheld GPS again and adjusted the Predator's
course.

'The *Eksund* and the *Bahiti* were public relations

disasters. Not just for the IRA, but for the Libyans as well. For Gaddafi, the final straw was Enniskillen – the only time PIRA deliberately targeted civilians. He had set himself up as the liberator of the masses, and at Enniskillen it was the innocent who died – eleven of them, God rest their souls . . .'

Ahead, I could make out a faint glow on the horizon – the lights of the Sardinian coastline.

Lynn saw them too, made another course adjustment and settled back into his seat. 'To cut a long story short, Nick, the Colonel threw Mansour into prison and he sat there under lock and key for the next five years. Not a particularly good time for him, no doubt, but it did tell us one very useful thing – that he had nothing to do with Lockerbie. In fact, prison, in a sense, was Mansour's saving grace.'

'What do you mean?'

'Because we knew he was clean, because he had to have been out of the loop over Lockerbie, we agreed to accept Mansour as an emissary when the Colonel decided in the late nineties he'd had enough of international sanctions. In 2001, Mansour flew to London on Gaddafi's orders and met with his counterparts in the Firm and the Agency.

'Because of what happened in '87, I obviously couldn't meet him personally, but I was there, in the background. By this time, the Colonel had already handed over the Lockerbie suspects for trial, enabling the UN-imposed sanctions on Libya to be lifted. But we wanted to take things further, especially after 9/11, by getting Libya to renounce its WMD and ballistic missile programmes.

'Unfortunately, the temptations of London proved too much for our old friend Mansour and he was covertly photographed in his London hotel suite with a prostitute. The Americans were all for hanging him out to dry, and because of his role in the PIRA shipments, there were a good many people on our side of the pond who'd have happily gone along with them.'

The look on Lynn's face in the reflection of the windscreen gave him away and in that instant the last remaining piece of the puzzle fell into place.

'You saved his arse?'

In his twisted, public-school view of the world, Lynn had believed that he owed Mansour one. Never mind that the Libyan had overseen shipments of weapons to the Republic. Never mind that Mansour was indirectly responsible for the death of God knows how many British troops – mates I'd served with and Lynn, too, in all probability.

This was why I hated spooks. Now I was lumbered with one that had gone soft in the head. And in a country where every pair of eyes would be on us and, if we put a foot wrong, we'd be dead.

'You still haven't answered the question. How are we going to find Mansour?'

'Oh, that's the easy bit. When we were monitoring him back in the eighties he showed himself to be a bit of a creature of habit. There was a *shisha* shop – a place where Mansour always used to go to smoke, day in and day out – in the Medina, the old walled city. It was called Osman's. His mosque was nearby. That's where we need to start looking.'

'He may not be sitting there with a welcome sign,' I

said. 'If he's still a player, he might well disappear for the next couple of days – or be completely swamped by security.'

72

Cagliari in the cold drizzle of a winter morning was a shit-hole – the hangover after the glittering Italian party the night before. We approached the harbour just before first light. A blue and white ferry, long in need of a lick of paint, blew its foghorn mournfully as we threaded our way through a set of rusty marker buoys towards the marina. The town loomed above us: banks of non-descript, colourless apartment buildings stared back at me from a hillside devoid of greenery except for a few moth-eaten palm trees.

'What do you mean? Why would Mansour suddenly be in the limelight?'

I told him what I'd read at the café. The British Foreign Secretary was hitting Tripoli either today or tomorrow, so if Mansour was still the man Gaddafi turned to when he wanted somebody to talk turkey with the Brits, our man was going to be down at the embassy nibbling at the vol-au-vents, not toking away in the *shisha* bar and waiting to invite us home.

The Secretary of State's visit couldn't have come at a worse time. However much 'liberalizing' had been going on in Libya in recent years, Colonel G would want to ensure that nothing marred the proceedings – which meant additional security and lots of it: around state buildings, embassies and on the streets themselves.

When I said as much to Lynn he just smiled. 'It's all in the lap of the gods, Nick. Why worry about what we can't change?'

Ahead of us lay a grey, businesslike harbour. A few fishing boats mingled with some of the rich boys' toys we'd seen in Italy. Maybe I was seeing Cagliari in the wrong light or through the wrong lens – blurred by the single hour's sleep I'd managed to grab during the night – but if I'd come here on a Club 18-30, I'd have asked for my money back.

I left Lynn to guide the Predator towards the filling station and went below to check on Gary and Electra.

I found her lying on the bunk in her bra and panties. She stretched like a cat and purred at me. 'Where are we?'

She knelt on the bunk and squinted outside.

I don't suppose Cagliari had ever loomed large on her list of Mediterranean must-see venues – unless, of course, its millionaire count was more substantial than first impressions suggested. A bouquet of unpleasant smells wafted in through the port hole. She shut it and lay back down on the bed.

'We'll be refuelling for an hour or so, then we'll be on our way again.' I turned to go.

'Hey, don't go . . .' She was getting more catlike by the minute. I guess that wherever you threw her, she'd land on her feet. 'Let me talk to you for a moment . . .'

I paused by the door and turned to face her. She was sitting on the edge of the bed, her thighs spread a little further than would be considered ladylike down at the Rose and Crown, let alone the Swiss finishing school her parents had probably sent her to. I could see she was thinking hard, preparing her words carefully.

'Listen. I don't know who you are and I don't really care. Whatever you want, it has nothing to do with me. Take the boat, do what you want to that arsehole. He's nothing to me. Just let me off here and I promise I won't say anything to anybody.' She let her thighs wander another inch or two apart. 'Deal?'

'Why should I trust you?'

'Because I'm good to people I like. *Really* good . . .'

'Big day out, I'm sure.' I turned back towards the door.

'I know some pretty powerful people.'

'Yeah? What are you doing with a big fat cunt like Gary then?'

The doe-eyed look vanished. The look she gave me now was meant to kill.

I switched off the light and closed the door.

I dragged Gary blinking into the galley and told him he could have a coffee and some toast for breakfast if he promised to be a good boy and help us out.

He nodded meekly. 'Sure. 'Course, mate. Anything. What do you want me to do?'

'Get ready with that credit card.'

As soon as he got dressed, I told him to get on deck, and, at the appropriate moment, help us to tie up alongside the refuelling station. I reminded him that I would be with him every step of the way and that I was still carrying a twelve-inch kitchen knife.

73

An hour later, we were hurtling southeast across the grey waters of the Med. Lynn had been monitoring Sky News on the Predator's flatscreen. They didn't say precisely when the Foreign Secretary was due to land, and they probably didn't know; it wasn't a full-blown state visit. But I knew the place would have been put on high alert: Gaddafi wouldn't want his admission to the Good Lads' Club to be screwed up.

Lynn had also had his calculator out. Judging by our timings over the previous leg, he reckoned that if we throttled back to twenty knots we'd be able to conserve enough diesel to enter Libyan waters with fuel to spare. Barring unforeseen incidents, it would take us another fourteen hours; we'd be in position, ready to deploy the tender and go ashore, shortly before midnight.

Along the way, we'd need to find somewhere to dump our two companions. Looking at the charts, we had a number of choices.

The island of Pantelleria was around 200 miles away as the crow flew. There was also Cap Bon, a deserted peninsula on the east coast of Tunisia. Or the west coast of Sicily.

But Lampedusa got my vote.

The tiny Italian island was famous for the moment when, in a fit of serious pique, Gaddafi had lobbed a Scud at it. The fact that nobody in NATO noticed until some hill farmers rang in to say that their goats had been spontaneously kebabed told me that by the time Gary and Electra found their way to whatever civilization existed there, we'd be long gone – and they'd be none the wiser about our destination.

Gary had already let it be known with a nudge and a wink that everything was cool by him. So was the fact that we were making our way towards the Adriatic, epicentre of drug-smuggling operations in the Med. He liked a bit of coke himself, he told me, and, since the boat wasn't his, good luck to us.

He reminded me about his wife and kids back in Barking and promised he wouldn't give us any trouble. I told him I'd bear that in mind.

With Gary stowed safely below deck, I ordered Lynn to get his head down. Given that it was daylight and I could navigate my way around a handheld GPS, I reassured him I could handle the boat.

'Just got to steer it, yeah?'

Five hours into the second leg, the sun came out. We passed a few tankers steaming between Tunis and Sicily, but otherwise the sea was calm and empty. From the driver's seat, I gazed past the bow of the Predator towards the North African coastline. The last time I had been in these waters had been in 2001, less than two months after 9/11.

I'd come ashore on the Algerian coast with two Egyptian nationals, deniable operators like me, to bring back the head of a forty-eight-year-old Algerian, Adel Kader Zeralda, owner of a chain of supermarkets and a domestic fuel company based in Oran. Why he needed to die, I didn't have a clue. It was a reasonable bet that with over 350 Algerian Al-Qaeda extremists operating around the globe Zeralda was up to his neck in it, but I wasn't going to lie awake worrying about that. All I cared about was carrying out the job correctly and on time. My American employers insisted I brought back his head. They were going to show it to some of his relatives to encourage a bit of *entente cordiale*.

The trick this time was much the same, to get in and get out, and fast. If we could track down Mansour without being grabbed ourselves, put the links in place between the *Bahiti*, the bomb-maker and Leptis, we'd know who was trying to drop us, and why.

We were still around fifteen miles from Lampedusa when, with darkness falling, we motored into a fog-bank. Our strobe navigation lights cast weird reflections off the mist and on the black surface of the water as the fog became progressively thicker. Lynn throttled back. The charts showed rocks on the run-in to the island. We couldn't take any chances.

We were both peering through the windshield when a beeping noise sparked up from the dashboard.

I looked at Lynn. 'What is it?'

'Proximity warning. Radar's tagged something. It's picking up a return off the port bow.' He stared at the radar screen for a second or two. 'To be absolutely honest, Nick, I don't really know what it is.'

'How far away is it?'

'Less than a mile. And closing.'

74

It was a fishing boat, but like nothing you'd find in Grimsby.

It looked as if she'd been built at the tail end of the nineteenth century – a hulk of a vessel, as big as the Predator, but streaked with rust and grime and with thick black smoke belching from a battered stack. As we drew closer, a breeze parted the mist and we got our first half-decent view of it. She had a bit of a list, about fifteen degrees to starboard, but that wasn't too surprising – there were around 150 people leaning over the rail, staring at us.

She was only a couple of hundred metres away, but in the diminishing light it was difficult – even through the binos – to make out the faded writing on her bow. The clues to her origin and purpose were a green flag, riddled with holes, that was flying from her stern mast and the people hanging off her side: I'd seen pictures of survivors from Belsen and Auschwitz who looked better fed.

Lynn chopped the throttles and we stopped dead in the water. He took the binos off me and raised them to his eyes.

The families looked like a meeting of the African Union. Sub-Saharan black faces, fine features and curly hair of the eastern Somalians and Arab North Africans. They had one thing in common: they were fucked and desperate.

'She's called the *Marhaban*. It means "Welcome".' He studied her a while longer and sighed.

I was about to tell him to open up the throttles and carry on heading south, when an image filtered into my mind of the champagne and caviar sitting in the fridge below decks.

I told Lynn to bring us as close as he could to the vessel, then shot downstairs and unlocked Gary's cabin. When he saw me, the fear reappeared in his eyes. He gulped. 'Yeah, mate. What?'

'There's a migrant ship. You ever seen one of them before?'

Gary shook his head.

'I'm letting you go, Gary.'

He nodded pathetically and walked over to pump my hand. 'Thank you, thank you . . .'

I stopped him in his tracks. 'Shut the fuck up and listen. This bit is important, because it might just stop you from winding up dead. Tell your friend Electra to wipe off her make-up, cover her hair and put on a pair of jeans and a long-sleeved shirt. If there's nothing in the wardrobe, lend her something of yours. Water – you'll be taking as much bottled stuff as there is on the Predator. Food too. And the first-aid kit and any other medicines.

289

Tell them that Electra's a nurse and that she can treat some of their kids. You got all that?'

Yes, he said earnestly, he'd got it.

'One more thing, Gary. I'm giving you our GPS and the charts. They're not going to harm you if you look like you're in charge.'

'What are they going to do to us?' The words frying pan and fire must have been bouncing around inside Gary's skull.

'We're around fifty miles from Malta, and a hundred from Sicily. Help whoever's driving that thing, Gary, and you'll have done your good deed for the day.'

Fifteen minutes later, we were on our way again. I watched from the back deck as the *Marhaban* slipped into the darkness. Lynn blipped the throttles and we accelerated away. It was now approaching six o'clock. Above us, the stars shone brightly out of a cold black sky. We had 2000 litres of diesel left, easily enough, if we maintained a steady speed of twenty knots, to get us where we wanted to be: twelve miles off the Libyan coast, with eyes-on the bright lights of Tripoli, sometime around 2300 hours.

75

The weather started to turn just as the lights of the Libyan capital pulled into view. Flashes of lightning lit up the sky over the coast, where the wind blowing in from the Sahara mixed with the chill air that had dogged us since Sardinia. We prepared to ride out the gathering swell.

While Lynn slept, I grabbed the Google Earth maps that he had downloaded when we were in Italy.

The downloads basically gave us two options for coming ashore. The first was on what looked like a deserted stretch of coast close to a suburb called Janzur. Tripoli, like most North African capitals, was a vast urban sprawl, bursting at the seams. The satellite imagery showed houses and industrial facilities extending ten to fifteen kilometres along a coastal ribbon east and west of the city centre – the old Medina – where Lynn told me our boy liked to disappear every morning for his regular *shisha* session.

Janzur was around thirteen kilometres west. The

photograph depicted a rocky headland dotted with small, sandy inlets, where we could easily come ashore without being noticed. There were no houses nearby. The coastal road, less than a kilometre away, led into Umar Al-Mukhtar Street, the artery that fed traffic towards the Medina.

But what then? Lynn and I would be forced into walking the road, conspicuous as fuck, as we tried to thumb a lift; or I'd have to nick a car. But as Arab cities never really slept, the chances of getting away with that were minimal.

Our other option was to tear the arse right out of it and come ashore in a densely populated, residential area.

I'd spotted a promontory on the satellite map around three kilometres west of the city. Three features identified it. The first was a small harbour dotted with boats. The resolution of the imagery wasn't good enough to tell me what they were, but they were probably fishing vessels of the *Marhaban* variety. The second was a large, T-shaped building with a car park at the front and a swimming pool on its roof; and, last but not least, a 400–500-metre stretch of beach, just west of the harbour and the building.

Lynn emerged from below as the first drops of rain started to hit the windshield. He made us both a brew and came and sat down beside me.

I showed him the Google map. 'See this? A stretch of deserted beach. And just here' – I pointed to the T-shaped building – 'is a hotel.' At least I assumed it was, judging by the pool on the roof. I looked at him. 'You recognize the place?'

Lynn studied the picture. 'I know the area. There used

292

to be a little seafood restaurant nearby. It served the best prawns in Tripoli. But the hotel is new.'

Twenty years ago, Libya was a closed society. Since the Lockerbie settlement, however, tourism was on the increase. There were a lot more white faces moving about the country but every one of them had to be accompanied by a 'guide' – tourist-board-speak for policeman.

Whereas there had only been a handful of border crossings in Lynn's day, there were many more now. I hoped that we'd find one that would pay a lot more attention to a fistful of dollars than a compromised passport and no visa.

Egypt, Tunisia, Niger, Algeria, Chad or the Sudan. I didn't fancy Niger, Chad or the Sudan much – and taking my chances again in Algeria, home of the headless Adel Kader Zeralda, didn't thrill me either. That left either Egypt or Tunisia, both tourist hotspots, so great cover once we were across the border. And with Lynn's knowledge of ancient history, we could always say we were on a tour of North African archaeological sites.

But first we had to find Mansour.

My plan was to wait until the worst of the weather had passed then take to the tender. It was around twelve miles to the coast. All being well, we'd reach the beach shortly before five. There was a cliff between the beach and the hotel, but the satellite overlays on the map showed what looked like a number of paths leading to the top. Once we'd disposed of the dinghy, we'd make our way to the hotel and grab a taxi to the Medina.

Lynn wasn't too keen but knew he had to do it.

'We have to appear as if we belong. It's a psych-job. It all starts and ends up here.' I tapped the side of my head.

293

'You have to convince yourself that you have a reason for being on those streets. If you convince yourself, you'll convince others. Humans – like animals – sense strength and weakness. If we seem in the least bit uncomfortable, they'll pick up on it.'

'I know what the manual says, Nick.' The fact that the boot was on the other foot and I was calling the shots still rankled with Lynn, but I didn't give a shit. This was no time for pride or hurt feelings.

'We've switched manuals here. In London, our primary objective was to lie low.' I studied his eyes to see if he was taking all this in. To be honest, it was pretty hard to tell.

'There won't be CCTV in Tripoli; at least, none to speak of. We'll need to take precautions all the same, conduct all the usual streetcraft. But we'll have to do it in a way that doesn't alert the man on the street. Third-party awareness is going to be a very big deal. We're going to be noticed everywhere we go. The colour of our skin, our clothes, everything about us will attract attention, because – there's no getting away from this – we're different. We just have to make a virtue of it; finding Mansour will give us a sense of purpose – it'll make it look like we belong.'

Lynn was clutching his brew, staring into the steam rising from the cup.

'Any of this making any sense?'

He nodded. 'Yes, of course. It'll make it look like we belong.' He even managed to sound like me.

I got to my feet. 'The alternative is just to turn the boat around. Go back to Italy. Stay tucked up in that nice, cosy apartment of yours while they track you down and then you're dead without ever knowing what the fuck this was all about.'

He shook his head. 'You're right. I'm sorry, Nick. I really should have told you. I'm—' He stopped. 'I've been living on my own so long I'm not really used to explaining myself.'

Something in the way he said it made me stop. I knew then that this was about his wife.

'You never separated or divorced, did you? What happened to her?'

76

He rubbed his eyes. When he looked up, they were red-rimmed and raw. Lynn stared long and hard at me. There was no anger, no resentment any more; just that increasingly familiar resignation. 'She's dead.'

He sat back in the big leather chair. The rain was falling harder. Rivulets ran down the Predator's windshield. 'You never did remarry, did you, Nick? At least, you'd successfully managed to avoid tying any more knots last time I checked your file.'

I shook my head. 'Strange, really. Nice, steady job, good money. Always saw myself as a bit of a catch. Can't quite think what went wrong . . .'

Lynn managed a bleak smile. 'I met my wife at Cambridge. We read Classics together. She was beautiful, but serious – serious when it came to her chosen subject, although as game as the next girl when it came to letting her hair down. She adored Italy. Had spent some time in Florence on a foundation arts course before she went up to Cambridge. I don't know what she saw in me, really.

Perhaps it was the fact that I was the only other student who shared her passion for all things Italian – not, funnily enough, that I had ever been to Italy when we met. I just loved the history – knew very little about the place itself.

'She promised me she'd show me all the things that she most loved about it; not just the stuff the tourists see, but the real Italy: the Etruscan tombs of Umbria, the Greek temples at Paestum, the place north of Naples where Aeneas came ashore, the food, the people . . .'

I still didn't know where he was taking this. I sat there and let him continue. Fuck it, we had to wait for the storm to pass.

'It didn't take us long after we graduated to tie the knot, much to the horror of her parents. Caroline was from a smart Norfolk family and, given the set that she used to socialize with, I knew that they had high hopes she'd marry a lord or a duke or an earl – of whom there are quite a few in that neck of the woods. Not for a moment, Nick, did they think that she would end up with someone like me.'

I said nothing, but the surprise must have shown on my face.

'It never bothered Caroline. It never bothered her that we lived in small, dingy junior officers' accommodation in Germany or Wiltshire or North Yorkshire. It never bothered her either that our two children came into the world in an NHS ward instead of some smart, private London clinic – the kind of place where she and her siblings were born.'

'You found the apartment together?'

'She showed me her Italy and because she had a little money we were able to buy the place outright – or rather,

I should say, she was. I didn't have a bean, other than what I was earning. That's why there is no trace to me. She bought it in her maiden name; she even had an Italian fiscal number. I had nothing to do with it at all.

'When I joined the Firm, she wanted us to have somewhere – a place we could retreat to if I ever needed to get out of the UK quickly: you know, if the shit ever hit the fan, as you put it. Nobody else knew about it. Not even the children. They still don't.'

'How old are they?'

Lynn's eyes glazed over for a moment. He seemed to search the roof for answers. 'Miranda's twenty-one and Freddie's eighteen. Good kids, both of them.'

'Why didn't you mention them before?'

'Patience, Nick. We're getting to the heart of my somewhat sad, sorry little tale. Caroline took responsibility for the apartment. It was her money that bought it. Her money that renovated it and furnished it – her time and energy that made it the place you saw. There were no footprints to me at all. When the children were at boarding school and I managed to get some time off, we'd often jump in the car and drive there. The kids, Caroline's family, our friends – still no one knew. The apartment became a refuge. Our place. Somewhere we could shut out the world.

'But then, you know how it is, the job started to take over. There were fewer and fewer opportunities for me simply to up sticks and get away. The hours and the pressures continued to build.

'I found myself spending more and more time away, weekend after weekend, when I never got to see Caroline or the kids because of some bloody flap or other – PIRA up to their usual bloody tricks or some Palestinian group or other hell-bent on killing Israelis in London . . .

'Caroline became seriously depressed. She started drinking. I knew something was wrong, but I thought it was just where we were. Then, suddenly, the kids were grown up. We were in our fifties. Ground down by life. It was the usual cliché; both of us staring at each other across the breakfast table and wondering how we'd pissed our lives away. But I never thought for a minute . . .'

His voice tailed away.

'The day after I retired, a Saturday, I was tinkering around on the boat when I got a visit from our local bobby. I knew what had happened the moment I saw his face. We'd known him as a family a long time. He didn't dress things up. He just gave me the facts. Miranda was down for the weekend from London. She had found Caroline hanging from a rafter in the attic. She also found the suicide note. Caroline had lost the will to live in my grey, murky, compromised world, which was so different from the gentler, more appealing landscape of ancient ruins, Roman art and architecture, and archaeological digs.' He took a deep breath. 'What made it worse was that she didn't attach any particular blame to me for what happened. It was, she said, just one of those things . . .'

I thought back over my life, how I'd never spent long enough in one place to think much, let alone meet someone and settle down. As a result, I didn't know whether I pitied Lynn or thought he was a dickhead for having it all – all the things I'd never had, but sometimes half wished for – and sacrificing it for some half-arsed ideological crusade.

The only thing I was sure of was that you could never, ever know what went on behind the closed doors of another man's life.

'I tell you this, Nick, for one reason only. I haven't made a habit of talking about it. There is, in actual fact, no one to speak to.

'My children have not addressed a word to me since the funeral and, needless to say, nor have Caroline's family. What's more, my kids have just told me, through a solicitor if you please, that they never want to see me again.

'Our friends were almost all Caroline's friends; thanks to the job, I never had time, really, to make any or keep those that I'd once had. So, what you saw when you poled up at my house a few days ago was me packing up what's left of my life. I didn't tell you for the same reason I haven't discussed it with anyone – I don't want, have never wanted, your pity, or anyone else's.'

For a long time, neither of us said anything. Then Lynn got to his feet. 'I'm going to go and get my things ready. I'll see you on deck.'

77

The storm had left the air fresh and still in its wake. Thick clouds moved quickly across the sky, allowing us every now and again to glimpse the thin sliver of the new moon. Lynn prepared the tender for launch while I opened up the hatch that led to the engine compartment. The Predator rocked at anchor with a corkscrew motion that made it difficult at times to maintain my balance, so I sat while I worked on the hatch catches. I was dressed in waterproof overalls – trousers and jacket – that I'd found during a rummage around the crew compartment. I'd grabbed a set for me and a set for Lynn.

The radar told us that there were no boats in the vicinity and the only lights we could see were the lights of Tripoli, which bobbed in and out of view.

With Lynn working on the tender, there was no one at the helm-station to monitor the radar or keep eyes-on the horizon for any approaching traffic. It would be fucking tragic to have come this far only to get caught with our pants down by Gaddafi's tin-pot coast guard. We were right on the edge of Libya's territorial waters – the nav-system said the statutory twelve miles – but I couldn't imagine the Libyans politely arguing the toss if they bounced us. We needed to move quickly.

A strong smell of fuel rose to greet me as the hatch came open.

I passed the torch beam around the engine room. The upper casings of the Predator's powerful twin diesels were about four feet below me. I slid down the ladder.

Before moving to the back of the boat, I'd closed off the cocks that fed seawater into the cooling system.

Standing between the power packs, hunched so my head didn't hit the roof, I swung the torch around till I found what I was looking for: a four-inch-diameter hose that led from the hull into the engine casing. I shouted for Lynn. His face appeared above me a moment later. This was the boaty stuff I did know about.

'You ready?'

He nodded, then handed me a spanner. I gave him the torch.

A large jubilee clip connected the hose to the engine casing. It took me about a minute to loosen it; another second or two to pull it free. The hose flapped uselessly and a trickle of brown, oily water dribbled onto the floor.

Lynn shone the torch across the floor until it came to rest on a lever next to the engine mounting.

I leant forward, wrapped my fingers around it and yanked back, hard. The hose straightened then writhed like a snake as water gushed in under pressure. I scrambled up the ladder and hauled myself back onto the deck.

Lynn played the torch around the compartment. The

floor rapidly became submerged under several inches of water.

A minute later, I couldn't see the base of the diesels.

Within five minutes, half the compartment was flooded.

The boat began to list to stern.

We went back into the deck saloon and retrieved the plastic bags that contained our possessions – money, credit cards, passports, towels, rucksacks and a change of clothes.

I told Lynn to tie his bag firmly to his belt, checked it was secure, then did the same myself. I took a last look around, allowing the torch to play across the leather sofas and armchairs. The only light on the boat was coming from the instruments at the helm station.

As we made our way towards the stern, water was already coursing over the top of the engine hatch.

Lynn jumped into the tender and I followed. As he readied the outboard, I leant over, untied the ropes and we drifted away as the Predator's arse end began to slip below the waves.

I liked destroying things that cost lots of money. It gave me the same satisfaction as firing, say, a Stinger that cost over a hundred thousand dollars. But over three million pounds? This was a good day out.

After a couple of minutes, I lost sight of the boat, then, when we were about fifty metres away, the clouds parted, giving us a momentary glimpse of the boat, up-ended, her bow pointing towards the stars.

With a rush of air and a gurgling sound, it suddenly slid beneath the water.

Lynn tugged the starter-cord and the outboard coughed into life.

78

I checked my watch. With the sun rising a little after six, we needed to make landfall within the next forty minutes to make maximum use of the darkness. The spray came hard in our faces and water made its way into every orifice, but we maintained a steady lick in the direction of the main harbour. After twenty minutes two sets of navigation beacons reared up either side of its large, natural entrance.

I tapped Lynn on the shoulder and pointed to the right. Without my having to say anything, he adjusted course.

Fifteen minutes later, we were close enough to the shore for me to be able to make out the headland west of the harbour that I'd used as the marker for our run-in. The lights of the city twinkled through the salt-spray crashing up from the bow. I could make out the head-lights of cars moving along the coast road.

A minute later, I spotted the big, T-shaped hotel and brought it to Lynn's attention by tapping him on the shoulder again. He gave me a thumbs-up and chopped the throttle.

As we slowed, the engine ticking over to mask our approach, I clocked the lights of a ship approaching the harbour to the east – nothing for us to worry about, but a reminder that there were vessels in the vicinity. Behind us, the horizon was black and empty. Only in front, just above the bow of the tender, was there any kind of definition – a skyline dotted with lights, rising and falling gently in the swell.

Beneath and to the right of the hotel, I could see a long dark expanse – an area devoid of lights that I knew must be the beach.

When we were around 500 metres from the shore, I told Lynn to kill the engine altogether.

There were two paddles in the side compartment of the tender. The headland masked the worst of the incoming swell, but as we came within a hundred metres of the shoreline, I could hear the steady crash of surf on shingle. I paddled from the front and Lynn from the rear. We worked hard to keep the dinghy steady as the water got choppier and the waves and the back-pull more pronounced.

A large wave hit us amidships and I thought we were going to tip over. We both leant hard to our right and the tender steadied.

A second or two later, I felt the propeller scrape some rocks. I jumped over the side, grabbed the rope and pulled us onto the shingle.

PART SEVEN

79

I yanked Lynn into a squat beside me and looked left and right along the beach. Fifty metres or so above us, at the top of the cliff, I could just make out the red neon sign on the roof of the hotel.

Lynn leant forward and whispered in my ear. '*Al Funduq Al Bahr Al Magrib*. It means the Hotel of the Western Sea. Definitely wasn't here in my day.'

We'd had to leave the tender on the beach; there had been no other options. There was nothing to link it to the Predator, and I was counting on it getting nicked long before it was reported.

We crept forward to the base of the cliff. I told Lynn to swap his wet clothes for the dry set in his bag while I recce'd for one of the pathways I'd spotted on the Google map.

It didn't take me long to find a flight of steps that led up to the hotel car park. Lynn had changed and was ready to go. It took me a couple of minutes to do the same. I removed the day sack from the plastic bag, opened it up and shoved everything inside – waterproofs, wet clothes, plastic bag, the lot. Lynn did the same.

I glanced at my watch. It was almost a quarter to six – first light in half an hour, perhaps less. I motioned at Lynn to follow me.

The steps had been dug into the cliff face and re-inforced with concrete. The safety rail was so corroded that it had parted company in places with its stanchions. I told Lynn to stay as far away from it as possible and to watch his step.

At the top I dropped behind a wall and scanned the car park for any sign of activity. Ten or twelve vehicles stood in line, slick with rainwater. The red neon sign reflected off the puddles left by the storm.

The main entrance to the hotel – about forty metres away – was protected from the elements by a flat, over-hanging roof. A doorman sheltered beneath it, smoking a cigarette. A policeman stood next to him holding a clip-board. Garish lights shone through the glass doors from the lobby behind them. There were people moving around inside.

I scanned left and found what I was looking for: a side exit leading from a ground-floor corridor into the car park.

I tugged at Lynn's sweater and pulled him close. 'Remember, you have to convince yourself . . .'

I headed for the door with Lynn close behind. I knew it was too dark for anyone in the bright lights of the lobby or the entranceway to notice us, but I checked over my shoulder just to make sure. No one, as far as I could tell, was behind us. It was going to be a different story in daylight.

The doorman and the policeman were too busy waffling to each other to pay any attention to us.

I still had one of the kitchen knives with me in case we had a drama. I thought I might need it to work the catch, but the side door was open. I pulled it back and pushed Lynn inside.

Lynn strode down the corridor as if he owned the place, and kept going until he reached the lobby. He manoeuvred between the guests and the bags and nodded imperiously to a concierge at the reception as he made his way to the main entrance. He pushed open the double doors and stepped outside, sniffing the morning air appreciatively. I kept a few steps behind him, hoping we looked like everybody else – a couple of tourists with backpacks setting off for a day's sightseeing.

The doorman dropped his cigarette and the policeman straightened.

'Sabah al-kheer.' Lynn's voice echoed in the still air.

The doorman touched his cap and bowed. 'Sabah al-noor, ya rayis.' He whistled and a white Peugeot pulled away from the rank to our left. It drew up alongside us, brakes squealing.

The doorman did his thing, opening the door and bowing several times as Lynn and I climbed in the back.

Libya's answer to Tom Jones, backed by an orchestra comprised entirely of reedy, high-pitched wind instruments, blasted from a couple of speakers sitting on the rear parcel shelf. Lynn slipped a dollar into the doorman's outstretched hand. It disappeared into his pocket with the fluidity of a conjuring trick. The door slammed. Lynn spoke to the driver and I waited for the taxi to go, but it just sat there, engine idling.

311

I glanced up. The policeman was standing next to the window, clipboard at the ready. He tapped the window with the end of his biro.

Lynn wound it down and examined the man's aggressive bloodshot eyes.

'*Taruh fein?*' A waft of onion breath filled the back of the car. The policeman's teeth looked as if he'd been chewing tar.

Lynn held the stare, smiled and gave him a bit of hubba-hubba.

The policeman glared back, eyes narrowing into slits.

I moved my hand onto the door handle, ready to do a runner back down to the beach and hope the tender was still there. If it wasn't, I'd just keep running.

'*Taruh fein?*' the policeman asked again.

Lynn jabbered a bit more then reached into his pocket, produced a five-dollar bill and nodded as Abraham Lincoln disappeared under the top sheet of the policeman's clipboard.

'*Shukran, ya effendi.*' He banged the roof of the cab and we set off in the direction of the Medina, just as the sun began to rise over Tripoli's myriad roofs and minarets.

'He wanted to know about our "tourist guide". I said we'd arranged to meet him at the Medina.'

'He believed you?'

'He believed President Lincoln – and that's all that matters.'

80

The taxi pulled up beneath the thick defensive walls of a castle.

'The old citadel.' Lynn looked up at it like a kid admiring a Christmas tree. 'Tripoli's most famous landmark. Riddled inside with a maze of alleyways.' He tapped the driver on the shoulder and gave him a burst of hubba-hubba.

The driver's face registered some alarm until Lynn dug a small wad of dollars out of his pocket. He held them under the driver's nose before slapping a ten-dollar bill down on the front seat. The driver picked it up, held it to his eye and appeared to sniff it. He nodded, satisfied, and we stepped out onto the cracked and crumbling pavement.

Traffic hurtled in every direction. Vast portraits of Colonel Gaddafi, inscrutable behind his Aviators, stared down at us from every corner. The Great Leader was represented in a variety of roles and poses: in military uniform, in tribal robes, and even in a blue nylon suit with lapels you could land a plane on.

Lynn gestured around us. 'This used to be Martyrs' Square until Gaddafi cleared it so his people could hold mass rallies in praise of his genius.' He pointed to a gap in the walls. 'We're headed in there, into the Medina. Most of the buildings are sixteenth to eighteenth century, the heyday of Libya's Turkish occupation, but a lot pre-date . . .'

This was scarcely the time for a history lesson, but I let Lynn ramble on. Anyone watching us, and there seemed to be plenty of them, would think we were doing the guided tour.

I told him to lead on.

We entered the Medina through a tall stone archway. It was still fairly dark and our warm breath swirled in the flickering street lights. It didn't take long for the noise of traffic from the square to recede. A hundred metres in, all I could hear of the outside world was the occasional car horn.

Ahead of us was a long, straight cobbled street with shops on each side and a minaret at the end. The puddles would have to wait until midday before the sun would reach in and dry them out.

The wail of a bloke calling the faithful to prayer sounded up somewhere close by, and was immediately answered by rallying cries from tinny, crackling speakers all around us. The dawn chorus gradually gave way to the clatter of shutters being thrown open for the day and shopkeepers gobbing onto the pavement as we passed.

Lynn went back into tour-guide mode. There were a number of *souks* in this part of the Medina. We were currently passing through the copper market. The gold, silver, jewellery, carpet, shoe, and even grocery emporiums were close by. You could buy anything you wanted here, as long as you didn't mind too much if it worked. 'The Gaddafi watch was all the rage in my day; they never managed to tell the right time.'

Lynn stopped, and I took the chance to scan behind me. The only people who were out and about looked like they really did have a valid reason for being here, but there was only one way to be sure.

'Take a left.'

We headed down an alleyway that was too narrow for cars. An old man in a long *gelabaya* wobbled alongside us on a pushbike then peeled away at the next turning.

We passed three houses with big, thick wooden doors and heavy, ornate iron knockers. One door was open. I saw a courtyard with a dried-up fountain in the middle. A young boy sat on its edge playing with a toy. A woman hung washing on a line stretched between two wrought-iron balconies. She stopped what she was doing to stare down at us. As soon as our eyes met she retreated into the shadows.

We moved on. Lynn pointed out items of interest: the white-washed walls, the tiles around the windows. He knew what he was doing: he pointed at stuff behind us occasionally, so I was able to do a scan. The only person who grabbed my attention was a guy with a load of cloth balanced on his head. I'd clocked him hanging around the main entrance to the Medina, seen him again on the main street, and now he was here.

Lynn pressed on. Copper-workers hammered plates into shape near the entrance to a mosque. I kept expecting to be pursued, as I'd been in every other Arab country I'd ever been to, by a small army of the curious and the persistent – kids, usually, tugging at your shirt and asking for *baksheesh* – but all we got here was the odd sidelong glance and the occasional stare.

We came to a crossroads. I nodded left down another narrow street, filled this time with shops and stalls.

We wove our way between food, shoe and CD stalls until we eventually reached another crossroads.

We took another left: the third side of the square. If the guy with the bundle of cloth on his head was still behind us, it was no accident.

He was nowhere to be seen.

81

We hit a wall of noise. Cars stretched nose to bumper down the main street, their exhausts belching thick, badly refined Libyan diesel. Horns blared. Pedestrians jostled past us and each other: office-workers in suits; old men in white robes; women in long dresses and headscarves.

Lynn glanced up and down the street, getting his bearings. 'Sharia Hara Kebir. The teahouse isn't far.'

'Mansour's local?'

Lynn kept going, talking as he walked. He kept his voice low. 'Went there every day. Military intelligence, the *Istikhbarat*, maintained a small office just off Sharia an-Nasr, about half a kilometre from here. It was from that office that Mansour ran the PIRA operation. We had it under surveillance. There wasn't much about the people who worked there that we didn't know.'

I thought about the images of Gaddafi I'd just seen. It was easy to rubbish these people as self-inflated; easier still to dismiss them as incompetent. But in Mansour the

Libyans had found someone who had successfully given PIRA the ability to carry on its war.

'Every day, at about eleven, Mansour used to walk from that office, pretty much taking the route we just have. He'd take an outside table if the weather was fine, order himself a glass of *shay* and a *nargileh*, and chill out, as my children would say.

'Libya is very tribal and Osman's is – or, at least, was – a popular hangout for members of the Al-Waddan tribe. Mansour could let his hair down there. He didn't need to look constantly over his shoulder, which is more than you could say for the offices of the *Istikhbarat*. The walls there had ears and they'd shop you for looking at Gaddafi's portrait the wrong way.'

'Got a plan for when we get there?'

I never liked being in somebody else's control, but until we found Mansour this was Lynn's world.

'I haven't thought beyond just waiting for him to turn up.'

If I'd had a better suggestion, I would have made it. I had no idea how long it would be before Gary and Electra were picked up, but, worst-case, I reckoned, was twenty-four hours – maybe thirty-six if we were lucky – before some bright spark at Vauxhall Cross or wherever put two and two together and realized where we'd been headed in the Predator. It wasn't much of a window, and if Mansour didn't turn up because he was needed to schmooze Britain's Foreign Secretary, there wasn't a Plan B.

We carried on, dodging traffic and people. The sun was bright by now and glared back at me off the tall white buildings each side of the street. I rounded a corner and turned to ask Lynn how much further we had to go, but he wasn't there. My gaze flitted in and out of the sea of faces around me. No sign of him. Smoke drifting from a kebab stall blew into my eyes and I lost another second or two.

Then I saw him – leaning against a wall, staring at something over my shoulder.

I doubled back, angry enough to give him a bollocking no matter who was watching us. He spotted me and must have read my face. He held up his hand. 'I know, Nick. I'm sorry. But it really does take the breath away, doesn't it?'

I looked back over my shoulder. 'What?'

'The Arch of Marcus Aurelius – the last intact remnant of the Romans' city. Legend has it that if anybody removes so much as a stone from the arch they'll be cursed for all eternity. That's why it's so beautifully preserved. You won't find a finer triumphal arch . . .'

I shook my head. 'How much further?'

'To Osman's?' Lynn looked surprised. 'We're here.'

He nodded in the direction of the smoke. Shimmering heat and smoke rose from red-hot coals in an oil drum, split down the middle and folded out, with a grill on top. A kid of about fourteen in a grease-smeared *gelabaya* was turning a chunk of what looked like goat meat on a spit. A group of people jostled around the makeshift barbecue, trying to attract the boy's attention. A few tables had been spread out behind them, along a narrow shop front. Its metal shutter had only been pulled halfway up, providing a glimpse of more people sitting at tables, smoking and talking in the cool, dark interior.

All in all, Osman's looked to me like a complete shit-hole.

82

Lynn ducked under the shutter and went in first. A scabby-kneed kid came and hauled the shutter open as I followed, allowing sunlight to spill inside.

I grabbed the table closest to the pavement and sat down with my back against the wall. From here I could watch the street as well as what was going on inside.

There were about twenty tables under cover and five outside. Approximate head-count: fifty males. No women.

The low murmur of conversation dropped still further as Lynn approached the bar.

The kid who'd opened the shutter came to take my order. I pointed at myself and Lynn. '*Shay.*'

I gave the whole area the once-over. There wasn't much to take in, unless you were the health inspector: an antique orange-presser on the bar counter that looked like it had squeezed its last around the time the Romans left, and a giant copper pot, tea-stained and beaten out of shape. A row of Turkish coffee pots bubbled away on a gas stove.

An old guy with a white handlebar moustache shooed flies away from a plate. He looked like he should have been flying Lancaster bombers over Nazi Germany. On the plate sat what looked like an over-sized haggis. I remembered they called this *osban* – a sheep's stomach filled with rice, herbs, liver, kidneys and other meats, then boiled. And the Jocks think they have a monopoly on all the delicacies.

Lynn started waffling away to the Wing Commander. A moment later, they shook hands.

The clientele, seeing this, visibly relaxed. People went back to doing what they'd been doing – smoking their hubble-bubbles, sipping *shay*, reading papers, playing draughts, talking.

The hubbub gradually filled the room again.

Lynn said something else to the Wing Commander. He nodded and produced a calculator from the folds of his *gelabaya*. The handlebars twitched alarmingly as he punched in some numbers and handed the calculator to Lynn. Lynn looked at the screen, muttered a couple of words and passed it back again. This charade continued for a minute or so, then the Wing Commander gave a big nod and they shook again.

Lynn handed over some dollars and got a fistful of local in return.

He waited a minute, then, above the background noise, I overheard him mention Mansour's name.

There wasn't a flicker of acknowledgement from the Wing Commander as he poured coffees from their little copper pots into some shot-glasses.

Lynn said it again, this time giving the full name – 'Mansour Al-Waddan?'

322

The Wing Commander shrugged and carried on pouring.

Lynn got to his feet. He clapped his hands and the conversation subsided. Then he started giving hubba-hubba to everyone in the room. Lynn's tone was apologetic and yet determined – I guessed that he was saying sorry for disturbing the peace, but had we seen his old mate?

The boy brought over our tea and Lynn carried on. At the mention of Mansour's name, I expected some kind of a reaction – something like the way the conversation had died when we'd entered the teahouse. But once everybody had got used to a foreigner talking to them in their native tongue, they just went back to what they'd been doing.

Lynn turned back to the bar, downed his coffee, put some money on the counter and walked over to me.

'Come on. I've paid for everything. We're leaving.'

I got up and followed him onto the street. We melted into the crowd on Sharia Hara Kebir. Lynn took a second to get his bearings, then motioned me to a table in front of an equally minging teahouse in the shadow of Marcus Aurelius's arch.

Lynn gave me the ghost of a smile. 'Let's see what that produces, shall we?'

As I sat down, I noticed that we had a perfect view of Osman's.

A waiter appeared. Lynn ordered *shay* and stretched back in his chair.

'Do you know the origin of the word Tripoli, Nick? It's named after the ancient Roman province of Tripolitania: from the Greek – "the land of the three cities". There was

Oea, Greek originally, then Roman – its ruins actually lie beneath our feet. Then there was Sabratha to the west of Tripoli and, of course, Leptis Magna to the east. Don't worry about what I did back there. Think about it: what choice do we have?'

The waiter arrived and placed our tea on the table. Lynn turned to me. 'Breakfast? I don't know about you, but I'm absolutely starving. I'm also betting on the fact that we may have a bit of a wait ahead of us.'

As he gabbled his order, I kept my eyes on the entrance to Osman's. Behind the activity around the barbecue, the teahouse was as we'd left it.

I took a sip of the very sweet mint tea instead of ripping into him for putting the message out over the tannoy. It wasn't the way I would have done things.

I didn't have a contingency plan, but we were going to have to think of one. 'Nobody in there had ever heard of Mansour, had they? We're going to have to find a telephone directory or something, or—'

'No.' Lynn shook his head. 'Like I told you, Osman's is Al-Waddan. The old boy behind the counter has worked there all his life. I asked him. Seventy years, man and boy. He is also Al-Waddan. And yet, did you see how he completely blanked me? It was like Mansour never even existed.'

'Or they're too shit scared to admit knowing him.'

Lynn's eyes played over the arch. 'Perhaps you couldn't see it from where you were sitting, but there was a chap in the corner, rather funny-looking. He was smoking a *nargileh* and had a lazy eye.'

The waiter arrived with bread. Lynn tore off a chunk. 'Of all the people in the room, Lazy-Eye was the only one who kept listening.' He put the bread in his mouth but kept talking. 'He knows, Nick. And I made sure everyone saw me doing my money-changing routine, so he also knows I've got cash. He's not going to be in a hurry. It might be an hour or it might be two or three – he won't want anyone to make the connection with us. But when he makes his move, he'll either go straight to Mansour, in which case we'll follow him, or he'll be out here, looking for us. You'll see; I know these people.'

83

Lazy-Eye made his move shortly after 1 p.m., when I was halfway through my fifth or sixth glass.

Lynn nudged me and pointed through the arch at a tall, thin man standing on the edge of the pavement outside Osman's. He was dressed in the worst mix-and-match combo I had ever seen, even by local standards – a cherry-red shirt, light green trousers and cowboy boots the orange side of tan.

Lazy-Eye glanced at his watch and peered anxiously up and down the street. Finally, he stepped off the pavement and joined a throng of people heading away from the arch down Sharia Hara Kebir.

Lynn slapped some coins on the table and we joined them, hanging back but close enough for me to cut him off if he had second thoughts.

We followed him for several hundred metres down the main thoroughfare, then left into the maze of alleys. The ground was dry; the sun had done its stuff.

I grabbed Lynn's arm. 'You stay with him and I'll

parallel and try to cut him off.'

I picked up my pace, walking another thirty metres along Sharia Hara Kebir before taking the next left turn. There were no shops here, only houses – I was back in the labyrinthine streets with the whitewashed facades and interior courtyards we'd passed by earlier.

Off the main drag, there were fewer people around, too – in winter, Arabs tend to finish working at 1 p.m., then go home for a siesta, returning to work at four and finishing for the day at around six thirty.

With no one behind or in front of me, I quickened my pace down the alley until I picked up the first junction. I took a right – no one there either – and ran down it. As I approached the alley where I'd left Lynn and Lazy-Eye, I slowed to walking pace, took some deep gulps of oxygen, regulated my breathing and listened.

Sure enough, there were footsteps ahead – the distinctive clip-clop of Cuban heels echoing off cobbles. They were coming from the alley that cut across mine.

Darting into a doorway, I shrugged off my day sack and unzipped the side pocket. I reached in and pulled out the knife, then peered around the brickwork just as Lazy-Eye's cherry-red shirt moved across my line of sight. I put the knife in the pocket of my cargoes and hooked the bag back over my shoulders.

As I reached the junction, Lazy-Eye rounded a bend in the alley, but I could hear the sound of his heels. He was no more than ten metres away.

I glanced to the left. Lynn was making his way steadily towards me. There was no one behind him. The street was still free of people – as empty as it was ever going to be. It was time to close this thing down.

I rounded the corner. Something made Lazy-Eye turn and he looked right at me. For a moment, he was frozen to the spot. Then he turned and ran.

He was never going to outrun me in those heels. The day sack bounced up and down on my sweaty back as I closed in on him, and I caught him before the next intersection. I grabbed his shoulders, pulled him hard up against the brick wall, clamped one hand across his mouth and pressed the flat of the knife against the skin under his right ear with the other. He needed to see the blade as well as feel it.

The good eye stared right at me, big and wide; the other swivelled in its socket like a compass in a magnet factory. I could smell the smoke on his clothes and the rancid odour of his skin.

'English? You speak English?'

I could feel Lazy-Eye's heart thumping against his ribcage as the weight of my body clamped him in place. He wasn't even going to shake his head too much to tell me he didn't.

An interpreter would be handy. Where the fuck was Lynn?

The good eye bulged and looked like it would jump right out of its socket. The bad one was in freefall. It looked like a fruit-machine wheel that wouldn't stop spinning.

Lynn strode into view at last. He took a few moments to tune in – and he didn't seem to like what he saw.

'Tell him what I'm going to do unless he complies.'

Lynn spoke to him low and fast. I watched for signs that the Arab was taking it in, but his body remained as stiff as a board.

Lynn gave him more hubba-hubba and Lazy-Eye spat into my hand in his rush to say yes. His good eye shuttled between me and Lynn. The blade moved a little as he did so, to give him an even better view.

The alley was still clear, but there would be unseen eyes. There always are. Somebody, somewhere might already be calling the cops or rustling up a lynch mob.

Lynn gobbed off again. Then, taking my knife-hand, he pulled it clear of the Arab's face. I felt Lazy-Eye's body give a little.

'You can take your hand away from his mouth, Nick, and start walking towards the main street. He won't give us any trouble.'

'How do you know?'

'Because he has information for us. He wants to do business. He was looking for us . . .'

'You established all that in thirty seconds?'

'Start walking, Nick, or somebody is going to round that corner and we're screwed.'

I pocketed the knife, but kept a sound grip on the handle.

I gave Lazy-Eye a shove in the back and pointed him in the direction of Sharia Hara Kebir. As the heels started to click, Lynn fell into step beside him. I took up position behind.

I just hoped we looked like two dickhead tourists accompanying a Libyan on our way to the market to buy a dodgy watch.

84

There were still plenty of people on the main street as we hit Sharia Hara Kebir and made a left.

Lynn leant towards Lazy-Eye and asked him something.

Lazy-Eye made an uncertain gesture with his hand and muttered a reply.

Lynn asked more questions for a good ten minutes and they kept waffling between themselves.

'What the fuck's he on about?'

'I asked him if he speaks English. He said a little, so you can take that basically as a no – Arabs hate to lose face. Yes means no, no means yes and a little means next to nothing. His name is Fawad. Fawad Al-Waddan. You need to listen to his story.'

I glanced between Lynn and Fawad. Lynn looked at Fawad and seemed to be asking for the Libyan's permission to continue. Fawad gave an almost imperceptible nod.

'There's an Arab word – *'ayb* – that's difficult to

translate into English. I suppose the closest approximation is "disgrace" – but it's much, much more than that. It's to do with shame and it's to do with the family. Remember, family and tribe are everything here.

'The idea that you can get on in life by succeeding is not a concept that's readily understood here. Despite all Gaddafi's reforms, blood is still thicker than water and probably always will be. It's not what you do in the Colonel's Libya, it's who you are and, far more importantly, who your father is – or was – that determines what you will be. Which is what made our man Mansour all the more remarkable.'

He was talking as if the 'who you are' system only worked here. I doubted if Lynn had ever been to a job centre.

'When Gaddafi grabbed power in 1969, the Al-Waddan tribe was not a part of the elite, his power base – they were outsiders. But then Mansour came along. He was refined, cultured, educated and exceptionally smart. He knew how to broker arms deals, he knew how to deal with the Soviets, he knew how to handle groups like PIRA; he even managed to keep the Libyans one step ahead of us and the CIA. Let's not forget he was the man who put together the whole *Bahiti* package.'

I checked Fawad's face to see if any of this was registering with him as he stumbled along beside us, but either the guy was up for an Oscar or his English was as good as my Arabic.

'So what?'

'So, on his own merits, Mansour rose to become part of the power elite. And as he gained Gaddafi's favour, so did the Al-Waddan tribe. My bet is that this guy' – Lynn jabbed a finger at Fawad – 'was twiddling his thumbs and minding his own business, when one day somebody told him he'd won the jackpot – that he'd landed a job in some ministry or other in Tripoli with a five-figure salary and an apartment chucked in. Not only that, but his brothers and cousins and uncles were all coming with him and they all had jobs, five-figure salaries and apartments too. And I bet some of them could barely even read or write . . .

'This is what Mansour did for them. It was like winning the lottery. Every member of the Al-Waddan tribe ended up with a winning ticket.

'Mansour also bought them the one thing that money couldn't buy: he bought the tribe the respect that it craved. He brought them into the Gaddafi elite.

'So you can imagine how they all felt, when – having tasted what it was like, having tasted the high life – the *Bahiti* operation went pear-shaped. Mansour was thrown into jail and everything was taken away from them. You see, Mansour brought *'ayb* upon the whole Al-Waddan tribe. He literally cast them back into the desert. It's clear that Fawad hates his cousin's guts.'

'He's Mansour's cousin?'

'Fawad's father is the brother of Mansour's father. He wants to help – and some cash reward at the end of it all, of course.'

Of course. We kept walking, away from the arch, edging ever closer to our point of entry into the Medina: Green Square.

Lynn and Fawad carried on walking and talking. It was as if they had known each other for years. The only

332

words I understood were '*aiwa*' – 'yes' – and '*la*' – 'no' – which batted back and forth between them.

Eventually, Lynn seemed satisfied. He turned to me. 'After the *Bahiti* operation, Fawad and his family were woken in the middle of the night and taken to a detention centre at the edge of the city. Fawad was separated from his wife and children and he was tortured. If there's a cock-up the suspicion is always that it's deliberate, orchestrated in some way – a conspiracy; a conspiracy by the Al-Waddans against the Supreme Guide . . .

'By the time they were released, Fawad had lost the sight in his right eye. His wife had been raped. Because of the '*ayb* on the entire tribe, it meant, too, that picking up work in the city was difficult, if not impossible. As a result, Fawad has relied almost entirely on charity for his and his family's survival for the past twenty-odd years. He's a proud man. You can imagine what it's done to him.'

'And they blame all of this on Mansour?'

Lynn put an arm around Fawad in a best mate sort of way.

'He's eaten up by his hatred of Mansour, but he's powerless to do anything about it. He can't kill him, because that would be a sin. However, if someone else were to do it for him . . . well, that would be God's will, wouldn't it?'

'That's why he thinks we're here – to kill his cousin?'

'I haven't exactly disabused him of that.'

'So where is he?'

Lynn stopped walking and gestured along the street with a sidelong glance. I followed his gaze. Ahead of us, at the end of the Sharia Hara Kebir, lay the Medina's boundary wall. In between I could see a mosque, a few tourist shops and a large square building festooned with balconies and shuttered windows. The building, which was around fifty metres away, immediately held my attention. With its onion domes and pencil-thin towers it was every Disney fan's idea of what a palace in this part of the world should look like. A crowd of people, all men, had formed around an archway that opened onto the street. There was a lot of jostling and some waved what looked like tickets.

Lynn spoke briefly to Fawad then he turned to me. 'Fawad does not know where he lives. The family has had no direct contact with Mansour for years. But that building ahead of us is a *hammam*, a bath house. According to Fawad, Mansour comes here on Tuesdays, Thursdays and Saturdays.'

Fawad was treated to another hug.

'And if this cousin is to be believed, he'll be in there right now.'

85

We should either have silenced our new best friend or kept him with us – anything to stop him roaming the streets, free to tell all and sundry about his encounter with the two foreigners who'd rocked up in Tripoli wanting to kill his cousin. But there weren't exactly any quiet spots round here to carry out the first option, and as for the second, Lynn insisted Fawad was telling the truth; if we brought him with us, we'd be actively signalling our mistrust and putting his back up.

'This is all about honour and trust, Nick.'

'Honour and trust? We're putting ourselves at serious risk because you think this lad is some kind of good egg?'

'Not entirely.'

I couldn't tell which of us Fawad was looking at as the words bounced between us.

'Nick, his story gels with what I already know. You have to go with my instincts. I really do know these people.'

The only extra that was required, Lynn said, was a

little something to seal the deal and then we could walk away from him and everything in the garden would be lovely.

We pulled into a doorway where Lynn peeled off a thick wad of American presidents and handed them over.

Fawad resisted the temptation to count the money in front of us, but I'd seen the spread of bills the same as he had. Lynn had presented him with at least $500.

We shook hands and Fawad walked away. I watched as he made his way through the traders, office-workers and shoppers clogging the main drag. Then he darted into a side street and disappeared.

Honour and fucking trust . . .

'Now what?'

'The bath house. Let's see if we've got our money's worth.'

'You said you trusted him.'

He shrugged, and headed across the road. By the time I'd caught up with him at the entrance of the *hammam*, Lynn had already worked his way through the crowd of jostling punters. A moment or two later, he returned shaking his head.

'Problem?'

'Too many people wanting to get in, not enough room inside. There seems to be some dispute, too, about who's next in line.'

'What do we do?'

'We wait.'

I said I'd need to do a recce of the building for any other ways in or out, but Lynn was ahead of me. He'd already asked at the ticket booth. There was only one entrance and one exit, he said, pointing to a doorway just beyond the arch.

There was nothing else for it but to sit down on a bench in the shade of the building and wait. I didn't like this one bit. Tourists sightseeing on the move was one thing; tourists static on a bench outside a bath house was completely another.

The rumble of raised voices was punctuated by the high-pitched tweeting of small, almost invisible birds in the trees we were sitting beneath.

I studied the rabble. I tried, but I couldn't get my head around it: a bunch of guys that couldn't form an orderly line for a bath house had once tried to take on the British government. One minute Gaddafi was arming PIRA with some of the most sophisticated weaponry on earth; the next he was cosying up to his former enemies, renouncing violence. And Mansour, the one-time golden boy, the man who went on to bring '*ayb* upon himself and his tribe, had been right in the middle of it all. To my mind, that marked him out as dangerous.

'Why didn't Gaddafi just wipe the slate clean when Mansour helped out post-Lockerbie?'

Lynn waved a fly away from his face. He rubbed his chin, which now showed more hair than his head. 'I suspect that Mansour became a visible reminder to Gaddafi of his many failures, not to mention the billions he was forced to shell out in compensation. The Colonel would have been grateful, but not to the point of forgiveness.'

Politicians in the West were forced to swallow their pride the whole time. But here, if our new mate Fawad was anything to go by, pride, honour and tradition were everything.

'And Mansour? You saved his arse in London.'

Whether it was a triumph of principle and loyalty, or a calculated move to put Mansour in his and Vauxhall Cross's debt, didn't matter. All that did was that Mansour felt honour-bound to return the favour.

'How grateful will he be when he sees you again?'

We were here because apart from the Firm, Lynn and me, Mansour was the only person on the planet who knew the significance of Leptis. And also because, in the Lesser-Duff-Lynn-me equation, he was the last man standing. I wanted him to repay the debt with hard information.

Lynn nodded thoughtfully. 'Did I ever tell you about my father, Nick?'

'He a history bore as well, was he?'

'Yes he was, and you could say he was also a spook of the old school, I suppose. When I was a boy, we were posted to Cairo. Of course, I had no idea then what he was – as far as I was concerned, my father was simply the military attaché and we had a very nice life, thank you very much – trips to the pyramids and lunch at the Zamalek Club and all that. It was the time of Nasser – Egyptian nationalism was rampant, King Farouk was hanging on by the skin of his teeth, and so, I suppose, were we Brits. The Egyptians wanted the British out. I remember we had to check under the car for bombs every time we went for a drive – exciting stuff for a schoolboy.

'Shortly before he died my father told me a story. Nasser knew, apparently, that my pa's mission in Egypt was to break up the cabal of young officers plotting to throw the British out. They put a price on his head – on the head of "Al-Inn", as they called him. A man named Sha'aban was the chief instigator behind the effort to kill my father and my father, in turn, was authorized by London to use any means necessary to "terminate" Sha'aban's operation.

'For a whole year they stalked each other like a couple of snipers. They came close to killing each other on a number of occasions, too. Sha'aban arranged once for a poisoned bottle of Nefertiti – the wine my father used to drink – to work its way onto his table at the club; my father responded by trying to blow up Sha'aban's plane. But they both survived.

'Years later, towards the end of his life, my father travelled to Cairo to meet Sha'aban. They talked for hours, apparently, about the old days, and at the end of the meeting they embraced and told each other they wouldn't have had it any other way – that it had been a good, clean fight. Old enemies, you see; mutual respect. That's the way the old school fought, and Mansour, Nick, is of the old school. The Middle East is a hugely nuanced environment – they're not all brainless diehards, as some people would try to have us believe. The British have always understood this of the Arabs.'

I was getting pissed off. 'Johnny Arab' was a lot more switched on than he'd been in the good old days, and a number of not insignificant events – 9/11, Iraq, Afghanistan for starters – signalled that the world had moved on . . . if, which I doubted, it had ever been where Lynn thought it had been in the first place – spy poisoning spy down at the country club.

Fundamentalists, rogue states, the cult of the suicide bomber and weapons of mass destruction had all conspired to make our world a very different place from the one Lynn romanticized about. There wasn't any call any more for Al-Inn, junior or senior, rewriting Lawrence of fucking Arabia.

But I wasn't able to take Lynn up on this – not here, at least. Because at that precise moment the crowd parted and Mansour made his appearance on the steps of the *hammam*.

86

I'd only ever had a fleeting glimpse of the Libyan, despite spending days studying him from Lynn's yacht before the *Bahiti* job, and that was why I knew he wouldn't have a clue who I was.

As Lynn dropped his gaze and pretended to rummage in his day sack for something, I lifted mine. The crowd parted further to allow Mansour to make his way down the steps. His light blue linen suit, without a hint of dodgy, Gaddafi-style lapels, looked expensive. It had been tailored in Savile Row, not the *souk*. And he might have put on a few pounds since 1987 and added a lot of grey to his hair, but he carried himself well. He looked distinguished – Omar Sharif stepping out of the Monte Carlo casino after a night at the gaming tables.

The sweat he'd worked up in the *hammam* glistened momentarily on his brow. As he took in the air, he produced a handkerchief from his top pocket and dabbed at his forehead a couple of times before moving away from the crowd.

The golden rule of surveillance is never make eye contact with your target – and I'd already allowed mine to rest too long on the man we'd crossed the Mediterranean to find. I lowered my eye-line as Mansour reached the bottom of the steps and, like Lynn, busied myself looking for something in my day sack. By the time I extracted my sun-gigs, Mansour had moved past us out onto Sharia Hara Kebir.

Lynn already had his day sack on, ready to move.

'No, he might recognize you. You've done your bit. Go back to the hotel, buy a guidebook. Wait in the lobby for me.'

Tightening my shoulder straps, I moved out onto the main drag. I made sure I kept him about thirty metres ahead of me and that plenty of bodies remained between us. The closer we got to Green Square, the louder the honking of car horns became. It was soon joined by the squealing of tyres, the hissing of air-brakes and the general hubbub.

As Mansour crossed under the archway in the Medina wall and moved into Green Square, he turned left and disappeared from sight. In the moment that I lost him, I wondered how he made his regular commute to the *hammam*. Did he have a car parked outside? Did he take a taxi? A bus?

The sun was high in the sky as I hit the square. I slipped my day sack off my shoulders and pulled out my printout of the Google Earth map. I caught sight of Mansour's light blue suit again, about halfway across. The giant portraits of the Great One looked down upon him.

He nipped between the converging lines of traffic. He

was making for the opposite side of the square, where six large avenues spread out into the city like the ribs of a hand-held fan.

Just over two hundred metres further on, Mansour took a right, past a large cemetery and into a quieter road, Sharia Sidi Al-Bahul.

I sat down at a bus stop by the entrance to the cemetery, watching Mansour as he moved steadily away from me.

The moment he disappeared from view, I jumped up and dodged a bus.

Tall trees shaded the pavement. A hint of a breeze blowing in from the harbour gave some relief from the heavy heat and the smells of diesel, sewerage, dust, decay and rubbish that had hung in the air since Green Square.

I found myself in a quiet residential area. The cars had transformed themselves from old rust-buckets into new-model BMWs and Mercedes. Apart from the occasional burst of birdsong, the street was quiet. I moved past three-storey houses shielded from the street by high walls and ornate railings.

I reached a junction and glanced to the left. Mansour was seventy-five metres away by a wrought-iron gate set into a high wall. He stood in a pool of bright sunlight, busy with a set of keys.

I slipped behind a tree and pored over my map until I heard the clang of the gate behind him. I stepped back onto the pavement and did a walk-past.

The wall was three metres high with broken glass set into the cement along its top. I glanced through the gate. The house – an old villa – stood in a lush, well-watered garden about six metres back from the street. It looked like a wedding cake, with white walls and pink window surrounds. I couldn't see the lower floor, but the windows on the upper two levels were securely barred.

A large satellite dish was mounted between a couple of balconies on the first floor. There was no immediate sign of motion sensors, alarms, CCTV or proximity lighting, but I didn't really expect any. Mansour had carried clout in military intelligence, and the locals knew it. The mob at the bath house had parted like the Red Sea for Moses. Everyone for miles around would know not to fuck with him. The lack of electronic defences could mean there were dogs roaming the grounds, or men in black leather jackets in the basement – but if he had bodyguards, they hadn't accompanied him to the *hammam*.

We didn't have a phone number for him and we couldn't risk just ringing the bell at the gate: if he wasn't in the mood to repay the debt he owed Lynn, we'd be fucked. The only plan I could come up with was to break in and grip him; there was no other way.

Palm trees circled the front and the side of the house. A creeper ran rampant up the right-hand wall. It would all provide valuable cover. I didn't have a clue how we were going to get in. I wouldn't be able to recce the locks on the gate until after last light.

I carried on walking. The house next door was a building site, another three-storey villa being pulled apart before being put back together again.

87

'How are we going to do it?'

There was an edge to Lynn's voice. He almost sounded excited.

We were looking into the garden of Mansour's house from a second-floor window in the building site. The windows had been stripped of their frames, all the wiring had been pulled out of the walls, light switches and power sockets had been removed. The place was a shell.

The front of Mansour's house was shielded by pull-down blinds, but there were plenty of lights on at the back: in the hallway on the ground floor, in what was probably a sitting room off the hallway on our side of the house, and in what was clearly a kitchen.

'Don't know yet. Wait.'

There was movement behind the kitchen window, and I could see that Mansour wasn't alone. Through the bug-screen on the kitchen window, in the glare of an unprotected strip-light, disembodied hands were preparing food.

I nudged Lynn. 'Is Mansour married?'

'He was married. We knew she was receiving treatment for cancer in Riyadh when Mansour was in London. She died around the time of the Lockerbie settlement.'

Staring out across Mansour's lush garden, looking at his big fuck-off house, remembering the cut of his suit, hearing that his wife had received expensive cancer treatment in Riyadh ... none of this seemed to gel with the profile of a public servant living out his retirement.

Lynn's take on this had been that Mansour had either skimmed off a few quid from the arms deals he negotiated with the Soviets, or he'd been given an unofficial thank-you present by Gaddafi after Lockerbie for making things sweet with the Brits and Americans.

Lynn watched through the binos as the owner of the hands revealed himself to be a boy in a *gelabaya*. He busied himself with some drying up.

'I'd say that the house-boy is Pakistani – Indian or Sri Lankan maybe. No Libyan I met here ever employed another Libyan, for fear they'd kiss and tell.'

I had other concerns. 'Will he have weapons?'

'Expect handguns – one in the bedroom and at least one elsewhere. They love cash. Mansour will have a bag of dollars hidden away, in case he has to make himself scarce.'

There was no street lighting so the garden remained largely in shadow. The light from the sitting room fell across a well-tended lawn, maintained by a sprinkler, which was switched off but visible in the middle of the garden. There was plenty of barking from around the neighbourhood, but none from down below, and I didn't see any turds on the grass. Things were looking up.

The only other sounds were distant traffic, the odd car on the street and an occasional aircraft taking off from Tripoli International a few Ks away.

A shadow moved behind the blinds at the front of the house. The kid was still in and out of the kitchen – worked off his feet. It was close to midnight by the time the light was switched off.

I waited. The boy didn't exit via the front door, as I expected. Instead, there was a creak from the back and a second later an outside light went on, spilling down a set of steps and some bins between the back of the house and the wall. There was a shriek of metal-on-metal, the tell-tale protest of a rusty hinge, as the boy paused to lift the lid on one of the bins, dropped a sack of rubbish into it, then turned and headed towards the gate.

So the kitchen quarters at the back of the house had their own separate entrance – and an outside light with a motion sensor.

I heard the click of the lock and saw the gate swing inwards.

If Mansour had ever rigged a light-sensor to the gate it was broken, or the bulb was, because it never triggered as the boy moved through it. The lights over the front door never picked him up either, which meant the sensors were angled inwards, specifically to cover the entrance. The ground from the side of the house to the gate was unmonitored by any kind of surveillance. Even better, the gate was fitted with a lever-lock:

opened by a key from the outside, a latch on the inside.

I turned to Lynn. 'Here's the plan. You're going to help me over the wall and then come back here. I'm going to lie low in the garden for a bit and see what else I can pick up inside the house. When Mansour heads for bed, I'll open the gate and let you in. Keep watching me and I'll signal you. As soon as you see it, make your move. OK? Once I let you in, sit tight, watch what I do and do what I say. Got it?'

His eyes gleamed. His jaw tightened and jutted. The fucker really was enjoying this. Maybe he relished being back in the world of spookery. Maybe it helped keep his mind off Caroline, and the life he thought he should have given her. It must surely have beaten the hell out of mushroom farming.

The lights in the front of the house were still burning brightly. I couldn't be sure, because I'd seen no movement behind the blinds for at least forty minutes, but I was almost positive Mansour was still on the ground floor. I'd been monitoring the window on the stairs, and no one had moved past it. It was conceivable that he had guests or bodyguards, but I'd been watching the boy prepare the food and, from the quantity, I was pretty sure he was on his own.

It was coming up to 12.30. I needed to get moving. The best moment to enter the house was within an hour and a half of lights-out – the time when Mansour, like the rest of us, entered the deepest period of his night's sleep.

I picked up a plastic carrier bag and part-filled it with builder's sand. 'OK, let's roll.'

88

Lynn and I moved downstairs and took up position by the wall.

I checked my pockets and handed Lynn my day sack. I put my mouth to his ear. 'Brace yourself against the wall. I need to stand on your shoulders.'

I climbed up, wobbling as Lynn found his balance. I edged my head slowly over the top.

The sounds of the city filled the night air. Everything was as I'd last seen it from the building site – the lights blazing from the front rooms, the rest of it quiet.

I pulled the knife from the side pocket of my cargoes and got to work, chipping away carefully at the cement on top of the wall. As I'd hoped, it was old, dry and loose. As each piece of glass came free, I placed it in the sand-filled carrier bag to deaden the sound.

It took me no more than ten minutes to clear enough space for my knees and feet. I hauled myself onto the wall, handed Lynn the bag and then lowered myself down the other side. The earth was still soft from the sprinkler.

Crouching low, I stopped and listened. A dog was barking further down the street – too far away to have heard me, but I stayed still until it stopped. Then I ran half-crouching to the cover of a palm tree and a group of immaculately sculpted bushes at the centre of the lawn.

I waited. Ten minutes later, the lights went out in the sitting room.

I checked my luminous dial. It was coming up for one o'clock. I glanced up as a shadow moved past the window on the stairs. At long last, the target was heading for bed. I waited another couple of minutes, then, keeping low, retraced the lad's route down the path along the side of the house until I was beside the kitchen window.

Two aircraft flew over in quick succession and I tracked their winking navigation lights against the stars as they headed out over the Mediterranean.

Eventually, at 1.45, Mansour must have grown tired of his bedtime reading and flicked off the light.

I gave it another forty minutes, then moved back out to a point on the lawn where Lynn could see me. I gestured for him to make his way to the gate.

Making sure that I stuck to the same line as the house-boy, I crept along the path, pressed myself into the shadows, and waited till I heard breathing on the other side of the gate. I double-checked it was Lynn then eased back the bolt of the lever-lock until it was clear of the restraining catch. Having heard the creak as the boy went out, I didn't rush the business of opening it.

Two minutes later Lynn was standing next to me, the gate firmly closed behind us.

At 2.37 by my watch, we were both standing in front of

the kitchen window. I moved my mouth to his ear again. 'Hands and knees this time.'

I pulled the knife from my cargoes. Standing on Lynn's back, I started to remove the four screws holding the bug-screen in place. They took me less than a minute each. As soon as I'd finished, I hid the screen in the bushes and dragged us both into the shadows.

I put my finger to my lips and pointed to the front left-hand corner of the house, where, by now, Mansour was hopefully asleep.

I caught the sound I was hoping to hear – distant, but unmistakable and growing in intensity.

I nudged Lynn and gestured for him to get over to the window and assume the position.

While the aircraft was still some distance away, I got to work with the knife, slipping it between the gap in the sash window and jiggling it until the tip pressed against the latch. I then waited until the plane was almost over-head before I exerted any pressure.

I pushed, gradually increasing the weight behind the hilt, until the spring-loaded mechanism gave.

I hoped that the click had been muffled by the sound of the airliner's four turbofans as they powered it up towards cruise altitude.

When the sound of the plane built to a crescendo, I raised the lower window. As soon as I'd got eighteen inches of clearance I slid part-way across the sill so that my upper body was balanced on the tiled work surface the other side.

Half in, half out, I moved quickly to clear a space. Just to my right were a sink and a draining board with some pots and pans on it. There was some kind of tea urn on my left, which I eased out of the way. Then, with the sound of the plane's engines still crackling in the distance, I swung my legs across the sill and dropped onto the floor of Mansour's kitchen.

89

I stayed perfectly still, letting the aircraft vanish over the Med, until all I could hear was the ticking of the battery-powered wall-clock and the soft hum of the fridge.

The white walls and ceiling picked up the little available light from outside. As my eyes adjusted, I was able to make out the more obvious details of the room. It was large, about six metres by ten, and entirely functional. Apart from the fridge, there was a cooker, a small table and some wall-mounted cupboards. The air was tinged with the smell of drains, grease and stale cooking. A handful of cockroaches scurried across the floor.

I edged towards the door, grasped the handle and twisted. Through the gap, I saw a passage leading into a large, open hall. Beyond it was the front door, flanked on either side by a tall strip of window. There was no carpet. Good; no pressure-pad. I knelt and touched the floor. It was tiled. Good; it wouldn't creak.

I stepped through. I made out tables with large objects sitting on them, and a series of less distinct shapes low down where the floor met the wall. I bent and touched one of them. It was a stone pillar around a metre high.

To my left, door open, was the sitting room. The dining room was on my right.

I was soon facing a wide, sweeping staircase. As my eyes adjusted to the ambient light I could see it split at mezzanine level – one half going right, the other left. I knelt and let my hand brush the bottom step. Tiled again.

I moved to the sitting-room door. No LEDs blinked on the walls or in the corners.

I moved inside. A large flatscreen TV was mounted on the opposite wall. And between the two windows was another stone pillar, several feet taller than the ones I'd just seen in the hallway. On top of it I could make out a life-sized bust. It was eerie in the half-light – like somebody was watching my every move.

As I turned back towards the hall I caught a glint from a table next to one of the large armchairs. I moved closer. A bottle. And next to it a tall glass. I gave it a sniff. Scotch. More good news: the target would be sleeping a little heavier tonight.

I crept up to the front entrance and ran my fingers down the crack between the jamb and the edge of the door. There was a chain, which I removed, and two bolts, top and bottom, which I undid. If everything went to rat shit, I now had a choice of exits.

90

I climbed the stairs slowly, following the right-hand sweep. A couple of steps below the top, I stopped.

I had heard a mumble. I stopped breathing, moving.

The background noise was still there – but what I had heard had come from inside the house.

Light streamed in through a window at the top of the stairs – starlight topped up by the thin sickle of the new moon: enough to reveal another window at the end of the long corridor and the two doors leading off the top of the stairs, left and right.

I moved into the shadows by the wall and listened, the fingers of my right hand wrapped hard around the knife.

I heard it again: the rasp of a whispered order. It had been close, but wasn't getting closer. I had to go forward and find out, or we'd be standing off all night.

When I reached the top of the stairs I allowed myself to start breathing again. Through a crack in the door to my left – the door that opened onto Mansour's bedroom – I could see the flicker of a TV.

I knelt and let my hand brush the floor. It wasn't stone or marble, but at least it was parquet; better than floor-boards.

I straightened and took stock. Mansour's bedroom door was to my left, a couple of metres from the top of the stairs.

The sound of his laboured breathing punctuated the waffle on the TV. Whatever he'd been watching, it was in English, because I could make out the odd word.

I stepped out onto the parquet and put my ear to the crack between the door and the frame. Mansour's breathing hadn't altered. I eased the door open. It swung soundlessly on its hinges.

Mansour's bed was against the wall to my left. Directly ahead of it, to my right, was a built-in wardrobe. One door was open to expose the screen of the TV. Mansour had been watching some eighties American cop show.

The light flickered across the bed. In the middle, propped up by several pillows, was Mansour. His head, which was turned towards me, had dropped onto his chest.

A small box with what looked like a button on top was mounted on the wall near the bedside table. An alarm bell went off inside my head.

Something wasn't right. Mansour. The way he was lying was totally unnatural. Worse, one of his hands was under the sheet where I couldn't see it.

The TV cop yelled a warning and I looked up to see that Mansour's eyes were open, fixed on mine, and as cold as ice.

91

Before I could move, Mansour threw back the sheet. He also shouted some kind of command, in a language that didn't sound like Arabic.

I wasn't going to spend a whole lot of time worrying about it.

Keeping his eyes and his pistol trained very firmly on me, Mansour brought his other arm across the bed and felt for the lamp switch by the table. If his eyes left me for a second, I'd take him – but they didn't.

There was a click and the light came on. Because the TV was behind me, I knew Mansour's vision would light-adjust quicker than mine, so I concentrated instead on the weapon – hoping by the time I'd taken in the details, I'd have thought of something.

It was a Makarov semi-automatic, the one-time standard Soviet sidearm. Like the AK47, it was designed to be used in some of the shittiest, most hostile theatres in the world, and nearly always went bang when you wanted it to.

His finger was very much on the trigger. The safety catch, just above the pistol grip on the left-hand side, was in the down position. In other words, off. The muzzle was threaded to take a silencer, but didn't have one in place. If he needed to use it against an intruder, he wasn't going to be fussed about waking the neighbours.

Mansour was saying something; this time it sounded to me like Serb or Russian. He didn't shout, and he didn't look remotely scared. Quite the contrary, as he motioned for me to bin the knife.

Had he already gone for the panic-button on the wall? The only thing I knew was that fifteen seconds into this fuck-up he still had the advantage, and inspiration hadn't come my way.

At last he tried English. 'Who are you?'

No way was I going to let him know I understood.

He waved me back with the barrel of the Makarov and swung his legs off the bed. Then, continuing to keep his eyes on me, and with the pistol pointed squarely at my chest, he pulled open the top drawer of the bedside table and took out a mobile phone. He moved back towards the window to put some distance between us.

If he'd pushed the panic button, why would he now need a mobile?

This was the best chance I was going to get – the moment Mansour took his eyes off me, however fractionally, to dial. But the fucker must have read my mind. He started punching in numbers without once looking at the phone itself.

The press tones were the loudest thing in the room right now.

Eyes on mine, pistol aimed at my centre mass, he was

still dialling when there was a loud crack on the window.

Mansour turned; I didn't.

I launched myself at him.

He brought the weapon up, but my punch landed so hard in his face that the shock made him drop it. As he fell to the ground, it clattered across the parquet and ended up somewhere in the shadows.

From down on the floor, a hand shot up and grabbed my crotch. He squeezed so hard I nearly screamed. I punched him again, hard on the nose. The back of his head snapped back and hit the floor. He went out cold.

I hobbled over to the dark corner. Retrieving the Makarov and knife, I went to the window. Lynn was looking up expectantly, like Romeo under Juliet's balcony.

I jerked my finger. 'The window – for fuck's sake climb in!'

92

We carried Mansour downstairs and tied him to a chair in the kitchen with a roll of clingfilm.

I left him in Lynn's care while I went through the rest of the house.

The most useful bits of kit I recovered were a second pistol – a .38 snub-nosed revolver – from the drawer of a desk in an upstairs study, and a set of car keys in the sitting room.

I opened up the garage to find a white, top-of-the-range Audi Q7 off-roader fitted out with all the trimmings – sat nav, CD/MP4 sound system, DVD player and a nice big sunroof. Where the fuck did this disgraced ex-spy get his money?

Mansour was beginning to come round by the time I got back. He did the same as I would have done: eyes down, mouth shut, play fucked. Lynn hovered anxiously close by.

I left them to it again and ran back up to the bedroom. Mansour had been on the point of calling someone. I found the mobile and scrolled the menu. He only had a few numbers on his contact list. But there was a problem, for me anyway: the alpha-numerics were in Arabic.

I jumped down the stairs and chucked it to Lynn. 'See who he was ringing.'

Lynn went through the motions, but I could tell his mind wasn't on it. He cleared his throat. 'Your methods, Nick . . .' He shook his head and threw a glance at Mansour. The Libyan's chin was back on his chest, only now his body hair was flattened beneath a layer of plastic and saliva.

'He was pointing a weapon at me. What the fuck do you think I should have done? Had a civilized conversation while I waited for you to come up and mediate?'

I pointed to the mobile. 'You sorted it?'

What Lynn saw on the screen clearly focused his thinking, because I saw him do a double-take.

'What?'

He frowned and shook his head. 'Well, he only managed to dial three digits, but they're a plus and two fours . . .'

'UK or Northern Ireland . . .'

I told him to check if it corresponded with any numbers in the address book.

Nothing. And the received, missed and dialled facilities had all been wiped.

'No matter. He's soon going to tell us.' I walked towards Mansour.

Lynn moved between us, raising his free hand. 'Is this absolutely necessary?'

Mansour had started to make a UK call. What went on in the heads of lads like Lynn? 'And your suggestion is . . . some George Smiley shit over sherry?'

'This is a cultured man, Nick. Take a look around you. Do you see what's on those plinths?'

'Who cares? We got big problems here.'

But Lynn wasn't in the mood to be diverted.

'Both of those stone heads are priceless. Busts covering the entire period of the Roman occupation of North Africa. Mansour isn't some fundamentalist plotting a car-bomb attack on a shopping centre. He has – or at least had – rank and status in this country and we need to show him the kind of courtesy that befits it; or, trust me, we will get nothing from him.'

As if on cue, Mansour started to move his head from side to side. He opened his eyes and blinked for several seconds under the glare of the lights. When he saw Lynn, the briefest of smiles played across his lips. He opened his mouth. 'Leptis . . .'

I leant down and grabbed his cheeks between my thumbs and fingers and squeezed. 'Who set up the Leptis call? Who called the station? Was it you?'

'Enough!' Lynn placed his hand on my shoulder, but I shrugged it off. I knew what I was doing.

Mansour would know all about interrogation techniques and how to overcome them. I didn't want to give him time to think – only enough to tell me what he knew.

'Why are we being targeted? Who set us up?'

Lynn grabbed me by the shoulder and pulled me round to face him. He was surprisingly strong. 'I will not be a party to this.'

My eyes burned into his. 'Then leave.'

'But—'

'No buts. Listen up. He is the only person who's ever

362

called you Leptis. That means he is connected – I want to know how. Second, I want to know who the fuck he was calling.'

My expression should have said it all, but in case it didn't, I spelled it out for him. 'Is he working for the Firm?'

Lynn held my gaze. Anger blazed in his eyes for a brief second. He shook his head. 'Please, Nick. Let's try it my way. Just once. If it doesn't work, well, I'll hand the reins back to you.'

'Fine.' I threw my hands in the air. 'Get the sherry out. But he gets to know nothing about me – understand?'

'Of course, Nick, I understand.'

Mansour watched intently as Lynn pulled up a chair and sat down in front of him.

'I need you to answer some questions, Mansour. Please make this easy on yourself. If you don't . . .' He paused and glanced at me.

Mansour looked at me then back at Lynn. 'Ask away, Leptis, my friend. I suspect we may be able to help each other.'

'Who were you trying to call? Who was it?'

The Libyan smiled. 'It should be abundantly clear to you.' His voice was calm, his English word perfect.

'It should? Why?'

'Why do you think? The number is yours.'

93

Lynn would have made a crap interrogator. Part of the job was never to react to any information given, but his cheeks flushed a deep shade of red.

Mansour's little bombshell had achieved its desired effect.

I knelt down, my eyes level with the Libyan's. 'Prove it. Tell us the number . . .'

Mansour was trying the oldest bluff in the book. The Libyan blinked innocently before fucking me off and shifting his eyes back to Lynn. 'I'm sorry, Leptis. You and I – we know each other of old. But your friend here. Why don't you introduce us? After all, you are both, in a sense, my guests . . .'

I stood up, wanting to walk away from this bad black and white movie. Where the fuck had these two been for the last twenty years?

Lynn was finally rejoining planet earth. His tone stiffened. 'You have no need to know that, Mansour.'

Mansour paused. I could see him assessing me,

weighing up how the power was shared out around here. He pursed his lips and narrowed his eyes. 'Country code four-four, then two, then oh, then seven, then two one eight . . .' Mansour paused.

I looked at Lynn. The flushed cheeks were turning white.

The Libyan reeled off the rest of the number. Lynn gave an almost imperceptible nod. 'That was my old number at Vauxhall Cross . . .'

'Ah, so you are retired now, Leptis. This I didn't know. I always thought that men like you and me, we never really retired . . .'

'How did you know my number? I don't understand.'

'You don't? Let's see. You are Colonel Julian Francis Lynn. Born fourth of September, 1949. Son of Brigadier Robert Anthony Lynn, the great "Al-Inn" of Cairo, scourge of Nasser's young officers' movement. You had a good, solid British education at a minor public school.' He stopped for effect and smiled up at Lynn. 'Three very respectable A-levels in Latin, Greek and English literature – good enough to get you a place at Cambridge, where you studied Classics, our mutual interest, of course. We have a great deal in common, Leptis. Like me, you decided to make the army your chosen career; and, like me, you switched to intelligence – not surprising, given your father's very considerable connections.'

I half expected him to bring out a red, leather-bound book and tell Lynn he was on Tripoli's answer to *This Is Your Life*.

'I know, Leptis, that you understand the Arab mentality. You know very well how we work, our methods, our thinking.'

He glanced at me now with the same look my school teachers used to give me. 'Not all of us are the dumb goatherds or fanatical hijackers portrayed in the Western media. There are many shades to us, just as there are many shades to you.'

He didn't seem to get that he was the one in the cling-film. Ignoring me, he turned back to Lynn. His tone was softer as he addressed a fellow gentleman.

'Of course, I'm not telling you anything you don't already know, Leptis. You know that I spent many years in custody at the pleasure of our Supreme Leader because of what happened that night. It was a stupid mistake. I should never have let it happen. Just as I should never have allowed my . . . feelings . . . to get the better of me in London when I was sent by our Great Guide as his special envoy over Lockerbie . . .'

Mansour paused to study his bindings. He raised his head to me and spoke in a voice people normally reserve for the waiter. 'Do you think I might have a glass of water? All this talking . . .'

I didn't move. It was Lynn who turned to the fridge.

A moment later, he lifted a bottle of Evian to Mansour's lips and the Libyan took a couple of gulps. He thanked Lynn, held his gaze and continued.

'I have no proof, Leptis, but I am sure that it was you who called off the dogs – or should I say the wolves – after that regrettable little incident.

'This, I believe, is what the new détente is all about. We were the best of enemies. But that is all in the past. I do not know what it is that has brought you to Libya – only that it is somehow meant. Men like you and me, Al-Inn, we live complicated lives. If you trust me, if the answers you seek are in Libya, then I can help.'

So, Lynn was the great 'Al-Inn' now. Nice touch. Flattery usually got you somewhere. But it wasn't going any further.

'A few days ago, I found an explosive device under my car. It had a very distinctive signature – the same as the devices on the *Bahiti*. Ben Lesser – that name ring a bell?'

'Of course . . .'

'That same day, someone left a phone message for me at a TV station in Dublin. Words to the effect that Leptis had the answers and I should go and see him. The only person who ever called Lynn Leptis was you. So I'm going to ask you again: did you set up that call?'

'No.'

'OK, then – who was Lesser's mentor?'

Mansour's brow furrowed. 'Mentor?'

'The person who trained him.'

'Ah!' A light went on somewhere in Mansour's head. He turned and looked at Lynn. 'After the failure of the *Bahiti* operation, so soon after the *Eksund*, there was a lot of . . . well, I guess you would call it soul-searching. People wanted to know what had gone wrong. These efforts to understand were led by the Supreme Leader himself. In the interests of self-correction – so that Libya could learn from its mistakes – I told them everything. Why shouldn't I? If it helped my country . . .'

Yeah, right. I knew all too well what they did to people like him in rat-holes like this in the interest of self-correction.

Mansour ploughed on. 'Reports were written and circulated. Your name – the name of Leptis – became well known in high circles, Al-Inn. You would expect it to. I remembered you from our encounter on the party circuit. I realized who you were – but you were careful and I could not prove why you were here.

'Afterwards, it seemed obvious. Given your connections with Libya, the time you spent here at the embassy, you must have been involved, somehow, in the *Bahiti* operation. You were even stopped at a roadblock near the docks on the night the ship sailed. And, naturally, you came to the attention of Lesser's mentor, because Lesser's mentor was also on the dock that night.'

I looked at Lynn, then at Mansour.

Mansour smiled. 'You seem surprised.'

Lynn pulled up a chair and sat beside him. 'He was there? You're sure?'

'He? Who said anything about a "he"?' Mansour was quite pleased with himself. 'Lesser's mentor was a woman.'

Despite being trussed up, he still managed to do a halfway decent impression of a cat who'd got the cream. 'During the time of struggle she ran the PLO's bomb-making school here. You'd have expected her to be on the dock that night. But she was there for altogether more personal reasons, too.' The cat's smile spread across his face again. 'Indeed, you could say she taught Lesser everything he knew.'

'How's that?' Lynn asked.

'She didn't just teach him how to make bombs, Al-Inn.'

94

Her name was Layla Hamdi. She was Palestinian, and she ran the training camp in Ajdabiya.

Lynn tilted his head in my direction. 'Eight hundred kilometres along the coast – halfway between here and Egypt.'

Mansour had more. 'In October 1985, after the PLO was attacked by Israeli planes in Tunis, the various factions that made up the PLO had decided to accept a clandestine offer from Gaddafi to relocate many of their significant activities, including weapons instruction, to Libya.

'Since Libya was already firmly on the West's radar screens for its support of foreign terrorist organizations like PIRA, the PLO's move here was picked up and tracked. But the Ajdabiya training camp and its leading proponents, including Layla, Lesser's teacher, weren't.'

He was happy to talk about it now, he said, because all of this was very firmly history; one of the many aspects of Libya's past that the country's Great Leader had freely renounced in the wake of the Lockerbie settlement.

Believe that and you'd believe anything. Mansour was waffling because he knew that the longer he talked, the more time he bought for himself. I'd have been doing the same.

Time for us, on the other hand, was ticking on. It was coming up to 5 a.m.: first light soon. Decisions were going to have to be made.

Layla Hamdi, he said, had trained as a chemist at UCLA, was incredibly gifted academically, and had shown no signs of radicalism until both her parents were killed by a stray IDF tank-shell that ripped through their quiet apartment in Gaza. The Israelis never apologized – Layla's parents were merely collateral damage in the Palestinian homelands; reason enough on its own, I thought, to turn Layla away from life as an academic and to the Cause.

When she returned from the USA she signed up with Force 17, another PLO spin-off, and soon discovered she had a natural skill as a bomb-maker.

Pulling in disparate techniques in the art of explosive-charge construction from right across the Middle East – including those taught by the British to the Mujahideen in Afghanistan – Layla rose through the ranks of the PLO to become its bomb-maker supreme. 'In the never-ending game of new countermeasures by us and then counter-countermeasures by you that characterized the bomb-maker's world, Layla was the person who kept the PLO and its fellow travellers state-of-the-art.'

She started out as Lesser's mentor and became his lover. Not long after that, she became his wife. 'When she first met him, Layla was already in her mid-thirties. Lesser was still in his late twenties, the tall muscled Irish boy with the unkempt hair.'

I pictured him in bomb class. He must have stuck out a mile in the company of his fellow students: Latinos from the Shining Path, Muj from Afghanistan, Arabs, and the odd Red Brigade Italian. Fuck knows what he and Layla had had in common, beyond bomb-making and sticking it to imperialist, bourgeois, capitalist regimes.

According to Mansour, it had been love at first sight. The Palestinian and the Irishman. It sounded like a bad joke . . .

When Gaddafi did his deal with the West, one of the conditions was that he gave up his support of terrorism. The bomb-making school was shut down and Layla suddenly found herself out of a job.

Now in her mid-fifties, and not in the best of health, she had decided to stay in Libya rather than go back to the West Bank. I couldn't say I blamed her. Ajdabiya, whatever that was like, couldn't be any worse than the Gaza Strip. Well, we were about to find out.

'How long to get there?'

'By car? If you take the coast road, maybe eight hours. But for you, that would not be an option. It runs through the oil fields and there are many checkpoints. Without papers, you would not get through.'

'Is there another way?'

'There is the desert road, but it will add another four hours to the journey. There are still checkpoints, but fewer. And the guards are more likely to accept *baksheesh*. The road, however, is still dangerous.'

'How so?'

'There are potholes – deep ones; deep enough to shatter an axle. And after a storm, the sand can bury several kilometres of tarmac, forcing you off-road. You would need a four-by-four, at the very least.'

Mansour must have realized, the second he'd opened his mouth, that he'd walked straight into that one. He added almost immediately: 'Of course, Al-Inn, you are at liberty to take my car. In fact, it would be an honour . . .'

I turned to Lynn. 'Grab whatever you think might help us on the road: a map, even if Mansour's Q7 has sat nav; water – lots of it; and food – as much as you can find, so we can eat on the move.'

I packed the revolver in my day sack and pocketed the Makarov along with Mansour's mobile phone.

Mansour told me where in his study he kept his spare mags and ammo. I went and took all I could fit into the day sack.

It was there that I also found his money – just as Lynn had predicted: a briefcase full of dollars – roughly ten grand's worth. Ten grand would go a long way in the *baksheesh* stakes – all the way between here and Johannesburg, if need be.

Lynn was still emptying the fridge of water bottles when I got back. I ripped at the clingfilm to release Mansour.

He rubbed his wrists. 'What are you going to do with me?'

I tapped my watch. 'You've got five minutes to get dressed. Then you're coming with us.'

PART EIGHT

95

We drove out of Tripoli into the rising sun.

I was at the wheel. Lynn was in the back, and Mansour was beside me, ready to take on any checkpoints. Nobody spoke much. Nobody needed to. All I'd had to do was reset the sat nav's voice commands from Arabic to English and load in Ajdabiya. According to Mansour, the house we wanted was located on the beach. His memory wasn't great. He'd have to point out the actual building once we got there.

We got past the city limits. I'd given Lynn the .38 and told him to keep behind Mansour's seat. On the coast road, with the sea on our left, the desert stretching away on our right, there weren't many opportunities for the Libyan to cut and run, but there was no telling what he might try.

I glanced across at him. 'What's with the Russian?'

'Excuse me?'

'You started to talk to me first in Arabic, then in Russian. Why?'

'I didn't know who you were. I *still* don't know who you are – only that you are British. When you were in my room, you could have been anyone. And a man like me has many enemies.'

Lynn leant forward. 'Why would the Russians be after you?'

Mansour kept his eyes on the road. 'I have always been a survivor, Al-Inn. But how could a man like me, with my background, survive in the new Libya? Our Great Leader had publicly renounced terrorism. He'd informed the world that Libya was ridding itself of its ballistic missiles, its weapons of mass destruction. I had emerged from prison with nothing. Nobody was interested in a disgraced former spy. What was I to do?'

'What did you do?' Lynn asked.

'All I had were my connections – contacts built up over many years – and my interests . . . *our* interest, Al-Inn. In the desert, there are treasures beyond your wildest imaginings – you know this – many of them still waiting to be discovered. From prehistory to the time of the Romans – the desert is full of these priceless remnants of my country's past. And there is only so much room in the Al-Jamaheri Museum . . .

'Now, many people come to Libya to look for these artefacts. I know what is out there, Al-Inn. I have spent years in the desert. The desert is my home. There are places I know that nobody else does. Why should some archaeology student from an American, Italian, British or French university be allowed to make these discoveries – to take these antiquities back home with them, supposedly for study? They are Libya's heritage and they should stay here.'

I couldn't see the problem. If some geek with a metal-detector discovered Septimus Severus's money box, he should be allowed to hang on to it. Finders, keepers.

But Mansour was getting sparked up. 'It is we who should decide what is to be bought and sold, what is to stay or leave my country.'

I loved how this guy twisted and spun. Now he'd recast himself as some kind of custodian of national treasures. It was fucking obvious he wasn't just squirrelling these objects away for posterity; he was trading them as well, and not on eBay.

I kept my eyes glued to the potholes that peppered the lumpy tarmac. 'And that's where the Russians fit in?'

'I am sorry?'

'The Russians. You decided that some of these price-less artefacts weren't quite Libyan enough, and that entitled you to do a little trading with your old mates?'

Mansour stared straight ahead, tuning me out.

I didn't want to let him off the hook. 'Let me see if I've got this right. In the eighties, Libya's foreign terrorist programme was up and running, and you were the guy who put it all together. The training, the weapons, the shipments . . .'

'If you want to put it that way, yes.'

'The market was big – PIRA, PLO, the Red Brigade, you name them. And the Soviets fell over themselves to supply you with all the kit. So there you were, top of the heap, pulling all the strings. Until the *Bahiti* op went to rat shit . . . And when you finally got out of jail, it wasn't just Gaddafi's little slice of paradise that had changed, was it?'

'No.'

Too right it wasn't. The Cold War was over. The Soviet Union didn't exist any more. But a lot of those GRU colonels Mansour used to deal with, his regular weapons suppliers, had grown rich – or, at the very least, had some extremely rich, well-connected friends.

I swerved to avoid another pothole that was deep enough to rip a wheel off. 'If there's something a wealthy Russian loves to spend his money on, apart from bling, powerboats and football clubs, I bet it's bits of old Roman bric-a-brac.'

Mansour bristled. 'The alabaster bust in my house is of Septimus Severus. It is one of a pair. The other one is at the Capitol Museum in Rome. On the black market, it would fetch millions.'

It explained a lot, not least the Q7, the briefcase of cash and the curious symbols I'd noticed on the sat nav's map display. Mansour had marked the location of these out-of-the-way archaeological sites. Nice work if you could get it. It almost made me wish I'd paid more attention at school.

Mansour turned and looked directly at Lynn. 'I was only ever prepared to sell things that didn't matter – a late classical statuette here, a bust from the Hellenistic era there. These things are two-a-penny, Al-Inn. You know that. But they always want more.'

'It's a Russian thing,' I said. 'Old habits die hard.'

He turned and watched the road. 'Some of my former contacts are still in the military and the GRU. Some now work for the FSB and Russian arms manufacturers. Many of them have a great deal of money. They also have some powerful friends.'

No surprises there. The Russian mafia were

everywhere. 'What did you do that means you have to sleep with a weapon?'

Mansour sighed. 'There were certain treasures, like the Severus bust, that I am not prepared to sell. They *should* remain in Libya. But the people you speak of are putting me under a great deal of pressure. Their clients – some of them well-known public figures – these men are extremely powerful, and they want only the very best. When they set their eye on something, they will stop at nothing to get it. I have started to become . . . nervous . . . There is no one I can turn to here. I needed the advice – the help – of someone I could trust.'

'So you decided to call Lynn?'

Mansour didn't answer. Something on the dead-straight stretch of road ahead had caught his eye. It had also caught mine.

Half a mile away, shimmering in the morning sunlight, was a checkpoint.

96

As we slowed to join the queue of waiting traffic, I told Mansour to put on his shades.

I tucked the Makarov under my thigh. 'Got that .38 within reach?'

Lynn shuffled about in the back.

'Make sure you can get to it.'

The old familiar feeling was crawling through my stomach – that sickening lurch, when you know you're in the wrong place at the wrong time and, worst of all, with no one and nothing to back you up.

'Get about $400 out of the case. Then keep it closed and under your feet.'

Our passports didn't have visas or entry stamps. To a guard who was even half alert we'd stick out a mile. But a few hundred USD might help us on our way.

I watched a sentry making his way towards us, past taxis laden to capacity, the odd private car and a couple of long-distance trucks headed for Benghazi and beyond. Immediately in front of us was a Toyota pick-up stuffed with farm produce. A goat stared vacantly at us from the tailgate, alongside a stack of bamboo cages filled with emaciated chickens.

I left enough room to pull a hard right into the scrub and loop back on the road to Tripoli if it turned into a gang fuck. We'd have to find another route to Ajdabiya. I wanted this sorted; I didn't want to spend the rest of my life looking over my shoulder.

The checkpoint was basic: a red-and-white-striped pole tied to a couple of sand-filled oil-drums. The sentry was picking vehicles out of the line at random and waving them through. A voice at the back of my head told me we weren't going to be one of them.

I'd normally expect guys like this, in the back of beyond, to be half asleep, bored or just pissed off. But he and his mates looked particularly switched on; they wore shades under their ball caps, crisply pressed green uniforms and carried AKs across their chest.

Mansour gave a low groan. 'Money will not help us.'

'Why not?'

'They are Kata'eb Al-Amn = Security Battalions. Gaddafi's men.'

I looked at Lynn. 'What's he talking about?'

Lynn spat something in Arabic. Mansour grunted back.

'What?' I hated being out of the loop.

'It's unfortunate.' Lynn's head appeared between the front seats. 'You don't usually find the Security Battalions at VCPs. They consider themselves above this kind of thing. Checkpoints are normally manned by the army or the People's Militia. Draftees. Eminently bribable. But not this lot.'

Unfortunate? Not quite the term I'd have used. 'Are they looking for something – us, maybe?'

Mansour sucked his teeth. 'Perhaps they had some trouble here. There have been protests over the price of bread and rice. They could be looking for troublemakers.'

'What are you going to tell them?'

'Quiet; I will deal with it.'

The guard reached the Toyota and started talking to the driver. Even the goat was starting to look uncomfortable. Mansour's time was up and I wasn't liking this one bit.

I turned to Lynn. 'Weapon?'

The strain was registering on his face too. 'On my lap.'

I checked. It was concealed by his jacket.

I nodded towards Mansour. The sweat was starting to trickle down his face. 'A word out of place, shout and I'll put my foot down. Then shoot him through the back of the seat.'

The guard handed back a fistful of papers to the driver of the Toyota. The goat celebrated by trying to bite the head off a chicken that chose that moment to stick its neck through the bars of its cage.

The guard turned his attention to us.

Our fate rested in the hands of a man who'd have slit his own mother's throat twenty years ago on the say-so of the Great Leader with the big lapels.

97

I kept my hands on the wheel so the guard could see them and so I could turn the wheel as soon as this went noisy. The automatic gearbox would do the work for me. All I had to do was shift my foot off the brake and onto the gas. The Makarov was still where I needed it – cold comfort in a rapidly worsening situation.

The guard swaggered up to the Audi and tapped the glass with the muzzle of his AK.

Mansour powered down his window. Warm, dust-laden air blew into the car as he beckoned the guard to his side of the wagon.

The guard bent down to give us a good look and I saw the pips on his shoulders. I wasn't hot on Libyan rank insignia, but I reckoned he was a captain or a major. His face was heavily pockmarked. A layer of black stubble showed beneath the ball cap. He stared at us over the top of his Aviators before finally addressing Mansour.

'*Taruh fein?*' Not a hint of deference; just a whole lot of suspicion.

I caught the word Ajdabiya in Mansour's reply.

There was another burst of questioning and I glanced in the mirror at Lynn. I didn't like the way this was going. By the look on his face, he didn't much either.

I ran my right hand down the side of the wheel so it was nearer the weapon.

The guard barked again and Mansour reached slowly into his inside pocket.

The guard's head moved a fraction; I was pretty sure the eyes behind the Aviators were looking straight at me. I smiled back.

Mansour handed over a small green carnet. More questions, more suspicion. The guard looked from me to Lynn, then switched his attention to Mansour's little green identity card.

I swore I heard the tick of the electronic clock on the Q7's dashboard as the officer scrutinized each line of Mansour's ID.

He glanced at the card, then at Mansour's face. Suddenly he barked at us, using a different tone altogether: '*Yallah, yallah, yallah.*'

The officer stepped back. I had no idea what was going on. Was he going for his weapon?

My hand moved towards the Makarov. I'd drop the guard before he could fire and then get my foot down.

Mansour realized what was going through my mind. He held his hand flat below the level of the window, where the guard couldn't see what he was doing. He was signalling for me to cool it. 'They're letting us through.'

The guard pressed Mansour's identity card back into his outstretched hand.

'Drive.'

I didn't need to be told twice. I edged past the vehicle in front.

More shouting. Lots of excitement. The sentry on the barrier snapped a smartish-looking salute as we passed beneath it.

Mansour hit the button and his window slid upwards.

I blipped the accelerator and the Audi's big engine purred as we headed back out onto the open road.

I checked the mirror, glancing back every so often as the checkpoint receded into the distance. Nobody was following us. It soon disappeared in a cloud of dust.

I turned to Mansour. 'What happened?'

The big, satisfied grin had found its way back onto the cat's face. 'Gaddafi still uses many Russian advisers. There are Russians everywhere in this country. If there is one thing that terrifies the Kata'eb Al-Amn as much as the Great Guide himself, it's the Russians he surrounds himself with. I got the idea from our conversation earlier.'

The relief in the car was so great I could taste it.

I told Mansour I'd heard him mention our destination: Ajdabiya.

'There's an oil terminal in Ajdabiya that's run by a big Russian petroleum company. I told the officer we were going there. Why else would I have two white faces with me?'

Lynn placed his hand on the Libyan's shoulder. He spoke softly – and with a degree of approval that left me feeling uncomfortable. 'Stroke of genius, Mansour. Well done.'

We drove on in silence. As we passed the town of Al-Khoms, I noticed a sign in English, pointing the way to

Leptis just a few kilometres to our left. I watched Lynn's reaction in the mirror. Needless to say, he knew exactly where we were. I studied his eyes as the sign slid past; he was like a kid catching sight of a disappearing ice-cream van.

At Misrata, we followed the road south for fifty kilometres, then took a right-hand fork and headed out into the Sahara. As we left the coast behind, the scrub became patchier and all traces of civilization gradually disappeared, leaving us with an endless flat landscape and a horizon that merged with the heat haze. The dark strip of tarmac stretched endlessly ahead of us, uninterrupted except for the odd rusting truck hurtling past in the opposite direction.

I'd crossed a lot of deserts, but nothing quite matched the desolation and loneliness of this particular stretch of the Sahara.

98

Several hours later we were down to a quarter of a tank. According to the sat nav there was a petrol station thirty-nine Ks ahead.

Mansour announced that our problems were going to start soon after it. The last time he'd driven this way, he'd encountered several roadblocks along one twenty-kilometre stretch. Rumours were rife of Russians buying huge tracts of coastline on which to build holiday homes. The police had been brought in to safeguard construction traffic and staff.

Mansour knew a way around the roadblocks. 'We can leave the road about ten kilometres after the filling station and use the old nomads' tracks. The vehicle can handle it.'

He turned in his seat. 'Al-Inn, I will show you something many, many times better than Leptis Magna. I found the bust of Septimus Severus very close to where we turn off.'

'How can you possibly say that?'

'You will see for yourself. Only a handful of people know about this place. I believe it to be the emperor's winter palace.'

I found myself tuning in. I now knew the value that antiquities could command on the black market. With a couple of busts in the boot, I could afford to disappear off the face of the earth.

As a boy, Mansour had been passed down stories from nomadic traders of ruins in the desert, north of Al-Waddan territory.

The traders had described the ruins as '*Roumi*' – Roman – but there were many strange sights in the Sahara: from the relics of ancient caravanserais – stop-off points for travellers plying the trans-Sahara trade routes – to downed aircraft from the Second World War, some still with the mummified remains of their crews in their seats.

The stories were part of the myth and folklore of the desert. Nobody in Waddan paid them much attention.

But the possibility of a long-lost Roman site wouldn't release its grip on the young Mansour's imagination. He became obsessed with the idea of finding it.

Years later, he was given a helping hand – from Gaddafi, of all people.

More than ten years after graduating from the University of Tripoli, when he was an ambitious young army major, he was sent into the desert to help train the 'freedom fighters'.

Collating information on all the possible locations for the lost site, Mansour constructed a grid. Whenever he could, he took off in a jeep and worked his way across it.

One day, following a particularly violent sandstorm,

he fell in with a band of Berber camel-herders who told him that they had recently passed some partially revealed ruins on the edge of a *wadi* around ten kilometres from the Misrata–Waddan road.

Following their directions, Mansour came across some half-buried columns. Then he found pieces of pottery and mosaic. For several weeks he excavated what he could, but in the wake of the US raids on Tripoli, the decision was taken to shift the 'freedom fighters' to camps further south.

Before he deployed with them, Mansour carefully triangulated the location of his find against some local landmarks, did what he could to conceal what he had uncovered, and promised himself that one day he'd be back. In the meantime, he told no one.

After his release from prison, he scrutinized archaeological notices for signs that his discovery had been compromised. It hadn't.

Recently he'd decided to return to the site and start excavating again. When he did, he realized that his discovery was even more significant than he'd first imagined.

To begin with, the complex was big. It comprised the ruins of a palace, a number of state rooms, a temple and a library. It had housed a dignitary of high rank.

I checked the sat nav. Another ten kilometres and we'd reach the petrol station. Good timing. From the rising note of excitement in Mansour's voice, I got the sense we were heading for the big reveal.

'I found inscriptions to a woman – a woman called Fulvia Pia, Al-Inn. *Fulvia Pia . . .*'

Lynn smiled. 'The mother of Septimus Severus.' He

leant towards me. 'She was Roman. His father was of Berber descent . . .'

Mansour broke through into what looked like an entranceway to an underground chamber. It turned out to be the opening of a tunnel. Imperial palaces employed them so that slaves could move around the complex without being seen by the emperor and his family.

'The bust had been wrapped in a leather cloth and placed in the tunnel, I believe, to conceal it from Berber raiders. I had found the remains of the palace of Rome's African emperor, Al-Inn.'

99

Twenty minutes after we filled the Q7 with fuel, costing all of about $8, Mansour's site loomed up on the sat nav, ten kilometres from the main road.

I turned off the highway. The terrain changed from flat as a billiard-table to rocky and undulating. After just ten minutes, the ground fell away dramatically and we drove down into a *wadi*. I swerved to miss a rock the size of a basketball and didn't see the pothole waiting to swallow the nearside tyre.

The Audi lurched and I heard the axle crunch. I put my foot down and powered out of it, but, with the car rearing, gave another huge boulder a glancing blow. As we grounded again the Q7's nose dipped and slewed. I braked to a halt.

'We've blown a tyre.'

I switched off the engine and got out. Our only piece of good luck was that the edge of the *wadi* kept the Audi below the level of the horizon, in case anyone happened to be playing I-spy from the road.

I opened the boot and the doors to allow what little breeze there was to blow through the car. 'You two need to get out while I jack it up.'

I took the .38 from Lynn. I didn't want him to hand it to Mansour on a plate while I changed the tyre.

The Libyan fucked around in the boot for a moment or two and came up with a foam-filled toolkit with cut-outs for the adjustable spanner, the screwdriver, the torch . . . all the things you'd need if you were unlucky enough to break down in the middle of nowhere.

'No point us getting in your way,' he said cheerfully. 'We might as well stretch our legs . . .'

They moved further down the *wadi* towards the clearly visible foundations of a house.

100

I found the hole in the tyre as I loosened the first nut. It was small, but deep. I eased the wheel off and struggled to replace it with the spare. It took a long, hot twenty minutes. I was soaked in sweat by the time I'd finished, and gagging for a drink.

I heaved the old wheel round to the boot. Lynn had stashed the water next to a large clear plastic box of tiny scrapers and trowels and stuff that the people on *Time Team* use to dig up Viking shit. Like the Q7 tools they each had their own little moulded spaces.

Voices drifted up from the *wadi* as I ripped the top off one of the bottles and got a litre or so down my neck. I peered around the back of the 4x4 and saw the two of them sitting on what remained of a wall. Mansour was waving his arms enthusiastically, pointing out various features of the site. Even at this distance I could see that Lynn was glowing with pleasure.

As I heaved the wheel aboard, I glanced again at Mansour's *Time Team* kit. Something wasn't quite right.

A little voice started screaming in my head. I lifted the lid and took a closer look.

There was an empty 3cm by 10cm recess in the top right-hand corner. A Nokia car-charger sat snugly in the space alongside it.

Fuck . . .

He had a back-up mobile for emergencies.

I didn't want him to know that I knew – not yet, anyway. I called Lynn up from the *wadi*. He joined me, still looking like his head was somewhere in ancient Rome.

'Has he been on his own at all while you've been down there?'

'Why?'

'Has he?'

'Yes . . . He needed to relieve himself. He went round the corner, but not for long.'

I showed him the empty space next to the charger. 'Did he have long enough to make a call?'

'Maybe, but I would have heard him.'

'A text, maybe?'

'There can't be a signal out here.'

'Wrong, mate.'

I showed him the phone I'd taken from Mansour's bedroom. Three bars registered on the left-hand side of the screen – a nice, fat signal.

'You can pick up a signal in the depths of fucking Afghanistan. Polar bears can get a fucking signal . . .'

'Well, maybe . . .'

Confronted by some old bricks, a few pillars, some shattered pieces of pottery and a two-thousand-year-old mystery, Lynn had abandoned any idea that Mansour might represent a threat – and had taken his eye off the ball.

'He's giving us the fucking run-around. That business about him trying to call you is bullshit. He's bullshitting about the Russians, too, and all this antiquities trading. And as for all his old enemies being his new best friends . . .'

Lynn's face flushed a deep shade of red. 'You know what, Nick? All your suspicions of Mansour are born of *your* myriad prejudices. They have a term for it; they call it paranoid projection. Any half-decent psychologist will tell you all about it if ever you have the good sense to go and see one.'

He paused for a moment, checking that Mansour was still out of earshot. 'There is no mobile phone, Nick. If Mansour had been bullshitting, there would have been nothing to see out here – no ruins, no imperial palace. We passed through that checkpoint because he bluffed it with the Kata'eb Al-Amn. I know. I listened to every word. What he told us about the Russians exactly matched what he told the officer at the checkpoint. He is trying to help us and I'm damned if I'm going to let you ruin everything with your paranoid delusions.'

He strode off downhill to collect his mate.

I closed the tailgate and jumped back behind the wheel. I signalled I was ready to leave by firing up the engine.

When Mansour appeared, he beamed at me like a cat that had swallowed not just the cream, but a whole fucking dairy farm.

He opened the door, ready to hoist himself into the passenger seat. I was tempted to grab him, spin him round and frisk him to within an inch of his life. But he wouldn't still have it on him. He was too clever for that. And besides, I knew I couldn't risk alienating him any more than I had already; he was the only one who could identify the Palestinian's house.

I put my foot down and we accelerated away in a shower of grit. Paranoid projection, my arse. I wasn't the one who needed the shrink here.

101

As the Audi bounced back onto tarmac I checked the sat nav. Ajdabiya was a little under 300 kilometres away – less than two hours.

I had no idea what we'd find when we got there. I had to hope that Mansour's line about Layla and Lesser wasn't just another king-size helping of bullshit.

All along, I'd operated on the assumption that the Chinese pigtails had been Lesser's signature, but if Layla had taught him, then Layla was the connection to the bomb under my car. Ghosts didn't make bombs. If Layla was real, she'd either be the bomb-maker, or know where I could find him. Then I'd keep following the trail until I knew who'd set us up.

If, if and when.

I checked the fuel gauge as another filling station loomed out of the desert. Masses; no need to stop. A BMW 4x4 sat by the pumps. We weren't the only gas-guzzler in this neck of the woods.

Mansour eyed the vehicle. He was probably reassuring

himself he'd made the right choice in the Q7. He shifted in his seat and turned to face Lynn. 'Al-Inn, I would like you to share something with me . . . in the spirit of co-operation and friendship that exists between us.'

Lynn nodded. '*Shukran, ya siddiqi.*'

'*Afwan, y'effendi.*'

In the spirit of cooperation and friendship that existed between me and Mansour, I offered my own little contribution.

'No fucking Arabic!'

They both shrugged.

Then Mansour kicked off again. 'There are certain things I would like to clarify to enable us, you and me, to move forward, Al-Inn . . .'

I glanced at the Libyan, distrusting him more by the minute.

'Prison gives you a lot of time to think. The *Bahiti* operation was watertight. I know: I set up the whole thing. After the *Eksund* compromise, we were especially careful. I say we – but in truth there was no "we"; it was all down to me. In the *Istikhbarat al-Askaria*, we did things very differently. Security came first for me – always. The Soviets taught me the value of compartmentalization – people knowing only what they needed to know. MI6, the CIA, the GRU . . . I had studied them all. Gaddafi expected the very best; he put his trust in me, and I swore I would not let him down. So many things in life come down to trust, wouldn't you say, Al-Inn?'

I looked in the mirror. Lynn shifted uncomfortably. 'Yes, I suppose so, Mansour.'

The old alarm bell started to ring somewhere in my head.

Mansour pressed on. 'For the *Bahiti* operation, I was the only person in Libya who possessed all the pieces of the puzzle: the contents of the shipment, the date of sailing, the identity of the crew, the route – everything. We knew you'd have our transmissions and codes covered. But there are advantages to working in a country that the West considers backward. Sometimes, simplest is best. No word of the operation was ever transmitted by any form of electronic medium.

'I was the only person who could have betrayed the operation – and I didn't. But the Great Leader had become so used to betrayal he assumed that the *Bahiti* had been compromised from within. When I heard the mission had failed, I knew it would only be a matter of time before they arrested me.'

I made to look in the rear-view to clock Lynn's reaction to all this, but Mansour swept his hand across the road ahead, as if the desert held all the answers. 'In my cell, by the Will of God, I knew that as the traitor wasn't Libyan, there was only one place we'd find him.'

The alarm bell in my head started to get a whole lot louder.

By now, Mansour was in full flow. 'But this raised another set of questions, Al-Inn. I knew, for example, that the *Bahiti* shipment, like the *Eksund* before it, had been planned by a small handful of men within the Provisional IRA's senior command structure. So who stood to gain from such a betrayal? I knew these men. They were all loyal, trusted Republicans. If this was a betrayal, it was not driven by the usual impulses. No one was being blackmailed. No one had been bought. I was looking at an infinitely more complex, infinitely subtler scenario. But subtlety, of course, is a British speciality, isn't it?

'I re-examined the events either side of the *Bahiti* and I noticed something interesting. In May, the IRA received one of its biggest military setbacks when eight members of the East Tyrone Brigade, several of them highly experienced, were killed in an SAS ambush when they tried to attack an RUC station at Loughgall.

'The Provisional IRA always maintained it had been betrayed; something the British denied, of course – the line MI6 takes to this day is that Loughgall was a result of communications intercepts.

'And that would be a very reasonable thing for the world to believe were it not for the *Eksund* and the *Bahiti*. These three events on their own, coming in rapid succession, were almost enough to cripple the IRA. But not quite . . .'

He paused.

'The IRA delivered the *coup de grâce* themselves.'

102

I'd had enough of this.

'You know what? I don't remember PIRA saying "enough" in '87. Enniskillen happened between the *Eksund* and the *Bahiti* – eleven dead; the biggest loss of civilian life in a single incident. PIRA wasn't exactly rolling over.'

Mansour's eyes sparkled. 'I was just coming to Enniskillen. What happened after the massacre? The entire world expressed its revulsion for what PIRA had done.

'Here, even our Great Guide declared his sympathy for the bereaved and his contempt for those who had perpetrated such a wanton, callous act.

'Despite their denials then and since, you can wager it was approved at the very highest level of the Provisionals' leadership. The most devastating blow to the Republican movement and it was *approved* from within . . .'

Mansour looked me right in the eye. 'Who in their right mind would have done this? Surely it could only have been an Irishman intent on bringing the reign of the bomb and the Armalite to an end . . .'

I said nothing. Lynn said nothing. Over the water, I'd just been a squaddie at the sharp end. But Lynn had occupied a privileged position within the intelligence community. He'd have been in a position to know.

Something clicked into place.

The car bomb. Ireland. Leptis . . .

When I turned up at Lynn's farm, convinced that the only organization with the means and the motive to kill me was the Firm, it had only been a gut-level assumption based on events stemming from the death of the Yes Man, and then fuelled by the instruction to seek out Leptis – the man with the answers.

But Lynn's first and only thought was that it *must* have been the Firm that was going for me – that was going for *us*. He'd been expecting this to happen . . .

Why?

When I replayed what Mansour had just told us, the pieces of the jigsaw puzzle started to tumble into place.

After Enniskillen, PIRA went into meltdown. Very soon afterwards, the leadership entered into secret talks with Downing Street.

Six years later, the culmination of those talks, PIRA announced a ceasefire and everyone gave everyone else a hug.

Four years after that the ink was drying on the Good Friday Agreement. PIRA disbanded. Apart from the odd bout of sectarian score-settling, the Troubles were over and there were even more hugs. An organization that had sworn never to give up the armed struggle until Ireland was 'free' had put its faith in negotiation with their sworn enemies. Looking back, it was little short of a miracle.

But miracles and PIRA didn't rub shoulders – not in my experience.

Mansour was watching me intently. He knew he was fucking with my head. 'You see now what I saw in my prison cell, Nick? An Irishman, a senior member of the IRA's leadership, did a deal with the devil – with the British government – because he knew that the armed struggle would never, ever amount to a solution. But he realized, too, that that simple concept – that there might be a peaceful way out of the Troubles – would never be accepted by his warmongering peers. So he set out single-handedly to show them that there was no hope in continuing what they were doing, that all their ventures were doomed to failure . . .'

Loughgall. The *Eksund*. The *Bahiti*. Each a large, compartmentalized PIRA operation, each a fuck-up and PR disaster. And that was because each phase was betrayed . . .

I glanced in the mirror. Lynn knew all this. He'd lived with this knowledge for years.

Mansour rubbed his hands. 'So, Al-Inn. I have shared a little. Now, please, it is your turn. Tell me, for old times' sake, about the *Bahiti* and why Lesser and his Palestinian whore are so important to you twenty years after the event.'

This time, not even Mansour's extravagant gestures could keep my eyes from the rear-view. But I never got as far as Lynn. My vision was too full of the vehicle sitting about half a K behind us.

Now I knew why the alarm had rung in my head.

It was the BMW 4x4 from the last filling station, and my subconscious had been trying to tell me that it had been on our tail ever since.

And each time I had moved to check my rear-view Mansour had done his best to distract me.

The fucker knew it was there . . . the fucker *had* made a phone call . . .

As I turned my eyes back to the road ahead, I saw that whatever problem we had developing behind us, it was nothing compared to the one that lay ahead.

103

The road was blocked by a JCB and a giant boulder that seemed to have fallen from its bucket.

I couldn't just head off-piste to avoid them. The road straddled a huge *wadi* with steep banks. The BMW was still about half a K away, but closing. No time to debate if this was a deliberate roadblock or a construction vehicle that had spilled its load.

I braked to a halt, simultaneously throwing the gearshift into reverse.

I accelerated back towards the BMW and kept the power on. Then I came off the power, transferred the weight to the back of the car, and threw the wheel hard right. The front of the car swung momentarily. Midway through, with the front wheels parallel to the road, I hammered the brake and clutch and wrenched the steering back the other way. As the car spun, I whipped the gearshift into first, came off the brake, applied some right foot and released the clutch. We'd done a complete 180 and were pointing back towards Tripoli. I put my foot down and accelerated hard.

The BMW driver was doing it the hard way, and was halfway through a three-point turn to get out of my way. I got a good view of him and his passenger as we closed. They were both wearing black leather jackets and definitely weren't locals. Then, while we were still about 100 metres apart, the passenger powered down his window and I caught a glimpse of an AK47.

I floored the accelerator and aimed straight at him. The Audi ploughed into his offside wing. The BMW slewed to the edge of the road, teetered for a second, and then toppled and rolled down into the *wadi*.

I jammed on the brakes and reversed until we were alongside.

Lynn screamed from the back seat as the AK reappeared through a shattered window.

The muzzle flashed.

Lynn threw open his door at the same time as I did, his .38 at the ready. I grabbed at Mansour as rounds started to puncture the bodywork. 'Out the fucking car!'

Automatic fire punctuated the frenzied shouts that echoed amongst the dunes.

Mansour twisted and tore away from my grip. There was another burst and he screamed once and dropped to the tarmac.

Lynn was to my right, static and firing at the muzzle flashes. He was calm and controlled, taking slow, deliberate shots. I ran further to the right to blindside them. Rounds zinged off the tarmac around my feet.

I jumped down into the *wadi* and ran towards the rear of the wrecked car. Shots were still being fired at Lynn.

I dropped to one knee, aimed the Makarov into the tangled metal and loosed off half a dozen rounds.

'Cease fire!'

The shout came from Lynn.

The silence was deafening.

I stared at the twisted metal. The BMW was lying on its left side. The driver was virtually decapitated. The passenger was crushed against the rock.

I moved forward a few paces to feel about for his AK amongst the mangled flesh and steel. What I saw stopped me in my tracks.

104

In Russian prisons, your life story is tattooed on your body, and this boy's was pretty much an open book.

The initiation tattoo of a new gang member is usually on the chest. I opened the dead man's shirt. The first thing I saw was a rose. He was Russian mafia. The ace of clubs nearby represented a warrior's sword. I didn't need to rip off his Levis to know there'd be a small star on each kneecap to show he would never kneel before anyone.

The tattoos were blue and blurred. The ink must have been improvised from a mixture of soot and piss, and applied without proper instruments. It was often injected into the skin with a sharpened guitar string attached to an electric shaver.

I scanned the rest of the wreckage. Both of our assailants were dead.

I made my way back up the side of the *wadi*, and as I crested the ridge I heard a single shot.

Lynn was standing motionless over Mansour's body, .38 in hand.

'What the fuck did you do that for? I thought he was your friend. Old enemies, mutual respect . . .'

Lynn looked up at me. His voice was steel. 'He knew.'

'He knew what?'

'The identity of the source. The man who betrayed PIRA all those years ago . . .'

'Who was it?'

'Nick . . .'

I thought he was about to fuck me off with need-to-know. Instead, he shook his head incredulously. 'You listened to Mansour's little speech. He was spot on. There's only one man who made the transition from acknowledged member of the IRA Army Council to democratically elected politician . . .'

'Isham? Richard Isham turned informer?'

'Richard Isham is a hero. He should have got a Nobel prize. Without him, there would be no Good Friday Agreement, no peace in Northern Ireland . . .'

'And all along, you knew this was why the Firm was after you – after us. But you said fuck all!'

'There is no higher state secret I know of . . .'

I kicked Mansour. 'Is that why you killed him?'

'One of the reasons, yes. Hadn't we better get going?'

He was right. This could wait.

We climbed back into the Audi and I gunned it another half K towards Tripoli until the *wadi* petered out and I could drive onto the sand and scrub. I turned the car and paralleled the road until we were past the JCB and rejoined it soon afterwards as the sun began to sink towards the horizon.

Lynn's time bomb had been ticking away quietly for years – retirement must do that to some people. You work for decades, you make it your life, and then – *boom* – one day it all stops and you get out the stamp album and the jigsaws, or in his case the mushrooms, and realize this is it – a one-way ticket.

When Caroline killed herself, he became an outcast. He must have been riddled with guilt. Even his kids had binned him. This dirty little secret was all he had left.

PART NINE

105

The dying rays of the sun picked out the target as we approached. I parked the Audi in dead ground, some distance away from it.

The house was large, walled off and in the middle of nowhere, exactly where the sat nav had said it would be. Mansour had lied about needing to point it out. He'd just wanted to stall us until he could summon his black leather reinforcements.

The entire area was only accessible via rough tracks.

It looked as if we'd wandered onto a landfill site. Newspaper and old plastic bags blew around the Audi. We were surrounded by burned-out cars, old clothes, discarded mattresses and – even fifty metres from the sea – fist-sized chunks of tar. It wouldn't have picked up any golden beaches awards, but fuck it, I wasn't here for the sandcastle competition.

I left the keys in the ignition and told Lynn to take the driver's seat while I did a recce. I told him he should drive back down the dirt-road if I didn't return within an hour, turn towards Tripoli and wait for me at the ERV. I'd pointed out the spot, a *wadi* a kilometre before the turn-off. I also told him that if he had to get out, he should lock the car manually to avoid bright yellow flashes giving us away.

I got out and took a lungful of air. There was an underlying tang of petrochemicals beneath the smell of brine. I was slap in the heart of Libyan oil-country and the Great Guide clearly wasn't any closer to going carbon neutral.

The hundred-metre dirt-road we'd just driven up had no fresh track marks on it. Layla's villa was a big, single-storey affair set in a couple of acres of scrub surrounded by a three-metre-high perimeter wall. The sea beyond it glowed red as the sun dropped below the horizon.

Flares burned in the darkening sky above the refinery further along the coast. I could make out the lights of ships in the bay and the glare of the Russian oil terminal.

If you were going to put a bomb-school anywhere, then this was the place – as unobtrusive, miserable and out-of-the-way as you could imagine.

I covered the two hundred metres down to the target. No proximity lights came on as I did a 360 of the perimeter wall. A pair of rusty steel gates, padlocked from the outside, provided the only access. Through the gap between them I could see a tarmac drive, maybe fifty metres long, leading to the main entrance. The ground either side of it, as far as I could see in the starlight, was just sand, rocks and more windblown litter. The place was shuttered and seemed completely deserted.

The padlock hadn't been disturbed since the last sandstorm. I could see no white light seeping out from behind the shutters.

I moved back to the Q7, killed the interior lights and opened the boot. I double-checked the contents of my day sack. I had my passport, a bit of local currency and a good few thousand of Mansour's dollars.

I reloaded the Makarov and Lynn's .38 with the spare ammo from Mansour's study then checked the chamber on the Makarov before tucking it into my waistband. I wanted to make sure it was ready to fire when I was.

Whatever Layla's place revealed, I'd head off-road for Egypt. The 4x4 would allow us to slip across the border undetected. Once there, mingling in a world of tourism and semi-civilization, I'd plan my next step. We'd have to wait and see if Lynn was included.

I fired up the Q7 and drove, lights off, down to the villa. I tucked the passenger side against the wall and switched off the engine. I clambered out, day sack over one shoulder. As I readjusted to the silence, Lynn shuffled back into the driver's seat. 'Same as before – if I'm not back in an hour, it's the ERV.'

The crescent moon rose above the desert horizon. I jumped onto the bonnet and then onto the Q7's roof. I took a few more moments to study the villa then climbed onto the wall, checked below me and jumped.

Another few moments to assess the silence and I was on the move again.

I walked up the front steps and put my ear to the door. Nothing.

I edged around the back, giving each shutter a pull as I passed. No obvious way in there either, so I came back round to the front. I checked under the cactus pots to see if Layla had left a key for me, but she hadn't.

Only one thing for it: the roof.

The house had been built Mediterranean-style – normally there was no insulation; nothing between the roof and the room below.

I hopped onto a water-butt fed by a down pipe leading from the gutter and hauled myself up. If anybody was inside, this was the moment I'd find out. They certainly wouldn't think it was pigeons.

I started to peel off tiles and stacked them carefully alongside me. When I'd created a decent hole, I dug out the toolkit torch from the day sack and lay down on my stomach.

I was four metres or so above the marble floor of a large, open-plan lounge. I could see armchairs, a sofa, a fireplace, tables.

Grabbing a supporting beam, I lowered myself through the hole.

I checked each room. I found food in the fridge – long-life milk, salami, stuff that would keep – but the place didn't look like it had been lived in for a while. There was a light coating of sand on the floor and the bed and the furniture in the master bedroom had been covered with dust-sheets.

I found some keys hanging from a board next to the fridge. One of them unlocked the front door. The shutters opened easily from the inside. If I needed to leave in a hurry, I was spoilt for choice. I pocketed the keys and moved back into the lounge.

I didn't know what I was looking for so it was hard to know where to begin. I shone the torch around the room and its beam swept across a desk by the fireplace. I walked over and started removing the drawers. They were filled with the crap you usually find in desks: pens, paper, paperclips, rubber bands and correspondence – lots and lots of it. I flicked through the letters. Most were in Arabic, but some weren't.

I stuck the light in my mouth and pulled out anything written in a language I might understand. I found a compliments slip and an invoice in German from a clinic in Oberdorf, Switzerland, clearly addressed to a Fräulein Layla Hamdi, and a letter, in English, also to 'Ms Hamdi', from the Cancer Research Centre of the Russian Academy of Medical Science in Moscow.

Thank fuck for the international language. I checked the dates. The Swiss invoice, for treatment of some kind, had been sent in November. The letter from the Russian Academy of Medical Science was more recent and definitive – it was dated the first week of December and was confirmation of an appointment booked two weeks earlier.

The first sentence of the second paragraph jumped out at me.

Due to the urgent nature of the treatment, we suggest that you check yourself in as soon as possible . . .

I was just too fucking late.

106

I put back the letters and closed the drawers. As I stood up, my torch beam brushed past a row of photographs on the mantelpiece. One was of a tall man with unkempt hair, dressed in jeans and a camouflage T-shirt, his left arm draped round the shoulders of a beautiful olive-skinned woman, several years older than him. A few strands of hair had been blown across her face by the wind. They were standing in front of a house – this house. It hadn't changed at all.

As I stared at Lesser's lank hair and her piercing, sea-green eyes, the years peeled back. The dock, the *Bahiti*, finning across the harbour . . . Layla disappearing down the gangway with Mansour . . . Big Ben sliced almost in half by the det cord . . .

I panned left and there he was in more familiar gear: khaki combat jacket, black beret and shades – the uniform of the Provisionals. He was out on some bog, in the middle of nowhere; low, grey clouds scudding in from the Atlantic behind him. He beamed from ear to ear, clutching an Armalite, draped in the Tricolour and flashing a victory sign at the camera.

My gaze shifted to the next frame: this time no guns, no uniform; just jeans and a T-shirt. It must have been dress-down Friday. A summer's day, outside a cottage just like Dom's. From the look of him, the cut of his hair – short – and the zips and chains on his jeans, the shot must have been taken in the late seventies, when Lesser was in his early twenties.

Next to him was a girl with a pale complexion and the same unruly hair – a little older than him; a sister maybe.

She took centre stage in the last photo. The backdrop was the same – the cottage in Ireland – but this time a smiling, olive-skinned schoolgirl was hanging off her neck. She looked about five or six, no more, but I was shit at guessing kids' ages. She had an awkward, gap-toothed smile and I had the uneasy feeling that I'd seen her somewhere before. I turned back towards the door and stopped.

Lesser and Layla. Lesser and the girl, and a kid with olive-tanned skin and jet-black hair – all on Layla's mantelpiece.

I ran down the corridor to the bedroom and yanked the dust-sheet off the nearer of the two bedside tables and there they were – the intimate shots you didn't put on public display: Layla, pale and drawn, clutching a newborn, olive-skinned baby to her chest; Layla and the baby again, this time in laces and ribbons; and then the infant with Lesser's sister . . . no sign of Layla at all.

I pulled open the drawer and found letters, tucked away in envelopes with Irish postmarks, with Layla's name and address – a PO Box in Tripoli – scrawled in big, loopy handwriting. I opened one and was confronted by the same writing and a wobbly drawing of a horse. *Dear Mummy* . . .

I opened another. Different drawing, same writing, a bit more mature. More letters, more drawings, the same story . . .

Hamdi and Lesser – they'd had a kid; and, by the look of it, given her up for adoption.

I moved round the opposite side of the bed and whipped the dust-sheet off the other table. Lesser, in a large, black and white portrait, surrounded by an ornate silver frame, stared back at me – at the time he'd met Hamdi in the desert, I guessed, every inch the young shit-stirrer, doing his best Che Guevara imitation.

And then there was a picture of Lesser standing beside the little girl, holding her hand – in the garden of the cottage again. The girl was seven or eight; Lesser now in his early thirties. It could only have been months, maybe even weeks, before he was dropped.

Another shot. The girl, in school uniform, giving the camera a self-conscious smile, braces on her teeth, the first signs she was developing into a young woman. And another. The girl on a pier or a ferry, leaning against railings, the sea behind her: teenaged, intense, angst-ridden, no smile, but more than a hint of her mother's haunting beauty. And finally, a big portrait, black and white again, like Lesser's – their girl all grown up.

And I had seen her before. I knew her. I'd *met* her.

My eyes flicked across the pictures again.

Lesser. Hamdi. The baby. The crofter's cottage. The

schoolgirl. The girl on the pier or the ferry, whatever it fucking was . . .

The *ferry*.

Little Miss Camcorder. Mairead O'Connell.

107

I sat on the bed and looked down at the picture in my hand.

Duff had gobbed off to the press about a Brit spy hidden away on his ship . . .

Lynn's nickname became common knowledge around the highest levels of Libyan spookdom . . .

We'd killed her precious dad . . .

Fuck . . . It wasn't the Firm cleaning house. It was this bitch.

I ran from the room, into the lounge and out through the front door. Clutching Layla's keys, I sprinted to the gate and produced the only one that would fit a large padlock. I shoved it in, gave it a twist and the chains fell away.

Lynn was already sliding back into the passenger seat. I jumped in and fired up the ignition. The engine caught. I sat there for a moment too long, air con kicking in, working everything out in my head.

Could the device have been her handiwork . . . ?

Her mother would have shown her the tricks of the trade.

I registered something out of the corner of my eye – a glint, nothing more: metal catching moonlight.

Something on the move; something coming at me – fast. I hit the gas.

Too late.

As the wheels spun I heard the scream of another engine a second before it rammed the Audi side on. It cannoned into my door, catapulting me off my seat and into Lynn as Mansour's car was slammed into the wall. In the same instant the airbags exploded and the side window shattered into a thousand fragments.

Sand and dust and yelling filled the air. The airbags pinned my body back against the seat and my arms to my sides. I couldn't get to my weapon. Boots crunched on the bonnet. Somebody was trying to pull the driver's door open, but it was too buckled to move.

There were urgent, angry shouts and a crowbar crashed down against the windscreen – once, twice, again . . . The lamination crazed like a spider's web, but the glass didn't give. The boots stomped across the roof as I struggled for the weapon. My door was still being pulled at, the distorted metal screeching against the frame.

More shouts, but not in Arabic.

The sunroof imploded. Glass rained down onto me like confetti, then something hard and metallic struck my shoulder then my head and I saw white starbursts in a sea of black.

I forced myself to fight it, but when I was grabbed by my arms and pulled towards the roof, I was too weak to resist.

The shouts were muffled now, but the blows weren't. And then, in the far distance, as I felt myself being lifted, I heard a woman's voice.

108

I came to on a hard, cold floor. As I struggled to focus, blurred pinpricks of light danced across my retinas. Stars. I was looking up through the hole I'd made in Layla's roof.

There was something sticky in my mouth. The taste of metal clung to the back of my throat. Blood, or the crowbar? The tip of my tongue did a quick inventory. As far as I could tell, I still had all my teeth.

I couldn't move my feet. They were tied to my wrists and elbows behind my back.

My eyes still wouldn't focus, even though I commanded them to. As the haze cleared, I found myself facing the fireplace and the rogues' gallery.

Seeing the pictures brought it all back again: Layla . . . Lesser . . . the daughter . . .

I heard a noise to my right and managed to turn my neck against the pain. No more than a metre away, and similarly bound, lay another prisoner.

Lynn had bruises on his face and cuts to his head that

had come from something a bit more vigorous than an open hand. He'd gone down fighting.

'It's Lesser's daughter.' I strained to get eye to eye. 'That fucking bitch is—'

'I know. She made me listen to her life story.'

'Tell me.'

He shifted a fraction to try and take some of the strain off his plasticuffs. 'Her name is Mairead. Likes to be called Mary. Don't try calling her any other names.' He grimaced. 'She doesn't take kindly to it.

'She was born in Libya, lived the early part of her life here – while Lesser commuted back and forth to the Irish Republic. But Layla became a prime target for the Israelis, and we had Lesser in our sights. So they moved her away.'

He nodded at the pictures on the mantelpiece. 'The childminder is Lesser's cousin. She never registered on our radar. Lesser, I suppose, visited the kid when he could, but when we took him out, any links we might have picked up between them vanished altogether. It was as if she'd never existed.'

'And now?'

'She's president of the Richard Isham fan club. Thinks the sun shines out of his arse – to the extent that she happily organizes drug runs to finance the cause. She's a zealot, Nick, devoted to the cause – but that's nothing compared to what drove her to this.'

'Don't tell me. She wants to avenge her father's death.'

Great. And Lynn and I didn't just have a ringside seat at Mairead's circus – we were the stars of the show.

'Who's she teamed with this end?'

'Russians. Mansour was involved, too, though

whether officially or as a freelance, I have no idea. After he got out of prison, it wasn't antiquities that took his fancy; it was drugs. I should have realized.'

'Realized what?'

'These guys are representatives of the new world order – drugs, politics and organized crime. They want to create Afghanistan on our doorstep – substitute Kabul for Belfast and you start to get the picture. The Mafia get a ready-made market for their heroin and cocaine. Guys like Isham get the financial backing to buy votes and swell their numbered Swiss bank accounts. Everyone's happy. Including the new boys at the Kremlin, who always like a bit of European instability. I don't imagine Putin's government will be actively taking measures to close down this operation.

'But that's the big picture. As for the here and now, her personal vendetta . . .' The look on Lynn's face told me the worst. Beneath the bruises, he looked like he knew we'd reached journey's end.

'She has waited a long time for this, Nick. She'd always known her father's death was no accident. Duff confirmed it after he saw the Basra incident on TV. From that moment, you were compromised. She just needed someone to lead them to me.'

I heard a noise somewhere behind me then a woman's voice and I knew that she was there, in the shadows, and had been all along.

109

Her footsteps drew closer and the hairs bristled on the back of my neck. She stepped out in front of us.

Mairead O'Connell . . . still holding that fucking camcorder. We were on *Candid Camera* . . .

'That, gentlemen, will play particularly well on the six o'clock news, don't you think?' She smiled behind the lens and I caught a glimpse of her perfect white teeth.

'How did you so elegantly phrase it, Colonel? "Lesser, I suppose, visited when he could, but when we took him out, any links we might have picked up between them vanished altogether." *When we took him out* . . . That's the part I like. When this airs, that statement will be beamed into every home in the UK; and then it'll be picked up by YouTube and go all over the world. The British government's shoot-to-kill policy confirmed in a breath – as Richard has been saying all these years.'

She lowered the camera. 'But that's just icing on the cake. This evening's proceedings are all about justice.'

Mairead took a couple of steps forward. She pressed a

button on the camcorder and rotated the little screen, holding it close to my face so I wouldn't miss a thing.

'I expect you're dying to see how I got to you?'

I found myself looking at close-ups of Liam Duff, bloodied, beaten, drilled full of holes. Through broken teeth, he mumbled that he had seen a face on TV. He recognized it as one he had seen on the *Bahiti* all those years ago. And that, he said, was when he realized that he had a story to sell.

It would only have taken her a couple of phone calls to discover the channel that first showed the footage – and that the face had been working for them in Basra.

The screen cut to a shot of Dom's TV station in Dublin. The picture was a little shaky to begin with; then it steadied. The microphone picked up the noise of the wind and the traffic. She'd been in a parked car – I could just make out a wing mirror on the edge of the frame. A group of people emerged from the building. One of them was Dom. It wasn't a presentation day; he was in jeans.

She would have put the building under surveillance and waited for Dom to appear. She had the perfect cover; if anyone challenged her, she'd have produced her ID and uttered the magic words Richard Isham. There wasn't a member of the security forces in Northern Ireland at the moment who would have touched her.

The picture jumped. I was now staring at the glazed front door of Dom's apartment block in Wapping. It had been shot on full zoom. Passers-by strolled between the camera and the building. A second or two later, the door opened and I stepped onto the pavement with Ruby's Christmas present and put it into the boot of the Merc.

And then . . .

There we were on the ferry. Ruby was talking into the camera, telling this woman what she was looking forward to about Ireland: green fields, horses, leprechauns, spending Christmas with Tallulah and Nick . . . it was all there.

She'd lowered the camera. What a darling little girl, she was saying. They were having such fun; didn't mean to frighten her, blah-de-blah-de-blah. But there, there . . . and I could imagine her reaching out to touch the little girl's head . . .

One of her mates from the World of Black Leather must have slipped the tracker under the Merc's chassis while it was parked outside the apartment block. It had led her to the cottage, where they'd placed the device – with a big enough hint in Lesser's Chinese pigtails to let me know this was no coincidence.

I looked up at her. 'The battery was flat.'

'I didn't actually want you dead, did I? I wanted you to introduce me to the Colonel.'

'The phone call about Leptis?'

'Somebody from the office. A Brit with the right kind of voice.'

'But *Leptis*?'

'Information provided by our mutual friend in Tripoli. I never dreamed we would all meet here. For that, I applaud your ingenuity and tenacity. I really thought we'd get you in Norfolk, then in Italy.

'When you surfaced in Tripoli, our mutual friend was kind enough to put in a call to let me know you were on the road. In exchange, he was going to receive a bonus on this particular shipment, but I gather you've saved me from having to pay out on that one.'

I wasn't sure how she'd picked us up in Italy – and I wasn't going to give her the satisfaction of telling me – but with passport-tracking technology it looked like anything was possible. Maybe Brendan's computer whiz-kid was on her payroll, too. He could have hacked into government databases, clocked us out of Gatwick and into Genoa, then hacked into credit-card databases and watched us hire a car. Then another government database in Italy, and bingo – our number plate exiting at Rapallo. After that, she'd have monitored both the card and number-plate recognition databases, and have eyes on the Rapallo turn-off. If the Firm could do it, then so could she.

I knew what was coming next. An elderly man lay slumped on a pavement, his face beaten to a pulp. I could only tell who he was by the packet of HobNobs scattered on the tarmac beside him.

But it didn't end there.

She shoved the screen right up close to my face. I was staring at the interior of something roomy and metallic – a shipping container, maybe.

The camera followed the point of a torch beam as it swept along the floor. The picture was fuzzy, because there wasn't much to focus on – until it latched on to a foot and a pair of bare legs. A woman's legs. Then, as it tracked upwards, the two legs became four. The second pair belonged to a child.

Tallulah and Ruby were huddled together, clinging to each other for warmth and comfort.

110

The camera panned to the right of them until I could see Dom holding Siobhan's face into his chest for protection.

Mairead froze the frame and placed the camcorder on a table beside her. She squatted down in front of Lynn. 'In a minute, Colonel, Stone is going to kill you, and then—' she held up a length of det cord, a battery, the whole enchilada – 'I'm going to kill Stone.'

She turned to me. 'For all the pain and suffering you have caused me and my fellow countrymen – for the distress that you caused my mother – I want you to know that after I've dealt with you, I'm going to kill them.' She nodded at the camcorder.

She waited for a reply, but she wasn't going to get one from me. How the fuck would that help?

'Has little Ruby ever tried cocaine? I bet her mother has. She looks the type.' She grinned. 'There was a couple I supplied once . . . they had a crack-addicted baby. She smiled a lot as she grew up, but only ever talked gibberish.' She rolled her eyes back in her head in case I hadn't got the message.

I didn't even flicker.

She stood up, pissed off that I hadn't given her the reaction she was hoping for. She called out for her boys to join her and a second later I was reunited with a couple of faces I'd last seen in Norfolk.

She turned, picked up the camcorder and walked out of the room.

111

Box-cutter's head had been shaved so the gashes down the back of it could be glued back together. The back of his neck was covered with dressings.

His feet, however, were undamaged. A boot flew into my stomach. I buckled to absorb it but it still drove all the air from my body. He grabbed my feet and started hauling me towards the door. I tried to keep my head off the floor as my chest slid across the marble. All that was left where Lynn had been lying was a small pool of blood-streaked saliva.

Light now flooded the area around the entrance to the house; Mairead was obviously still in Spielberg mode.

Box-cutter brought out a blade and cut me loose then forced me onto my knees by the threshold. Lynn was getting the same treatment a couple of steps below me. His face was no more than a few inches from mine. He looked into my eyes. 'Nick, for God's sake don't tell her . . .'

Box-cutter gave him a heavy backhander across the cheek.

I didn't know what he was on about but I'd go with it. This wasn't over yet: neither of us was dead.

Mairead sneered from behind the camcorder. 'You still think you're in with a chance, don't you?'

Box-cutter grabbed as big a handful of my hair as he could, pulled back hard and ground the muzzle of his weapon deep into my neck. I could still make out Lynn's face at the very edge of my vision.

She bent down beside me and treated me to a waft of her lemony perfume. The tips of her perfectly manicured nails brushed my face. Her other hand pressed a pistol into mine.

'There is a single round in the magazine. You will load the round, point it at his forehead, count to ten and then pull the trigger.'

She gobbed off in Russian and the weapon came away from my neck. Box-cutter was clearly used to doing as he was told. Lynn was also released and we were left on our knees facing each other.

She lifted my chin. 'Liam Duff told me how my father died. He saw his body when it was brought up on deck. Blown almost in half by detonator cord.'

She stood and started filming once more.

'Kill me, Nick. Just promise me you won't tell her . . .'

I finally saw where he was going with this. Actions weren't going to get us out of this, he was telling me. But words might.

I jerked up my head. 'It didn't stop with Lynn, you know. It went higher.'

Did I detect a momentary hesitation?

'Right to the top. There was a source – a PIRA source. Someone senior in the leadership. It wasn't just the *Bahiti* ... he gave us Loughgall, the *Eksund*, the whole organization . . .'

I heard a strangulated sound coming from Lynn. 'Nick, no, *no* . . .'

Mairead lowered the camcorder. Her brow furrowed, but only for a split second. She wasn't hooking into this as fast as I'd hoped.

'Kill us and you'll be looking over your shoulder forever. Release us and I'll tell you. In fact, I'll do better than that. You can film my confession. I'll do the whole thing on camera. Not that dinky little thing – a proper, grown-up camera in Dom's TV studio. I'll give you chapter and verse on the *Eksund*, the *Bahiti*, Loughgall, Enniskillen. And I'll name the source. But I want to see all four of them alive. Let them go and I'll tell you. I'll tell everyone. The name of your traitor will be broadcast across the world, and the British government will be seriously compromised.'

She still wasn't convinced.

'Think about it, Mary. The leadership knew they had to go the political route. But they also knew that people like your dad, the diehard Republicans, wouldn't see it that way. They'd see it as surrender. So they had to be dealt with before the leadership could become respectable and have their pictures taken kissing babies.'

I was getting to her. Her face said it all.

'I know – shit, isn't it? But get us to Dublin, release the others and I'll tell you everything you need to know.'

Lynn choked with rage. He was good at this. 'You *bastard*, Stone!'

436

For a second, our eyes locked. He knew, I knew. We understood each other. For the first and last time.

With a roar, he grabbed my hand and pulled the semi-automatic from my fingers.

For a moment, everybody froze. Mairead stood there, silhouetted against the light, still filming.

Lynn pointed the pistol at her and pulled the trigger.

There was silence. It wasn't made ready; the round was still in the mag.

Then the loud bang I'd been expecting finally came, and blood and brain tissue spattered my face. A red flower bloomed on his right temple and he fell forward across the steps.

Box-cutter shoved his pistol back into his jeans and turned away.

PART TEN

112

My head throbbed. I tried to lift my eyelids but they seemed determined to stay glued together. I was dry and thirsty, but my mouth felt too furred up to let anything through again.

I thought I could hear diesel engines, big ones, but for all I knew they could be inside my head.

I took as deep a breath as I could manage and forced my eyes open.

My vision blurred and my head spun. It was like having a lifetime's supply of hangovers in one hit.

At least I was aware how bad I felt; I took that as a good sign.

And wherever I was, it was hotter than hell.

I remembered the first injection, and a couple of the others I'd been given since to keep me under. Rapid heartbeat, dry mouth, vision beginning to go hazy ... It all happened so quickly it had to be a scopolamine and morphine cocktail. The mix depresses the central nervous system. I'd treated a few targets to it, but never thought I'd be getting the good news myself.

Attempting to get my head into real-life mode, I checked inside my jacket. They'd had everything away: the Richardson passport and the card and the money. It wasn't worth worrying about; worrying wouldn't bring them back.

My eyes were starting to focus but my fingers were numb. I looked around me, flexing both hands as the pins-and-needles kicked in and they slowly came back to life. I was sitting on a sheet of steel. Some kind of bunk. There was no bedding, only the bunk fixed to the wall, and a slim wardrobe just big enough to hang a jacket in. Next to it was a tiny stainless-steel sink.

The bunk lurched and my head rolled onto my right shoulder.

I wasn't travelling first class. The whole cabin was layered with grime.

There was no porthole. I was probably below sea level and near the engines.

Where's Lynn?

Oh yeah, I remembered.

I rubbed away at days of stubble on my grease-coated skin. My eyes were gummed up and my mouth tasted stale and acidic.

I turned my head towards a steel door, painted to look like wood panelling. The stench of diesel was overpowering.

I dragged myself to my feet and stumbled to the not-so-stainless-steel sink. My knees buckled and I had to grip the rim to stop myself collapsing.

I pushed down on the tap. Water dribbled out. I bent down and sucked in a mouthful.

I staggered to the door.

The handle wouldn't budge. I'd known it wouldn't, but I had to try anyway.

I went back to the sink. I unbuttoned my jeans, tucked in the sweatshirt, pulled up my socks. If I could sort myself physically, maybe I could sort myself mentally.

I was definitely on a boat, and it was moving. On its way to Ireland? Maybe she'd bought the idea of me appearing on TV.

I stooped and sucked again at the trickle of water.

The image of Lynn sprawled across Layla's steps forced its way into my mind. His dad would have been proud of him, giving up his life for something that he believed in. I felt admiration and anger, in equal measure. Nobody was ever going to know what he'd done, and this time next year nobody was even going to care. Nobody apart from me. If I got out of this shit alive.

The door rattled.

Somebody was working the handle.

I took the couple of paces back to the bunk and lay down. What else could I do?

The door swung open. Box-cutter filled my field of view, but he wasn't alone. More than one pair of hands reached down and yanked me off the bunk and onto the floor.

I tensed every muscle that would still pay attention and curled into a ball. I took a hard kick in the back, and then my world became a frenzy of black leather. All I could do was stay foetal and take it. The drugs still had a hold. I'd be too slow to escape or retaliate. I'd have to bide my time.

Each time a boot connected, my whole body

443

convulsed. The drugs were an advantage. I felt I had a barrier against the worst of the pain, at least for now. Tomorrow I'd be suffering. But at least I now knew that tomorrow *would* come.

The flurry of kicks and punches seemed indiscriminate, but none of them were landing on my face.

113

Lemony perfume did momentary battle with the diesel fumes and the attack stopped as suddenly as it had begun.

The throbbing of the engines increased. She had left the door open.

I opened one eye. A line of bright white det cord ran down the middle of the knackered red lino out in the corridor.

She hunkered down alongside me. Luxuriant brown hair brushed fleetingly across my cheek.

'Who betrayed us, Nick? Who gave up the *Bahiti* and my father?'

I kept looking down, waiting for a slap, a punch, a kick, but nothing came. She sounded very calm, very collected, but I could feel the anger burning in her eyes.

'You're dead anyway, Nick. It's not as if you're helping yourself. The woman and that wee little girl, and those two friends of yours from Dublin – they're the ones you can save.'

I stayed clenched, ready to accept the punishment.

I gave it a few more seconds.

'I'm giving you fuck all until I'm sure they're safe.'

Her breath whistled as she stood up. 'You're giving me precisely what I want you to give me, or your friends will die in the most painful ways even you can imagine.'

She stepped back into the corridor.

Box-cutter grabbed my right arm and forced it up. Not even bothering to roll up my sleeve, he jabbed an autojet into the bicep.

My world went into slow motion again. Even his shouting against my ear was muffled and blurred.

I felt myself drift away as my central nervous system closed down and there wasn't a thing I could do about it. The urge to sleep was just too strong.

Fuck it, I needed the rest anyway.

Fifteen seconds and I was gone.

PART ELEVEN

114

It was like an oven in here. My throat was painfully dry and my head thumped like a bass drum. I tried to sit up but was too fucked and dizzy and out of it. In the end I rolled off the bunk and used the wall to pull myself upright.

I worked my way over to the sink and slapped my hand on the press-button tap. I sucked at the tiny trickle. It took forever to get a mouthful of warm, brackish water.

I swayed back to the bunk. How long had I been out? No idea. I remembered getting injected, filled in, dragged about, no more than that.

I lay back on the bed and rested my eyes. Everything was still fuzzy and hazy. But I became aware that below the thud of the bass drum in my head, the chug of the engines was softer. They were doing no more than ticking over.

I struggled to my feet. The motion of the ship was definitely calmer, but it didn't feel like we were in dock. I tried the door and it was locked.

I went back and lay face-down on the bunk. Now that I'd recovered enough to notice such things, my stomach was aching. Was it the water I'd drunk? Was it the kicking? Or the fact that I hadn't eaten for fuck knew how long?

There was a bang on the side of the hull, then another. The scrape of metal. The odd shout. A couple of minutes later, a mechanical whine. I remembered the sound from the *Bahiti*. A crane kicking off. They were unloading.

That must mean we were near the coast: making an RV on the open sea would have been difficult for a ship as small as this one.

It also probably meant it was dark.

Ten minutes later, I heard shouts. The Russians. Then a young girl's cries. I was sure they passed the door.

I got up and stumbled towards it. I was about to put my ear against the steel when it burst open and caught me on the side of my head. I toppled backwards, banging my lower back on the edge of the bed.

115

Box-cutter followed, a whirlwind of punches. He caught me in the stomach and I crumpled onto all fours. My body wanted to vomit but all that came up was watery bile.

Another body came in behind him and got to work with his boots.

I went down.

I felt a hand on the back of my head. It grabbed a clump of my hair and yanked it up. I didn't need to focus big-time to see the box-cutter in his free hand.

He tapped the handle against my forehead. 'Later.'

The English was heavily accented and he wasn't smiling.

Two sets of hands grabbed my arms and dragged me fast along the floor. My chest banged over the threshold and then, agonizingly, my knees and shins.

116

I felt the difference in temperature the moment we were out on the red lino. They hauled me through another doorway, over another threshold, and my breath immediately clouded.

Were we outside?

There were lights either side of me, and I could hear the sea.

I could also hear a girl sobbing, and then a woman's shout. 'Bring them over! Bring them over!'

I lifted my head. I was in the cargo hold of a small ship or the cold store of a fishing trawler. Lights ran down two sides of an eight- by six-metre space. The deck was three or four metres above me. It was a small vessel, but you didn't need that much room to cart around a few hundred kilos of white powder.

In the far left-hand corner of the hold, towards the bow, was a huddle of bodies. I could see the back of the head of the one who was crying. Ruby. Holding her, protecting her, was Tallulah. Her eyes were fixed on me.

Dom and Siobhan were there too, holding each other. All four were cuddled up, sharing body warmth. All they had on were jumpers.

Mairead stood over them. She turned as I was dropped onto the cold steel floor of the hold. I saw the camcorder in her hand. She came over and shoved it into my face.

'Now's your time, Nick. Now you get to tell everyone what you know. Tell the truth and they all go free. They all get on the boat with me. Everyone else has gone. The crew's gone, the shipment's gone. We're the only ones left. You're staying here – you know that. Accept it. But tell your story, and if I believe it they go free.'

My face rested on the freezing metal. Running along the skin of the hull, I saw four dustbin lids held in place by gaffer tape. Det cord ran up into the lids and back out again.

The ring main.

I moved my head, but I could see no detonator on that side, no TPU. Maybe there wasn't one. Maybe she had a remote control: they'd get on a tender or something and fuck off before pressing the button.

And in that moment, I knew beyond any doubt that none of us were going to get away from here. All five of us were good as dead.

117

I lay watching the two Russians' boots pace up and down. I turned my head when Mairead told one of them to rig up some arc lights.

I made eye contact with Tallulah. She had Ruby in her arms, head into her shoulder so she couldn't see me. The little one was shivering and sobbing.

I made myself cut away. I didn't want the Russians to see that we cared for each other. And in any case, I was just too exhausted, and I needed to think.

One. I hadn't seen any weapons apart from the box-cutter.

Two. They must have another boat tied up alongside for Mairead and the two Russians. Or was she so hell-bent on revenge she just wanted to hear me say the magic words and then blow us all to hell?

118

The bow end of the hold was soon bathed in light.

I got slowly and painfully to my feet when told to do so.

Mairead turned to Dom. 'You too.'

She filmed us both as we made our way to what had been transformed into a well-lit performance area and stood facing each other.

I saw Tallulah over Dom's shoulder, still trying to console Ruby. She cuddled her, rocked her back and forth in time with the movement of the boat.

I glanced at Dom. His eyes told their own story.

He nodded in the direction of the camera. 'What is it you want me to do?'

I kept my head down, focusing on the position of the two Russians. Their top halves had disappeared into the shadows thrown by the beams of light directed at me and Dom, but I could see their boots.

'You're going to interview Nick. Ask him about the *Bahiti*.'

'*Bahiti?* I don't understand—'

'You don't have to. Your man's going to tell you. Nick, I want you to speak to the camera. Dominick, when he's told you, you're going to ask him a direct question. Ask him if he was the man who killed Ben Lesser. And Nick, you're going to say yes.'

'Ben Lesser?'

'My father. Nick murdered my father.'

The camera zoomed in on me.

'Isn't that right, Nick? You're going to tell us the truth for the first time in your sorry little life. If not, everybody dies.'

Tallulah could contain herself no longer. 'I've got a child here, for God's sake! She doesn't have to watch this. Let her go.'

Mairead turned and filmed her. 'Oh but she does. She needs to know. She's the age I was when Nick took my daddy away from me.'

The time had come. I wasn't exactly match-fit, but I was running short of choices.

119

I lunged at Mairead, screaming at the top of my voice.

Her face didn't register surprise or fear, just anger. She tried to back away. I grabbed the camcorder with both hands. My eyes were fixed on her face as I swung it down onto her head. She screamed and fell, her body colliding against mine as she went down.

Box-cutter was a metre away, going for a weapon in the waistband of his jeans.

I yelled at Dom: 'Take the other one!' and threw the camcorder at Box-cutter. It bounced off his shoulder.

I dived at him as the weapon came up, slammed into him and made a grab for his arm. His roar echoed around the hull as we hit the deck.

I had two hands on his bicep, trying to force his hand down at the same time as he tried to bend his arm to shoot.

The weapon went off.

I dropped my head and sank my teeth into his cheek.

He screamed and bucked like a wild animal, shook his

head left and right. His whole body arched, desperate to throw me off.

His left hand swung round and grabbed my hair and wrenched me off his face.

The weapon clattered onto the steel and spun away into the shadows.

I scrambled towards it, kicking and punching behind me as his arms closed round my leg.

Then Tallulah shouted: 'Run! Run! Run!'

A small pair of legs rushed across my field of view, heading for the door.

The sudden pain was excruciating; sharp, deep, intense; exploding outwards from the top of my thigh.

It got even worse as the Stanley knife plunged in again and this time carved its way down the back of my leg.

120

I twisted and thrashed to escape the blade.

I had to get to the pistol.

The blade dug in again. I squirmed and it gouged its way out. I half turned and saw it raised once more.

That blade was my whole world now. I grabbed his wrist with both hands and wrenched it towards my face. I twisted it until the back of his hand was against my mouth. I opened my teeth and bit into taut skin and tendon.

He screamed as he pulled his other hand free and hammered his fist on the back of my neck.

I butted him with the back of my head, again and again, yelling like a madman. I found a bit of extra strength and jerked both my hands clockwise. There was a crack as his wrist snapped.

The blade dropped free.

I let go of his wrist and it flapped like a broken wing. I

grabbed the blade and punched hard into the back of his neck, and pulled.

There was a gush of air and a wobbling, rasping sound from the hole in his windpipe.

121

The two women were all over Mairead, fists flailing as anger poured out of them and into her curled-up figure. Primal forces were driving Tallulah; what she was doing was beyond her control.

Dom staggered to his feet. He was a big lad but so was the Russian who now lay motionless on the floor. It must have been quite a battle.

I took a couple of laboured steps towards them. I was aware of what was happening but the software was taking too long to kick in.

Tallulah looked up. 'Find Ruby! For God's sake find Ruby!'

122

I turned left along the corridor, following the line of det cord. I needed to know how she planned to detonate the Semtex before going on to find Ruby.

The cord ran up the wall next to a set of steep metal steps. I saw what I was looking for: a TPU just like Daddy used to make.

I clambered upwards.

I could hear sobbing. Ruby was on the bridge.

A sliding door opened onto the deck. She was tugging uselessly at the handle in an uncontrolled frenzy. Whether it was because the door was locked or too heavy, she couldn't budge it no matter how frantically she tried.

I ran over to her. 'Ruby! It's me, it's me.'

She was still fumbling at the door.

'Ruby! It's OK. It's me, Nick.'

She wasn't listening; she was in a blind panic.

I put a hand on her shoulder.

Finally, she turned, and the moment she saw me her

body went rigid. She screamed at the top of her voice.

'It's me . . . it's Nick . . .'

Then I realized: my head, face and hair were covered in blood. The deck was reddening round my feet.

I didn't know what to do. Did I just pick her up, or what?

'It's OK, Ruby. Everything's going to be all right. Calm down, please, it's all right.'

I started throwing open drawers looking for a first-aid kit. There should be a good one on a boat this size. But all I could find was a sort of wooden shoe box with a couple of bandages and bottle of cough mixture inside. It would have to do.

Looking out of the bridge window, I could see a four-seat fibreglass powerboat bobbing alongside us in the swell. We couldn't be that far out to sea.

The door had a weather latch on the top. I threw it. There was no way she was getting out. 'Just stay there, darling – I'll go and get Tally.'

I hobbled back down the stairs. There was nothing more I could do for her right now.

123

The hold looked like a battlefield.

Mairead lay in the corner where I'd first seen the four of them. There was no movement from her. The two Russians lay where they'd died.

Tallulah ran up to me. 'Where is she?'

My leg hurt big-time. 'Upstairs. Go and talk to her. Go look after her.'

She looked down. 'Oh my God, Nick!' She put her arms out, whether to hold me or help me, I wasn't sure. Her breath clouded around us.

'I'm OK. She's up on the bridge. Keep her up there. I haven't finished down here yet.'

Dom hugged Siobhan under the arc lights. I pointed. 'Go with her, help her. Then wait up there for me, OK?'

I dropped the medical box and I followed it onto the deck. Dom let go of his wife and ran over to me.

'Pressure, mate. I need pressure on the wound.'

He didn't need any second bidding. He knelt down and tipped the contents onto the floor.

I looked over at Mairead. 'She dead?'

'Nearly.' He shook his head. 'But not nearly enough.'

He started bandaging my leg tightly to stop the leaks.

I leant back, my hands flat on the steel. I suddenly became aware of how cold I was. Dom shivered as he tied off the bandage.

I gripped his forearm. 'Check through their gear. They've got to have some clothing here somewhere. Get some warm stuff on. There's a boat parked up next to this thing. Get the girls wrapped up, get them all in it.' I nodded over to Mairead. 'I'm going to sort her out and then let's fuck off. Have a look at the nav gear; find out where land is.'

124

Her legs moved.

'Go – get everything sorted and I'll be up there to meet you.'

He tucked in the last of the bandage just above my knee. 'Are you going to kill her?'

I didn't answer.

He stood up and held out a hand. I pulled myself up.

We grabbed an arm each and started dragging her out, just the same as the Russians had dragged me. She bounced over the threshold and into the corridor, then along the red lino and over the cabin threshold.

I ripped off her duvet jacket, checked the pockets and lobbed it at Dom. 'Get this on Ruby.'

125

I leant down and gave her a couple of slaps to bring her round. 'Come on!' I wanted her to be fully aware.

I felt in her jeans pocket for the knife or whatever it was she'd been going to unscrew the TPU lid with.

I found a stubby flat-head screwdriver.

'Come on, wake up.'

She was sort of there. I sat on the bunk with her at my feet.

Next door, the engines idled. I was getting warm again. My ears and hands stung as they came back to life.

I stared down at her. Her mass of hair glistened with blood and was matted against her head.

I didn't blame her for being pissed off with me. If I'd been close to my dad I'd have felt the same. And I understood, too, why she'd want to know the traitor who gave up the ship to the British in the first place. I didn't even have a problem with the car device, now that I knew that it was just a ploy. In fact, I admired her for not giving up. I'd admired her dad for the same reason. They might have been the enemy, but they were solid.

The only reason I was still sitting here and she was on the floor was that she'd brought the other four into it, and they had nothing to do with the world that she and I moved in. They were real people, and none of them would be safe unless I put an end to this.

She'd also killed Lynn. He died doing his job, even though it wasn't his job any more. He was one of the old school. We needed more like him. I would make a point of contacting his kids and telling them what had happened. They needed to know how the man they despised had met his end.

126

She began to come round.

I eased myself off the bed. The pain in my right thigh had begun to register in my brain. It seemed that these deep, clean cuts really were every bit as painful as any other kind. Blood oozed from the dressings. It was going to be hospital time very soon. I'd have to go in and complain about these drugged-up muggers who not only took all my cash, but also seemed to take pleasure in slicing me up.

I couldn't kneel because of the pain. I had to stoop, one hand on the edge of the steel frame of the bunk as I leant down.

I pulled open an eyelid. The pupil reacted. She could hear me all right.

'It was Richard Isham.'

She took a big, involuntary breath and sobbed.

'Yeah, you know, the one who's always been up for the cause, the local hero, ready to fight to the death. But you know what, he was on the make, just like everybody else.' I leant a bit closer so she didn't miss a word. 'He saw what was coming and made sure he was one of the survivors. What would your dad think of that? But he can't think anything, can he? Because while Richard is sitting behind a big fat desk with an expense account to match, your old man is dead.'

She kicked out her legs.

'It's a fucker, isn't it? But you know what? I agree with you. A traitor is a traitor, in anyone's book, including mine. I have more respect for you than I do for him.'

She was still sobbing but it wasn't from pain or fear of dying. She was a player; she had more bollocks than that. She was grieving.

She should have spent five minutes with me over a brew some time. I could have put her straight: never trust those fuckers, and don't waste your faith in them. They're always in it for their own ends, no matter what side of the fence they're on.

'But the problem is, you're the enemy.' I pushed myself up using the side of the bunk. 'Regardless of what I think of you, we both know what that means.'

I limped into the corridor and locked the door behind me.

127

The TPU box was made of wood and the lid was screwed down tight. Four screws, of course. And there were a good two metres of loose det cord before the detonator was attached, in case it was contaminated. She'd learnt her lessons well.

The screws came out easily.

I turned the Parkway to the full hour, and the plastic disc fell to the floor.

The timer ticked gently as the spring started to unwind.

PART TWELVE

128

Dom drove the powerboat. Siobhan sat shivering one side of him and I stood behind, a hand on a shoulder each to brace myself as we bucked through the waves.

Everyone but me wore a mish-mash of bloodstained fleeces and black leather jackets. I had a duvet draped around me like a cloak.

Little dots of light began to sparkle in the darkness ahead.

Dom half turned his head and shouted against the wind. 'Terrible timing.'

'What's that?'

'Biggest story of my career and it has to break when everybody's away.'

'What do you mean?'

His face broke into a grin. 'Don't you know what day it is? Merry Christmas, Nick.'

He turned back to concentrate on the sea. 'You know you're welcome to finish your holiday at the cottage.'

'No offence, mate, but I've got a place in Italy. For a while anyway . . .'

I sat down next to Siobhan.

She smiled weakly. 'What are you going to do, Nick?'

I shrugged. 'I might go into the antiquities business. It seems there's a lot of rich guys who pay good—'

'No.' She tilted her head to indicate behind. 'What – are – you – going – to – *do*?'

I knew what she meant, but I didn't know the answer. Tallulah hadn't exactly been all over me when I got into the boat, and I could understand that. She had an eight-year-old priority desperately holding onto her.

I got up and moved back a row. Ruby was still curled into her stepmother, no longer crying, just staring into I didn't know what. Her hair was being blasted about in every direction.

I leant over to Tallulah as she put a protective hand to Ruby's head. 'Listen, she's going to need lots of care now, to get over this, and to get things right. I know, I've seen it before. If you want, I can be there and help her – and you.'

The expression I got back wasn't the one I was hoping for. There were no nods or smiles, nothing encouraging.

Her lips moved, but I didn't hear the words. A brilliant flash of light arced across the sky from behind us, and seconds later came the short, sharp, dull sound of *brisance* as the steel of the hull took the full impact of the shaped charges.

I tapped Ruby's shoulder. 'Not the best Christmas fireworks you've ever seen, but give me points for trying?'

A little smile creased her face.

'And look at that lot.'

We were approaching a small Irish port. A group of carol singers gathered around a Christmas tree on the quay. Their clear voices reached out to us across the water. A cluster of houses were lit up with Santas and reindeer behind them.

Tallulah sank her head into Ruby's hair.

'Sorry, Tallulah, what did you say just then?'

I still wasn't getting the expression I had hoped for, but I guessed it was the words that were the most important.

She looked up at me and nodded slowly. 'I said, yes, Nick. I would like that.'

Ruby had the faintest hint of a smile on her face. She started to sing along.

O tidings of comfort and joy,
comfort and joy,
O tidings of comfort and joy . . .

ANDY McNAB

is back...
The original, the best...

At last, the long-awaited sequel
to the international bestsellers,
BRAVO TWO ZERO and
IMMEDIATE ACTION

SEVEN TROOP

They were like a band of brothers...

In 1983 Andy McNab was assigned to B Squadron, one of the four Sabre Squadrons of the SAS, and within it to Air Troop, otherwise known as

SEVEN TROOP

This is Andy McNab's gripping account of the time he served in the company of a remarkable group of men – from the day, freshly-badged, he joined them in the Malayan jungle, to the day, ten years later, that he handed in his sand-coloured beret and started a new life.

From the pen of the man who invented the modern military memoir comes another storming battering ram of thrill-packed, unforgettable drama. Never before revealed operations and heartbreaking human stories combine to create a new classic of the genre and a book that takes us back to where it all began...

Out now
from Corgi Books

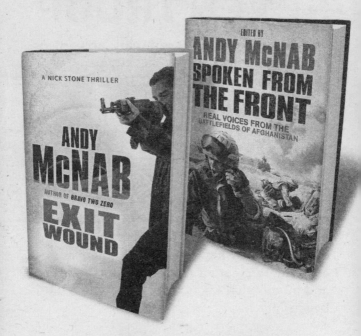